The Lebensborn Alliance

The Lebensborn Alliance

Book II

Joyce Yvette Davis
Author of The Lebensborn Experiment

Copyright © 2019 by Joyce Yvette Davis
All rights reserved.
No part of this book may be used or reproduced by any means, graphic, electronic, or mechanical, including photocopying, recording, taping or by any information storage retrieval system without the written permission of the author except in brief quotations embodied in critical articles and reviews.

ISBN: 9781670327673 (se)
ISBN: 9781689450188 (e)

Any people depicted in stock imagery provided by Pond5 are models, and such images are being used for illustrative purposes only.

This book is dedicated to my son

Brandon Jossef Davis
And
My Grandson
Brandon Jossef Davis, Jr.

Chapter One

*How thin and sharp is the moon tonight
How thin and sharp and ghostly white
is the slim curved crook of the moon tonight?*

Langston Hughes

Saturday, February 4, 1956
Charlottesville, Virginia

A thin layer of fresh snow lay across the long open road. It was well past midnight. A 1956, two-tone, dark brown and beige Nash Rambler station wagon made its way down the two-lane highway, traveling north towards Michigan. Former WWII officer's Sergeant Kapp Johnson and his wife Clare, Lieutenant Milton Taylor and his wife Olivia, and Private First-Class Ray Wilson and his wife Charmaine were in the car. They had just come from the annual reunion of the 761st Tank Battalion held in the University of Virginia gymnasium. Kapp was driving. Clare sat next to him, and the other four occupied the back seat.

Like every year, the reunion was a formal affair with all the ladies dressed in long flowing evening gowns like glamorous society matrons. Clare wore a spaghetti-strapped dress of shimmering gold silk with a large matching bow adorned to the front of its high waistline. Her long black wavy hair was parted on the right and combed to one side, cascading over her shoulders. This year, Kapp surprised Clare with a beige mink stole for the occasion. Ray's wife, Charmaine, wore his favorite color, red. The bare-shouldered, tightly fitted dress sparkled with sequins. Her auburn hair was styled in a sassy short cut that framed her small, oval face. Lieutenant Milton Taylor and his wife Olivia could have been twins. They were both tall and lanky with a coffee and cream complexion and long thin necks. Olivia's sandy brown hair of curly ringlets was pinned up on top of her head in a cluster. She wore a sleeveless V-neck dress of avocado green chiffon with a thin belt and a pleated skirt that flowed to her ankles.

Most men wore black tie and tux, except for those who, like Milton and Ray, wore their military uniforms.

Kapp didn't like wearing his uniform. It reminded him of the way his brother Paulie died, and the strange, unexplainable changes to his body. He was sure his condition caused Clare's miscarriages. The doctors couldn't find a medical reason for her inability to carry a baby full term. Now, after ten years of trying, the couple had become reconciled to the likelihood that they may never have a child of their own.

Ray and Milton wore their uniforms proudly at any and every occasion. Both had boys, one each, ages eight and ten, respectively. Milton and Ray relished their status as World War II veterans and never missed an opportunity to boast about serving under General Patton. Ray especially loved holding listeners captive with soaring tales about the heroism of the 761st Battalion whenever he wasn't sticking his nose in somebody else's business.

"What were you and Captain Carter talking about so intensely in the corner?" Ray asked.

Kapp shrugged his shoulders. "Nothing, just catching up," he replied.

"There's not that much catching up in the world. The two of you were locked in each other's embrace for practically the entire evening. Even Clare noticed it. It's not like you two don't communicate all year long. It seems like every reunion you and the 'Cap' are huddled in a corner somewhere all by yourselves. One would think you two are hiding something. Got a secret? Do tell. I'm still wondering how you got sprayed with all those bullets in Straubing and emerged without a scratch," confessed Ray.

After all these years, this was the first time what happened in that ravine in Germany had been mentioned, at least, to Kapp. Hearing it now made Kapp's heart skip a beat. His body stiffened, and he suddenly couldn't feel his fingers. The steering wheel turned on its own as the car skidded to the right and off the road.

"Kapp!" Clare screamed, reaching over and grabbing her husband's arm. Kapp quickly regained his composure and guided the station wagon back on the pavement.

Slowly breathing in and out, Clare kept holding onto Kapp's forearm but didn't look at him. Kapp fought the urge to glance at Ray in his rearview mirror. There was an awkward moment of silence followed by whispers between Ray and Milton before Clare abruptly switched on the radio.

"This is Walter Cronkite. After 30 days, the bus boycott in Montgomery, Alabama, continues. With nearly a hundred percent of Negro residents participating, there are no signs of letting up. The conflict ignited one cold December evening last year after Mrs. Rosa Parks, a department store seamstress, stepped onto a bus and sat in the fifth row, the first row of the "colored section." When more patrons boarded, the white bus driver, James Blake, asked Mrs. Parks and three other riders to give up their seats to the white passengers. But Mrs. Parks refused and was arrested."

"My Uncle Leo was one of the four riders, and they were told not asked," corrected Clare.

"No Joke! I can imagine what that redneck cracker said," quipped Charmaine. "I bet it wasn't nice."

"He told them to move, that he wanted those two seats. My uncle and the three other men got up immediately and walked to the back of the bus. Uncle Leo said his face turned white when he saw Mrs. Parks still sitting there. My parents and uncle attend the same church as Mrs. Parks and her husband. The bus driver raised his hand as if he was going to slap her, but my uncle heard Mrs. Parks tell the bus driver, 'Don't you dare.' The bus driver didn't, thank God. Knowing my uncle, he would have intervened and ended up dead."

"So, what happened next?" Milton's wife, Olivia, asked.

"The driver just walked back to his seat. He radioed for the police, and they came and arrested Rosa Parks," Clare revealed.

"Whew! I'm sure glad I'm not living in the south," said Milton.

"Oh! Like Chicago is such a bastion of racial justice." retorted Kapp.

"I'm not saying that. But it's better than the south. At least, we got some recognition for serving in WWII by getting better jobs. Before the war, it was unheard of for a Negro to be a bus driver in Chicago, much less get hired as a welder, working for the railroad like me. And look at Ray and the number of other Negroes working for the first time in Detroit in the automobile industry. It may have taken killing Nazis to make whitey finally display an ounce of fairness. But an ounce is better than nothing, which is what most Colored soldiers from the south received when they returned. That's why so many migrated up north after coming home. Lucky for you, there's a lot of Negro colleges down south. You don't think your position as assistant football coach at Morehouse College would be possible at Georgia Tech, do you?" asked Milton.

Kapp didn't answer. He was no longer listening. Instead, his eyes were fixed on the approaching vehicle, speeding towards them in the oncoming lane. The headlights were too big for a car but too small for an 18-wheeler. *Must be a pickup*, he thought.

Kapp slid his hands from the bottom of the steering wheel to the top and tightened his grip.

"What is it?" Milton and Ray both asked, leaning forward in their seats simultaneously to peer out the front window.

Kapp just shook his head from side-to-side and passed his wife a glance. Clare knew the drill. She clicked off the radio, then reached under the dashboard on the passenger's side and pulled out Kapp's Colt 45 and placed it inside her gold silk purse. Every American Negro knew an oncoming car on a lonely road in the dead of night, particularly in the south, could mean you weren't coming home that night in one piece or perhaps ever again.

"These damn reunions! Why do we always have to be the last ones to leave every year?" Ray's wife, Charmaine, complained.

Swoosh! A red pickup truck zoomed past. Kapp checked his side-view mirror and watched as it sped away in the opposite direction.

"Looks like a Ford jeep," said Kapp.

After looking back, everyone else let out a sigh, and Clare immediately clicked the radio on again.

"No more Walter Cronkite, please. Let's have some music," said Charmaine cheerfully.

Clare switched to a station playing: "What A Wonderful World" by Louis Armstrong, and suddenly, everyone broke out singing…

"I see skies of blue and clouds of white, the bright blessed day, the dark sacred night. And I think to myself, what a wonderful world."

Bang!

Clare and the other wives screamed as the bright lights from the vehicle behind them beamed into their car.

"Got Damn it! That's a rifle. Thank God they missed," Milton shouted as he reached over the front seat and grabbed Clare's purse and took out Kapp's gun as Ray retrieved his revolver from the inside breast pocket of his uniform.

Milton, who was sitting in the backseat directly behind Kapp, rolled down the window on his side of the station wagon and fired several shots at the red Ford, now chasing them. Ray did the same and shot out of the window on his side.

"Milton!" Olivia screamed.

"Shhh honey, get down! All of you," Milton ordered Olivia and the other wives. They obeyed.

Kapp pressed the gas pedal to the floor. The arrow on the speedometer shot to 100. A flashback of himself running through the woods in Germany popped into his mind. Kapp couldn't help but think how much faster he could run on foot.

Suddenly it began to snow. The highway quickly became a road of slippery slush, causing the Rambler to slide between lanes.

Hell, I can't see a thing! Kapp thought to himself. Words he didn't want to say out loud. *Damn it! If only our wives weren't here, I'd turn this car around and kick some redneck ass! But our wives are here, so just stay calm and get them home safe.*

Visibility grew worse as the snow rained down even harder. So far, Kapp kept a considerable distance ahead of the Ford. But then he felt the curve in the road bend first left, then right, then left again. He slowed down with each twist and turn. That allowed the riders in the pickup to cut the distance and get close enough to fire off their rifle again.

Bang burr bang burr bang! The sound of bullets slicing through the icy cold air, echoed loud and shrill through the night.

Kapp glanced at his wife, crouched down partially under the space between the dashboard and the seat. She was crying with her face buried in her arms. His mind was riddled with questions.

Is this what we fought a world war for and risked our lives to come home to this? Are we forever to be chased down and brutalized and maybe killed like wild animals because some other race can't accept our existence?

Before Kapp realized it, he crossed his left hand over his right hand, eased his foot onto the brakes and turned the steering wheel. The car skidded as it spun around into the oncoming lane heading south towards Virginia. Kapp then zoomed pass the Ford pickup, now going in the opposite direction in the next lane. Kapp made another sharp U-turn until his Rambler was once again heading north toward Detroit. But this time, he was chasing the truck.

"Yes, yes, that's what I'm talking about!" Ray shouted as he pumped his fist in the air. Milton just patted Kapp on the back. Ray and Milton both stuck their heads out of their windows and fired continuously at the red Ford. The pickup swerved back and forth across the two-lane highway.

"Niggers!" shouted an angry male voice from the truck. Then, someone in a white pointy hood poked his head out of the window on the passenger's side, looked back, and held up his middle finger.

"I got your niggers right here!" Ray shouted and then fired his gun again. The bullet went straight through the top of the man's pointed hood and hit the roof of the vehicle. The driver suddenly lost control, and the truck swirled around until it finally stopped facing the Rambler.

With the vehicle's headlights beaming into his station wagon, Kapp couldn't see.

"Oh, sh_ _!" yelled Kapp as he slammed on the brakes. "Clare, get up! Everybody put on your seatbelts!"

Afraid the driver would ram the truck straight into them, Kapp immediately turned the steering wheel left and hit the gas.

"What the hell are we going back to Charlottesville for?" Ray objected.

"He's right," said Milton, "there's far too much road ahead of us. We'll never make it all the way to Michigan with them in pursuit. It's better to go back to the city where people are. If Kapp can keep far enough ahead of them so firing their rifle will be useless, we've got a chance. I'm all out of bullets anyway. What about you?"

Ray checked the chambers in his revolver. "Empty," he announced.

Once again, Kapp was speeding down the highway at 100 miles per hour. His brand-new Rambler would do 120, but Kapp hoped he wouldn't have to drive any faster than his current speed. The snowy road conditions already made it too dangerous.

"It's a good thing their Ford is a much older model than your Rambler," said Milton, "or we probably wouldn't be able to outdrive them."

Kapp didn't reply. He focused on the highway ahead as they approached the section of the road that curved. Kapp didn't want to, but he had to slow down.

Everyone braced themselves as Kapp took the first bend in the road, then the second and the third. With uncanny physical prowess, he maneuvered the curves while only decreasing the speed by 10 to keep the Rambler pushing ahead at 90 miles per hour. Kapp never lost control of the car and not once did the car skid or swerve.

Clare and the others clapped and cheered. It had stopped snowing, and the highway sign to Charlottesville read 10 miles ahead.

"Hey, you all, no more headlights," said Olivia, as she peered out the back window.

Kapp glanced in his rearview mirror while everyone else turned and looked out the back window.

"Yea, I guess ole speed demon here left them in the dust," said Milton.

"You mean in the snow," chuckled Ray.

Twenty minutes later, Kapp turned off Highway 29 and drove down Ivy Road towards the University of Virginia. They were hoping to spend the night again at Tarver House on Massie Road, a twelve-room lodge not far from the University, where they stayed for three days while attending the reunion events. Owned by a Colored family since 1902, it was the only establishment in the city where Negroes could stay.

The streets were empty. With sheets of snow blanketing the landscape, the city looked like a winter wonderland. The glow from the streetlights made the snow sparkle and luminesce.

Kapp drove at a steady pace, careful to stop at every stop sign and red traffic light. If the city of Charlottesville was anything like the city of Atlanta, a few beat cops were parked inconspicuously along the main thoroughfares to catch late-night joy riders or deviants trying to commit whatever crime they could perpetrate.

Heading north on Ivy was Copley Road. But in the opposite direction, heading south, the name of the road changed to Alderman. Copley was now just a block away. Kapp accelerated, hoping to make the green light before it changed to red. At the intersection of Copley and Alderman, Kapp turned left onto Copley. He hadn't made the turn completely, when, out of the corner of his right eye, he saw the red Ford speeding towards them from Alderman.

Attached to the front fender of the pickup truck was a massive metal rail. Boom! It all happened so fast. The red Ford slammed into the passenger's side of the Rambler. The force of the impact was strong enough to hurl the car three feet into the parking lot fence on the corner. The vehicle then tore through the silver wire before it tipped over on its side.

Kapp's head crashed against the door window breaking it. Though he felt no pain, and there was no blood, the smell of blood was all around him, mingled with the heavy odor of gasoline. His head lay outside on the cold snow. He couldn't feel his legs. Kapp slowly turned his face to the right. Lying unconscious next to him was Lieutenant Milton. Like Kapp, the lower half of Milton's body was still inside the car. Blood soaked the lieutenant's uniform.

Oh God! Suddenly, Kapp became aware of the silence. He lifted his head slightly off the ground.

"Clare! Are you all right? Clare!"

"She's dead nigger, just like you gonna be in a second," said the hooded man who suddenly appeared as he walked around the right side of the Rambler.

There was a bullet hole in his hood. Sewn on to the upper left corner of his white robe, was a small circular black cloth with the words Knights of the Ku Klux Klan stitched in white. In his right hand, he held a rifle positioned upright against his shoulder.

"Ha, ha, ha," giggled another hooded member, approaching from the opposite side.

"Hold the nigger's nose," said the one with the shotgun.

The other obeyed, kneeled, and squeezed Kapp's nostrils together so that Kapp couldn't breathe. But Kapp didn't open his mouth. Then Kapp felt a hard jab to his stomach as the unexpected pressure from the rifle butt forced Kapp's mouth to open.

The one holding the rifle quickly jammed the barrel of the shotgun down Kapp's throat. The gun went off when the one squeezing Kapp's nose stood up.

"Come on, Bubba, we better get moving. I see flashing red lights. The police will be here any minute. Come on, what ya waiting for?"

"But look at him, Jonesy. That bullet should have blown his head off. You can't even tell I shot him."

"You plugged him all right, and he's good and dead. There's no way he ain't. So you can stay here, baffled if you want, but I'm leaving."

Kapp's eyelids closed as soon as the bullet exploded in his mouth, but he was still conscious. He heard everything around him, such as the sound of police sirens in the distance. He listened to the two Klansmen talking, and he heard them drive away. The bullet felt like a tiny fireball barreling down his throat. It punctured his larynx, ripped through his lungs, and tore a hole in his stomach until it lodged itself in his intestines. But it didn't settle there. The pointy-tipped lead piece quickly churned its way back up his body until it reached his throat again. Kapp coughed and spat it out. Opening his eyes, Kapp immediately reached up with his right hand and snatched the bullet out of the air.

There was a sudden tingling sensation in his legs, and Kapp wiggled his toes. He then sat up and flexed his feet.

"Holy hell, how in God's name did this happen?" wondered one of the policemen out loud.

Kapp shut his eyes again and lied back down. The sound of crunching snow under the feet of the police grew louder as the two officers approached. Then, the crunching stopped.

"Ugh, figures, just a bunch of niggers, probably drunk. Serves them right," said one of the policemen.

Kapp sensed that one officer was standing directly over him.

"Look at this one," said the second policeman. "He's wearing a military uniform. Wow! Look at all the medals on his jacket. Hey, there was a reunion at the University for World War II veterans. I bet they attended."

Is he alive? Check his pulse, you redneck pig! Call for an ambulance.

"I can feel a faint pulse. This one is still breathing, but barely. You check the others while I radio for an ambulance. We're going to need a lot of them for all these bodies."

Oh Yes! Thank God. Thank you, Jesus. Maybe they are all alive. Oh God, please let Clare be alive!

Kapp suddenly felt a pair of cold fingers pressing on the carotid artery of his neck.

Not me, you fool! My wife! Check my wife, the woman in the front seat!

"He's alive too," hollered the first officer to the second.

Kapp kept his eyes closed and pretended to be unconscious even after the ambulances arrived. God answered his prayer.

"They will all need emergency surgery for internal bleeding, except the male over there in the tux. He's just unconscious, though, he may have a concussion due to blunt force head trauma," said one paramedic to the other. "We won't know for sure until a doctor examines him."

Kapp felt one paramedic grab his feet as another grabbed him under his shoulder blades and lift him onto a gurney. The paramedics continued to talk as they loaded him into the ambulance, closed the door, and inserted an IV drip into his veins.

"The other five are going to need blood transfusions, at least, one or two pints, if not more," said one paramedic.

"The hospital doesn't have that much blood in storage, do they?"

"I don't know about back in the Colored section. It's usually short-staffed and short on supplies. If they don't, I doubt any of them will survive."

Kapp moaned. He moved his head slightly from left to right before slowly opening his eyes.

Chapter Two

"For the life of the flesh is in the blood…"

Leviticus 17:11
New World Translation of the Holy Scriptures

The paramedics remained silent after Kapp regained consciousness. Their initial reaction, for the first few seconds, was to stare directly at Kapp as if surprised he was alive. Kapp heard the driver radio the hospital that he was awake. One paramedic took his pulse. After that, the paramedics ignored him and fiddled with the medical equipment as if he wasn't there.

Ten minutes later, the ambulance arrived at one of the back entrances to the University of Virginia Hospital. The door to the Colored section was just a plain single wooden gray door without identification. It was a far contrast to the double glass doors the ambulance driver drove pass in the front of the hospital where white patients enter.

After rolling him inside, the paramedics left Kapp strapped to the gurney in the small receiving area and left. There was no one staffing the reception desk. Kapp looked around. It was a cold, austere room with pasty white walls and no furniture. He sneezed as the strong smell of rubbing alcohol irritated his nose.

"Hello! Is anyone here? Hello!" Kapp called out.

Ever since Kapp returned home from the war, he followed Captain Carter's advice and made it a point not to draw attention to himself. That meant he always kept his physical impulses in check. The changes to his body made Kapp abnormally strong and fast. But he never displayed his strength, not even to his wife. Kapp now realized that would have to change. He regretted not using his power more decisively tonight with the two white supremacists. He knew if he had, his wife and friends would not be near death now.

Oh, Clare, I'm sorry, baby, he scolded himself. *I should have protected you better. If you survive this, I promise I will from now on.*

Kapp pressed his arms against the gurney straps, splitting them in two. He pulled out the IV Drip from his left arm, and then rose and walked over to the only other door. It was locked. He knocked then banged on the door. No one answered. Gripping the knob firmly with his right hand, Kapp yanked. The screws in the door hinges popped out and fell on the floor. Carefully, Kapp placed the door against the wall. He made his way down the long corridor, checking each room as he went. There were patients in every room, but none were Clare or his friends. When Kapp reached the end of the hallway, he had to decide between turning left or right. He chose left. Suddenly Kapp heard muffled voices coming from the room straight ahead with the double doors. One door was slightly ajar.

Walking fast, Kapp rushed toward the room. But a tall, bald white man dressed in a long white cotton coat grabbed his arm just before he reached the double doors.

"Wait a minute!" spoke the bald gentleman. "You can't go in there. Who are you, and what are you doing here?"

Kapp noticed the stethoscope around the gentleman's neck. He had just stepped off the elevator to the right and caught Kapp off guard.

"My wife and friends were brought here in ambulances a few minutes ago," said Kapp as he studied the white doctor's face. There was something about him that Kapp couldn't quite put his finger on.

"Oh, yes, the car accident, bad scene, terrible, well, I am Dr. Henderson. I'm here to assist Dr. Franklin and

Dr. Mason in performing the surgeries. That is if we can find enough blood donors. All of them have severe injuries and have lost a lot of blood. We need at least five pints of blood for the surgeries, one for each patient. Unfortunately, we have only two pints on hand. The two women we have prepped for operations are suffering from subarachnoid and intracerebral hemorrhages in the brain. Subarachnoid bleeding occurs in the space around the brain; intracerebral is bleeding within the brain tissue. We must operate quickly to prevent brain swelling and death."

"Is one of them, my wife?" Kapp asked.

"I don't know."

"Excuse me, Dr. Henderson," a nurse, dressed meticulously in a starched white uniform with a matching white cap, suddenly interrupted them as she came out of the room with the double doors. Her hazel eyes complemented her smooth golden complexion. Her brown hair with honeysuckle streaks was pinned in a bun at the nape of her neck. The badge fastened to the right breast pocket on her uniform read, Ernestine Russell/Head Nurse.

"Two of the female patients from the car accident are ready for surgery," said the head nurse in a soft voice.

"Is one of them, my wife? Does one of them have long, wavy black hair?"

The nurse looked at the doctor as if she was asking his permission to speak. Dr. Henderson returned the look with a nod.

"No, one has short black hair and the other light brown hair," she replied.

"Excuse me, but the woman matching your wife's description is under heavy sedation," said a doctor walking towards the three."

Kapp turned to his right and saw another doctor approaching them. On the lapel of his long white coat was a badge with the name, Curtis Franklin, MD. Dr. Franklin stood only five feet six inches tall. He was slim with dark brown eyes and a dark chocolate complexion. The doctor reminded Kapp of a shorter version of Ray Wilson. Like Ray, the doctor's hair was straightened and slicked back on his head with pomade.

"Your wife has a subdural hematoma due to a traumatic brain injury, which is common with victims in automobile accidents. The condition occurs from a collection of blood between the skull and the peripheral tissue that covers the brain called the Dura. Of course, surgery is necessary to relieve the pressure by draining the clot. Your wife's injury can be life-threatening if it is not taken care of within the next 24 to 48 hours," explained Dr. Franklin.

"Excuse me, but I must go," interrupted Dr. Henderson before entering the room with the double doors. Nurse Russell left with him.

"My name is Kapp Johnson, and my wife's name is Clare, The other two women, Olivia and Charmaine, are the wives of Milton Taylor and Ray Wilson. The three of us served in the war together. How are they?"

"One has a collapsed lung as well as a spinal injury and may be paralyzed for life. They both have sustained concussions. The other has severe kidney damage. They also must be operated on as soon as possible and will need blood transfusions."

"I can give blood. I can give it to my wife and the others. I'm Type O negative."

"Good, that makes you a universal donor. Most adults have between 8 to 12 pints of blood in their body according to their body size. A person can lose up to 5 pints without dying, and it is possible to donate as much as 1.5 liters or up to 3 pints without going into shock. But the standard set by the American Medical Board is that we are only allowed to take one pint per person. And as a blood donor, you must wait at least 56 days before we can extract another pint. We need blood as soon as possible. You were also in the accident, correct?"

"Yes," Kapp nodded.

"Then, under the circumstances, it may not be medically feasible for you to donate blood right away. You may feel okay, but I assure you, your body has undergone a traumatic experience and still may be in shock. Even when donors are considered healthy, we perform a mini-physical, checking their temperature, blood pressure, pulse, and hemoglobin to ensure it's safe for them to give blood. I will have to insist that you receive a complete physical and wait at least 8 hours before donating. That will give your body time to recover."

"I don't think that long a wait will be necessary."

Upon hearing a familiar voice, Kapp turned around. His heart leaped at the sight of Captain Carter approaching from the same hallway he entered. The captain was still wearing his tux under a long gray wool overcoat. He walked in with his bow tie untied and his shirt unbuttoned, all except the last three buttons.

"Dr. Carter," said Dr. Franklin, "I am so glad you changed your travel plans to assist us with this emergency. It's a blessing I caught you before your flight to New York. We need all the help we can get. I assume you and Mr. Johnson know each other?"

"Yes, very well. We served in the same tank battalion together."

"Oh, yes, the famous 761st, I've heard so much about, which was commissioned by General Patton."

"By the way, the door in the reception area is off its hinges, did you know that?" asked Dr. Carter to Dr. Franklin.

Kapp opened his mouth to confess when another nurse with brown eyes, short black hair and the name Eula Bernard printed on her badge, rushed out from room 10.

"Excuse me, doctors, but you are needed immediately. The blood count of the third female patient from the car accident has suddenly dropped to 3.4, and her oxygen level is now at 30 percent."

"That's my wife!" shouted Kapp as the four ran towards the room. Clare was hooked up to monitors with tubes attached to both arms. There was a blue tinge to her skin. Her eyes were closed, but her face was dripping wet with sweat.

"My God Cap is she...!?" Kapp asked with a look of fear and concern on this face.

"No, but we must act quickly, or she will be," replied Carter.

"She's hemorrhaging," said Dr. Franklin after pulling back the cover and seeing the bloodstained sheet. They turned Clare over on her right side, lifted her gown, and found a deep puncture wound oozing blood. There was a horizontal slit a half an inch in diameter above her hip between her stomach and her diaphragm.

"That wound leads directly to her liver. Good Lord, how did we miss this!?"

"No time for blame now. We must operate immediately," shouted Dr. Carter. "Get her ready!" he ordered Nurse Bernard.

"But we have no more blood, doctor," she replied.

"We have all the blood we need right here," said Dr. Carter turning to his right and tapping Kapp on the shoulder. "Her husband is a universal donor."

"I suggest we perform a direct transfusion from his veins to hers. It will be quicker," said Dr. Carter as they helped the nurse disconnect some of the tubes and roll Kapp's wife to the operating room.

"Yes, I agree," nodded Dr. Franklin. "I would also like to perform the operation to relieve the clot in her Dura cavity after we cauterize the bleeding in her liver."

"Hell! It is risky to perform two delicate surgeries, one right after another, but we have no choice," said Carter.

Dr. Franklin again nodded in agreement.

After Kapp donned a patient's gown, surgical mask, and cap, Nurse Bernard worked quickly to prep him. Kapp found himself in the operating room, reclined in a bed beside his wife with a tube attached to his right arm. A machine drew blood from his vein into a tube attached to his wife's left forearm. Nurse Bernard explained that the device would beep when a pint of blood was extracted, but she controlled the speed and flow of blood from his vein to his wife's with a hand pump. Kapp watched as Dr. Carter worked quickly to cauterize the wound to Clare's liver. Afterward, Dr. Franklin, assisted by Dr. Carter, operated on Clare's brain. First, Clare was shaved bald. Then Dr. Carter drilled a hole into the left side of Clare's head and placed an intraventricular catheter in her skull to monitor the intracranial pressure.

Kapp looked on, holding his breath as Dr. Franklin made an incision, like a reverse question mark on the frontal, temporal region of Clare's skull. Next, Franklin gently and ever so carefully made an incision to open the Dura. Using a surgical suction and irrigation pump, he removed the clot. He later utilized biopsy forceps to subtract what the pump couldn't.

After seven hours of surgery, Clare was rolled into the recovery room alongside Olivia and Charmaine.

"The surgeries went well, right?" Kapp asked Dr. Carter as they both stood and looked at Clare while Nurse Bernard hooked Clare to a heart and oxygen monitor and changed her IV Drip.

"You were there; you saw what happened."

"Yes, but she's going to be all right, isn't she?"

"As long as there are no complications, she'll be okay," assured Dr. Carter. "Now we must see to Milton and Ray. They need transfusions too."

After Nurse Bernard finished with Clare, she walked over to where Kapp and Dr. Carter stood near the entrance to the recovery room.

"How do you feel, Mr. Johnson? Wouldn't you like to sit and rest a little longer? Can I get you more orange juice?"

"Don't make such a fuss nurse. This man survived a war. He's fine," insisted Dr. Carter. "In fact, I want you to prepare…no, that's all right. I'll do it myself. This way Johnson." Carter led Kapp out of the recovery room into a smaller room down the hall, the blood lab, where he closed the door and took two more pints of blood.

"There, now we can proceed with the operations on Ray and Milton," said Carter, as he placed the two blood filled component bags in a white refrigerator half the size of a normal one.

Dr. Carter then turned to Kapp, still seated. The doctor looked concerned. "You know, son, giving your blood to your wife, and the others may cause them to…." Dr. Carter suddenly paused and froze in place.

"What is it?" Kapp asked.

"Shhh, listen." The doctor put his finger to his mouth before quickly walking over to the door and opening it.

As soon as he did, the sound of the patient's emergency buzzer was heard loud and clear. Two alarms were going off. Dr. Carter peeked out and saw Doctors Franklin, Mason, and Henderson running into the critical care unit where Ray and Milton lay. Immediately, Carter retrieved the two blood component bags from the refrigerator.

"What is it? Is it Clare!?" Kapp asked.

"No, it's either Milton or Ray or maybe both. You stay here," said Carter as he hurried from the room.

Kapp rose from the chair only to flop down again, overcome with fatigue. His eyelids felt like bricks. Still, he struggled to stand. He didn't want to rest. He wanted to be there when Clare awakened. But the more he tried to keep his eyes open, the heavier they became. Kapp took deep breaths to fight his drowsiness. It didn't work. He finally gave in and leaned back. Slowly his eyes closed, and his head dropped forward.

Chapter Three

*Sometimes memories sneak out of your eyes
and rolled down your cheeks*

Unknown Author

The Battle of the Bulge, December 1944

If it weren't for the sound of his rapidly beating heart, Kapp Johnson would have sworn he was deaf and blind. Surrounded at night by an army of giant pine trees with thick branches loaded with foliage and covered in snow, he lied on his back in a trench engulfed in total darkness. Kapp couldn't see anything which compelled him to blink continuously to prove that his eyes were open. He couldn't move either. It was also hard to breathe. Something heavy was pressing down on his entire body, something big and hard. He kept thinking that a large piece of tank casing must have blown off and landed on top of him. The last thing he remembered was standing thigh-deep in a foxhole shoveling dirt.

That tedious task had commenced at 1100 hours on December 16th, Saturday morning. It began one hour before Hitler launched a sneak attack against American and Canadian troops along a hundred-mile stretch in the hills of Belgium. And Kapp had thought his most significant concern that day was the weather.

"Damn, it's cold enough to freeze hell out here," Kapp growled to himself as he looked out over the turret hatch of his M4 Sherman. The cold air felt like tiny bits of glass cutting his face. He was leading a long convoy of battalion tanks through the Ardennes Forest in the worst winter imaginable. It had to be at least ten below. The snow was so thick it covered everything with layers of milky white flakes two inches high. Everything from the roads to the trees, to the highest mountain peaks to the deepest gullies, lay beneath a blanket of white. During the hours of heavy snowfall, visibility was impossible. The ground was frozen solid, which made trying to maneuver a tank through the heaps of snowy terrain a tumultuous feat.

That was during the day. The night was even worse; the temperature dropped to twenty below. Because the ground was so hard, to dig foxholes, TNT had to be used along with pickaxes to break up the ice before using a shovel to remove the dirt. When Colonel Baker radioed the command to halt the convoy, the digging quickly began before dusk fell. It took a quarter pound block of trinitrotoluene to crack the frozen crust. Kapp's tank crew took turns bombing, digging, and excavating two dugouts. Kapp took over to take his turn at the second foxhole when snow suddenly began falling, only this time, German bombs fell with it.

Kapp saw an explosion of light and then felt his legs lift from under him. He fell backward immediately, and his body hit the ground hard. The sound of wounded soldiers screaming was excruciating--the sound of bomb blasts, deafening. Kapp looked up from the dugout and saw blurry visions of soldiers flying across the sky like jet propelled missiles. After that, he heard only his heart beating as nightfall slowly claimed what remained of the day. The voice inside Johnson's head kept telling him, *Stay awake! Don't close your eyes. You're going to be all right. You're not deaf. You're not blind. It's nighttime. It will be daylight soon.*

When morning came, Kapp felt his eyes slowly open. He realized he must have lost consciousness sometime during the night after all. Everything looked fuzzy at first, but as his eyes gradually adjusted to the daylight, his view came into focus. He now saw what was weighing him down. There had to be at least fifty dead bodies of his fellow soldiers lying on top of him. The body of one of the soldiers was that of Major Tom Whittlecat. His carcass lay on top of all the others. The major was spread out on his stomach, but his head was twisted sideways and tilted slightly upward in an awkward position, so officer Whittlecat's bloody face was facing Kapp. The top half of the major's skull was blown off, and one eyeball was gone. The eye that remained was open and staring directly at Johnson.

"Ahhhh! Ahhhh! Ahhhh!" Kapp screamed as his body jerked and shook uncontrollably.

Chapter Four

"A man is not completely born until he is dead."

Benjamin Franklin

"Ahhhh! Ahhhh!"

"Wake up! You're having a nightmare! Wake up, son!" Dr. Carter shook Kapp Johnson vigorously as the former sergeant slept in a chair in the blood lab. When shaking didn't work, Carter slapped Kapp across both cheeks. Johnson awakened, rubbed his hands over his face and sat up straight. Tears remained in the corners of his eyes until Kapp quickly wiped them away, then glanced at his watch. He couldn't believe that he had slept for nearly four hours.

Johnson looked up at the captain, but Dr. Carter didn't meet his gaze. Instead, the doctor stood with his shoulders slumped, looking down.

"What is it?" Kapp rose from the chair. He could feel the muscles in his stomach tighten.

"Is it Clare?"

Carter remained silent.

Kapp grabbed the doctor by his shoulders and shook him once. "Tell me!"

Reluctantly, Dr. Carter gave in and lifted his gaze to Kapp's face.

"Yes. It's Clare..." Carter paused for a second. "...and Ray... and Milton, they are all dead."

Kapp felt his legs buckle before he collapsed back down into the chair. Thump! He was lying in that foxhole again. But this time, it was the bodies of his two best friends and his beautiful wife on top of him. He had little time to grieve. Less than a minute later, Dr. Franklin burst into the room.

"Dr. Carter, come quickly! Something incredible has happened. They're alive!"

Chapter Five

*The untold want, by life
and land ne'er granted,
Now, Voyager, sail thou forth,
To seek and find.*

Walt Whitman

Vancouver, Canada
Noon Monday, February 6, 1956

"We should send at least one reporter to Alabama to report on the bus boycott, don't you think?" The Senior Editor and Investigative Bureau Chief, Carl Richardson, asked.

There was silence. As if suddenly noticing another person, the managing editor quickly stopped looking at his wrists and rolled down his shirt sleeves before placing both hands under his desk.

Reading the manager's body language, Richardson immediately changed the subject.

"I suppose your baby brother will have an editor position once he graduates from Harvard and joins the paper this summer," remarked Richardson.

Hans Weiss, Managing Editor of the Vancouver Daily Press, finally looked up from his desk at Carl seated directly across from him. The two were sitting in the managing editor's office surrounded by glass walls that looked out onto the newsroom floor. Since becoming managing editor of the Daily Press, six years ago at 23, Hans purposely grew facial hair to make himself look older. He started with a mustache, but last year he added a beard, cut close, and meticulously trimmed to the diamond shape of his face. It complimented his thin, straight nose and his full cheeks, as well as his pointy chin and neatly cropped, wavy red hair. In April, Hans turned 29-years-old. The beard made him look more distinguished, especially today when he wore his favorite suit color combination, a tailor-fit navy blue suit with a light blue silk shirt, and a red striped silk tie.

Carl Richardson was one of only two Negroes employed by the newspaper. He was a middle-aged man with a narrow face, bushy eyebrows, a thin black mustache and curly black locks with gray hair around the edges. Although Carl was light-skinned, he couldn't pass for white. His thick lips and sizeable broad nose with flared nostrils gave his ancestry away.

"No," Hans replied as he leaned back in his high-back black leather chair. "I prefer for my brother Adok to begin as a cub reporter, the way I did."

"Oh."

Hans could tell by the skeptical look on Carl's face that the senior editor didn't believe him. Mr. Richardson was hired eighteen years ago after an unsatisfying stint as a reporter for the Washington Post. His job there entailed writing obituaries for four years. Like many native-born Canadians, Richardson sought higher education in America, where the colleges were much more prestigious and well-known. For Carl, there was also an additional reason. Attending school in the U.S. allowed him the opportunity to study at an all-black university, of which there were none in Canada. Richardson graduated summa cum laude from Howard University in Washington, D.C., in 1931.

Hans understood the reason behind Mr. Richardson's inquiry and skepticism. Richardson wanted the next open editor position to go to his daughter, Nola, who joined the newspaper five years ago after graduating from the School of Journalism at Columbia University in New York. Nola was indisputably the best investigative journalist at the Daily. Nola's series of articles on the growing conflicts over the Suez Canal that the U.S. and Great Britain had with Egyptian President, Gamal Abel Nasser, won her the Pulitzer Prize last year. Unlike her father, Nola looked Caucasian. With long bleached blonde hair, light brown eyes, thin lips, and a peaches and cream complexion, Nola looked like an attractive 26-year-old white girl. But to Hans, the stature and form of her body revealed her heritage. No white woman Hans had ever seen had hips as broad and formidable and a butt as round and plump as Nola Richardson.

"The copy Nola submitted on the VII Winter Olympic Games has been excellent. How is she enjoying her working vacation in Cortina d'Ampezzo, Italy?"

"She loves it. Thanks for extending her stay a week after the Olympics are over to sightsee. But I was hoping..."

"I know, Carl. You want Nola to be an editor. But is that what the paper truly needs? She's doing an outstanding job as an investigative reporter. With all that's happening in the world, the paper needs someone with your daughter's tenacity and detective instincts to cut through the stonewalling and get to the truth. I know she was disappointed about not getting the deputy editor position in foreign affairs last year."

"Yeah, beat out by another reporter hired only two years ago. How fair was that?" Carl interrupted.

"It wasn't, and I told both of you so. But it wasn't just my decision."

"And why wasn't it just your decision?" asked Richardson.

"You know that a committee does all the hiring and promoting, and I have only one vote. The procedure was implemented to ensure a fair and unbiased selection process."

Carl grunted, then stood up. "Ok, boss." He walked toward the glass door but turned around before leaving. "All I have to say is, if being the best reporter on the paper stops my daughter from getting promoted to an editor, then maybe she should be a mediocre one, like all the other reporters around here."

Before the last word dropped out of Carl Richardson's mouth, the phone rang. Hans immediately picked it up, knowing who was on the other end.

"Is Carl still upset about Nola not getting that editor position?" Adok asked. "Isn't this the third time he's brought up the subject? That's why we need to add the no nepotism clause to the hiring rules."

"If I were to add the no nepotism clause to the hiring guidelines that would also prevent you from being hired this summer as well, so let's drop the subject brother. Besides, you are supposed to be in class, not gazing out at the ocean involving yourself in the affairs of the paper. You will be working here soon enough," said Hans.

"I am in class. Well, no, I'm not in class; I'm in the office of one of my professors, Professor Hydelman, the one I'm always talking about. He's teaching my philosophy class this period. I'm just retrieving some papers he left in his office that he asked me to fetch."

"Hmm, then your ability to see more than two hundred miles away across land has increased, and you don't need water as a reflector to bring the images closer. How long have you been able to see so far... Adok!?"

"Two years," Adok finally replied. "I would have told you only you don't like to talk about our special abilities. I understand that you want us to be normal, brother, but we aren't normal, and we never will be, no matter how much you wish it."

"Yeah, well, we can talk about that later. Go back to class."

As Hans hung up the phone, he felt his heart sink. Adok's enhanced vision meant that his baby brother probably saw what Hans had heard two nights ago when the sound of gunfire and crashing automobiles woke Hans up in the dead of night.

"Clare! Are you all right? Clare!" The man called out. It was the same voice Hans heard in the castle tower, the same voice of the Negro soldier on the U.S. military ship who was greeted by his wife, eleven years ago.

"She's dead nigger, just like you gonna be in a second."

Hans couldn't stop those words from repeating in his mind. Then there was that last gunshot. Hans cringed at the sound of it as the memory of it firing played in his head. Hearing it was terrifying enough, seeing it must have been even worse. Hans couldn't wait until Spring break to talk to Adok about the matter. He had to speak to his brother now, face-to-face.

Hans clicked the switch on the intercom box for his secretary. "Mrs. Clifford, see if you can get me a flight to Boston for tomorrow morning."

"Yes, sir."

Chapter Six

"Because brothers don't let
each other wander in the dark alone."

Jolene Perry

Mrs. Clifford booked Hans a flight later that same day, and he arrived at Boston's Logan International Airport at 11:25 that night. Hans drove his rental car straight from the airport to the campus, too eager to check into a hotel first. The seven-mile drive through the Ted Williams Tunnel and around the I-90 West Turnpike took only eleven minutes.

Hans switched on the light in his brother's dorm room after he knocked and found the door unlocked. Walking inside, he found the room to be the average 11 x 15 dorm size, with the usual layout arranged like a galley kitchen. A washbasin with a mirror above and a cabinet underneath was to the left of the door. Two closets flanked both sides of the room, followed by bunk beds positioned against the north and south walls. A chair and a desk filled the space at the end of each bed with three extended bookshelves stacked overhead. A large window occupied the west wall. Against the south wall was Adok's bunk.

Hans expected Adok to be in bed asleep. His brother wasn't there, and neither was his roommate, Ross Duncan. *Where could they be on a Monday night?* Hans didn't like Ross. Hans thought Ross was a bad influence on his brother. Adok had excelled academically during his first two years at Harvard, but ever since Adok joined the secret male club, Porcellian, his grades had been slipping, and so had his brother's behavior.

Within the last year and a half, Adok had been caught smoking reefers and patronizing strip clubs where he often drank too much and became unruly. Duncan, also a Porcellian member, was always right by Adok's side. Those were minor offenses compared to his brother's involvement last year in the gang beating of Bobby Seymour, the only Negro basketball player on the Harvard Crimson team. The incident happened Halloween night on the Quad lawn, a vast park-like area surrounded by student dorm buildings. Although the fight occurred at four o'clock in the morning, several students were still awake to witness it from their dorm room windows. Adok and the other boys involved were all wearing vampire costumes and masks. Though outnumbered three to one, Bobby Seymour managed to land a single blow to the face of one of his attackers. The punch knocked off Adok's mask, exposing him to the lamppost lights. Four students, including Bobby, recognized Adok. The skirmish cost his brother his position as an editor on the Crimson student newspaper. When Adok refused to identify the other two students involved, the school threatened to expel him. Thankfully, Ross and Stu Kramer, another Porcellian member, voluntarily turned themselves in to keep Adok from being tagged a snitch.

All three boys wrote a formal apology, which appeared in the student paper, and Hans and the other boys' parents paid restitution to Bobby Seymour to avoid criminal charges.

As Hans stared at the picture on Adok's desk of the two, taken eleven years ago on the ship that sailed them to Canada, he couldn't help but recall the day they became brothers. Hans would never forget the sorrowful look in Adok's doe shaped blue eyes as he peered up at him after Mr. Polanski told them about how the Nazi soldiers dragged Adok's parents and his baby brother out into the street and executed them. Adok was such a vulnerable little boy then, so fragile and innocent.

He's not that fragile or innocent anymore.

Hans shook his head from side-to-side. "No, he's not," He admitted to himself out loud.

Hans also had to admit that perhaps he had been a little too lenient with Adok. He recalled the many restrictions his father placed on him when he was growing up.

What hard, non-negotiable rules had I demanded of Adok? None. But it's too late for me to discipline him now. He'll turn twenty-one in May, and he's almost as tall as I am.

"Still, something will have to change," Hans mumbled.

"What's will have to change?"

Hans flinched, startled by the sudden sound of Adok's voice. Hans turned toward the door. *Don't back down.*

"You, young man, you're going to have to change."

Adok walked in wearing black slacks with a red, button-down Cardigan over a black turtleneck. He had grown up to be just as handsome a young man as he had been a cute, adorable little boy. Gone were his blonde locks. Adok's hair was now cut in an Ivy League Clip, long on the top, and parted on the side. His square chin and broad shoulders made him look even manlier than his age. Behind him stood his roommate, Ross, who was wearing a pair of gray corduroy pants and a dark blue pullover wool sweater. He was the athletic type, with a thick twenty-inch neck, muscular arms, and a beefy chest. Ross played football in high school until he busted his knee during a game in his junior year, which ended his football playing forever. Though he looked like the typical dumb jock with a butch haircut, he wasn't. He was a math major. And unlike Adok, Ross handled the antics of being a bad boy on campus without letting his grades suffer. Like Adok, Ross was blonde, and the two were also the same height--5 feet 11 inches tall.

"I think I'll camp out in Stu's room tonight so the two of you can talk."

"That's a good idea, Ross," said Hans as he took off his black tweed overcoat. Hans was still wearing the navy-blue suit he wore to work that day.

As Duncan opened the door, Hans laid his coat over the back of the chair in front of Adok's desk. As soon as the door clicked shut, Hans turned and faced Adok. Tension immediately flooded the room.

"You seem so uptight, brother, what's wrong? Are you still hearing muffled voices and whispers in the night?" Adok gestured with his hands as he asked the question with a touch of sarcasm. Hans could smell the alcohol on Adok's breath.

Hans clamped his hands together behind his back to restrain his anger. He had never hit his brother before, nor had Adok ever given him a reason. Growing up, Adok had always been an obedient and respectful child. But, at that moment, Hans wanted to knock Adok's perfectly aligned teeth out of his brother's stinky, whiskey-smelling mouth. At the same time, Hans wanted to wrap his arms around his baby brother the way he used to when Adok woke up at night screaming, 'Alenka,' his mother's name.

Not knowing what to do or say, Hans just stared at Adok and remained silent. Hans felt anxious, angry, and alone. He didn't know why. All he knew was that something was wrong. In his gut, Hans sensed that terrible things were happening and that Adok was somehow involved. Hans suspected his brother of keeping secrets. Occasionally, one of the muffled voices he heard was Adok's. It frustrated Hans that he could not clearly discern what was said.

Adok stepped forward and placed both his hands on Hans' shoulders, and then leaned in so close the two almost touched noses.

"Come on, big brother, talk to me," Adok teased, slurring his words. "You flew all this way for a reason. Now tell little brother what's wrong," Adok giggled as he patted Hans on the cheek.

Hans pushed Adok's hand away.

"You promised me that you would stop drinking and improve your grades. But a month after returning from Christmas recess, you get put on academic probation. To date, your grade point average is a 'D.' Instead of graduating at the top of your class, you'll probably graduate near the bottom. If you even graduate, that is."

"I know what my GPA is. You don't have to tell me. And don't push me. How dare you push me? You are not my father, and guess what, you're not my real brother either. You know what you are…"

"Adok!" Hans tightened his jaw as his eyes narrowed.

"You're just what, Paul Opus, the former owner of the Vancouver Daily said you were, after you stole the paper from him, a Jew, a stinking Jew."

Hans felt his fingers curl into a fist as his right arm rose from behind his back and extended the distance between him and Adok. The blow landed on Adok's right cheek. Adok's head snapped back. His baby brother looked stunned as he fell backward. Hans reached out with both hands and caught Adok by the tails of his Cardigan. Pulling his brother into his chest, Hans wrapped his arms around Adok's upper body.

As Hans held Adok close, Adok wept, a little at first, and then a lot. Hans soon realized that his brother's tears had nothing to do with the punch he just received. "You saw it didn't you, two nights ago--the crash?"

Adok shook his head up and down as his face lay buried in the side of his big brother's neck.

"You have to tell me, Adok. You have to tell me everything you saw, now, brother."

Chapter Seven

*When the past no longer illuminates the future,
the spirit walks in darkness*

Alexis de Tocqueville

With his arms still wrapped around Adok's waist, Hans helped Adok sit down on the bed. Minutes passed in silence with the two locked in a brotherly embrace, holding on to one another as if neither could breathe sufficiently without the other. Once again, they were in Slupsk, Poland, sitting on the floor in Adok's bedroom. Hans realized they would never leave that room unless the two confronted their past. The courage to face it was the test he had for so long avoided, which they must now overcome together. But, where to begin? Suddenly, Adok spoke and supplied the answer.

"It started two years ago when my vision increased, and I no longer needed to be looking out across an ocean for the water to reflect distant images. Before, I could see only 200 miles across land without water, and it took a lot of time and considerable effort to do so. I would have to stare into the distance for at least thirty minutes or more before I could see anything at all from that far away. Now, whenever I want to, my eyes travel across masses of land thousands of miles away as if I am an eagle soaring in the sky. It's not a problem because I can control it. The problem started when flashes of images began to pop into my mind unexpectedly."

"I see strange things, mostly of death, brief incidents of people getting beaten up, stabbed, strangled, shot, and blown to pieces. The images appeared to come from other countries, but I don't know where. The faces of the people dying are distorted. Sometimes there's one killer, other times two or three. The killers always wear long black hooded coats. With the hoods covering their heads, I see only their nose and mouth. And yet, their features look familiar. Then, two days ago, Friday, everything changed. It was midnight. I was writing an essay for my English class when I glanced out the window, and the sidewalk winding through the Quad suddenly became a road. Speeding down the road was a dark brown and beige Rambler station wagon. It was snowing heavily.

The vision was so vivid and close; it was as if I could touch it. I did reach out, but, of course, there was nothing there. Inside the vehicle was the same Negro soldier I saw running through the woods the night we fled from the castle. The soldier was driving, sitting beside him was the lady that met him on the ship. You remember?"

"Yes, his wife, Clare. Kapp is the name she called him," recalled Hans, suddenly transporting his mind back to that day on the ship.

"There were four other people inside the Rambler sitting in the back seat, two men and two women. A red Ford jeep was chasing them. The two men in the Ford were members of the KKK. They were wearing white robes with white pointy hoods. Suddenly…"

Adok paused, stood up, and walked over to the window and drew the scene on the glass with his finger. "All of a sudden, the soldier cut the car left into the next lane, sped forward passed the Ford, cut another sharp left until he was behind the jeep, and was now chasing the truck. The two men in the back seat rolled down their windows and began firing back at the jeep. One of the bullets made a hole in the top of the passenger's pointy hood in the Ford. The jeep quickly spun around and stopped, facing the Rambler. The black soldier hit the brakes, and then immediately turned his car around and headed back in the opposite direction."

Adok stopped drawing on the window and turned and looked at Hans, still sitting on Adok's bed.

"The Rambler was doing 100 miles per hour," said Adok. "They passed a sign that read Charlottesville, Virginia 10 miles ahead. By then, it had stopped snowing, and the Ford was no longer chasing them. The driver of the red jeep turned off the road and drove west across an open field of snow a few miles back. But after the jeep turned off the highway, something amazing happened that had never happened in my visions before."

"What?" asked Hans.

"I was still able to see them. My eyes followed the Ford."

Hans immediately rose and walked over and stood beside Adok. Now the two stood with their backs leaning against the windowsill.

Adok continued. "And not only that, when the riders in the truck took off their hoods, I could see their faces clearly, just like I could see all the faces of those in the Rambler. They both had to be no older than eighteen or nineteen, maybe twenty. The one driving the jeep had brown hair that was slicked back on both sides and combed in a high pompadour on top of his head. The hairstyle, together with his oblong face and red blotchy skin, made the driver look funny, like a cartoon character. The other guy could have been Elvis Presley's twin.

His black hair was greased with Brylcreem and combed back in a ducktail with a sprig of hair hanging over one eye. The two drove across the open terrain for at least five minutes before they got back on a different road. They passed a few houses along the way. Then, at the same time, the Rambler was turning left onto a street going in the opposite direction. The truck rammed into the passenger's side of the station wagon. The Rambler tore through a silver wire fence and landed on its side in an empty parking lot. It was an awful sight. The head of the soldier's wife, Clare, slammed into the dashboard and then hit the steering wheel when the vehicle tipped over."

"The soldier's wife was unconscious and bleeding from her nose, mouth, and forehead. The two KKK members put their hoods back on before they got out of their jeep and walked to the crash site. Elvis Presley walked over to Kapp. The driver walked around the wreck on the opposite side and stood over the man dressed in a lieutenant's uniform in the back seat behind Kapp. The lieutenant's upper body was lying outside in the snow, but his lower body was still inside the car. The white driver looked down at the lieutenant for several minutes and then walked over and stood beside Elvis. Kapp was conscious, and it looked as though the Klansman with the hole in his hood was trying to get Kapp to open his mouth. Elvis said a few words, and the driver bent down and squeezed Kapp's nose. Then Elvis jammed the butt of his rifle into Kapp's stomach, causing Kapp's mouth to open. That's when Elvis rammed his rifle down Kapp's throat and pulled the trigger after the other Klansman released Kapp's nose and stood up. The two talked back and forth as they stared down at Kapp's lifeless body and then left. Only Kapp wasn't dead. Once they drove away, Kapp opened his eyes, and then his mouth and out flew the bullet. The last thing I saw was Kapp reaching up and plucking the bullet out of the air. The vision got hazy after that and slowly faded."

"So Kapp wasn't dead?"

"No," Adok repeated. "It didn't even look like he had been shot."

"Have you seen any more visions since?"

"No," said Adok.

Hans put one hand on his chin and lowered his head. "Hmm," he muttered, closing his eyes. Suddenly, he opened them and looked over at Adok. There was a look of revelation on his face. He placed his left hand on Adok's right shoulder.

"I'm sorry, brother. I'm so sorry. All this time I thought your association with Ross and the Porcellian Club members was the reason you were acting up. I didn't know. I wish you would have told me."

"I wanted to many times. But there never seemed to be the right moment, and you never seemed open to hearing it. The visions always occur late at night because that's when the murders take place. But the images stay with me for days. The most recent one will pop into my head during moments when I'm concentrating, like when I'm taking a test or reading a book for class. It has gotten so I can't study, and I dread going to sleep afraid that I will see another vision."

"Do you remember everything you see?"

"No. The flashes disappear too quickly. I can tell you that someone was stabbed or shot or strangled, but I don't see all the details of what takes place or what led up to it."

"But I thought you said you see the same apparition over again days later. And you just recalled the one with Kapp."

"Yes, that's what's so weird. Before Kapp, all I saw were flashes of images that burst into my mind."

Pop, Pop, Pop, Adok snapped his fingers. "That's how quickly the images appear and disappear. The first image occurs at night, then over the next day or two, I see flashbacks of that same apparition. The flashbacks occur at different times during the day, but always when I'm focused on something. That is, until I see another image. Once I see another vision, the prior vision never repeats.

It's like my memory erases all previous apparitions from my mind. My mental picture of the scene never lasts long enough for me to describe with specificity exactly what happened."

"So when did you see your first vision?"

"The twenty-eighth of July, the same day, Alenka died."

"Your Mother, I thought Mr. Polanski said the execution of your family took place in September?"

Adok didn't answer. He looked uneasy and began to crack his knuckles.

"Brother, talk to me."

Adok inhaled one long, deep breath before slowly exhaling. "Alenka was a girl I knew at the Lebensborn Home. She was also kidnapped. She, she was my best friend," Adok revealed, still cracking his knuckles while staring down at the floor.

Hans didn't ask what happened to her. By Adok's demeanor, Hans knew she was dead. He wouldn't ask how, not today anyway. He could tell Adok was still affected by her death and didn't want to talk about it, even after all these years. Until now, Hans assumed when his brother cried out the name 'Alenka,' it was for his mother. He knew now that wasn't always true.

*But why hasn't he ever mentioned this girl before, and what else is he keeping from m*e? *It's time to come clean,* *brother. Maybe I should tell him that one voice I hear is his. No, not yet. That will be one secret I'll keep.*

"So when did you start hearing voices?" Adok asked.

"It was the same night, the twenty-eighth of July," stated Hans.

"Good," replied Adok. "That means you must be hearing what I'm seeing."

"Yes," agreed Hans, "and there must be a reason. We must discover the reason and decipher what you're seeing, and I'm hearing. Didn't Professor Hydelman arrive at your school around that time?"

"Yes," Adok answered. "He started teaching at Harvard in the spring of 1954. Before that, he was a professor at Cornell University. Why do you ask? What does he have to do with anything?"

"I don't know," said Hans. "I'm just trying to figure out what could have triggered these visions. We need to write a list of all the new people we've met in the past two years and any unusual events that occurred during that period."

"I don't think this has anything to do with the previous two years. I believe it all has to do with Germany eleven years ago. Isn't that the reason you heard, and I saw what happened to the Colored soldier? He's someone we both knew from the castle," said Adok.

"Remember how fast I saw him running through the woods the night we escaped. No normal human being can run that fast, which means your uncle must have given him the serum too. That's the only way this makes any sense. That's the connection."

Hans shook his head vigorously from side-to-side. "My uncle wouldn't have given any Colored man the serum, particularly one from America. That's impossible!"

"Then why didn't Kapp die when Elvis shot him in the mouth?"

Hans placed his right hand on his forehead. *Oh, my God, that's right.*

"What if your uncle injected Kapp by mistake? Do you recall everything that occurred that night in the tower?" Adok questioned.

Hans walked back over to Adok's bed and sat down. He wasn't accustomed to dwelling on the past, at least, not that past. Since the war ended, Hans had conditioned his mind not to recall the bad things that happened. Occasionally, he thought about his life with his parents before the war. Those were happy times. Everything else he blocked out. The days with his uncle were the easiest to forget because he wasn't in his right mind. Now he had to remember, and he didn't want to. He was feeling a headache coming on. Hans leaned forward, rested his elbows on his knees, then raised both hands to his forehead and massaged his temples.

Adok paced the floor, back and forth between the door and the large window overlooking the Quad. "Of all the people we know, Mrs. Dexter, our housekeeper of ten years, Nola and her father, not once have we ever had a vision about either of them. Our link to Kapp is the serum that runs through each of our veins. I'm certain of that, which is why we both were able to see and hear what happened to him that night. Therefore, it's only logical to conclude that the serum must be the reason for the flashes as well."

Hans stopped massaging his temples and looked up at his younger brother in disbelief.

"What are you implying? Are you saying that all those people that were killed were also given the serum?"

Adok stopped pacing and stood directly in front of Hans. With a stern piercing gaze, he looked down straight into his older brother's eyes.

"No, it's not the people that were killed, it's the one's doing the killing. They must have been given the serum too," Adok revealed.

A chill suddenly ran through Hans' entire body. Adok was right. He knew it, and before he realized what he was saying, he opened his mouth and blurted out the names, Arnulf and Dag.

"I remember now. Those were the names of the two young Nazi soldiers that were with us when we fled the castle. The youngest one, Dag, was driving the jeep. They were also with us just before my uncle died at his house in Switzerland. Uncle Josef gave them some money and sent them away."

Hans stood up, "Oh, my God! The Nazi Colonel, his name was, was--Strauss. My uncle told me that he had given him the serum. He was sitting in the chair dead. The colonel had not yet awakened, and I wrapped his body in barbed wire. How could I have forgotten all of this?"

"Because you didn't want to remember," said Adok.

Hans nodded his head up and down, acknowledging the truth of Adok's words. At that moment, Hans felt like the younger brother.

"My uncle didn't tell me, but he must have also injected Arnulf and Dag. That must be who the hooded men are. And, of course, the third one is Colonel Strauss. That may also be why their features look so familiar to you."

Hans stared at Adok in silence for a moment, then stood up and walked over to the window and looked down upon the Quad lawn. The lamppost was positioned directly below the window several feet away. Hans gazed at it while disturbing thoughts pounded his brain.

You idiot, your baby brother figured this all out. And perhaps, he has been in contact with Strauss in Germany. That would account for why every time you hear Adok's voice, your brother is saying 'hello' as if he is answering the phone. After that, Adok's voice becomes muffled like the voices on the other end of the line.

"Did you see the colonel awaken?" Hans asked.

Adok walked up to the window and stood beside Hans.

"Yes, eleven years ago. It was two days after we saw Kapp and his wife on the military ship. It was on Sunday, at sunset. I entered our cabin out of breath. You asked me what was wrong and where I had been. I told you I just finished my tennis lesson and rushed to change for dinner--not true. I completed the session an hour earlier. I was just strolling about on deck bouncing my tennis ball on top of my racket when an eerie feeling came over me, compelling me to walk to the edge of the ship and peer out at the ocean. As my eyes scanned the curling waves, a house gradually came into focus. Suddenly, I was peering through the open window on the second-floor of your uncle's cottage. Inside sat the colonel in the black leather chair still wrapped in barbed wire. Due to decay, the barbed wire hung loosely off his bony, emaciated body. The vision was so real I even imagined smelling his rotting flesh, and I placed my hand over my nose to lessen the stench. I wanted to run away, but my feet were like blocks of concrete. I couldn't move. So I watched shivering and scared."

"I watched as the colonel's body twitched, a little at first, and then a lot, until finally, his sunken eyes, surrounded by thick black circles, popped open. Slowly, he rose from the chair, straightening his legs more and more. Higher and higher, his body ascended until the joints in his knees snapped, and he was standing straight up. The silver wire slid to the floor as the top of his head bumped against the ceiling. The colonel was a giant, taller than seven feet. He bent down low, stepped from the wire, and turned to leave. As he walked out the door, the vision slowly disappeared. Finally, able to move, I ran as fast as I could to our room."

Why didn't I hear anything? Hans wondered. "Did he speak?" Hans asked.

"No, not a word, he didn't open his mouth. That's probably why you didn't know when he awakened," said Adok.

Hans felt betrayed. He couldn't believe how much Adok hadn't told him. The two were all each other had-- brothers created by fate and the tragic circumstances of war. But that wasn't enough to get Adok to confide in him. Hans knew that now, and the realization made him swell up. Hans wiped a tear from the corner of his eye.

Hans then felt Adok's hand slide across his back and grip him firmly around his shoulder.

"I know I should have told you all of this before brother," spoke Adok in a soft voice. "At first, I was like you. I didn't want to think about those days. That's what I decided the day I saw the Nazi Colonel rise. I reasoned, asking myself what could we do about it anyway? We're on our way to Canada to start a new life. So just forget about it. Let it go. No need to tell you. We will never meet that colonel again anyhow, I told myself."

Adok drew in a deep breath, then slowly exhaled. "Now, I realize I should have told you everything from the beginning. We might have a better handle on what's happening now, and I wouldn't be on the verge of flunking out of college."

Hans could hear the sincerity in Adok's voice. For better or for worse, Adok was his brother, and he loved him.

"I bear a lot of the blame. I encouraged your silence. It was a mistake to think that we could put what happened during the war behind us. You knew we couldn't, and told me so more than once, but I didn't listen. Well, I'm listening now, brother, so from now on, we tell each other everything. No more secrets. We must find out what's going on before the world is plunged into another global conflict."

"You don't think it will lead to another world war, do you?"

"I don't know what to think. I just know bad things are happening, and I think it's going to get worse."

Hans held up his wrist to check his watch. "It's 2:00 am and you have a 7:30 class in the morning. So for now, let's just get some sleep. We'll talk about this tomorrow."

Chapter Eight

"Most truly I say to you unless anyone
is born again, he cannot see
the Kingdom of God."

James 3:3
New World Translation of the Holy Scriptures

2:00 am February 4, 1956
Charlottesville Hospital, Virginia

"They're alive!" Those words echoed in Kapp's mind repeatedly as he rushed toward the recovery room on the heels of Dr. Franklin. Before he reached the doorway to the critical care unit, Dr. Carter grabbed Kapp's arm and pulled him aside.

"You know what has occurred, don't you? It's your blood transfused into their bodies. They are just like you now," said Dr. Carter as he and Kapp stood in the hallway a few feet from the recovery room.

"Did you know this would happen?" asked Kapp.

"I wasn't a hundred percent certain, but I thought there was a chance that it might," said Dr. Carter.

"What do we do now?"

"I don't know," Carter replied. "We just have to play it by ear."

Kapp and Dr. Carter entered the recovery room. Ray, Milton, Clare, Charmaine, and Olivia all lay in beds lined against the south wall. Ray and Milton were sitting up in bed as if they had just awakened from a good night's sleep. Though alert and looking about, Clare was reclining quietly. Olivia and Charmaine were still under heavy sedation.

"Wow, doctors! Whatever drug you gave me, it's working triple time. I feel like I'm soaring above the clouds and will soon be able to touch the face of God," Ray mused, with puffy smiling cheeks.

Milton just nodded his head while giggling in agreement.

Kapp bypassed the two and walked straight over to Clare. Tenderly, he took his wife's hand while, at the same time, kissed her cheek.

"I know you can do better than that," Clare responded flirtatiously with a gleam in her eyes. Despite the bandage wrapped around her entire head, Kapp couldn't help noticing how fresh, radiant, and full of life his wife looked. Kapp grinned, then bent down and planted a long passionate kiss on his wife's lips. He almost forgot where he was and was ready to climb over in the bed with her.

"Uh oh, looks like there's a bull in the barn," hollered Ray.

Any other time Kapp would have told Ray to mind his own business, but this time Kapp was too embarrassed to speak and merely flashed Ray a "shut up" glance.

Still holding his wife's hand, Kapp watched as Doctors Franklin, Henderson, Carter, and Mason gathered around Ray. The car accident caused a severe laceration to Ray's left kidney, requiring surgery. Ray also sustained several substantial cuts and bruises that needed bandaging. Head Nurse Russell untied Ray's hospital garment, then lowered his bed. As Doctor Henderson removed Ray's gown from Ray's upper body and undid a large bandage on Ray's arm, Doctor Carter glanced back at Kapp, who froze and held his breath. For a second, the two locked eyes before Doctor Carter turned his attention back to Ray. The physicians standing around Ray's bed partially blocked Kapp's view, but Kapp finally exhaled when he saw Doctor Carter lower is shoulders.

"Does that hurt?" asked Dr. Henderson, gently touching the area around the stitched wound with one finger.

"Just a little stinging," Ray responded.

"Well, everything looks good. It's still quite red, but the swelling has gone down, which means the penicillin is already working. That's a good sign," said Dr. Henderson. "Let's hope your kidney mends that quickly. We'll wait another day before we check it, and if all is well, seven days from now, we may be able to take out the stitches."

After a brief examination of Milton, who needed an emergency embolectomy to surgically remove a small blood clot in one of his lungs, the doctors gathered in a corner on the opposite side of the room. Watching them, Kapp immediately became afraid.

What are they saying? They seem engrossed in a heated discussion. Did they want a more intensive examination of my wife, Milton, and Ray the way Doctor Carter examined me the day after I rejoined my unit? That would expose my secret and who knows where that might lead.

Kapp was relieved to see that whatever the doctors were suggesting, Doctor Carter was adamantly shaking his head and waving his hands against their requests.

Minutes later, the other three doctors left the room. Doctor Carter walked towards Kapp, who met Carter before he reached Clare's bed. The two stood several feet away in the center of the floor.

"What was that all about?" Kapp asked in a whisper. "Do they want more tests?

"Yes, of course, they do. Resuscitation rarely occurs after a person has been dead for more than fifteen minutes. A person's brain cells start to die after only four to six minutes, so revival usually happens before that. Your wife was dead for 56 minutes. Ray and Milton revived after 38 minutes. That's a phenomenon that's hard not to want to investigate, especially when it happened to all three of them. That's extremely usual," Dr. Carter whispered.

"What did you say?"

"I agreed to the testing."

"What!?" Kapp shouted. He looked back at his wife and then over at Ray and Milton. He then lowered his voice again. "Why did you agree to it?"

"Because," explained Dr. Carter, "I convinced them to let me do it at my hospital in New York where we have the better testing equipment and a more extensive research lab. I told them that since we served in the same unit, Ray and Milton trust me and will be more willing to agree to intensive examinations. With me doing the testing, I can ensure that all their results turn out normal. Because of the serum, your hemoglobin cell count is abnormally high; it's 25.5, instead of 15.5 to 17.5 for the average male. With a red blood count that elevated, you should have polycythemia vera, a rare disease that occurs when your bone marrow produces more red blood cells than it should, causing your blood to thicken, which makes it harder for it to flow through your arteries and veins. That increases the risk of blood clots, which can lead to strokes and heart attacks. A person with prolonged polycythemia vera will develop Acute Lymphocytic Leukemia. Your high hemoglobin count has not thickened your blood, or cause Leukemia. Your INR or International Normalized Ratio that measures the time it takes your blood to clot is 1.0, the same as most healthy people. Before the transfusion, Ray, Milton, and your wife's blood count were below average due to excessive bleeding. If we test them now, I'm certain their counts will register at the higher levels," said Dr. Carter.

"I also convinced the other doctors to keep the resuscitations a secret until I complete the research because revealing what happened to the medical world may backfire if there's nothing significant to report. As I told my three colleagues, there have been rare cases where persons have been pronounced dead even sent to the morgue and found alive hours later. A delayed reaction to adrenaline, the drug used to resuscitate, is one explanation. I stressed to the three of them that as Negro doctors, we don't have the luxury of making those kinds of mistakes. It's difficult enough for Colored physicians to get a residency at major hospitals now. If this gets publicized, and the result is that we made an error, residency acceptance for Colored doctors may cease altogether. With that argument, they all agreed to keep quiet and let me handle it."

"Dr. Henderson is white. They would believe him," said Kapp.

Dr. Carter let out a halfhearted laughed. "Well, Dr. Henderson has secrets of his own to keep."

"What do you mean?"

Dr. Carter just passed Kapp a look with raised eyebrows. It took only a second for Kapp to get the hint.

"Oh, he's one of those. Do Doctors Franklin and Mason know?"

"Of course, they do. Franklin and Mason told me. But they haven't let on to Dr. Henderson that they know he's passing."

"Hmm, I guess that's the reason he shaved off all his hair at such a young age. It's rare to see a baldheaded man in his thirties," said Kapp. "The naps would have given him away. I knew there was something about him the first time I saw him, but I couldn't quite put my finger on it. He reminds me of my 5th-grade teacher, Mr. Samuels, who had the same tan complexion. Only, Professor Samuels never hid the fact that he was Negro."

"Hey, what are the two of you whispering about over there?" shouted Ray. "You two are always whispering. Let us in on the secret, why don't ya."

"It's time we moved the three of you to different rooms," said Dr. Carter, ignoring Ray's request. "Remember, your wives are still in serious condition."

Ray and Milton's jovial spirit quickly vanished as the two, along with Clare and Kapp, glanced over at Charmaine and Olivia.

"Will they be all right? Are they going to recover?" Milton asked.

"Both operations were successful, and all their vital signs are stable. The next 24 hours are crucial. We will have a better prognosis tomorrow," replied Dr. Carter.

Kapp leaned in closer to the doctor and whispered, "Why don't you just transfuse them too?"

"No, we can't keep having patients die and come back to life," replied Dr. Carter. "Persuading the other doctors not to run blood tests on your wife, Milton, and Ray was difficult enough. It's a good thing that their wounds were still visible and hadn't disappeared the way yours does. The reason maybe because they didn't receive the serum directly. Dissemination of the serum through a transfusion may not enhance a person's abilities to the same degree as direct injection of the serum into the body. Dr. Mason wasn't totally on board with the delayed adrenalin explanation. He suggested the phenomenon might have something to do with you since all three of them received your blood. If the same thing happens to Mrs. Taylor and Mrs. Wilson, it will increase the doctor's suspicions."

"Okay, I see what you mean," said Kapp.

Head Nurse Russell, along with Nurse Bernard, walked into the room.

"We are going to move the three of you to different rooms now," announced Nurse Russell.

"Ladies first," said Nurse Bernard as she and Nurse Russell walked over to Clare's bed and unhooked Clare from the monitors. Working quickly, the nurses moved all three patients to new rooms in less than thirty minutes--Clare to a room by herself, and Ray and Milton in a space together.

Chapter Nine

*When you can't remember why you're hurt,
that's when you're healed.*

Jane Fonda

Noon Thursday, February 9th
Charlottesville, Virginia

It snowed the entire morning on the day that Kapp Johnson's wife and friends were released from the hospital. But by noon, when Kapp arrived at the back entrance to the Colored Section of the University of Virginia Hospital, the sun shined with all the brightness of a summer's day in June. Kapp stood quietly as he leaned against the wall in the small reception area. Kapp was wearing a tan suede cap and a double-breasted brown Marl tweed peacoat with wide notch lapels and side slash pockets over a gold wool turtleneck sweater and dark brown corduroy pants. The door he pulled off the hinges seven days ago was now fixed.

"I don't want you to come into the room and get me when I'm released. I want you to sit in the waiting area until I come out," said Kapp's wife. Reluctantly, Kapp agreed. He overheard Nurses Russell and Bernard talking about how Clare wanted to surprise him with a new dress and a new hairstyle, so he submitted to his wife's request.

Kapp looked at his watch; it was now 12:48. "What's taking them so long?" Kapp mumbled as he paced the floor. He heard the door creak and stopped. Suddenly, the door flung open. A male Negro orderly dressed in a light blue hospital uniform walked out and held open the door. Behind him appeared Charmaine in a wheelchair pushed by her husband Ray immediately followed by Olivia in a wheelchair pushed by her husband Milton, but no Clare.

Several bruises and scars were still visible on Olivia and Charmaine's face, while Ray and Milton, both wearing black wool overcoats and black Fedora hats, looked the picture of health. Charmaine tried to cover the purplish bruise on her right cheek with a red silk scarf wrapped around her head and tied under her chin. She kept touching the small nick over her left eye. She wore black slacks and a red swing cashmere overcoat and black leather gloves. Olivia wore a Carmel Tam hat covering her entire head with a matching Carmel wool fur collar coat and beige slacks. Olivia seemed less concerned about the horizontal scar across her forehead and her puffy upper lip as she joked, "Well, here I am, scar faced and all. Al Capone has nothing on me. Now all I need is a Tommy Gun."

Everyone laughed except Charmaine. She was too busy staring Kapp up and down. It was the first time she saw Kapp without being under the influence of drugs since the collision.

"You too--I don't understand how it is that all of us were in the same accident, but the three of you look as though the crash never happened," Charmaine ranted.

Kapp just shrugged his shoulders in response.

Oh God! Wait until she sees Clare.

Just then, the door opened and out stepped his wife, escorted by Nurse Bernard. Clare was a vision at five feet, nine inches tall in tan pumps, a silk, long sleeve pink dress with tapered lapels accented by an oversized butterfly collar. The dress fitted which at the waist, hugged her breasts, and then flared into a poodle skirt. Her long black hair that once flowed below her shoulders was now two inches shorter with loosely flipped curls. Long and short pixie cut bangs framed her forehead. Draped over her shoulders was the light brown mink stole she wore at the reunion. Red rouge highlighted her high cheekbones, which complimented the deep red shade of her glossy lipstick meticulously applied to her full lips. Black eyeliner accentuated her large almond-shaped eyes. Her cinnamon complexion was smooth and flawless.

"Here I am," Clare beamed, flashing her pearly white teeth as she stepped from the doorway and made a full turn in place. Kapp stood with his mouth gaped open, and so did everyone else. Kapp then whistled as Charmaine gasped.

"I thought we were going home, not to a Hollywood movie premiere. I do believe you're overdressed darling," snipped Charmaine.

"I think she looks gorgeous," rebuffed Olivia. "I hope to look as good in a few months once my hair grows back. It's a good thing you didn't have a head injury and need your head shaved, Clare."

"But she did get her head shaved," said Nurse Bernard, who immediately put her hand over her mouth. "Oh, excuse me, I shouldn't have revealed that. Sharing a person's medical information to non-family members is against hospital policy. I'm so sorry. I hope you will forgive me, Mr. and Mrs. Johnson."

"Don't worry. We won't tell. It's no big deal. Right, honey?" spoke Clare.

"Not to us, unless they object," Kapp replied, glancing around the room at the others.

"Why should we care," said Ray. "It wasn't our medical info she divulged."

"If you got your hair shaved, how could it have grown back so fast?" inquired Charmaine.

"My hair has always been fast-growing," Clare answered.

"But to grow that long in, what, six or seven days, that's impossible" Charmaine replied.

Clare shook her head, causing her hair to swoosh from side-to-side. "Obviously not that impossible," she jabbed.

With tightened jaws and steely eyes, Charmaine shot Clare a jealous look.

"Enough with the hair," said Milton. "Let's go home."

Milton wheeled Olivia toward the exit as each couple filed out the door and into Kapp's station wagon with Nurse Bernard and the male orderly's assistance.

"Well, here we are again," said Milton as Kapp turned onto the same highway they drove on the night of the accident.

"How many miles is it from here to Chicago?" Olivia asked her husband as Charmaine whispered to Ray.

"About nine hundred, I think," said Milton, "but I may be wrong."

"No, you're close," replied Kapp, glancing back at them in his rearview mirror. "It's 612 miles from here to Detroit and another 282 miles from Detroit to Chicago, making it a total of 893 miles. We'll reach Detroit in a little over nine hours. From there, it will take only 5 hours to arrive in the Windy City."

"I don't know," whispered Ray to his wife in an irritated voice. "As she said, her hair grows back fast."

"Are you still talking about Clare's hair?" asked Olivia, who sat beside Charmaine in the back seat.

"Yes, I am because I don't believe that's her real hair. You all forget I'm a beautician; I do hair for a living. I've shaved clients almost bald, leaving only peach fuzz, so that I can get their damaged hair to grow back evenly. Not in one of those cases has a client's hair grown back that long in just seven days, not even close to that long. It takes months for our hair to grow half that length-- months and months."

"Well, there's only one way to find out," said Olivia as she reached over and gently pulled Clare's hair. "It's definitely not a wig."

Clare turned her head and looked back at Olivia. "Thank you," she said and smiled.

"Huh!" Charmaine grunted.

Kapp just shook his head and remained silent, so did Milton and Ray. The three were married long enough to know not to get involved in arguments between wives.

Then suddenly Clare screamed: "Ouch!"

Charmaine had reached over with both hands and gave Clare's hair a hard yank from its roots.

"Now, I'm satisfied," replied Charmaine after letting go.

"Honey, I think you better pull over," said Clare in a seething voice.

"Now baby, let's calm down and think about this. If I stop and the two of you start arguing out here on the highway, and the police come by, what do you think will happen?" Kapp asked.

"We'll probably all end up in jail," answered Milton.

"That's exactly what's going to happen," affirmed Ray, "and we don't need another incident, we just need to get our black asses home."

"Then maybe your wife should apologize," said Kapp, glancing at Ray and Charmaine in his rearview mirror. He saw Ray nudge his wife in her side with his elbow.

After several seconds passed, Charmaine finally apologized. "I'm sorry," she blurted out before bursting into tears.

Clare sobbed too, and so did Olivia.

"What the heck are you crying about!?" Milton asked Olivia.

Ray just leaned back, scooted down into the seat, and folded his arms. "Looks like it's going to be a long ride home," he said before positioning his hat down over his eyes.

Chapter Ten

Find joy in everything you do.
Every job, relationship,
Home... it's your responsibility to love it,
or change it.

Chuck Palahniuk

Thursday, February 23, 1956
Atlanta, Georgia, 6:15 AM

Kapp walked into the kitchen of his three-bedroom two-story, craftsmen style brown brick house wearing black slacks with a white, open-collar shirt. He sat down at the small round kitchen table in front of the bay window while his wife fixed him a plate piled high with scrambled eggs, bacon, toast, and cheesy grits. Still, in her nightgown and robe, Clare handed the plate to Kapp along with the morning newspaper, The Atlanta Journal-Constitution. Kapp set the plate down and unfolded the paper.

"Well, they've done it," said Kapp as he viewed the front page.

"They've done what, honey?" asked Clare while standing at the counter and loading up her plate with double portions of everything she had given her husband.

"Yesterday, the police arrested Dr. Martin Luther King Jr. in Montgomery, Alabama, along with ninety-eight other black leaders for leading the bus boycott."

"Well, we knew it would happen eventually. What else were the authorities going to do? Allow Negroes to exercise their right not to ride the bus and cause the financial ruin of its cities' white-owned bus company?" replied Clare as she set her plate on the table and sat down.

Kapp noticed her plate piled high with food but said nothing. Instead, he placed the newspaper on the seat of the empty chair beside him and reached over and locked both his hands into both of hers. The two then bowed their heads. Kapp only said the words: "Dear Lord, thank you...," before the doorbell rang. "Thank you for the food we are about to receive, Amen," prayed Kapp quickly before getting up to answer the front door.

"Who can that be this early in the morning?" Clare asked.

Kapp peeked out the window. The sun was rising, splashing gold streaks across the sky, but it was still too dark to see clearly. All Kapp could make out were two robust male figures standing on his snow-covered porch wearing Fedora hats and large overcoats.

As Clare attacked the food on her plate, Kapp walked through the hallway and opened the front door. His eyes widen.

"President Mays and Reverend King, what an honor, please come in," he said, directing them into the living room to the right passed the staircase.

The two men walked inside. The living room was olive green. Beige curtains with a floral print of tiny red roses attached to multi-colored stems with leaves of wintergreen, lime, and chartreuse hung from the large picture window facing west. In front of the window was a twill moss green Chesterfield, roll arm sofa. Two highback juniper green and mint paisley printed chairs flanked each side of a glass and walnut coffee table. A red brick fireplace surrounded by white bookshelves dominated the north wall.

"Please, have a seat," said Kapp. The two obeyed and took off their hats before sitting on the sofa as Kapp sat down in the chair near the hallway. They unbuttoned their coats but kept them on. Underneath, they both wore suits and matching colored ties with the President of Morehouse College wearing navy blue and Reverend King clad in dark brown.

"We won't take up too much of your time. You must be anxious to know why we have come here so early in the morning. Reverend King and I have a proposition we would like to present to you," said President Benjamin Mays. He then looked to his right at Reverend King.

The Reverend leaned forward. At 57-years-old, Martin Luther King Senior was a broad-shouldered man with course carefully cut salt and pepper gray hair and gold rim glasses. His baritone voice was deep and authoritative.

"Let me get straight to the point, Coach Johnson. I would like to enlist the skills you acquired in the white man's army fighting the white man's war to help protect my son in his righteous quest for civil rights for our people."

Kapp sat speechless as his heart raced. He didn't know whether to be honored, excited, or scared. A hundred thoughts flooded his mind all at once.

What about Clare? The way she is eating, she must be pregnant. She's not going to want me to leave her alone if she's expecting, and taking her with me, maybe too dangerous. Neither she nor I want to risk another miscarriage. And what about money? Am I going to get paid, or am I expected to do this for free? We're still paying the mortgage on this house. But how can I refuse after the way Reverend King put it. I fought the white man's war to free other people, people I didn't even know, from oppression and tyranny only to come back home to face the same old racism, prejudice, and social ostracism. What about my people? Who's going to fight for us if not me and others like me?

"I know you have a wife to support, not to mention the mortgage on this house. So we are not suggesting that you do this for free," explained President Mays. "What I'm suggesting is that you take a one-year paid sabbatical. When submitting your request, you can say you wish to research the best ways to help more high school Negro athletes qualify for college."

"Yes, that's a good idea and is sorely needed, but what exactly are you asking me to do for your son, Reverend King, be his bodyguard?"

"Yes," said Martin Luther King Sr. "Now that my son is the leader of the boycott, Martin doesn't drive himself anywhere for fear he may get into an accident or be run off the road and crash his car. Before the protest, my son was stopped over 25 times for speeding. A man of color driving a car is an easy target for police to harass. So one of your responsibilities as his bodyguard will be to drive him everywhere. My son's house was bombed last month, as you have heard. Thankfully, no one was hurt. Now that the court indicted Martin for instigating the protest, things will get even more heated, and he and his family will need some real protection. Someone who knows how to handle himself in intense situations without panicking or over-reacting is essential. What better person to enlist than a battle-harden soldier who also knows how to lead men?"

"So there will be other men protecting your son as well?

"Yes, some local men, but not with your experience," replied Reverend King.

"Well, it all sounds okay, but I will have to talk to my wife before I agree to it."

"That's the other reason we thought you would be perfect for the job," said President Mays.

"Your wife has family in Alabama, doesn't she?"

"Yes, her parents and an uncle live in Montgomery, and her aunt lives in Selma."

"Good. So staying with your wife's relatives wouldn't be a problem then, would it?" inquired the President.

"I don't think so, but I'm not sure my wife will want to leave our house vacant for that long."

"Of course she wouldn't," said Reverend King, "that's why I've taken the liberty to make a list of several suitable couples from the congregation who you and your wife can interview to rent your home. All the couples have good steady jobs and can afford the rent, and none have children, so your house will remain as tidy and well maintained as it is now."

Reverend King reached in his coat pocket, pulled out a sheet of paper and handed it to Kapp.

"Well, I see the two of you have thought of everything, but I still will have to talk it over with my wife. You see, we may be expecting a baby, though we haven't gotten it confirmed by a doctor yet. But if we are, we would have to consider that as well. You understand?"

There was silence. Seeing the disappointed looks on both their faces compelled Kapp to give them some reassurance. "But even so, I'm still inclined to accept. Don't worry, my wife and I will talk it over, and I'll let you know for sure this Sunday after church."

"Good, then we will leave it in the Lord's hands," said Reverend King.

"And with that, we'll take our leave and let you finish your breakfast and get to campus," replied President Mays as he and the Reverend stood up.

Kapp walked them to the door. He stood on the porch and watched them drive away, waving goodbye. Minutes later, Kapp was still standing in the same spot with his hands tucked into his pockets, shivering from the cold and wondering how to tell his wife and what to say to get her to agree. Just when he decided to let it ride and merely inform her of his decision, he heard Clare's soft, soothing voice.

"I just got off the phone with mom and dad. They said we can stay with them if we like. Now, all we have to do is choose one of the couples on Reverend King's list and pack."

Kapp turned around. Clare was standing in the doorway.

This is why I love this woman so much. She's always on my side and always ready to support me, no matter what. She overheard everything that was said. What wife wouldn't eavesdrop on her husband's conversation, especially when it's taking place in the living room of her own house? I couldn't have been prouder of her than at this moment.

Kapp walked over to Clare and placed his arms around her waist.

"What about the baby? It may be a little too early for a doctor to tell you with certainty, but are you sure you want to risk it? It won't be easy. It could be dangerous."

"I'm sure. It will be all right; everything will turn out fine. Like I know I'm pregnant, I know I'm going to carry this baby to full term, and whatever happens in Alabama, we'll survive. This time is different. I feel stronger, somehow. Ever since the accident, I've felt as though my body has gone through, I don't know, a sort of metamorphosis, as if every cell has undergone a rejuvenation. It's hard to explain, but lately, I feel like nothing can go wrong. I've been too afraid to tell you or say it out loud. But the truth is, I feel invincible."

Kapp didn't answer. He just pressed his wife's body against his chest and buried his face into the side of her neck.

Yes, darling, you have changed. Now we are both invincible.

Chapter Eleven

Where is the Jim Crow section
On this merry-go-round,
Mister, cause I want to ride?
Down South where I come from
White and colored can't sit side by side.
Down South, on the train, there's a Jim Crow car.
On the bus, we're put in the back—but there ain't no back
to a merry-go-round!
Where's the horse for a kid that's black?

Langston Hughes

1:00 PM, Thursday, March 1, 1956

Vancouver, Canada

Hans walked into the newsroom on the 10th floor of the Vancouver Daily Press building after having lunch at a local restaurant and was immediately flanked on both sides by Carl and Nola Richardson.

"This just came over the AP. This morning the Alabama legislature voted to ask the U. S. Government for federal funds to have all blacks in Alabama deported to northern states," said Carl holding up the AP wire for Hans to see. "I think it's time we send a news crew to Alabama, don't you?"

Hans chuckled and shook his head from side-to-side as he continued to walk to his office. "That's never going to happen."

"Whether or not it's going to happen is not the point. The point is we are the only newspaper in the world that's not covering what's happening in Alabama. Even the German press is covering it. You didn't want to send a reporter to Alabama when they arrested Martin Luther King or bombed his house. Now, when all the Negroes in the state may get deported, you still have this newspaper sitting on its hands. Why?"

Hans stopped, turned to his right, and looked at Carl, who stared at him with a creased brow. Hans knew Carl's question implied that he didn't want to cover the story because Negroes were involved. Carl was right, but not for the reason the senior editor thought. Kapp wasn't prejudiced; he was scared. Hans always knew that one day, he, Adok, and Kapp would meet. Hans feared what that might mean. He didn't want to facilitate that meeting sooner than necessary. Despite the significance of the Negroes fight for equality in Alabama, Hans couldn't shake the feeling that sending reporters there somehow would force the meeting with Kapp. Nor could he shake the feeling that all the killings his brother saw were also connected to Alabama. After all his talk to Adok about stopping another world war, Hans didn't have a clue about how they would achieve such a formidable task. Their unique abilities didn't make them supermen.

Hans knew Kapp lived in Atlanta, Georgia, and attended Ebenezer Baptist Church, the same church where Martin Luther King's father was a pastor. He also knew Kapp was now in Alabama. The morning Reverend King, Sr. and the Morehouse president visited Kapp, Hans heard their conversation. Whenever anything significant happens in Kapp's life, good or bad, his enhanced hearing perception kicks in. Ever since that day on the ship, eleven years ago, a connection between the two was forged. It was a connection he didn't even share with his brother. With Adok, only when trouble was about to occur was his senses alerted, and sometimes not even then.

Why he had such a bond with a Negro soldier, Hans didn't know. Perhaps it was because he and Kapp were alike. They were both peaceful men at heart and tried to avoid confrontation. They were both God-fearing men even though Hans no longer practiced the faith that he once shared with his parents. For two years now, he read a few chapters of the bible every Sunday night before retiring. Though, he still couldn't bring himself to pray.

Hans entered his office, took off his brown trench raincoat, and hung it on the eight-hook coat stand along with his black suit jacket before sitting down at his desk. Both Carl and Nola followed him in. He motioned for them to take a seat at his desk across from him. Hans loosened his gold silk tie, looked at Carl then at Nola, and then abruptly turned his chair slightly right to gaze out the window at the rain that suddenly came pouring down outside.

I know my paper must cover what's happening in Alabama eventually, still…

"I've been in contact with Bayard Rustin, one of Martin Luther King's key advisers. I met Rustin and got to know him well while I was attending Columbia U. I met him at a social justice meeting in Harlem," said Nola. "He's an amazing man. He's been a social activist for years. Rustin helped organize the March on Washington in 1941 to press the government to end employment discrimination. So, if I'm sent to cover the story in Montgomery, I'll have an 'in.' I won't be just another reporter on the outside writing about the same events. I'll have an insider's perspective."

Hans turned his chair back towards his desk. "Ok," he blurted out. His quick approval surprised even him.

Nola became ecstatic and jumped up out of her chair. "You mean, I can go? And you won't change your mind later?"

"I just might if you keep asking me. So, if you are going, go. I want some good pictures, so you must take Sands with you. His pics of the winter Olympics were outstanding."

Nola's smile faded. She glanced over at her father, who glanced back at her. There was a concerned look on both their faces.

"I don't know if having a photographer with her is a good idea," said Carl. Particularly if the photographer is white. Dr. King and the other pastors may think Nola is spying and may not be willing to…"

"Look, to tell a compelling news story about a social movement, people must be moved, and nothing does that more effectively than pictures. Words alone are not enough. We're a newspaper, not a wire service." Hans flashed Nola a stern look. "You must give me pics, or it's a no go. I don't care how you get them, just get them.

Every story you send me, I want at least ten accompanying photos."

"Ten! That's way too many. How about five?" Nola replied.

"Ten!"

"Ok, I will try to get ten, but I will only guarantee you five pictures per story--deal?" Nola held out her right hand to Hans.

Hans hesitated as he looked up at her standing on the other side of his desk.

If I hold out for ten, maybe she'll refuse to go. No, that's not fair. I've never put a picture quota on any of my other reporters.

After several seconds, Hans finally extended his hand. "Ok, five it is. Now get packing, I want you in Alabama by tomorrow."

Chapter Twelve

…Get up, get out from
among my people…
(Pharaoh said to Moses)

Exodus 12:31
New World Translation of the Holy Scriptures

6:00 PM, Friday, March 2, 1956
Dexter Avenue Baptist Church
Montgomery, Alabama

Kapp heard the members of the Dexter Avenue Church talking in the background as he waited for an usher to get his wife to come to the phone. Although the telephone was in the office off the main entrance, he heard the loud, high-pitched voices and imagined the church filled with adults and children all discussing the possibilities of being deported to cities up north.

"Hey babe, how's it going?"

"It's a madhouse in here," Clare replied. "Everyone is scared that the state will send us to some God-forsaken place in a remote northern state where no one else lives and force us to live there the way the American Indians have been forced to live on reservations. You don't think that could ever happen, do you? You don't think the federal government will really deport all the Negroes in Alabama up north as the members of the Alabama State Legislature requested yesterday, do you?"

"They could if we let them. For a long time, no one in America believed the Jews were being sent to concentration camps and exterminated until we saw it for ourselves. Anything is possible when people don't fight back. But, don't worry, neither Martin nor any of the rest of us will allow that to happen."

"So, you're calling him Martin now and no longer Dr. King?"

"Martin insisted that I call him by his first name. Besides, protecting someone's life is personal. If you can't be on a first-name basis for a person you're willing to take a bullet for, then when can you be?"

Clare didn't reply. Silence filled the airwaves. Kapp immediately realized he shouldn't have spoken so literally. He never explained the dangers of being a bodyguard. Nor had he told her that nothing could kill him. The honor of the position was all the two ever discussed. Now, for the first time, he sensed Clare's fear.

Kapp spoke his wife's name, strong and with confidence. "Clare."

"Yes," Clare replied in a weak, raspy whisper, barely audible.

"It's going to be alright, babe. I'm going to be fine. We're going to get through this just like you said, remember?"

"Yes," Clare uttered in a louder, more measured tone. "Uh, hum," she cleared her throat. "So, when is Martin coming? The congregation is getting restless."

"Oh yeah, that's why I called. The baby has a fever, so Martin isn't coming. They think she may have an ear infection, but they won't know for sure until Dr. Hayes arrives. The doctor should be here soon. Reverend Abernathy will officiate over the meeting tonight. He's on his way."

"Wow! Being a Civil Rights Leader has its perks, I see. You can get doctors to make house calls. It must be nice. On the other hand, the congregation won't be pleased. All these people came out on a cold wintry evening to see and hear Dr. King, not his second in command."

"I'm sure once Reverend Abernathy tells them that little Yolanda is sick, they will understand and won't be too upset.

"Excuse me a minute, honey," said Clare to her husband. Clare turned her head toward the door. "Yes, may I help you?" asked Clare, lowering the phone from her mouth while standing beside the black office desk positioned in front of the only window in the room.

"Yes, I am looking for Mr. Bayard Rustin. He told me to meet him here."

"And you are...?" inquired Clare.

"Nola Richardson. I'm an old friend. I met him years ago in New York at college."

"He's in the main auditorium straight ahead through the double doors. Since the two of you are such old buddies, I'm sure you will know Mr. Rustin when you see him."

"Thank you."

"Your welcome," said Clare as she rolled her eyes and lifted the phone back to her ear.

"Who was that?" asked Kapp.

"Some black girl with bleached blonde hair passing for white."

Kapp chuckled. "Where is Rustin? Is he even there?"

"Yes. When I came to answer your call, Mr. Rustin was standing in the back of the hall in a corner, holding up the wall as usual. I know Rustin is supposed to be a good organizer, but I don't trust him. There's something about him I don't like. Anyway, he's just the type that would know a fake white girl."

"Excuse me, but this fake white girl can't find him."

Clare looked up from the phone to meet the smirk on Nola Richardson's face as Nola stood ten feet away from Clare with her arms folded. Dressed in a white silk blouse that tied in a huge bow at the collar, Nola's black A-line skirt hugged her wide 48-inch hips. Nola sashayed closer and stopped three feet in front of Clare. Nola's long shapely legs were spread apart in a defiant stance. On her feet were a pair of black patent leather, pointed-toe spike heels.

Click!

Clare dropped the phone on the hook without saying goodbye to her husband. Mrs. Johnson then looked Nola up and down while placing both her hands on her bigger 52-inch hips. Wearing a violet turtleneck, long-sleeve, sweater dress that accentuated every rise and curve in her body, Clare took one step forward, staring directly into Nola's light brown eyes. In Heels, they were both the same height. Although she was two months pregnant, there was only a slight baby bump.

Nola glanced down at Clare's rounder, wider hips, and instinctively straightened her shoulders and arched her back.

"So, you can't spot your old friend in a room where most everybody is seated," remarked Clare. "Tis, tis, tis, what's a fake white girl to do? Seems to me, being such good old friends with Mr. Rustin, he would have spotted you and made himself known, or perhaps he didn't want to acknowledge a phony white girl in a room full of Colored People."

"Maybe the reason he didn't acknowledge me is that he isn't there."

"Well, if he isn't there, what do you expect me to do about it, snap my fingers, and make him appear?"

"No, of course not, you don't possess such abilities. Just tell me where Rustin is."

"Huh hum, excuse me sistahs, I'm right here."

Both Clare and Nola turned their heads simultaneously and peered at Rustin, standing in the doorway.

"We're not sisters," they both replied in unison.

Rustin walked towards them. He was a tall, attractive, middle-aged man of medium brown complexion with a thin black mustache and a black, two-inch high, neatly cropped afro. He wore a white shirt with a light gray tie and dark gray suit pants. Around his slim waist was a thin black leather belt with a silver buckle. The sleeves of his wrinkled shirt were rolled up to his elbows. In his right hand, dangling between his fingers, was a pair of black-rimmed, wayfarer-shaped eyeglasses. He immediately put them on as he stopped and stood between Clare and Nola. He looked tired as if he hadn't slept the night before. His breath smelled of cigarettes.

"You may not look like sistahs, but you are sistahs, and there's more important fish to fry here than for you two to be fighting like a pair of alley cats. So acknowledge it and move on."

"Why should I acknowledge it when she doesn't? She's only black when she wants to be. How many "Colored Only" water fountains have she taken a drink from? How many hotels have turned her away?" Clare glared at Nola. "Tell me, 'sis-tah,' are you staying downtown on 5th Avenue at the Molton Hotel? Where the distinguished Commissioner of Public Safety, Mr. Eugene "Bull" Connor, spends his mornings at the bar sipping shots of Ole' Grand-Dad bourbon? And, where Colored people are only allowed in the back entrance if they are bellhops or maids?"

Clare waited for Nola to reply. Nola stood silent with her eyes looking elsewhere as Clare shot Rustin a condemning glance. "Of course, she is. And you want me to claim her as my sister, I don't think so," said Clare switching from the room with one hand on her hip.

As soon as Clare was out the door, Nola buried her face in her hands and cried. Bayard pulled Nola into his arms and held her against his chest as the two stood in front of the desk.

"As much as I hate to admit it, Mrs. Johnson is right. There's no passing for white down here," said Rustin.

Nola lifted her head and looked up at him. "But you have a few white people working for the cause. I met several of them this morning. Why can't I be just like them?"

"Because you're not just like them. And by now, I'm sure Mrs. Johnson has told every black woman here about you."

"Of course, she can't keep her big mouth shut."

"Don't be so naïve. Even if you had been able to fool Mrs. Johnson, someone else would have recognized your Negro heritage. Either way, you were going to be exposed. You've been living a lie, and it's time to face reality."

Nola backed away from Rustin. "Face reality? My father is black, and my mother is white. I'm both races. That's my reality. I look more white than black. Therefore, I have chosen to be white. So how am I living a lie?"

"Okay, suit yourself. But you can't stay at the Molton Hotel. It's where the Klan holds their meetings. And if they get so much as a whiff that you are passing, you will be on your way back to Canada in a box."

"You don't mean they would kill a white woman?"

Rustin looked at Nola with raised eyebrows but didn't answer.

"Juliette Hampton Morgan is a white socialite who has written articles in the Montgomery Advertiser against segregation," said Bayard. "I'm sure she wouldn't mind hosting you during your stay here. Your association with Miss Morgan will give you creditability with our, my people."

"What about my photographer?"

"I think she has room for him too. I'll call her now." Bayard turned around, reached across the desk, and pulled the phone to him. As he was talking to Miss Morgan, one of the female ushers rushed into the office and announced that Reverend Abernathy just arrived. Bayard hung up the phone.

"Everything is set. Here is the address and Miss Morgan's phone number," Bayard said, handing Nola a small slip of paper. "I've also written the directions on the back. Miss Morgan will be expecting you tonight."

Chapter Thirteen

"Courage is the most important of all the virtues because without courage, you can't practice any other virtue consistently."

Maya Angelou

Monday, March 5, 1956
8:00 AM

"You take the bus to work?" asked Nola to Juliette as she followed Miss Morgan out the front door and down the long walkway of Juliette's large white Georgian style house. Although it was a cloudy morning and the ground was still saturated from the downpour of rain from last night, Nola wore only carmine red heels with a matching carmine, shoulder strap purse, nude stockings, and a hip-length, navy blue, box wool coat over a pink blouse and burgundy A-line skirt.

At age 42, Juliette Morgan was a spinster and worked at the Montgomery Public Library as the director of research. She wore her black hair cut short and combed back off her forehead, which complimented her long angular nose, dark brown eyes, and the oval shape of her face. Juliette was a stylish and meticulous dresser. She paired a long gray swing coat fastened with three silver buttons down the front, welt pockets at the hip, and shoulder darts in the front and back with a soft felt, pewter, wide brim cloche hat. The hat encircled by a three-inch ribbon band had a side bow. Miss Morgan protected her black heels with a pair of maroon front lace-up galoshes, trimmed in rabbit fur. She also wore matching maroon leather gloves while carrying a black tubular handbag. Both Miss Morgan's parents were dead. She lived in that big house all by herself. Miss Morgan employed a negro woman, Mrs. Alberta Smith, as her cook and Mrs. Smith's 19-year-old daughter, Tessie, as her maid.

"Driving doesn't agree with me. I get too nervous and suffer from bouts of anxiety. Riding the bus is much safer."

"But you can afford to hire a driver," said Nola, trying to keep up with Juliette's long strides while dodging the sometimes large puddles of water, and bracing herself against the frequent gusts of wind that sent her long blonde locks swirling over her head.

"Yes, I can. But for an unmarried white woman to have a Negro chauffeur is frowned upon in these parts. It tends to lead to accusations and gossip."

"Oh, I see," said Clare as she walked down the street one step behind Miss Morgan.

Sands walked behind the two with his camera around his neck, occasionally taking pictures of the neighborhood. The 28-year-old photojournalist's first name was Bonneville, so he preferred to be called by his last name. Because he stood only five feet, four inches tall, and was skinny with small facial features, light brown eyes, and curly brown hair, people often thought he was just a kid and didn't notice him. That made it easy for him to blend in and move in and out of crowds taking close-ups and photos from unique angles and perspectives. When Sands was on assignment, he always wore denim blue jeans and a white T-shirt, which aided in the perception that he was a teenager, no older than sixteen or seventeen. Today his attire was no exception. Only, against the cold, he donned a mid-length, brown leather overcoat with a zip-to-top China collar, and matching brown leather, newsboy cap.

After walking three blocks down Knox Drive, the three arrived at the bus stop on Day Street, one of the city's main thoroughfares. They didn't have to wait long. The bus rolled up seconds later. The multi-colored bus was painted white on top with a six-inch wide strip of army green paint around and below the windows. The rest of the bus was pumpkin orange.

As soon as Nola stepped onto the bus, she froze. With her eyes locked on the signed that read "Colored Only," she no longer felt her feet. The sign was still posted on the rail above the back of the tenth-row seat even though there were no Colored riders on board. Nola could hear herself breathe as she imagined seeing the chiseled, stoic faces of Negro passengers all crammed in the back of the bus, many of whom would have had to stand due to lack of adequate seating. Only white passengers were on board today. There were five white patrons, including Juliette, Sands, and herself. The other two riders were an elderly couple, Mr. and Mrs. Reynolds, sitting in the first-row seat opposite the driver. The couple and Juliette were members of the same church, St. Peter's. Realizing that she was the only one still standing, Nola finally sat next to Juliette closest to the aisle after paying the ten-cent fare.

The driver was a middle-aged, blonde man with a neatly trimmed mustache and a butch haircut wearing a bluish-gray uniform. His shirt was lighter than his pants. The name tag pinned above the right pocket on his shirt read, Guy Buckman. As the bus driver pulled away and continued, Nola kept glancing back at the sign until she noticed Negroes on the sidewalks. Men and women, young and old, on their way to work, kids on their way to school, some riding bicycles but most walking, all moving in different directions on both sides of the street.

There's so many. Nola thought to herself as she looked across Juliette out the window. She tapped the thumb of her right hand against her left palm as she silently counted the number of blacks. She stopped counting after three hundred, no longer able to keep track.

There's so many.

"I imagine they don't have very many Negroes in Vancouver," said Juliette.

"No, maybe half a million in all of Canada," Nola replied. Suddenly realizing that she was fidgeting and probably appeared nervous to Miss Morgan, Nola stopped tapping her thumb. Yesterday, the church was full of Colored People. That didn't seem to bother her. Why did the sight of Negroes rattle her so now?

Maybe it was because of the setting. I was in church. Everyone was waiting for Dr. King to appear, and I knew nothing bad would happen. Maybe my excitement about being there overcame my fear. I don't know. I don't know.

Nola shook her head.

"Are you all right, honey?" asked Miss Morgan.

Nola flashed Juliette a smile. "Yes. Why wouldn't I be? It's not like I haven't been around Negroes before. I'm well acquainted with Mr. Rustin, remember? And my father is…"

Nola suddenly paused.

"Your father is what?"

Nola shook her head again. "Nothing," she said. Nola stopped looking out the right-side window and cast her gaze straight ahead. But out of the corner of her eye, Nola still saw the concerned look on Miss Morgan's face. She was relieved when the bus stopped, and the door swung open. That diverted everyone's attention. It surprised Nola, and everyone else, to see a Negro woman step onto the bus.

Nola's first impression of the woman was that she was middle-aged, perhaps in her forty's or early fifties. But after the woman quickly dropped two nickels in the slot and turned around, Nola got a full view of the passenger's face. She was a young female, perhaps nineteen or twenty with a smooth, chocolate complexion, round, plump, cheeks, full lips and stunning brown eyes. It was the clothes the Colored girl wore that made her appear older than she was. She had on a long dusty, tweed coat with a ratty, dark brown, fur collar, and an equally ratty white knitted hat with a big, knitted ball on top. The cap was pulled down over her entire head with only a few strands of auburn hair showing. The hat even covered part of her face. The overcoat was two sizes too big with thick, padded shoulders that hung well below the young woman's natural shoulder line. Black tights covered her thin legs, and on her feet were a pair of run-down, black, granny, lace-up shoes. She carried a small, narrow, red purse with a single thin strap that looked old and frayed and didn't match the rest of her attire.

Nola expected the girl to proceed down the aisle. Instead, the girl got off and walked back along the outside of the bus.

Nola looked at Juliette, puzzled.

"They must board by the rear door once they've paid," whispered Juliette.

Nola turned her head and followed the girl with her eyes. The girl stopped and waited in front of the side door. The door opened suddenly but closed just as quickly as the driver pulled away, leaving the girl standing on the curb.

Miss Morgan immediately hopped up from her seat and pulled the cord for the bus to stop.

"Excuse me, driver, but you forgot your passenger."

"My passenger," the driver said with a nasty smirk on his face. "Slavery is over, remember? I don't own her. I have a schedule to keep. I can't help it if she doesn't board the bus quickly enough. I can't wait all morning for just one rider."

"That's right! He has a schedule to keep. My husband and I have doctor's appointments this morning, and we don't want to be late," said Mrs. Reynolds.

"Yeah, slow, lazy niggers, they always want special treatment," ranted her husband. "And you, Miss Morgan, sticking up for them. I've read your articles in the Advertiser—shameful! I know your parents wouldn't approve. I bet they are turning over in their graves right now."

"Better my parents then Saint Peter for keeping silent and not standing up for what is right. How would the two of you like to pay your fare and then be made to get off the bus to board in the rear, only for the driver to leave you? Would you like to be treated that way? The bible says, "do unto others as you would have them do unto you," or don't the two of you believe in the bible, being such good Protestants," spoke Juliette, passionately.

The elderly couple both made a scoffing sound but didn't reply.

"That's right! And if you pay your fare, you should be able to sit wherever you want," shouted Sands. Nola watched as Sands got up from his seat directly across from her and Juliette and walked to the last row in the back of the bus and sat down.

"Excuse me," said Juliette. Miss Morgan slid pass Nola and walked to the back of the bus also and sat beside Sands.

The driver shook his head at the two.

"Suit yourselves," he said. The driver then looked in his overhead mirror at Nola.

"Aren't you going to join them?" he asked.

Suddenly Nola felt weak. A lump formed in her throat. Her chest began to burn. Her mouth was suddenly dry, and her tongue expanded. She felt a chill creep slowly down her back. She couldn't speak or move the slightest muscle in her body. Nola sat still and silent with her knees pressed together, and her arms pinned to her sides, listening to the sound of her heart pounding loudly in her ears.

Chapter Fourteen

"Failure should be our teacher, not our undertaker.
Failure is delay, not defeat.
It is a temporary detour, not a dead end.
Failure is something we can avoid only
by saying nothing, doing nothing, and being nothing."

Denis Waitley

As she sat among the group of activists, ministers, and community leaders in the basement of the Dexter Avenue Baptist Church where the Montgomery Improvement Association gathered to organize the bus boycott, Nola Richardson felt small and insignificant, a failure to everyone gathered there, and most of all, to herself. Nola occupied one of the many chairs positioned against the wall of the meeting room. She didn't remember saying goodbye to Juliette Morgan when the bus stopped and let Miss Morgan off on High Street at the Montgomery Public Library. She didn't remember when she and Sands exited the bus and entered the church building thirty minutes ago at 8:45 am. Nor did Nola remember when Bayard Rustin introduced Sands and her to the group. She recalled none of these details because disconcerting thoughts so rattled her mind that she could no longer function normally or think of anything else but what happened on the bus earlier that morning.

I'm a coward. Why didn't I speak up like Juliette and Sands? Why didn't I join them and sit in the back of the bus? I'm a coward. They're not even Colored; I'm half. They found the courage to say something. Why couldn't I?

Nola wanted to cry. She covered her face with her right hand and lowered her head. She was about to when she heard a familiar voice.

"So, you're a reporter and staying with Miss Juliette Hampton Morgan."

Nola immediately lifted her head. Standing in front of her was the woman she had a run-in with two days ago in the small office upstairs. The woman with hips wider than hers, and who Nola now noticed bore a striking resemblance to the Colored actress Dorothy Dandridge. Nola merely nodded her head without speaking. She was in no mood to engage in a verbal two-step with the Dorothy lookalike today. Despite Nola's tepid response, the woman gracefully lowered her big hips in the empty chair next to Richardson. Nola immediately inhaled, breathing in the faint scent of the woman's jasmine perfume. The smell was soothing. It mad Nola feel better.

"My name is Clare Johnson. My husband, Kapp, is Martin's, Dr. King's bodyguard." Clare nodded her head in her husband's direction. Her husband was standing directly behind Dr. King. The Reverend, wearing a black suit and tie, arrived two minutes ago with Mr. and Mrs. Johnson and was sitting at the head of the long conference table in the center of the room. Also seated at the table were Civil Rights Attorney Fred Gray, Reverend Ralph Abernathy, Edgar Nixon, the local chapter President of the NAACP; Reverend E. N. French, Ella Baker, NAACP Field Secretary, and JoAnn Robinson, Teacher and President of the Women's Political Council, along with six other members.

"Please to meet you," Nola responded with a half-hearted smile. *So, your husband's Dr. King's bodyguard, and I guess you think that makes you something. By the smug look on your face, that something is queen. Look at you, sitting all poised and proper, with your back straight, your hands clasped together in your lap, and your legs crossed at your ankles. That long sleeve, button-down the front, gold, silk-looking blouse your wearing with the open-fly collar is fake, not real silk, like mine. My burgundy A-line skirt is pure wool flannel. Your black A-line skirt is a cheap synthetic. Yeah, you do favor Dorothy Dandridge a little. But I've often been told I look like Marilyn Monroe, and we both know which of the two is a bigger star. So, you can take your red-lips, diesel-hips ass, and get out of my face, Mrs. Johnson.*

Nola flashed Mrs. Johnson another cheesy smile before she rose ever-so-gracefully from her chair and walked over to where Sands was standing in front of the closed-door taking pictures.

"Wow! I'm getting some great shots. I hope your copy is just as good," said Sands.

"Why? What's going on?" Nola asked, suddenly noticing how almost everyone in the room was holding what appeared to be a legal document in their hands and intently reading it.

"You mean you haven't been paying attention. What have you been doing all this time? Dr. King and the other leaders arrested in February must pay a $500 fine or spend 365 days in jail. They are charged with instigating a boycott and interfering with a business under a 1921 ordinance. There were 99 leaders and ministers apprehended that day. Only fourteen are here. You should have gotten most of their names and bios by now."

Nola's face turned bright red. Standing 5 feet 9-inches tall in heels, she stared down at Sands and replied with an edgy-politeness attached to her words: "I've won a Pulitzer. I know how to do my job; thank you very much, Mr. Bon-ne-vill."

"Then do it!" Sands shot back before walking away.

Nola watched Sands move to the other side of the room and couldn't help but think what a little man he was.

I bet if I bumped my hips against his skinny, weasel body, he would fall to the floor and probably never get up. If Mrs. Johnson slammed him with her hips, the little weasel would be dead before he hit the ground.

Nola giggled as she glanced over at Clare Johnson. Mrs. Johnson was still sitting in the same chair against the wall. But sitting next to her was a heavyset Negro woman with reddish-brown hair in a white knitted pullover sweater, a wintergreen wool skirt, and black flat-heel boots. On the floor next to the woman's chair was a large brown grocery bag. She and Mrs. Johnson were huddled together, whispering like best friends sharing a secret. Suddenly they shot a look Nola's way. Without thinking, Nola immediately walked over to them.

"Are you two talking about me, Mrs. Johnson?"

"Yes. We were. By the way, this is Mrs. Maddie Wilkins. The Klan lynched her husband a year ago," said

Clare as her eyes quickly scanned the room before speaking again. Mrs. Johnson and Mrs. Wilkins both stood up.

"Why don't you join us in the ladies' room," Clare whispered. "And by the way, you're right. If I bumped that photographer with my hips, it would kill him," Clare smiled.

Nola's eyes widened. "What?"

Chapter Fifteen

> I raise up my voice—not so I can shout,
> but so that those without a voice can be heard...
> we cannot succeed when half of us are held back.
>
> Malala Yousafzai

As soon as Nola entered the church's first floor ladies' room behind Clare and Mrs. Wilkins, Clare spoke.

"It's curious, isn't it that there are so many ministers and community leaders here, and the one person who started it all, Mrs. Rosa Parks, isn't."

"Yeah, especially since not one of those ministers were willing to support more than a one-day boycott when Edgar Nixon first recommended it," revealed Mrs. Maddie Wilkins, "and that's including Dr. King. Nixon had to shame them into it."

"Nixon, he's the president of the local NAACP, correct? How was he able to persuade them?" Nola asked Maddie.

"Nixon told them that every congregation member in their flock works hard for the meager wages they receive, and still manages to support their church financially, so much so that the ministers can afford to buy new cars while their flock must ride the bus. Now that their congregations need their ministers' help, the pastors are unwilling to give it. Nixon even called the ministers cowards. After that little speech, Dr. King proclaimed he wasn't a coward and volunteered to lead a more sustained campaign," said Maddie.

"Oh, I see. So, what are you saying, that Mrs. Parks has been shut out and not allowed to come to these meetings?"

"Not entirely shut out, she still attends more times than not. It's more like she's getting pushed aside. And it's not only Rosa but all the women," said Clare. "It's the women who arranged the carpools and pies and cakes sales to fund the car rides. The women set up the meetings and rally's and contact the people to attend them. Many of these women are involved in labor organizing and voter registration drives, which often means teaching applicants to read. In fact, most NAACP members are women. That's why we are proposing that you interview Mrs. Parks and some of the other female leaders like Septima Clark and Ella Baker. They are doing good work. They risk their lives just like the men and are getting no recognition for it," said Clare.

"Unfortunately, our men prefer it that way. If there's one thing that's common in all races, its male chauvinism," confessed Maddie.

"Will I also get to interview Mrs. King too?"

Both Maddie and Clare shook their heads.

"No. I don't see Coretta agreeing to it. She might have agreed before their house was bombed. But not now," said Clare.

"And Mrs. Parks, she's on board with being interviewed?"

"Definitely, at the first mass meeting after the boycott started, Rosa wanted to address the assembly, but one of the ministers, who shall remain nameless, told her, "'I think you've said enough already,'" Maddie relayed.

Nola's jaw tightened. "That's not fair. Any woman courageous enough to stand up to injustice has the right to be heard."

"Of course, they do, and we are going to make sure they are," said Clare as she handed Nola a small blank sheet of paper. "Now, I want you to write a note to your photographer, Sands, telling him to meet you in the upstairs hallway by the restrooms, immediately. Maddie will pass your note to him while I tell my husband that I'm tired and that Maddie is going to drive me home. Since I'm pregnant, he won't think it unusual. We'll drive the two of you to Rosa's house. You must interview her first before her husband gets off work. Septima and Ella, and several of the other women will meet you at Maddie's house later this afternoon. We want the interviews to be published as one story, a kind of synopsis of all their efforts. That way, the focus and ire that will surely come from the male leaders won't rest on the shoulders of just one person."

"Several of the neighbors are certain to notice us," said Maddie. "We look out for each other because the KKK is always up to something, especially now since the boycott started. If two white people are observed entering the Parks' house, the news will be all over Montgomery before lunch. So, we brought you a pair of black slacks and a long black wig, along with another jacket and cap for your photographer to wear. I don't know of any Negro in Montgomery that can afford a genuine leather coat," said Mrs. Wilkins. She handed Nola the giant paper bag with the items in it, and then glanced at Clare who gave Maddie a nod.

"Oh yes, there's one more thing you'll need, here," said Clare, handing Nola a jar from her purse.

Nola took the jar from Clare's hand. "What's this?"

"It's black camouflage paint. Soldiers smear it on their faces during combat," said Clare.

Nola frowned. "Is this really necessary? Why can't I just wear a scarf over my head and keep my head down?"

Clare flashed Nola, a mischievous grin. "Because we didn't bring you a scarf," Clare jeered. "Don't worry hon, it washes off easily."

Suddenly, Nola noticed something black sticking out of Mrs. Wilkins's skirt pocket, and immediately reached over and pulled it out.

Nola held it up. "You don't mind if I borrow yours, do you, hon?" Nola asked Maddie, dangling Maddie's scarf in the air.

Clare huffed and rolled her eyes before passing Maddie a disapproving glance. "Come on, we don't have all day. Let's get this done," Clare fumed.

At 11:00 am, Maddie Wilkins pulled up in front of the house of Mrs. Rosa Parks in a black and gray, 1952 Ford Crestliner.

Clare and Maddie turned and looked at Nola and Sands in the back seat. Nola adjusted the black scarf to cover more of her face while Sands made sure he tucked all his curly light brown hair under the black knitted cap he was given. Unlike Nola, before he left the church, Sands smeared the camouflage paint all over his face, including on his mouth and eyelids. Up close, Sands looked like a white boy in blackface, but from a distance, no one could tell he wasn't Colored.

"Okay, we're here. Both of you should exit on the curbside," said Clare. "Maddie and I will get out first and flank the two of you while you guys walk in between us." Clare looked at Nola. "And I want you to hold his hand like he's your son. Don't forget to keep your head down."

"What about the photographer's camera?" asked Maddie, pointing to the Nikon hanging from a strap on his chest.

"Here, put it in this paper bag," said Nola to Sands as she retrieved the bag from the car floor and passed it to him. Sands took the camera from around his neck and placed it in the sack. He then rolled up the bag and clamped it under his left arm.

"Are we ready now?" Clare asked. Everyone nodded.

Maddie and Clare opened their doors and got out of the car simultaneously. Clare waited until Maddie walked around the back of the Ford and was standing on the curb before she lifted the front seat to let Nola and Sands out. Nola stepped from the car first. As Nola waited for Sands, she kept her head down. As soon as Sands got out, Nola grabbed hold of his right hand.

"Come on, son," said Nola in a motherly tone. Nola suddenly realized she wasn't wearing gloves and quickly shoved both her hands, along with the hand of Sands, inside her coat pockets. Together, the four walked up the walkway at a steady, even pace. Maddie and Clare waved hello to neighbors on both sides of Rosa Parks' house, who were peeking out their windows or who stepped out on their front porch to get a better view of the visitors.

Oh, my God! I hate to admit it, but Mrs. Johnson was right. Perhaps I should have smeared on some camouflage paint. The neighbors are everywhere. Just keep your head down, Nola. Don't look up.

To Nola, the walkway seemed to go on forever. When they finally reached the porch, the four climbed the five steps in unison—right, left, right. Once they ascended the last step, each softly sighed before walking up to the door. Clare rang the doorbell. Within seconds, the door opened, and Mrs. Rosa Parks appeared.

"Hello," Mrs. Parks smiled, "Come on in," she said as she stepped aside to let them by.

Nola was the first to enter. The front door led directly into the living room. Once inside, Nola finally lifted her head and removed the scarf. Her eyes automatically rested on the face of Rosa Parks, who was still holding the door open as the others walked in. Nola had expected a much older woman. Instead, she saw a woman who looked to be in her late thirties or early forties stylishly dressed in a tweed, high-waisted, midi pencil skirt.

Tucked into her skirt was a long-sleeve, white blouse with small black polka-dots. Mrs. Parks' black hair was parted on the right side and combed back in a bun off her face. She wore thin, round, wire-rim eyeglasses and stood five feet, three and a half inches tall in black pumps.

Once everyone was inside, and Mrs. Parks closed the door, Clare quickly introduced Nola and Sands.

"Please sit down. Can I get you all something to drink and perhaps some cookies?" Rosa asked.

Clare shook her head. "No, thank you, we don't have that much time. The sooner we do the interview and leave, the better," said Clare before anyone else could speak.

Everyone sat down except Sands. Sands entered the house and retrieved his Nikon from the brown paper bag and took pictures. Nola and Clare sat in the two armchairs in front of each end of the coffee table. Rosa sat on the couch positioned against the wall below the large gold-framed mirror, while Maddie walked into the adjacent dining room and sat in one of the dining chairs.

No one said a word for several minutes as everyone stared at Nola rummaging through her purse. Nola knew they were all watching her.

I've interviewed heads of state and didn't get this nervous. What's wrong with me? Get it together, girl.

Finally, Nola remembered where she put her pen and notepad and unzipped the side pocket inside her purse.

"Ahh! Here they are," sighed Nola with a smile as she held up the Bic ballpoint pen and small Mead notepad. "Now, we can begin."

Out of the corner of her eye, Nola saw Clare shaking her head, but Nola decided that she would proceed as if no one else were present except her and Mrs. Parks.

"First, let's get some background information about you, like where you were born, your grade level, your full name and family, etcetera."

Rosa: I'm 43-years-old. I was born Rosa Louise McCauley in Tuskegee, Alabama, on February 4, 1913, to Leona and James McCauley. My mother was a teacher, my father, a carpenter. I have a younger brother named Sylvester. When my parents separated, I moved with my mother and brother to Pine Level and lived on the farm with my maternal grandparents. I went to Highlander Folk School and Alabama State Teachers College for Negroes. I married my husband, Raymond Parks, in 1932. He's a barber here in Montgomery.

Nola: Were you involved in civil rights activities before the bus incident?

Rosa: Yes, along with my job as a seamstress, I'm a secretary for the local chapter of the NAACP. As secretary, I investigated the rape of Recy Taylor, who was kidnapped by a gang of young white men in Abbeville, Alabama, in September of 1944. Mrs. Taylor and I founded The Committee for Equal Justice. The committee tries to help Negro women reclaim their bodies against sexual violence and interracial rape. It has 18 chapters across the U.S. Some of the members include W.E.B. Dubois, Langston Hughes, Mary Church Terrell, and Oscar Hammerstein.

Nola looked surprised.

Nola: You mean, Oscar Hammerstein of Rodgers and Hammerstein, the music and songwriting duo?

Rosa: Yes. My husband and I are also members of the Voter's League, which helps Negroes register to vote.

Nola: Wow! That's impressive. Now tell me about your experience riding the bus before the incident last year. Did you ever pay your fare and then get left by the bus driver?"

Rosa: Yes, James Blake, the bus driver that radioed the police was also the same driver that left me several years ago standing in the rain after I paid. There's probably not a Negro who rides the bus that hasn't been left behind at least once. Although there was only one white passenger on the bus when this occurred years ago, I had to exit the bus after paying and re-enter in the rear. If no white riders are on board, we can walk directly down the aisle to the designated Colored Section.

Nola: But last December, you decided not to sit in the rear in the Colored Section, and you took a front-row seat.

Rosa: No, I was sitting in the Colored Section that day.

A crease appeared on Nola's forehead as she shook her head.

Nola: Then, why did the driver ask you to vacate your seat?

Rosa: Where the Colored Section begins depends on how many white people are on board. As the bus fills up with white passengers, the sign is moved back further and further to make room for them. Whites get to sit, no matter what. That day, the Colored Section started five rows back. The entire bus was full, which meant, if I gave up my seat, I had to ride the rest of the way standing.

Nola: Did you ever have to ride standing before?

Rosa: Yes, often.

Nola: So, what made that day in December of last year different? What made you not want to comply? Were you tired that day?

Rosa: That's what many people believe. But that's not true. I was not tired physically, no more tired than I usually was when a working day ended. The only tired I was, was tired of giving in. I was tired of being treated like a second-class citizen and giving in to segregation laws designed to humiliate Negroes, strip us of our dignity, and make us lesser human beings. Growing up in Pine Level, Alabama, school bus transportation was unavailable to us. I remember the school bus picking up the white kids to go to their new school while all the Colored kids had to walk. I'd see the bus pass every day... but that was a way of life; we had no choice but to accept that as the custom. The segregated bus system was how I realized there was a black world and a white world. But there's only so much injustice a person can take before they either go insane or fight back. And the more we gave in, the more we complied with that treatment, the more oppressive it became. I didn't want to go to jail. But I didn't want to be deprived of a seat I had paid for either. I guess it was the accumulation of years of mistreatment endured by my people that led me to refuse to give up my seat that evening. Earlier that year in Mississippi, two white men brutally murdered 14-year-old Emmett Till for supposedly flirting with a white woman. Emmett's killers abducted him from his great uncle's house at night and beat and mutilated him before shooting him in the head; then, they tossed his body in the Tallahatchie River. Can you imagine how terrified that child was? How he must have screamed and hollered and cried for his mother? I was thinking of Emmett Till that day, and how that could have been my son.

Nola didn't wipe away the tears from her cheeks. All while Mrs. Parks spoke, Nola visualized Rosa's words in her mind. She recalled her father mentioning that a Negro boy from Chicago was visiting his relatives and was killed in the Alabama in August of last year. But her father didn't go into detail, and the Vancouver Press never printed the story.

Out of the corner of her eye, Nola saw a hand extend to her. Nola turned her head to the right. The hand was holding a handkerchief. As Nola took the hankie, she locked eyes with Clare. It was as if Nola saw Mrs. Johnson for the first time. Clare's eyes were also red.

"Thank you," said Nola.

Clare just nodded and didn't speak.

"I think you have enough for the article," said Mrs. Wilkins as she stood up. "What do you think, Clare?"

After wiping her eyes, Clare rose again from her chair. "Yes, I agree. We better go now. We've been here a little over an hour," said Clare looking down at her watch, "just long enough for a nice visit and short enough for the neighbors not to get too suspicious and wonder what's going on."

Nola re-positioned the scarf on her head as Sands put his camera back in the brown bag and clipped it under his arm. Walking to the car was less stressful than walking into the house. This time, only two neighbors watched the four as they left.

"You two won't need to wear your disguises at my house. I live on a farm, and there aren't any neighbors that close by. It's about a 25-minute drive outside of town."

"Do you live by yourself, Mrs. Wilkins?" asked Sands as he wiped the camouflage paint off his face. Nola pulled off the shoulder-length black wig, placed it on her lap, and then unpinned and combed her blonde hair.

"No. I live with my youngest brother and his wife and two little kids. They are in school now, and my brother and his wife are at work. They moved in after my husband was killed by the KKK."

Sands scooted up to the edge of the back seat and leaned forward. "Why did they kill him?"

"For being a better farmer than all the white farmers around here," said Maddie. "He grew corn, and every year his crop came in yielding large kernels of beautiful, healthy, yellow cobs. He always got a high price. Hardly ever did my Jimmy have a bad harvest. With the money he earned, he was able to buy himself a new truck and me a new car. We got the house painted and bought some new furniture. None of this went unnoticed by the whites in town. They claimed we were getting too uppity which is code language for: "who do you niggers think you are making a lot of money and trying to live a good life like white folks."

Maddie made a sharp right turn, drove a short distance then stopped. "We're here," she announced.

"It looks like Ella is here too," said Clare, noticing the white, 1950 Pontiac Catalina with a red top parked in the long dirt driveway beside Maddie's Ford. The four got out and walked inside the yellow wood-framed, two-story house.

"Where is she?" Nola asked as she and the others stood in the living room looking through the dining room into the kitchen. The house was quiet and still. Suddenly, they heard the faint sound of laughter.

"Oh, they're in the basement," said Maddie. Maddie led them through a small hallway between the dining room and the kitchen to an open door leading to the basement.

As the four descended the stairs, the laughter grew louder.

"You ladies are having entirely too much fun down here," joked Clare as she stepped down from the last step into the cellar. "Don't you know you're Colored Women, and that's not allowed."

"They must be getting too uppity," teased Maddie.

"Yeah, how dare you black girls giggle and carry on like white girls," Juliette chimed in.

Nola was surprised to see Miss Morgan but happy she was here. She was glad she wasn't the only white female present.

Juliette introduced Nola to Septima Clark. Nola already met Ella Baker and JoAnn Robinson earlier that day.

The cellar was divided into three rooms with the staircase in the central area adjourned by two smaller spaces--one slightly bigger than the other. The walls of the basement were salamander with scenic pictures of trees, and green mountains from around the world hung on the walls. Against one wall was a floor to ceiling walnut bookshelf stacked with books and magazines. In front of the bookshelf were two red and beige, floral-printed, sling-back armchairs, and a small round walnut table positioned between the chairs with a red-shaded lamp. Against another wall was a matching floral-printed sofa with a large square coffee table in front of it. Opposite the couch was a dark brown recliner. Above the couch was a long, rectangular window, three and a half inches wide. The high-polished, black and white checkered linoleum floors in all three rooms were shiny enough to see your reflection.

Once again, Clare was eager to get started. "Which one of you wants to be interviewed first?" Clare asked.

Jo-Ann Robinson put up both her hands. "I don't want to be interviewed at all. I'm just here for moral support," Mrs. Robinson replied.

Septima looked at Ella. "Why don't you go first."

Miss Baker agreed, and everyone took seats around the coffee table. Nola sat in the recliner while Sands directed Mrs. Clark and Miss Baker to sit in the armchairs in front of the bookcase to make it easier for him to take pictures of the two at different angles. Septima and Ella complied, leaving Clare, Maddie, Juliette, and Jo-Ann to sit on the sofa.

"Where would you like me to begin?" asked Ella, sitting in the chair closest to the couch.

Nola: "Why don't you give me a little background on yourself, like where you were born, your age, etcetera?"

Ella: I am 53 years old. I was born Ella Josephine Baker on December 13, 1903, in Norfolk, Virginia, to Georgiana and Blake Baker. My grandmother, Josephine, was born into slavery. I remember listening to her tell stories about slave revolts. Once, she was whipped for refusing to marry the man her slave master chose for her. I graduated from Shaw University in Raleigh, North Carolina, in 1927. After college, I moved to New York, where I worked for the *American West Indian News* and then as an editorial assistant for the *Negro National News*. I also married my college sweetheart, T.J. Carter.

I began my involvement with the NAACP in 1940 as a field secretary and then served as director of branches from 1943 to 1946. I've traveled extensively, especially throughout the South, raising money, recruiting members, and organizing local chapters. I've worked alongside A. Philip Randolph, W.E.B. Dubois, and Thurgood Marshall. I also worked on the campaign to free the Scottsboro Boys, and I protested Italy's invasion of Ethiopia.

Nola: You are married, but you don't take your husband's last name, why?

Ella: I have adopted the practice of dissemblance, which is simply to conceal my private life so I can be accepted as an individual. Men don't need to hide their marital status. But for women, it's different. A woman with a husband is often viewed as having to get her husband's approval for everything she does. To men, this means a married woman is limited as to what she can commit to and what her job can expect from her. The prevailing view in society is that a married woman's life is not her own to control, and neither is her mind. She may have strong beliefs, but her husband may forbid her to act on those beliefs. She may think one way is right, but her husband may persuade her to think the reverse. That's why I rarely discuss my marriage.

Nola: Then, why reveal it now?

Ella: I don't want my marriage to define who I am and what I can achieve. But you asked me to share my background and personal facts about myself. So how can I leave out the fact that I am married?

Nola: Do you think your practice of dissemblance has worked? Isn't the reason for this interview because you, Septima, and even Mrs. Rosa Parks are getting overlooked by the male members of the movement?

Ella: Yes and no, prejudice is a hard demon to fight, whether it's named racism or chauvinism. None of us working to desegregate the public bus system believes that if we win, racism will be eliminated forever. We will never rid the world of sexism or racism completely. However, we can remove the effects such prejudices have on our lives. But only the actions by the victims of discrimination can bring it about. The boycott is one way to stop racial hatred from negatively affecting the lives of Negroes. The practice of dissemblance is the way I've chosen to lessen the effects that male chauvinism can have on my professional career as a woman. But it's not a cure-all. What works for me may not work for all black women, and that's okay. My sisters don't have to imitate what I do precisely. They should stand up and find the courage to fight. Courage comes from within. It springs from a profound conviction inside your heart that causes you to act. Your firm resolution motivates and propels you forward even when you don't have the support of others. It doesn't depend on someone else. I'm talking about the mettle Henry O. Flipper had to become the first Negro cadet to graduate from West Point in 1877. Now that took courage because he was all by himself. It's hard for me even to imagine the racial hatred Henry Flipper must have faced day after day, year after year. But he endured it without the rhetoric of soaring speeches laced with eloquent words of support. That's why I'm critical of charismatic leadership that centers solely on the personality and oral communication skills of one person to define the civil rights movement and determine its success.

Nola: So, you don't think Martin Luther King, Jr. should be the leader?

Ella: Martin is the right leader for this movement at the right time. He has been effective, and I don't want to cast dispersions on that. But that doesn't mean I don't see the pitfalls and can't have a different opinion about how things should proceed. I merely don't believe that a top-down movement is sustainable over the long haul. The best way forward for the NAACP is to be a grassroots organization that gives each community and its members the power and ability to advocate for themselves. Chapter leaders should be members with the grit, passion, and determination to do things regardless of their sex, profession, or educational background.

Nola nodded as she finished writing her notes.

"Okay, I think I have enough." Nola turned to Septima. "Would you like to begin now, Mrs. Clark?"

Septima: "Well, I was born in Charleston, South Carolina, on May 3, 1898, to Peter and Victoria Poinsette. In two months I'll be 58 years old. My father was born a slave on the Joel Poinsette farm near Georgetown. Although my mother was also born in Charleston, she was raised in Hatti by her uncle, who took my mother there when she was a baby along with her two sisters. My mother, Victoria, was never a slave. After the Civil War, she returned from Hatti and eventually met and married my father. Of course, back then, as it is now, working as a maid, cook, or nanny for white folks was common, and practically the only job a Negro woman could get, especially in the South. But my mother never allowed us to work in the homes of white people because she wanted to protect us from sexual harassment, which occurred quite frequently and still does. My mother took in the laundry but never worked in a white home. I graduated from high school in 1916 and was eventually able to get a B.A. Degree in teaching from Benedict College in Columbia, South Carolina in 1942, and later, an M.A. Degree from

Hampton University in Hampton, Virginia. I married my husband, Nerie Clark, in 1923.

Nola's eyes widened.

Nola: You have a master's degree. Wow, that's phenomenal, given your circumstances. I thought white colleges didn't allow Negroes to attend their schools.

Septima: No, these are both black schools.

Nola: Oh, I see. That makes more sense. Still, I didn't know there were so many institutions of higher learning for People of color in America. My father wen...Anyway, when did you get involved in Civil Rights?

Nola almost revealed that she was black. She wondered if the others caught the slip. Nola perspired. She felt a bead of sweat rolling slowly down her side from under her right armpit. She knew her slip of the tongue didn't go unnoticed by Clare. Sands knew, but he also knew not to tell. Nola kept her head down, looking at her notes, afraid to look at Mrs. Clark or over at the other women on the couch. Her heart was beating so rapidly now that she could see her chest fluttering up and down.

Oh, God! I think I'm going to faint.

Nola suddenly felt a hand on her shoulder. Nola looked to her left, and Clare was bending over in front of her, holding a cup of hot tea.

"Here, honey, it looks like you need this. Have you eaten anything today?"

Nola shook her head. "No, I had only a cup of coffee this morning."

"No wonder you look like you're about to collapse. Maddie went upstairs to set up for lunch. Here's tea, and there are pastries on the table. Help yourself," said Clare.

"Thank you," Nola replied softly. She took a sip. It was chamomile, her favorite. Nola took a deep breath, inhaling the aroma into her nostrils. Immediately, she felt relaxed, and her heart rate decrease. Nola picked up a Danish. She hadn't realized how hungry she was until she bit into the light, flaky crust with apple filling. She could tell it was homemade and not store-bought. The buttery crust melted in her mouth. As soon as she gobbled it down, she had another.

Nola: Hmmm! These are delicious. Let's continue Mrs. Clark, shall we? When did your fight for Civil Rights begin?

Septima: I first heard of the NAACP while I was teaching on John's Island in 1916. John's Island is one of the many islands off the South Carolina coast and is separated from the mainland by the Stone River. In 1919, I left the island and returned to Charleston to teach sixth grade at Avery Normal Institute, a private school for Colored children. Then I first became a political activist when I gathered 10,000 signatures in one day. The signatures were for a petition to allow Negroes to be principals at Avery and any public schools in Charleston. We won the right in 1920. In 1945, I worked with Thurgood Marshall on a case led by the NAACP to obtained equal pay for black teachers, which we also won. I am now the vice president of the NAACP Charleston branch. In 1954, I was hired as the director of workshops at the Highlander Folk School in Tennessee. The school's focus is on social justice training and literacy courses to increase black voter registration. Rosa Parks was a student.

Nola: Oh, I didn't know that. When did Rosa attend Highlander?

Septima: In the summer of 1955.

Nola: And later that same year, Mrs. Parks put what she learned into action. Apparently, you taught her well, Mrs. Clark.

Septima smiled.

Septima: Apparently, I did.

Nola: Besides obtaining equal rights and better opportunities for your people, what else do you hope the movement will achieve?

Septima: I believe unconditionally in the ability of people to respond when told the truth. We need to be taught to study rather than believe, to inquire rather than to affirm. Education is the long-term goal and the key to a successful future. Yes, we need motivational and inspirational leaders, but where would we be without teachers to instruct us on how things should be done and lawyers to defend our rights. What we are working for is an educational program that will become a resource and rallying point for scores of brave southerners leading the fight for justice and better race relations in these crucial days.

Nola: Malcolm X doesn't believe in non-violence. Don't you think Negroes should show their anger over segregation and the unjust treatment you have suffered for so long?

Septima: I never felt that getting angry would do you any good other than hurt your own digestion, and keep you from eating, which I liked to do.

"On that note, let's have lunch," said Maddie as she stood on the stairwell looking down. Everyone agreed and headed upstairs.

"Hmmm! It all smells and looks so good," said Sands as he entered the dining room first. A banquet of crispy fried chicken, creamed corn, okra in lemon and butter sauce; collard greens seasoned with smoked ham hocks and a large platter of fried hot-water cornbread filled the table. On the walnut buffet was a four-layered chocolate cake.

"Man, if this is lunch, what's for dinner?" Sands asked.

Everyone laughed.

"One thing you'll learn about Colored women in the South," said Juliette as the eight sat down, "when Colored women cook, they don't play around."

Chapter Sixteen

Why do women have smaller feet than men?
So they can stand closer to the kitchen sink.

Unknown Author

Noon, Wednesday
March 14, 1956

When Nola saw the brown United Parcel Service truck pull up in front of Juliette Morgan's house, she didn't wait until the delivery man got out of his vehicle and rang the doorbell. Nola rushed out of the house in her stocking feet and retrieved the parcel. When she saw the large vanilla envelope from Canada, she was so excited she jumped up and down.

"It's here!" Nola yelled upstairs to Sands from the vestibule the minute she walked back into the house, shivering from the cold. Sands rushed downstairs and joined Nola in the living room. The two sat on the couch in front of the large window overlooking the front yard as Nola opened the envelope. Inside was the front page of the *Vancouver Daily Press*. Nola quickly unfolded it. There, front and center, was the article she wrote accompanied by several pictures of Rosa Parks. There was also a photo of an Alabama city bus and Rosa's mug shot taken at the police station. The headline across the front page read: Rosa Parks Speaks, with the byline, Nola Richardson. Sands was only interested in the pictures. Wisely, Nola's father sent two copies of the newspaper. Nola handed Sands the extra copy before reading her story. To her chagrin, her article was only six paragraphs long.

"Where's the rest of it? There's no mention of Septima or Ella. This isn't what I wrote. They cut my story. Why did they cut it?"

Furious, Nola hurried to the library and dialed long distance to Vancouver. "I know who did it. It was that little prick, Craig Marshall. I should have gotten the job as editor instead of him," Nola fussed to herself as she stood listening to the ringtone next to the large cherry oak desk in front of a tall window with long flowing, pleated, gold curtains.

"Hello. This is Mrs. Clifford, secretary to Hans Weiss, Managing Editor of the Vancouver Daily. How may I help you?"

"Hi, Gloria, this is Nola. I need to speak to Hans right away."

"You mean, Mr. Weiss," Mrs. Clifford corrected in a stern voice. "He's conducting the weekly editor's meeting. No, wait, it looks like it's over. Everyone is coming out of his office now. Okay, I'll put you through."

"Hello, Nola. Your article on Rosa Parks was fantastic. We ran it four days ago in the Sunday Edition, and the feedback has been outstanding. Craig's idea to write a side piece about Oscar Hammerstein being a member of the Committee for Equal Justice, founded by Mrs. Parks, gave the story an extra edge. In fact, AP picked it up, so the articles will run in many U.S. newspapers as well as overseas."

Nola looked at the paper in her hand again and noticed the side piece Hans was referring to for the first time. The article was nearly the length of her story, accompanied by a headshot of Mr. Hammerstein smiling. The caption read: Oscar Hammerstein Assists Rosa Parks in her Fight for Civil Rights with the byline, Adok Weiss, Cub Reporter. Nola wanted to cry, scream, and shout.

Instead, she sulked and remained silent for several minutes.

"Nola, are you there? What's wrong?"

Finally, Nola blurted out. "This is not the story I sent. What happened to the rest of it? What happened to what I wrote about Septima Clark and Ella Baker?"

"Who are they? No one knows who they are?"

"That was the whole point of my article, to highlight the accomplishments of other women in the movement. It's what Rosa Parks wanted. She's a humble woman. She didn't want the piece to be just about her."

"Craig made an editorial decision, and I agreed with him. A newspaper is a business, Nola. It's the business of selling information. But it must be information people want to read, which means that not all information is saleable. Sure, other black women may have done as much or even more than Rosa Parks. But their efforts didn't galvanize a people and start a protest that has made the entire world sit up and take notice."

"Well, it was still the wrong decision."

"No! It wasn't. When the board chose Craig as editor over you, I thought they made a mistake. Now I see they were right. You're not ready to be an editor, Nola. Like I..."

"Oh, kiss my ass and go to hell!" Nola slammed down the phone and turned around. She noticed Sands lurking in the doorway watching her.

"How long have you been standing there?"

"Long enough," said Sands.

Nola placed both her hands on her hips. "So, you got something to say?"

"No, not a word. It's your career, not mine."

With both hands still on her hips, Nola walked towards the doorway. She lowered one hand. Just as she passed by Sands, Nola swung her butt to one side, bumping her right hip into Sands so forcefully; Sands immediately lost his footing. His bony body hit the wall then dropped to the floor. Nola smiled and giggled as she sashayed through the living room into the entry hall and upstairs to her bedroom. Less than five minutes later, there was a knock on her door. It was Tessie, the maid, informing Nola she had a telephone call. Nola walked back downstairs to the library to answer it.

"Hello," said Nola as she stood in front of the desk.

"What the hell do you think you're doing talking to Mr. Weiss that way!? Have you lost your mind?"

Upon hearing the anger and disapproval in her father's voice, the realization of what she said to Hans finally hit Nola, and she felt her stomach drop. Mortified, she hobbled back behind the desk and sat down.

"Daddy I...I," Nola didn't know what to say and immediately started to cry.

"That's right, cry. Tears are the only response women have when the shit hits the fan, isn't it? Women want to act like a man, do a man's job and receive a man's pay and respect, but when it comes time to answer for your mistakes the way a man has to, how quickly women abandon their demand for equality of the sexes and fall back on their femininity. But all the tears you and your mother can shed together, won't help you this time. As the Investigative Bureau Chief of the Daily Press, Nola Selena Richardson, you're fired, effective immediately. Pack your bags and come home!"

Thirty minutes after her dad hung up, Nola was still sitting at the desk, holding the phone up to her ear, numb and silent, unable to move. Although her body was frozen, her mind wasn't. Nola kept hearing her father's angry voice uttering the words, "Nola Selena Richardson, you're fired." The words repeated in her head like a broken record along with the sound of the loud click when her dad slammed the phone down on the hook. Nola would have sat in that comatose state all day if Tessie hadn't walked into the library carrying Nola's shoes, coat, and purse, reminding Nola of her appointment. Tessie was a dark-skinned girl with thick long woolly black hair, pulled back in a ponytail and tied with a rubber band. She always wore a black maid's uniform. It was a loose-fitting dress with short sleeves trimmed in white with a white collar and a white apron tied around her waist.

Without thinking, Nola slipped on her black pumps, took her jacket and bag from Tessie, and walked out of the house, and into the light blue and white Buick Riviera parked in the driveway.

Nola and Sands couldn't rely on public transportation to get them around town to cover events. So they both rented vehicles at the newspaper's expense. Sands rented a dark brown Ford Jeep. Juliette appreciated finally having someone drive her to work every morning. Nola and Sands took turns chauffeuring Miss Morgan.

Nola was on her way to Maddie's house, where she arranged yesterday to meet Clare and Maddie for lunch. By the time Nola reached Maddie's farm, she had convinced herself that she could win back her job and that everything would be all right.

Act natural as if nothing has happened. Don't let Clare and Maddie know you've been fired. What would they think of you if they knew?

"They didn't publish the story the way I wrote it. The information on Septima and Ella was cut," said Nola as soon as she walked into the kitchen of Maddie's house. Clare and Maddie were sitting at the kitchen table, sipping tea and eating tuna salad sandwiches and homemade donuts. Maddie poured Nola a cup of tea and passed it to Nola.

"We know," Clare admitted, holding up the front page of the Montgomery Advertiser.

"I'm so sorry. I feel awful," Nola apologized as she sat down and took the cup from Maddie's hand.

"You can't beat yourself up over such things, darling, or you'll spend the rest of your life feeling battered and bruised," said Maddie. "The life of a black woman is defined by disappointment."

"Maybe yours, but not mine," refuted Clare, "at least, not always."

"How are Ella and Septima? Are they upset?"

"No, of course not, they're fine. The person we need to worry about is Rosa," said Maddie as she stood up and walked over to the stove. Maddie opened the oven door, took out four cake pans, and set them on the countertop next to the eight other cakes cooling on racks. She then turned off the oven.

"Are you making cakes to raise money for the carpools?" Nola asked.

Maddie nodded.

"You write well," said Clare as she sat reading Nola's article for the second time. The Montgomery Advertiser ran only one photo of Rosa Parks along with the picture of Mr. Hammerstein on the front page.

"How many people have seen it? Has anyone said anything?" Nola asked.

"It's all everybody is talking about," Clare stated. "I drove several groups of boycotters to work early this morning, and most of them had a copy of the Advertiser. They were reading it as I drove."

"What did they say?"

"Oh, they loved the article. People thought Rosa's comments about racial injustice were spot on, and that Rosa expressed herself well. Many were impressed that the article originated from a Canadian newspaper. "'If the world didn't know what was going on down here and that Negroes are fed up and not going to take it anymore, they know it now,'" said one rider. But many of the male commuters wondered why there was no mention of Dr. King."

"Yeah," said Maddie, "my brother wondered why the entire article wasn't about Martin since it's Martin that's leading the boycott. "'Rosa Parks ain't leading nothin,'" said my brother Charles. Sissy, his wife, disagreed, vehemently. She said that without Rosa, there would be no boycott for Dr. King to lead, so why should all the spotlight focus on the Reverend. The two sat at the breakfast table, arguing until they left for work this morning."

"So why did they exclude Septima and Ella from the piece?" Maddie asked as she walked back to the table and sat down beside Clare.

"Because despite all of Septima and Ella's efforts, none of what the two of them accomplished resulted in a boycott that garnished worldwide attention," replied Clare before Nola could respond. " Am I right?" asked Clare, looking at Nola sitting directly across from her.

Nola nodded. "That's almost the exact reply my managing editor gave."

"So all that sneaking around was for nothing," said Maddie. "Poor Septima and Ella overlooked again. Well, we tried. Now Rosa will have to take the heat alone."

"I would like to apologize to Mrs. Parks in-person. I know Rosa didn't intend for the article to be just about her," said Nola. Nola watched Clare take a sip of tea and then noticed a smile flash across Clare's face before Mrs. Johnson lowered her cup.

"Well, I guess we better get busy and decorate these cakes," said Maddie, rising from the table again.

Clare and Nola spent the next four hours helping Maddie ice six cakes--two German chocolate, two coconut cream, and two with vanilla icing with lemon filling. When they finished decorating, Clare and Nola left together. Their cars were in the driveway, parked one behind the other with Clare's car first in line. Before Nola reached her car, she stopped and confronted Clare.

"You knew the paper would only publish Rosa's story, didn't you? You coaxed Rosa into doing the story, knowing that all along."

"Who said I had to coax her?"

"So Rosa was in on the scheme? I don't believe you. I certainly know Ella and Septima weren't."

"Look, there was no scheme. When I suggested the interview, Rosa was happy to do it. She wanted Ella and Septima to have their day in the sun too. If your paper published the article about the three of them, everyone would be happy. But your paper didn't. That doesn't mean Rosa didn't want her story to print. And yes, Septima and Ella are disappointed, who wouldn't be? But they are grown women. They'll get over it. The question is, will you? You seem rather naïve to be such a seasoned reporter, and much too sensitive."

This is the third time today I've been told I'm not acting like a professional, and that I'm deficient. Can they all be wrong? What am I going to do? How am I going to get my job back? There's one thing I know for sure, I'm not packing my bags and coming home, daddy!

Nola didn't respond to Clare's comment. She just got into her car and drove away, leaving Clare Johnson standing beside her Rambler looking on. Clare finally got into her car and drove to her parent's house. A storm was brewing, and it wasn't only going to pour down from the rain clouds hovering in the sky. Clare's husband wasn't pleased about Rosa's article either when he read it during breakfast this morning. Clare couldn't forget the frown on Kapp's face, and the look he gave her as he tossed the paper aside on the table.

"What's wrong?" Clare asked him. Her husband's first reply was silence. His second reply in a sharp, terse tone was, "we'll talk about it later." Kapp always kissed Clare goodbye before going to work, but not today. Not getting a goodbye kiss bothered her. All-day long, Clare worried about what her husband would say. She drove home, not knowing what to expect when she arrived. The closer Clare got to Hayneville Road, the more nervous she became.

On weekdays, Clare's father, Simon, drove Kapp to Dr. King's house before her dad went to work, and he also picked Kapp up on his way home from work, leaving Clare the station wagon to transport protesters. Kapp chauffeured Dr. King from place to place in the Reverend's car. When Clare didn't see her father's 1945 light brown Oldsmobile parked under the carport, Clare felt relieved. It meant Kapp was still guarding Dr. King. Usually, Clare entered her parent's house through the front door. That evening, she walked around the back and came in through the kitchen. She was startled to see Kapp sitting at the kitchen table waiting for her.

"You had something to do with this article, didn't you?" accused Kapp, holding the rolled-up newspaper in his hand and waving it at Clare as soon as she stepped inside. Clare shut the door behind her.

"Sure, I did. I wrote it. Didn't you read the byline?"

Kapp jumped up and was suddenly in Clare's face. His movement was so swift, Clare didn't see him walk over to her. The massive size of her husband's, muscular, six-foot, two-inch, chiseled physique towered over her like a skyscraper. Clare standing five foot nine in heels, timidly gazed up at him as the two faced each other. There was a look in Kapp's eyes Clare had never seen before, but she understood its meaning. The look said: I am your husband and the man of the house. You are my wife and just a woman. I am in control. So never challenge me and never forget it. Clare backed up and slithered her way over to the sink in front of the kitchen window. Kapp followed. This was the first time Clare felt threatened by her husband, the first time she felt Kapp was perhaps angry enough to hit her.

"Don't you ever answer me that way again," said Kapp glaring down at her. "Now, I asked you a question."

"Darling I...I." Clare placed her hand on her stomach as her eyes teared up.

Kapp glanced down at his wife's slightly protruding belly. Clare noticed the muscles in her husband's face soften as he stepped back.

Clare exhaled. "Yes, honey, I set it up. I was just doing what Mrs. Parks' wanted. She wanted the interview to happen. She wanted to be heard."

"You set it up the day you lied and told me you weren't feeling well, and Maddie was supposed to take you home. You had that photographer made up in blackface, pretending to be a Colored kid. Old man Ross who lives next door to the Parks, saw you and the other two getting out of Maddie's car that day."

Clare nodded her head, vigorously. "Yes, yes, but I didn't think I was doing anything wrong."

"Really? Then why did you sneak around? Why did you go to the trouble of hiding what you were doing if you thought it was all right? Why didn't you tell me? Answer me, Clare!"

Clare put her hand to her forehead and rubbed her temple. "Well, because I...I don't know. Mrs. Parks and some of the other women thought that Rosa was getting pushed aside. So they thought it best that no one know about the interview until after it published."

"Rosa Parks and which other women?"

Clare turned away, suddenly overcome by strange feelings. Every corpuscle in her blood rippled through her veins like lightning bolts. She was overwhelmed with a sense of fearlessness. No longer did she feel threatened or afraid. Instead, Clare perceived herself to be strong, strong enough to take on anybody, even her husband. The intense sensations of power and control were both exhilarating and frightening. One part of her wanted to stand her ground. The other part wanted to surrender. Clare lifted her shoulders and arched her back. She was about to give a reply to her husband when the fetus inside her kicked not once, not twice, but three times.

"What does it matter now, honey?" Clare asked in her softest, meekest voice. Clare turned around and gazed lovingly into her husband's eyes.

"I don't understand why no one wants Rosa to talk. If it weren't for Rosa, there wouldn't be a boycott for Martin to lead. She courageously took a stand. Shouldn't she be allowed to speak?"

"No one denies Mrs. Parks' courage. But it takes a lot more than one courageous act to effect change for every Negro in the country. And stop pretending that Rosa hasn't spoken. The woman has done at least two interviews since the boycott started. Rosa didn't initiate the boycott. It was Edgar Nixon's idea, and Jo Ann Robinson printed 3,500 flyers the next day to publicize it. Do you see either of them giving interviews? After Edgar and Clifford Durr posted bail to get Rosa out of jail that evening, Rosa went home to her husband. She never contemplated staging a protest. She even said so during a radio broadcast."

"Not only that, Rosa wasn't even the first woman to refuse to give up her seat. In 1946, Irene Morgan was arrested in Middlesex County, Virginia, for the same thing. Thurgood Marshall argued Irene Morgan's case, and he won the lawsuit in the U.S. Supreme Court. But that decision didn't erase bus discrimination in Alabama or anywhere else, nor was it highly publicized. What's the difference between the 1946 case and now? --the bus boycott initiated by Nixon, together with the lawsuit filed by Civil Rights Attorney, Fred Gray, in combination with the charismatic leadership of Dr. Martin Luther King, Jr. Without their coordinated efforts, Rosa Parks' refusal to give up her seat would be nothing more than a footnote in history."

Much to Clare's surprise, her husband's argument had merit.

"I see your point, honey, and I'm sorry. Perhaps you're right," Clare admitted.

"Perhaps?"

Clare smiled and wrapped her arms around her husband's waist. "Okay, darling, I give in. You're right."

Finally, Kapp smiled and embraced Clare. "Now that's the wife I know and love. And since we're back on the same team, I want you to call that reporter tonight and have her and her photographer meet us at Dr. King's house at ten o'clock tomorrow morning."

Clare beamed. "Oh, I see. You're going to have Nola interview Martin. What a great idea. I'll call her right now."

Clare hurried to the telephone stand by the staircase in the front hallway.

"Hi, Nola, guess what? To offset the objections many of the male leaders have about your article on Rosa, my husband wants you to interview Dr. King. So meet us at Martin's house tomorrow morning at ten, okay? Great, see you then."

"Yes!" Nola shouted as she hung up the phone in the library. Now, she was guaranteed to get her job back. No way her father and Hans would reject her exclusive interview with the leader of the boycott. Nola rushed upstairs to the bedroom Sands occupied. She knocked, then walked into his room before Sands could answer. Sands was standing with his shirt off in front of the tall wooden Armoire with mirrored double doors examining the enormous red bruise on his left side above his hip. Nola pretended not to see the mark.

"I hope you got a lot of film in your camera, Sands darling because tomorrow morning we're going to Martin Luther King's house to interview him and his wife. Isn't that great!"

Sands looked at Nola with disdain.

"It would be if you were still a reporter working for the Vancouver Press. But you've been fired, remember? So the paper is sending Adok to replace you. I'm picking him up tomorrow at the airport. He's arriving at 9:30 am."

Nola's jubilance instantly faded. "Oh, I see. All right then," Nola said and walked out. She lingered in the hallway for a second then quickly ran downstairs and into the sunroom where Miss Morgan reclined every evening around this time to read and relax before supper.

"Miss Juliette, do you have a minute? I have a problem and need your advice."

Miss Morgan was lying on a white wicker divan wearing purple silk lounging pajamas.

"Sure, honey, come on over here and sit down." Miss Morgan made room for Nola on the settee.

Nola told Juliette everything. They talked for two hours until Tessie announced dinner. Nola entered the dining room excited and scared, knowing that tomorrow, her life could change forever.

Chapter Seventeen

"The first step in getting somewhere
is to decide you're not going
to stay where you are."

J.P. Morgan

4:00 pm Thursday
March 15, 1956
Vancouver, Canada

"So, when is Nola coming home?" Hans asked Carl. Hans and Carl were sitting at the round conference table in Hans' office, reviewing the markup of news copy to publish in next week's paper.

"I don't know. I haven't spoken to Nola since I fired her yesterday, and neither has my wife, Elsa. It's going to take a while for it to sink in. I don't expect to hear from my daughter anytime soon. In three or four days, she'll probably call her mother. I doubt she will want to talk to me for a long time," said Carl.

"Firing your daughter took guts. I know it wasn't easy, and I really appreciate how quickly you handled it."

"Well, it had to be done. Nola's behavior to you was unacceptable and couldn't be tolerated. I know if a reporter talked to me that way, I would have demanded their ouster. So how in good conscience, could I excuse Nola. She deserved what she got, and no one is to blame but herself."

Hans and Carl quickly turned their heads towards the door when Craig Marshall suddenly rushed into the room.

"Nola's on TV interviewing Martin Luther King, Jr.," announced Craig as he pointed to the three TV monitors mounted in the newsroom on the farthest wall from Hans' office. Hans and Carl jumped up immediately. The two hurried into the main newsroom and stood in the center of the office where they watched the 15-minute broadcast with the entire, forty-five-member news crew.

"This has been Nola Richardson, Special Correspondent for CBS on assignment in Montgomery, Alabama," said Nola at the end of the segment. Nola looked stunning in an all-white dress with a V-neckline and her blonde hair flowing over her shoulders. She was standing in the living room of the King house when she signed off.

Most in the office clapped, and a smile spread on Carl Richardson's face as Nola's former colleagues commented on how well Nola handled herself and how great she looked.

"She's a natural," remarked several staffers while shaking Carl's hand or giving him a pat on the back.

Craig Marshall's only reaction was a tepid nod to Carl before returning to his cubicle. Craig was a 31-year-old nerd with a full head of black curly hair and a thick black mustache. He wore black, half frame, horn-rimmed eyeglasses and always looked just a little disheveled with part of his shirttail never tucked inside his pants and the knot in his necktie slightly crooked.

"Well, I guess Nola isn't coming home after all. I wonder how she snagged a job like that so quickly?" Hans asked Carl as the two made it back to the office and resumed their review of the markup.

Five minutes later, Mrs. Clifford entered.

"Your wife is on the line, Mr. Richardson."

Carl stood up. "I'll take the call at my desk," he said and followed Mrs. Clifford out.

From his office, Hans sat watching Carl Richardson's exuberance while talking to his wife about their daughter's TV appearance and couldn't help but be a little ticked off. Livid was the only word to describe the way Hans felt at how Nola spoke to him over the phone yesterday. Hans downplayed just how angry he was. Since Richardson immediately fired his daughter, Hans was satisfied that her blatant disrespect of him hadn't gone unpunished. But it didn't seem right now to see Nola, the next day after she was let go, on a major news network with a better paying, high-profile job as a television news reporter. Hans felt cheated. If the other senior editors and bureau chiefs had their way, Carl would have been fired too. They all felt Nola took liberties. They complained that Nola was hard to work with and often overstepped her authority. They believed Carl spoiled his daughter, making her lousy behavior partly his fault. The executive staff wanted both father and daughter gone. But Hans didn't think that was fair and wouldn't agree to it. He also believed Carl's race had something to do with their objections. Hans liked Carl. He felt Richardson performed his job well and was always willing to work as late as necessary to put an edition to bed. When Hans became managing editor, Carl showed him the ropes and helped him the most. But despite his genuine regard for his investigative bureau chief, Hans couldn't erase from his thoughts the inclination now to fire Richardson.

"There's no way Nola could have landed a job at CBS that quickly, just a day after her father fired her," said

Craig to Hans as he entered the boss's office. "She must have already had the job set up."

"What are you saying, Craig, that Nola actually planned to get fired?" Hans questioned, even though the thought also crossed his mind.

"Yes!"

"Okay, so you think Nola would take the time to compose a beautifully written article, knowing part of it would get cut just so she could call and curse me out and her father could fire her? Wouldn't it have been easier for Nola just to quit?"

"I know it sounds farfetched, but that's what makes it so plausible. You know how those people are; they can be very manipulative."

Hans squinted his eyes as he gazed up at Craig standing across from him. Craig was leaning forward with both hands on the table.

"What people are you referring to?"

Craig stood up straight. Hans could tell Craig wanted to reply. Thankfully, Marshall had enough sense not to say another word. Hans wasn't in the mood to handle any more drama today. The palavers of the past weeks left Hans feeling emotionally drained. After dropping off his brother today at the airport at five in the morning, Hans wanted to go home and crawl back into bed. Hans didn't want Adok to go to Montgomery. He didn't think his brother was ready for such a big assignment. But Adok begged and pleaded, and Hans finally gave in. What Hans feared finally happened. Harvard kicked Adok out of school. Adok claimed he dropped out when he suddenly showed up at the newspaper two weeks ago without notice. That was unlikely. No one in their right mind would drop out of college with only three more months until they graduated unless they had to, especially not from an ivy league school. Hans never tried to press his brother for the truth. He figured Harvard would notify him. The college did. Two days later, Hans received a letter. Adok hadn't attended any of his classes in three weeks and was flunking every course.

When Carl walked back into the office and sat down, Hans didn't notice Carl until Richardson spoke.

"Elsa said Nola called to tell her about the broadcast and that she was now a TV reporter. Nola told her mother she didn't know when her broadcast would air in Vancouver. Of course, her mother revealed that Nola's interview with Dr. King just aired on the four o'clock news. My wife asked Nola how she got the job, and Nola told her that Bayard Rustin arranged for Sands and her to stay with a Miss Juliette Hampton Morgan, a rich socialite in Alabama. Miss Morgan knows Babe Paley, the wife of the co-founder of CBS, William Paley. Mrs. Paley and Miss Morgan went to the same girls boarding school,

Westover, in Connecticut. Nola told Miss Morgan that she landed an interview with Dr. King, but she no longer had a job at the Daily Press. Miss Morgan made a call to Babe Paley and set the whole thing up. The CBS producer told Nola if her interview with Dr. King went well, she had a job. CBS already had a news crew in Alabama covering the boycott, so the interview that was already in the works for this morning took place without a hitch."

Carl shook his head. There was a smile on his face twenty inches wide. "That's my daughter. She's always been a go-getter, won't let anything stop her from succeeding. She handled that interview like an old pro, didn't she? Walter Cronkite couldn't have done better."

Carl paused as he sat, still smiling, proudly reflecting on his daughter's performance.

"So, have you spoken to Adok yet? Did he arrive in Alabama safely and get settled in?"

"I don't know. I'm still waiting for his call," Hans replied.

"Well, he has some big shoes to fill. I hope your brother can handle it."

"Of course, he can handle it," said Hans. "Adok is an excellent writer and a good reporter, just as good as Nola."

"Nah, I wouldn't go that far. Adok's a fair writer. Craig rewrote a lot of the copy Adok submitted on

Hammerstein. Marshall was complaining to me about how many syntax errors there were. I doubt Adok would even have a job as a reporter, much less get a top assignment if it wasn't for you. I mean, let's face it, the boy can't even graduate from Harvard. How can he be trusted to…"?

Boom! Hans hopped up out of his seat so fast his chair fell over.

" You're fire!"

"What!?" Carl looked up at Hans, shocked.

"You heard me, get out! Your check will be mailed to you. Get the hell out of my office and out of my sight!"

Hans stood with his right hand extended and his index finger pointing towards the door. The glass door to the office was open, and all the employees in the main newsroom stood or sat at their desks watching.

Angrily, with his jaws clenched tight and his nostrils flared, Carl Richardson flung his red pen across the table and rose from his chair. With his fists balled, Carl turned to leave. Hans noticed Carl's demeanor, and Hans immediately felt the muscles in his neck, shoulders, and arms tighten. Hans was a peaceable man. Engaging in confrontation wasn't his natural inclination. But at that moment, something inside him snapped, and Hans wanted to pound Carl into pulp.

"You and your daughter are just alike," Hans growled before Carl was out the door. "Neither of you know when to keep your mouths shut or can recognize when someone has done you a favor. All your fellow bureau chiefs wanted me to fire you after Nola's insubordination. But I wouldn't do it. I used my position to over-rule them. But with all your insight and knowledge of what goes on around here, you didn't know that, did you? If you had, perhaps you would have shown a smidgeon of humility when you walked back into my office ten minutes ago instead of gloating over your daughter's TV appearance. Perhaps you wouldn't have had the gall to badmouth my brother to my face. You're standing there with your fist balled like you're ready to fight. Well, come on! But take note, there will be only two blows--one when I hit you and the other when your ass hits the floor!"

Like two boxers in a ring, Hans and Carl stared at each other long and hard without blinking, neither willing to be the first to back down. But as soon as the incident started, Mrs. Clifford called the police. When the officers arrived, Carl had no choice but to stand down.

Two seconds after Carl Richardson was escorted out of the building, Adok called.

"Wow brother, everyone in the office now knows not to mess with you. I was unpacking when the image of you and Carl facing off beamed on the wall of my bedroom like a giant TV screen. I never liked Carl anyway, him or his daughter."

"And why is that?"

"Because Richardson and Nola think they are better at their jobs than every employee at the Press, even you."

Perhaps they felt that way because they are, little brother. It may have been challenging to work with Nola, but the articles she submitted were always superbly written and packed with interesting details. She didn't know how to write fluff. Nola is the only reporter on my staff that has ever won a Pulitzer. And Richardson, well, he could do the work of two editors in one day and often did. Oh, Lord! What have I done? I've lost my two best employees over what?

"Why has it taken so long for you to call, Adok? You arrived in Alabama at 10:30 this morning. It's now 4:40 here, so it's 6:40 in Alabama. You're just now unpacking. What have you been doing for seven hours?"

"Sands and I have been catching up," said Adok. "He's been showing me around Montgomery."

"I didn't send you there to visit bars and strip joints. You're there to report on the boycott. I expect an excellent copy free of spelling, grammar, and syntax errors. If what you send me isn't up to par, you will be going the way of Nola. But I don't think you'll find another job as easily as she did. Nola didn't just go to college, she graduated. Now put Sands on the phone," Hans demanded before his brother could reply.

"Hello, Mr. Weiss; how are...?"

"Sands, did Nola tell you about the interview with Dr. King?"

"Yes, she came busting into my room yesterday evening, wondering how much film I had in my camera for the interview today."

"So she expected you to accompany her and take photos. That meant she intended to submit the article to the Press. So why didn't you go with her? Didn't you think it was good for the Press to feature the King interview?"

"Well, yes sir, I guess, but she was no longer working for the paper, and I was picking up your brother the next morning."

"Adok is not a child. He could have taken a cab. By the way, who told you Nola was fired?"

"Craig Marshall, sir. He called and told me shortly after her dad gave her the ax. Mr. Marshall said I wasn't to help Nola in any way from now on. Marshall also said that he wanted your brother to replace Nola. He called your brother and told Adok to ask you to send him here. Mr. Marshall made it sound like it was crucial that Adok get the assignment."

"Hmm, I see. From now on, Sands, you don't talk to anyone on the paper but me. Not any of the other editors or bureau chiefs, just me, and especially not Craig Marshall. Do you understand?

"Yes, sir."

"I want daily progress reports on the stories Adok is working on and the people he is seeing, and where he goes. Where are you staying, still at Miss Morgan's house, I hope?"

"Yes."

"Good, remain there. I will have my lawyers contact her and make payment arrangements for you and Adok's room and board."

"If I may suggest, sir. I think it would be better if you contact Miss Morgan yourself. Down here, it's not so much about legality or contracts as it is about friendship. If they like you, they'll help you. All it takes is your word. It's as simple as that. Although Miss Morgan is fond of Nola and helped her get the job at CBS, she likes me too. Miss Morgan isn't stupid or naive. She asked me if I thought the paper was justified in letting Nola go, and I told her yes. Miss Morgan didn't ask me to leave just because Nola and I are no longer co-workers. I'm sure Nola would like me to go. But I'm still here. I suspect Miss Morgan is lonely and enjoys the company. I have already asked if Adok could stay, but it would be proper if you called Miss Morgan and ask her yourself."

"I understand and thank you for the tip. When would be a good time to call and talk to Miss Morgan?"

"Now, she is in the sunroom. I will get her. Oh, by the way. If you want privacy, you might ask Miss Morgan if you can pay for putting another phone upstairs in the bedroom Adok and I are sharing. Except for the phone in Miss Morgan's room, Nola and I use the downstairs phone in the library. It's going to be very inconvenient for all of us to use the same telephone."

"That's a good idea, and thanks again, Sands."

After talking to Sands and Miss Morgan, Hans felt better about Adok being in Alabama. He was frank with Miss Morgan and told her about the mischief his brother was prone to get into. Miss Morgan was easy to talk to and a person you wanted to be honest with. Juliette promised Hans she would look after Adok like he was her younger brother, for which Hans was thankful.

Immediately after Hans finished speaking to Miss Morgan, he called Carl Richardson. Hans apologized and offered Carl his job back. Carl also apologized and agreed to return.

"So, I will see you on Monday."

"Right boss," Carl replied.

Hans smiled as he hung up the phone. That was easier than he thought it would be, but Hans knew they both realized they were wrong and regretted what happened.

There was one more thing Hans had to take care of before he went home today. What Sands said about Miss Morgan not being stupid or naïve stuck with him. Hans dialed the extension to Marshall's desk.

"Craig, please come to my office."

Hans was sitting at his desk in front of the window overlooking the street and had a big smile on his face as Craig sat down in the chair on the other side of the office desk.

"You've been doing such an excellent job as an editor; I've decided to make you the next bureau chief at our London branch. Ralph Lester, who holds the position now, wants to retire. I know you will only have two people under you, a reporter and a photographer, unlike here, where you are overseeing the assignments of at least five reporters, but I think this will be a good fit for you. Okay, so I'm going to give you a week's vacation starting this coming Monday, which means you can start your new job the following Monday on March 26th. The vacation will give you time to pack and get your affairs in order here. By the way, you will also be getting a 10 percent salary increase."

Hans stood up and extended his right hand to Marshall.

"Congratulations, Craig, and keep up the good work."

Hans couldn't help but noticed the confused look on Marshall's face as Craig shook his hand without saying a word. Craig even seemed mad as he turned and walked away. Hans didn't like the way Craig went behind his back and told Adok to vie for the Alabama assignment. Why was it so crucial to Craig that Adok replace Nola? It wasn't Marshall's place to tell Sands that Nola was fired or to order Sands not to give Nola any assistance.

When Hans went home that evening, he was so exhausted; he went straight to bed without eating. As soon as his head hit the pillow, he was fast asleep. That night Hans dreamed he was a boy again at a religious meeting with his parents. Hans and his parents were standing, singing praises to God along with the other members in the congregation. Although everyone's mouth was moving, there was no sound of music or singing. Instead, a deep voice in German kept repeating, "Das sind 181421126 bis 15202015. Das Flugzeug wurde abgeschossen." Unlike the voices he heard when he was awake, the words were not muffled and indiscernible. In his dream, the voice was crisp and clear.

Hans woke up and clicked on the light on the nightstand beside his bed. He grabbed the pen and notepad from off the table and quickly wrote what he heard in his dream: "This is 181421126 to 15202015. The plane has been shot down. Repeat, the plane has been shot down."

Chapter Eighteen

"Racism is man's gravest threat to man –
the maximum
of hatred for a minimum of reason."

Abraham Joshua Heschel

1:15 pm, Friday, March 15, 1956
Chicago, Southside

Milton Taylor worked the graveyard shift from four o'clock in the morning until one o'clock in the afternoon. He was one of only four Negro welders, all WWII veterans, employed by the Illinois Western Railroad. He just completed his shift and was two blocks away from the yard when he heard a police siren and pulled over to the curb.

"What's the problem, officer?"

"You failed to stop at the stop sign at the last corner," answered the stocky policeman.

Milton glanced up and checked his rearview mirror.

"There is no stop sign at the corner officer," Milton said.

"There is if I say there is," snapped the policemen. He held out his hand for Milton's driver's license. Milton handed over his license and watched the cop write the ticket.

"Just because you're lighter than most of your race, don't mean you ain't a nigger," said the policeman to Milton.

"Just because you're white, don't mean you still ain't a dirty Irish Mick," Milton replied in his head. He knew it was foolish to argue with someone carrying a gun with authority to use it. He didn't want to end up dead over a traffic ticket. This was the third time in two weeks that the police stopped him on his way home from work to give him a bogus traffic violation. Usually, there was only one patrol officer. Today there were two. The older cop was doing all the talking while the younger policeman stood slightly behind the elder cop watching. The young officer, with blonde hair, gray eyes, and skin as white as

snow on the ground, looked to be in his mid-twenties. He was a rookie in training. Unfortunately, part of his training was learning how to be a racist and harass Colored folks.

Milton gave the officer a quick nod after taking the traffic citation.

"You gotta keep these niggers in check, or they'll take over," Milton overheard the senior policeman say to the younger one as the two officers walked back to their patrol car.

Milton started the engine and drove away in his 1955, two-tone, light and dark blue Chevy Bel Air. He bought the car last year after he was promoted to lead welder to the displeasure of the white welders, most of whom were also Irish. Milton knew a few had relatives that were policemen. Milton was sure his promotion was the reason for the frequent police stops he received since his advancement. But what could he do about it? *Nothing*, the voice inside his head replied. Milton's cheeks burned. He was thinking about how he fought for freedom for others but still didn't have, and probably never will have, full citizenship in his own country, and that made him angry. Milton considered joining Kapp in Alabama to protect Dr. King. At least he would be advancing the cause of his people. His wife opposed the idea. She lived through years of fearing Milton would die in WWII, leaving her to raise their son alone. After months of pleading, Olivia finally persuaded Milton to quit the Army.

The prospect of her husband now dying at the hands of racist rednecks was just as probable. Milton knew it would be even harder for his wife to bear if the KKK killed him than if Milton died in the war. His wife wanted an ordinary life. No more moving from place to place and living on military bases. Olivia wanted their son to grow up in a neighborhood where he could establish long-term friendships. So going to Montgomery to fight for the cause was out of the question.

Milton yawned. He was tired and wanted the day to end. But today was payday, which occurred every other Friday. That meant it was also grocery day. Milton was going home but only to pick up Olivia. Ordinarily, his wife did the shopping without him and their son, Theo, who was still in school. That changed two weeks ago due to a string of robberies occurring all over Chicago. Six men dressed in black with guerrilla masks were robbing banks and grocery stores. Now Milton accompanied his wife grocery shopping.

The "Guerrilla Bandits," the press called them. The bandits were quick and professional. From the time they entered a store, it took under five minutes for the bandits to empty not only the safe but all the cash registers and walk out, reported the Chicago Tribune. The police didn't have a clue who the six men were and trying to catch the robbers in the act was proving just as difficult without knowing where the 'Guerillas' would strike next. The police didn't have the manpower to put patrol cars at every supermarket and bank in the city.

"I am so sick of the snow and the wind," said Olivia, as Milton made a left turn off East 87th Street into the parking lot of the local supermarket, Potash Brothers. It snowed all morning and stopped only an hour ago, leaving an inch and a half of snow on the ground. "I wish we would have settled in California instead of Chicago. Maybe after Theo graduates from high school and goes to college, we can."

Milton didn't answer. He was too busy trying to find somewhere to park. He drove around the lot twice before he finally spotted an empty parking space at the far end of the third aisle. Milton got out of the car and walked around the back of his Chevy to the passenger's side and opened the door for his wife. He then proceeded cautiously, looking around the parking lot at all the cars and mentally noting the face of everyone he saw getting in and out. Inside, the store was packed with people, mostly Colored women, and some whites. The Southside used to be predominately Irish. The Irish still lived in pockets of the neighborhood. But it was slowly turning black as more Negroes migrated from southern states to other northern states like Chicago and whites moved to the suburbs. Twenty years from now, Milton predicted, the entire Southside would be black.

"You go ahead. I'm going to stay by the front entrance and look out for anything suspicious," said Milton, standing in front of the wall of windows. He kissed his wife and watched as Olivia pushed a shopping cart down the first aisle to his left. Olivia was an elementary school teacher but could only get a position working part-time teaching kindergarten in the mornings from eight o'clock to noon. She was still wearing the gold pleated, full skirt and white nylon, long-sleeve blouse she wore to work that day under a black wool swing coat. She wore clear rubber galoshes over her black pumps. Her hair had grown back since the accident. But it wasn't nearly the length it was before being shaved. Today, she wore it pinned up in a bun on top of her head. Milton hadn't changed out of his work clothes either and was still wearing his black steel-toe work boots and dark green coveralls under a heavy brown, corduroy, midlength coat.

As Olivia disappeared down the first shopping lane, Milton noticed several customers rushing to the front of the store from the last aisle to the far right of him next to the produce section. The shoppers were bumping into each other as if they were trying to escape from someone or something. All the shoppers standing in the checkout lines, and the cashiers and baggers, watched and wondered what was going on. When a fat elderly white woman fell running, Milton and three of the six baggers rushed over to help her.

"It's a dog!" shouted a black female customer, appearing from the far-right lane. "There's a dog loose in the store."

By that time, the store manager had come out of the front office to see what was causing all the commotion. The name tag on his shirt read, Ralph Cookman. Mr. Cookman was a short white, middle-aged man with a prominent forehead and a partially bald head.

The three male baggers helped the elderly lady to her feet as everyone else, including Milton, watched. More customers became frightened when the appearance of a dark brown Pit Bull suddenly emerged from the same far-right aisle. Just the look of the canine was scary with its wide, muscular jawbones, straight box-like muzzle, broad shoulders, and large rib cage. The dog was showing its teeth while growling low and deep as it slowly walked forward. The focused and intense stare in the Pit Bull's small, deep-set eyes signaled that it was ready to attack.

The same elderly woman that fell screamed as did many of the other female shoppers and some children sitting in the shopping carts that were being pushed by their mothers in the checkout lines.

The Pit Bull stopped at the sound of their shrieks and wagged its tail. Its manner changed suddenly from threatening to happy. It then turned and trotted between the vegetable stands in the produce section before scampering to the back of the store again.

"Shoo, go away!" Several shoppers could be heard telling the canine as it dashed from one end of the store to the other in the rear of the supermarket.

"Go get that mutt!" ordered the manager to the three baggers. The baggers obeyed.

Milton's wife loved dogs, and dogs loved her. No matter what the breed, Olivia befriended them. Even mean mongrels warmed to Olivia overtime. They had a Golden Retriever at home, aptly named Goldie, that followed his wife around the house. Goldie laid at her feet wherever his wife sat. Olivia just had a way with dogs. Still, Milton wondered if his wife was all right. He wanted to look for her, but he also wanted to warn the manager.

Milton walked over to the storekeeper. "I think you better call the police."

"Oh, I'm certain we can handle it. It's just a wild dog on the loose."

"Are you sure? Then why isn't it barking? And wouldn't a wild dog run all over your supermarket instead of only patrolling the back of the store?"

"Patrolling?" Mr. Cookman passed Milton a thoughtful glance as if a light bulb had just gone off in his head. Cookman turned and started towards his office. He never made it.

Bang! The sound of gunfire transported Milton back to his days in the war.

"This is a holdup! If everybody remains calm, no one will get hurt," said a sharp, loud, slightly distorted voice.

Milton turned to his left. Standing in the front of the store were six men dressed in black carrying rifles with guerilla masks over their faces. The assailants were different heights, from 5 feet 6 inches to 6 feet 2 inches tall. No area of their skin was exposed. They wore black knitted ski caps on their heads and black leather gloves, and black sunglasses.

Damn! These guys are good. They used the dog as a diversion. The Pit Bull so distracts everyone that no one noticed when the robbers entered the store. The dog is well trained. It growls instead of barks and behaves to frighten some, but not enough to have all the customers scared and screaming and running out of the store. That would bring too much attention and might cause a business owner from across the street to call the police.

"Now, I want everyone to freeze. Don't move a muscle," demanded the tallest robber. "If I see anyone make the slightest move, I'll shoot."

Three of the masked men quickly emptied the six cash registers. One of the shorter bandits walked to the back of the store and shouted to everyone to line-up against the back wall while the other two robbers stood guard in front. The Pit Bull was running back and forth, growling at the shoppers.

Milton regretted not going to find his wife sooner as the tallest robber who told everyone not to move walked in Milton's direction, pointing his gun.

"Open your safe," ordered the bandit to Mr. Cookman. The manager was standing two feet from his office door but didn't budge.

"Now! Before I blow your head off," shouted the masked man.

Mr. Cookman immediately opened the door and rushed inside. Within seconds, the robber came out of the office with a brown sack full of cash. He tossed it to one of the other bandits who put the sack of money into a large brown shopping bag with the rest of the loot. He stacked several loaves of bread, taken off the counter of one of the check-outs stands, on top of the money. All six of the robbers were now standing in front of the store.

As if in collusion with the thieves, it started snowing. The heavy snowfall gave the thieves cover as they escaped.

"I want everyone to stay where they are, don't move. Look at me, not at them," said the tallest bandit pointing his rifle at the customers in the checkout lines standing as stiff as boards. The Pit Bull suddenly emerged from one of the aisles. It ran to the front of the store and walked back and forth as it growled. One-by-one the robbers exited the store. The tallest bandit was the last to leave. He opened the glass door, whistled, and then ran out the door. Each robber got into separate cars parked directly in front of the building. The other five robbers drove away before the last bandit hopped into his vehicle. Milton noticed the last thief take off his mask once inside his white Oldsmobile. The robber looked like a young white man with brown hair, but it was hard to see his face through the deluge of snowflakes pouring from the sky.

Even after the last thief drove away, the customers in the store didn't budge. The Pit Bull was still growling. When the loud blast of police sirens were heard from several blocks away, it dashed back down the same aisle it came from.

Mr. Cookman stumbled out of his office, rubbing the back of his head. "The robber clubbed me with the butt of his gun after I opened the safe," said Mr. Cookman to Milton when Milton rushed over to help him. "The blow stunned me but didn't knock me out, so I was able to lift myself off the floor and call the police."

Many shoppers left, some with groceries, some without. Most of the white patrons headed for the door.

"It's all right now. As you can hear, the police are on their way," assured Cookman to the customers.

"We didn't have this problem until they moved in," complained the fat elderly white lady, tilting her head toward the Negroes still standing in the checkout lanes just before she hobbled out the door.

Most of the black customers stayed and continued shopping. Milton went to look for his wife. As he searched for her, he wondered what happened to the Pit Bull. Milton found Olivia back in the meat department trying to decide which package of pork chops to buy. She didn't appear to be the least bit unnerved by the ordeal.

"Are you all right, honey? Do you want to go to another supermarket?" Milton asked.

"Why? Do you think the bandits will be dumb enough to come back and robbed this market again with all the cops arriving?"

Olivia could see the front door as she glanced down the center aisle. Milton followed her gaze. At that moment, four cops rushed into the building with at least ten more police cars entering the parking lot from every direction. By the time they all arrived, there were over twenty policemen in the supermarket questioning the manager and employees. All the cops were white. Some officers, with frowns and mean stares on their faces, lined up against the wall of windows in the front of the market as if the robbers were still there, and they were preventing the thieves from escaping. Milton noticed that none of the cops bothered to query the Negro customers about what they may have seen. To this, Milton just shook his head.

No wonder they haven't caught the bandits yet.

Ignoring the urge to search for the dog, Milton took over, pushing the shopping cart from his wife. He slowly walked alongside Olivia, keeping an eye out for the Pit Bull as his wife filled the cart, and they went up and down every aisle until they reached the produce section. Milton could see the manager's office at the front of the store and the entrance to the stockroom in the rear of the building. He kept watching the double, swing doors to the stockroom. Above the entryway, it read, "Employees only."

Milton figured that the dog must have left by the loading entrance in the stockroom since it was the only other way out. If the Pit Bull was still in the store, it must be hiding in the backroom somewhere between the shelves and stacked boxes. A trained dog could slip by unnoticed while workers unloaded the produce truck. Milton wanted to go to the stockroom and look, but dared not, fearing that the police might misconstrue his curiosity and implicate him as an accomplice.

The police are eager to pin these burglaries on someone. I won't give them a reason to accuse me.

"That's him, that's the one who suggested I call you about the mutt."

Milton heard Mr. Cookman's voice. He turned his head and saw two policemen walking towards him while the store manager stood behind and watched. It was the same two officers who stopped him over an hour ago. Milton felt his stomach churn. He had a feeling this could go wrong if he weren't careful. He braced himself as the cops approached.

"I remember you. You're the same nigger we gave the traffic ticket to earlier today," said the young officer.

"Excuse me," interrupted Olivia. "My husband's name is Milton Taylor. He was a lieutenant in WWII for the 761st Tank Battalion, which was commissioned by General George Patton, and he received two silver and two bronze medals for bravery in battle. He is not now, nor has he ever been a nigger."

As Milton's wife spoke, several other law enforcement officers gathered around the two.

"Well, he's not in the army now, and a lot of men served in the war," said the young officer.

"No, but he is a veteran and deserves to be addressed properly by mister or sir," Olivia insisted, not backing down.

One, two, three seconds passed in silence while the young officer looked at his partner and the other cops as if he wanted them to tell him what to say next. No one did.

"Well, Mr. Tay…"

Before the young cop could finish pronouncing Milton's last name, one of the other policemen interrupted. He was a husky cop with black hair and dark brown eyes and a large black mole on one cheek.

"How did you know the dog was with the robbers?"

There were now five policemen facing Milton and staring him down. Two stood with their arms folded while the other three, including the rookie, had one hand on the handle of their holstered gun. Milton felt his whole body suddenly stiffen. He felt a rush of adrenaline surge through his veins. Milton wanted to beat the hell out of them all. He was confident he could take the five on and survive without so much as a scratch, even if they shot him. Milton couldn't explain the reason he felt so sure of himself. He just did.

Go ahead, shoot me, and I'll take your pistols and rammed them so far down each of your throats, your guns will pop out your ass.

Out of the corner of his eye, Milton noticed his wife move in closer to him. She then slipped her hand into his palm. Milton took a deep breath, forcing himself to calm down.

"Ten years of army training," Milton finally answered the officer. "We are taught to notice the unusual," Milton replied. "How often do stray dogs enter supermarkets? It was strange that the Pit Bull never barked, just growled a little, and stayed mainly in the rear of the building. Besides, the German Army used dogs to perform specific tasks. The U.S. Military trains canines and utilizes them in combat as well. Police use dogs too, don't you?"

"This is the first time the robbers have used a canine. So we are looking for a dark brown Pit Bull?" asked the same officer.

"Yes," replied Milton. "But if the dog left, it didn't leave with the bandits. At least, I don't think it did. All the bandits went out of the front door. The dog didn't. The Pit Bull must have entered and escaped through the stockroom. Or, it might be still back there hiding."

"We better check," the husky cop said to the others. Just as they were about to look, they heard the dog barking in the stockroom. All five cops ran to the back room, along with the other officers still in the store. Milton noticed that Mr. Cookman was with them.

"*Get out of here, now,*" the voice inside Milton's head said. Milton turned to his wife. "I hope you got everything because we're leaving."

Olivia didn't argue. "There are a few more things on my list, but I can get them later," she said.

The two walked briskly to the checkout stand. The last lane on the left had no shoppers waiting. Milton and Olivia quickly entered that lane and unloaded their cart. Thankfully, the cashier was quick and efficient. She took only a few minutes to tally up all the groceries. Olivia paid the cashier in cash as Milton, and a male bagger filled six bags with food and loaded them into the cart while the sound of the Pit Bull barking, and the noise of police officers shuffling about in the stockroom, was heard.

"With all those cops after it, you'd think they would be able to catch that dog or have sense enough to call a professional dog catcher," Milton's wife commented as the two walked toward the door. Milton was pushing the shopping cart as his wife led the way. As they approached the exit, the glass door opened automatically. Olivia went through first, but Milton stopped for a second. He didn't hear the dog barking anymore. *Good, they must have caught it.* Milton continued out the door.

The snow was still pouring down, making it hard to see. Milton maneuvered the cart through the parked vehicles in the first and second lanes while thinking how stupid it was for the police to spend so much time trying to catch the bandit's dog instead of the bandits. Milton laughed to himself, realizing that the robbers planned it that way.

"There's our car," Olivia said, pointing to the seventh car down the row at the end of the third lane.

"I think I saw it over there!"

Milton and Olivia both stopped. They turned their heads toward the voice they heard shouting; it was Mr. Cookman, and they saw a group of policemen running out of the stockroom side entrance of Potash Brothers. The cops were running away from them toward the side street at the other end of the parking lot. Milton noticed that several officers had their guns drawn.

"Come on!" Milton directed his wife. He pushed the cart ahead of her and quickened his pace. Olivia followed close behind. As Milton swung the shopping cart around in the back of his Chevy and went to open the trunk, the Pit Bull emerged from underneath their car and barked at him aggressively. There was blood on the dog's teeth and a determined look in the dog's eyes.

Milton knew if he showed any sign of fear, the dog would attack him.

"Get behind the cart. Hold on to the handle and keep it in front of you," Milton told his wife. But this time,

Olivia didn't obey. Olivia had reached into one of the grocery bags and grabbed the doggie bone she bought for Goldie. She was now holding it out to the dog.

"Come here, come on, no one's going to hurt you. You can have it," said Olivia to the Pit Bull in a calm, soothing voice. The Pit Bull ceased barking and wagged his tail before it walked up to Olivia and took the bone from her hand.

"Here it is!"

Milton and Olivia turned around simultaneously and saw the young cop limping towards them with his gun drawn, pointing it at the dog. There was blood on the young cop's pants leg.

"No! Stay back!" Milton yelled to the rookie. But the officer kept coming. So did the other policemen running behind the young cop. Immediately, the Pit Bull dropped the bone and barked. It then growled right before it went charging towards the young officer at full speed.

Without thinking, Milton jumped in front of his wife just as the rookie fired his first shot, then another. It all happened within a millisecond. Milton was facing the cops with both his arms stretched out to shield Olivia. The rookie aimed his gun at the dog, but the mutt plunged into his chest and sunk its teeth into the officer's arm as he was firing his weapon. The first bullet hit one of the parked cars. It ricocheted off the vehicle's hood and landed in Milton's stomach. Milton felt the shell slice through his flesh. The bullet went straight through him. Olivia screamed. Milton turned around and caught his wife before her body hit the pavement. Blood stained her coat. Tears filled the corner of her eyes.

"Olivia!" Milton shouted as he lowered his wife's lifeless body to the ground.

"Oh, God, no! No! No!" Milton cried and moaned and cried. He gasped, feeling his breath suddenly leave his lungs. Then everything went black.

Chapter Nineteen

Once the soul awakens, the search begins, and you can never go back.
From then on, you are inflamed with a special longing that will never again let you linger in the lowlands of complacency and partial fulfillment.
The eternal makes you urgent. You are loath to let compromise or the threat of danger hold you back from striving toward the summit of fulfillment.

John O'Donohue, Anam Cara
The Book of Celtic Wisdom

4:30 pm

Seconds before Milton awakened from death a second time, he heard muffled voices all talking at once.

He opened his eyes and was looking through a white sheet covering his body from head to toe. Shadowy figures moved back and forth around him. He felt stiff and so very cold as he lay stretched out on the ground. It was a deep chill he never experienced before. The very marrow in his bones felt like ice sickles. He lay there unable to move or remember anything. His mind was blank.

Where am I? Who am I? What am I doing here?

He wanted to get up, but his entire body was rigid and weak. He couldn't move his fingers.

Where am I? Who am I? What am I doing here? He kept asking himself repeatedly. Minutes later, he felt himself being lifted by his legs and his armpits and placed on a gurney. He began to move. He saw vague images through the white sheet. He was put in a van. The word "ambulance" popped into his mind. He heard the vehicle door slam shut. It was quiet, too quiet. There was no one in the vehicle with him. The roof of the van was low. Milton suddenly realized; he wasn't in an ambulance but a hearse.

They think I'm dead. Why do they think I'm dead? I'm not; I'm alive.

He tried to concentrate, to recall the events of his life. But his mind was filled with only dark space. There were no images he could conjure up of his existence, not even a memory of how he looked. He kept commanding himself to rise, to sit up, but his body wouldn't obey.

Say something. Speak, shout.

He opened his mouth and moved his lips to form words, but no sound came out. He was going to the morgue, and there was nothing he could do about it. So he laid there and waited to arrive at the city medical examiner's office.

When he pulls back the sheet, the coroner will see that I'm alive, and that will be that.

It seemed to take forever to get there. When the hearse stopped, the beat of Milton's heart pounded rapidly. He felt himself being pulled out of the hearse and rolled inside the building. When the rolling ceased, he was placed on a hard surface. Milton saw the bright light from the ceiling shining down on him. He heard voices, but the words were still barely audible.

"Is this the other victim?" The coroner's voice was deep and gruff.

"What did he say? Are there other victims?"

"Yes, this is the husband. The bullet went straight through him and into her," said the driver of the hearse.

"Huss, is that my name? I can't hear you, speak louder!"

"I know. I just removed the bullet. It ruptured the woman's liver," said the coroner. "A police detective will be here soon eager for a report. So I'll undress him and start with the examination immediately. Good day sir."

"Good day," replied the driver.

"Good, what?"

Milton could hear sounds clearly but not words. He listened to the driver leave and heard the coroner wash his hands and put on gloves. He then heard the clip-clop of the coroner's footsteps walking towards him.

"Now, let's see what we got here," said the coroner to himself.

Through the sheet, Milton saw the medical examiner reach over his head and grab hold of the top end of the coverlet with both hands. The anticipation of his face finally being revealed suddenly made Milton afraid, and he shut his eyes.

Don't close your eyes, you fool, or you'll be slit from pillar to post like a dead fish.

Milton opened them immediately just as the coroner pulled the white sheet from his forehead. He held his breath as the rest of his face was finally exposed.

"Oh, my God! This man's alive!" The coroner shouted. "How the hell did this happen? Don't the police know a dead man from a live one?"

The coroner was bent over peering directly into Milton's eyes. The examiner was a middle-aged man with a long nose and thin black hair mixed with gray. The silver metal eyeglasses he wore were positioned on the tip of his nose.

"Hello, Mr. Taylor, can you see and hear me?"

Milton nodded his head automatically without thinking. He could hear now. He felt the stiffness in his body dissipate. Milton moved his fingers and wiggled his toes. But he still wasn't strong enough to sit up.

So my name is Mister Taylor?

"I am going to call an ambulance, and have you transported to Cook County Hospital, Mr. Taylor."

The coroner walked into the next room. Milton looked up at the white ceiling and the large moon-shaped, white opaque glass light fixture. When he heard the coroner speak, Milton turned his head to one side. He could see the coroner talking on the phone in his office through the glass window. He watched the medical examiner for a while until he sensed the presence of the body lying on the examination table on the opposite side of him. Milton didn't turn his head immediately. A minute passed before he shifted the direction of his focus. Slowly, slowly, he rotated his head from right to left. Milton lowered his eyes. He was looking at the floor once he stopped turning his head. Milton heard his heart thumping against the wall of his chest. The beats grew louder and louder as he lifted his gaze to meet the face of the body lying across from him.

Like a current of water rushing down a waterfall, the memory of what happened now flooded all his senses. Suddenly, within a few seconds, he could see, hear, feel, and smell everything that occurred earlier that day. The most potent recollections were the burning sensation Milton felt as the bullet burrowed through his flesh and holding his wife's body in his arms. Milton immediately sat up and swung his legs off the table and onto the floor. His legs buckled when he stood. For support, he held onto the exam table. Trembling, Milton hobbled over to his wife. He took four steps to reach her naked body. She was covered with a white sheet from her shoulders down. He peered at his wife's lifeless face, and the voice that eluded him in the hearse now wailed up inside him and spewed out of his mouth in a soul-wrenching, deep, and mournful cry.

"Ahhhhhhhhhhhhhhhhhhhhhh!" he screamed before his legs gave out. Milton remembered the coroner helping him back onto the table and feeling the pinch of a needle in his arm. He instantly felt calm as his eyelids became heavy.

The next day, Milton woke up in Cook County Hospital. It was late afternoon when he regained consciousness. Ray and Charmaine Wilson were standing by his bed. Ray was on one side and his wife on the other. They had driven for five hours straight from Detroit early that Saturday morning after Olivia's mother called them with the tragic news.

"Kapp and Clare are on their way," said Ray. "Captain Carter is coming too."

Milton responded with a slight nod of his head. Underneath the covers, he was touching his abdomen with his right hand, trying to feel the hole in his body made by the young cop's bullet, but the wound was now bandaged and wrapped.

"Where's my son?" He then asked.

"He's in the waiting room with your mom and mother-in-law. The two have been alternating between sitting with you and watching Theo," said Charmaine. "Would you like to see your boy now?"

"Yes."

Charmaine immediately left to fetch Theo. During the moments alone with Milton, Ray wailed against the police. Ray was never one to suppress his opinions. Ray was the militant one in the group.

"What the hell were the cops doing shooting at a dog? They shouldn't have been chasing that Pit Bull in the first place," Ray fussed. "The dog didn't rob the supermarket. Smart cops would have known the dog was just a diversion."

Ray's rant brought tears to Milton's eyes. Milton passed Ray a sad but sneering glance. Ray got the hint.

"Okay, man, I know. Now is not the time to discuss all that," Ray acknowledged. Ray handed Milton a Kleenex from the nightstand. "Here, wipe your eyes. You don't want your son to see you crying."

As soon as Theo entered the room, Milton sat up and held out his arms. Theo ran to his father, sobbing. Milton scooped his boy up onto the bed with him. With his son's face buried in the side of his neck, Milton squeezed Theo as tightly as he could. Their embrace lasted for several minutes until Kapp and Clare entered the room, along with Dr. Carter. The three gazed sympathetically at Milton. No one spoke. Clare walked over and kissed Milton on his cheek, then took Theo in her arms and led him to the empty chair in front of the window. She sat the boy on her lap. Clare rocked him gently as Theo laid his head on her chest. Kapp opened his mouth to speak but was interrupted when the attending physician walked in.

"Hello, Mr. Taylor. I am Benjamin Amiel, your doctor. I have taken x-rays and would like to discuss your medical condition. If your friends don't mind leaving the room, I will share them with you."

Dr. Amiel was Jewish and the same height as Dr. Robert Carter, five feet six inches tall. But the two were of different body sizes. Dr. Carter had broad shoulders and a thin waist, a big nose with flared nostrils, and a round face. Dr. Amiel had an oblong face and was thick around the waist. Though curly, Dr. Amiel's black hair was course. He had bushy eyebrows, dark brown eyes, and long eyelashes. Dr. Amiel had the classic Jewish hook nose with an arched nasal bridge and a downward turn at the tip.

Everyone left and gathered in the waiting room down the corridor. On the way, Kapp pulled Dr. Carter aside and down a different hallway away from the others.

"We should have transfused Milton and Ray's wives with my blood too. If we had, Olivia would be alive today."

"It seemed too risky at the time. But now, I wish we had," regretted Dr. Carter.

"Don't you think you should be in there with Milton. Dr. Amiel may ask Milton some questions he can't answer."

"And how am I supposed to answer them?" Dr. Carter replied. "If I try to furnish reasons why Milton is still alive, it may only make the doctor more suspicious. No, it's best just to let him do his job and wait and see what the doctor says."

"You two are whispering again," Ray chimed in suddenly. Kapp and Dr. Carter turned around.

"All these years, you two have been huddled together away from everybody else whispering. I always wondered why. I'm not wondering anymore. Now I know." Ray reached into his coat pocket and took out a cigarette lighter. He flicked it on and held his palm over the flame. The flame was burning Ray's hand, but Ray didn't flinch. When he turned it off, the entire inside of Ray's left hand was bright red and emanating smoke. The three watched as the redness of Ray's palm darkened and became black. Then, rapidly, the blackness disappeared, and Ray's hand looked healthy and normal again.

"Look, Mommy, my boo, boo is all better now," said Ray, flashing his palm in Carter and Kapp's face. "I've slit my wrist, sliced my arm, and stabbed myself in the thigh with a six-inch butcher knife. Not only did the wounds heal within seconds, but I also didn't feel anything, and both of you know why. Fess up, Kapp, you did get shot full of holes in that ditch in Straubing, Germany, didn't you?"

"If you know the answer," replied Kapp, "why ask the question?"

"I just want to hear you admit it."

Kapp didn't reply. A Colored nurse stared at the three as she walked by. As soon as she turned the corner, Ray got up in Kapp's face.

"So admit it," Ray said with an attitude.

"Come on, you two, break it up," Dr. Carter intervened, pulling Kapp and Ray apart. "Now is not the time to argue. We're here to support Milton. This can wait. We'll discuss all of this after Milton gets out of the hospital, and we bury Olivia."

"What did the doctor say?" Carter asked Milton when he, Kapp, and Ray entered Milton's room again. The three saw Dr. Amiel talking to Milton's mother, Carol, and his mother-in-law, Grace, in the guest lounge and was eager to discover what the Jewish doctor said. Kapp was standing on one side of Milton's bed, Ray on the other, while Dr. Carter stood at the foot of the bed.

"He said that it is a miracle that I am still alive and that it's incredible how quickly my wound is healing. In fact, he said I am well enough to go home today. The doctor asked if I fought in the war and wondered if I was a survivor of a German war camp, which I thought was curious. I told the doctor, no, and asked him why he wanted to know. Dr. Amiel just shook his head. I know the doctor was hinting at something, but he didn't want to say. He asked the question as if it had something to do with my rapid recovery."

Kapp and Dr. Carter passed each other looks. Milton noticed their exchange but said nothing.

Two hours later, the hospital released Milton. A Negro male orderly rolled him to the parking lot in a wheelchair. Milton was driven to his parent's home by his mother. His son and mother-in-law were with him. Milton's father died five years ago from Tuberculosis. Milton agreed with his mom; it was too early for him and Theo to return to their house. Instead, Kapp, Clare, Ray, Charmaine, and Dr. Carter would stay at Milton's home until the funeral.

That night, while asleep, Milton felt restrained and irritated by the bandage covering his wound and woke up. He knew he didn't need it anymore. Milton clicked on the light on the nightstand and got out of bed. He opened the closet door. Fixed to the inside of the door was a long mirror. Milton took off his pajama top and unwrapped the bandage around his waist. He gazed at his bare torso in the mirror then touched the area where the bullet entered. His skin was smooth. All evidence of the injury was gone. It didn't even look like he had been shot. Ever since the car accident in Virginia, Milton had been feeling strange, different somehow. He couldn't describe the feeling. Only that, Milton had a sense of invincibility, that he couldn't die. Milton never told Olivia or anyone else. He thought about telling Kapp and Ray. But what would he say? I'm invincible. They would laugh at him. It wasn't until Dr. Amiel questioned him that Milton believed there was something to the way he felt. That bullet went straight through his liver and should have killed him. Why didn't it? The way Kapp and Dr. Carter glanced at each other when he relayed his conversation with Dr. Amiel made Milton wonder if the two knew something.

Maybe what Ray has been saying all these years was true. Maybe Kapp was sprayed with bullets in that ditch in Germany. It's not natural for a bullet wound to heal like this. Something is going on, and it's about time I discovered what it is.

Chapter Twenty

Three things cannot stay long hidden:
the sun, the moon, and the truth.

Buddha

10:00 am, Tuesday, March 20th
Hermon Baptist Church

There were over two hundred people at Olivia Taylor's funeral. Because her death resulted from a police shooting, reporters and news cameramen were also there. The church services lasted two and a half hours. Milton, Kapp, Ray, Dr. Robert Carter, and Olivia's older brothers Vincent and Stan Barnes were pallbearers.

The repast was held at Milton and Olivia's home. Clare and Charmaine helped Olivia's two younger sisters, Donna and Gloria, prepare food. Olivia's father, Henry Barnes, was blind due to an accident that occurred at his job ten years ago when acid, one ingredient in making liquid drain cleaner, splashed in his eyes.

Mr. and Mrs. Barnes sat near the front door, greeting mourners as they arrived. Most guests arrived between one-thirty and two o'clock. At two-thirty mourners lined up in the dining room to get their food from the banquet spread out on two, long side-by-side tables. Plates and other eating utensils were on the buffet. The basement was set up as a dining area with white cloth tables and foldable chairs. Milton, Mr. and Mrs. Barnes, and the rest of Olivia's family, as well as, a few close friends were served first. Clare also helped serve the food along with several women from Hermon Baptist Church. She was putting a large bowl of macaroni and cheese on one table in the dining room when a person she didn't expect to see came walking through the front door. Clare immediately went to inform her husband.

"What's he doing here?" Clare whispered to Kapp as he stood at the back of the line. He would eat last with his wife. Kapp looked at Clare, puzzled.

"Who?"

"The physician from the hospital, Dr. Amiel."

"What!?" Kapp looked shocked. He peered through the den into the hallway, and there was Dr. Amiel dressed in a black suit and tie, a white shirt, and a black wool overcoat standing in the vestibule looking around. The doctor was fiddling with the black hat in his hands. He looked uncomfortable. It was evident that the doctor was nervous about being in the company of so many Negroes.

Kapp hesitated. He didn't know what to do. Should he get Robert? It was evident by the questions the doctor asked Milton at the hospital, he suspected something. But Kapp felt Dr. Amiel had to be more than just suspicious to come to the repast of his patient's wife, a patient he met only once last week. Kapp knew he had to tell his secret to Milton and Ray, eventually. Kapp hadn't even planned to reveal it to his wife yet. So he would not divulge it to a stranger. Kapp finally spoke to the doctor.

"Dr. Amiel, what a surprise," Kapp extended his hand to the physician. "I am Kapp Johnson. We met briefly at the hospital.

The two shook hands.

"Oh yes, you're the one who was captured by the Nazis and escaped."

Kapp noticed for the first time the doctor's heavy accent. Dr. Amiel was a German Jew.

"How do you know that?"

"Milton told me. We've talked several times over the telephone since he was released from the hospital. Milton invited me to the funeral. I'm sorry, I'm late. I was in surgery and came as soon as I was done. Where is Mr. Taylor?"

He's calling Milton by his first name as if they're old friends. And why the hell is Milton talking about me. If Milton wants to tell strangers his business, that's fine, but not mine.

"When did you leave Germany, before the war, during or after?" Kapp asked.

Since you know about me, doctor, it's time I discover something about you.

"After," replied Dr. Amiel. "Milton tells me the Nazis performed experiments on you and your brother. I would like to…"

"Milton is downstairs. Follow me," Kapp interrupted the doctor.

Kapp led Dr. Amiel to the basement and over to the table where Milton sat. All of Olivia's immediate family sat at one long table in the center of the main cellar room. Milton sat at the head of the table with his son Theo to the left of him and Olivia's father at the other end. Milton's mother sat next to Theo. Ray, Charmaine, and Dr. Carter dined at a smaller, round table against the wall.

Kapp beamed Milton a hard, sustained stare as he approached with Dr. Amiel behind him.

Milton stood up when he saw Dr. Amiel and didn't notice the intense look on Kapp's face. Before he could greet the doctor, Kapp walked up to Milton, stepped to one side, pressed his right shoulder against Milton's shoulder, and whispered in Milton's ear.

"Why are you talking to him about me? How dare you tell this man my business!"

Afterward, Kapp brushed by Milton, knocking his shoulder against Milton's shoulder before walking over to Dr. Carter.

"We have to talk," Kapp said to Carter. Kapp led Dr. Carter upstairs and out the side door to the backyard. Ray followed. The three walked to the end of the yard near the alley and stood next to Milton's garage. Kapp noticed Ray was with them. Any other time Kapp would have insisted this be a private conversation. But today, he was too pissed to care.

"Did you know he talked to that doctor about me?" Kapp asked, angrily.

"No, not exactly. This morning, Milton told me seconds before the memorial service began that he invited Dr. Amiel. I asked him why, but Milton didn't say. So I knew he must have told the doctor something. Since it didn't appear as though Dr. Amiel was going to show up, I thought it best not to mention it."

"Hmm, that's interesting, because I never told anyone that the Nazis performed experiments on Paulie and me.

That was the line we gave our superiors. I told no one else that lie."

"First of all, it's not a lie. You were given an experimental drug of some kind. Your body couldn't sustain fatal wounds before. I think you were probably given the drug by mistake. But that doesn't matter now. Second, I told Milton. The day he was released from the hospital, he phoned me late that night at the house. He asked a lot of questions, and I told him. I told him everything, how your abilities passed to him, Ray, and Clare when your blood transfused into their bodies. There was no reason to keep it from him now. It never occurred to me that Milton would tell Dr. Amiel anything."

"And you might as well know, Kapp," said Ray. "Everything the captain told him, Milton revealed to me the next day, so there." Ray raised his hands.

Kapp shook his head and threw up his arms. "Did you tell Clare, too?"

"No," Dr. Carter replied. "I figured you could do that in your own time."

"Why not? You've seen fit to tell everybody else my business."

"Yo, business!? It's not just yo business anymore. We're all affected by this," shouted Ray. The veins in Ray's temples were bulging. While Kapp stood with his fists balled. Once again, Dr. Carter had to separate them.

"Stop it, you two, and lower your voices. You're going to have to calm down and get a grip. I've noticed that aggression appears to be a symptom of the condition. Both of you are flying off the handle over the slightest thing. And you seemed to be disagreeing about everything. I don't know what other side effects the four of you might develop over time. But I do know this. I can't deal with it all by myself. I'm going to need help. So if Dr. Amiel can assist me, I say, let's use him. Who knows? Together, we might be able to find a cure."

"What do you mean, find a cure? We already have the cure," said Ray. "Having bodies that can heal themselves from fatal wounds and diseases is the desire of every human being on the planet. And our bodies are now capable of doing just that. So, finding a cure is not something we need to worry about."

Kapp nodded his head and turned to Dr. Carter. "For once, I agree with Ray. But you are right too. We will need help understanding and overcoming any adverse symptoms that may be the result of our condition. And I'm sorry for not realizing the burden that you knowing my, our secret, has on you. So if you want to bring Dr. Amiel into the fold, I'm okay with that."

"I'm not sure I'm ready to disclose everything to Dr. Amiel yet," said Dr. Carter. "We need to talk to him and hear what he knows first and what exactly Milton told him. Then, we can determine if he will be of use to us. More importantly, we need to find out if we can trust him. I wasn't expecting to deal with all this on the day of Olivia's funeral--two or three days from now, perhaps, but not today. But since Milton has invited Dr. Amiel here, it appears Milton is ready to deal with it."

"Yeah, well, that may be because Clare and I must drive back to Montgomery early tomorrow morning so that I can be there Thursday," Kapp replied. "That's the day Martin must appear in court for instigating the boycott. I told Milton about it Sunday night. Milton seems keen on going back to Montgomery with us to help me protect Dr. King. Milton says he needs to do something meaningful that matters. There's no way he can go back to just being a welder. He said it's either go to Montgomery or rejoin the army. I didn't try to talk him out of it. Clare and I discussed it later that evening. We figured Theo should live in one place rather than travel from one military base to another. That's not the life Olivia wanted for their son. So my wife called her parents and asked if Milton and Theo could stay there until Milton can get a job and find a place of their own. The two must sleep in the same room, but that will be good for Theo, I think. The boy needs his dad more than ever now."

"Well, I guess it's all settled then," said Carter. "We'll talk to Dr. Amiel and take it from there. In the meantime, let's try to get through the remainder of the day without another flare-up between you two, or anybody else."

Kapp and Ray both nodded their heads. As Dr. Carter walked back to the house ahead of Kapp and Ray, Ray grabbed Kapp's arm. Kapp slowed his gait to hear what Ray wanted.

"By the way, man, we gonna need some more of yo blood."

Kapp looked at Ray and frowned. "What!?"

"You know, for Charmaine and my boy Mickey."

Rolling his eyes, Kapp just walked away.

Chapter Twenty-One

There is a sacredness in tears.
They are not the mark of weakness, but of power.
They speak more eloquently than ten thousand tongues.
They are the messengers of overwhelming grief,
of deep contrition, and of unspeakable love.

Washington Irving

9:30 pm, Tuesday

The mistress of 116 Champagne Street was gone never to return. The wide veranda, two-story, bungalow-style house seemed to sense the permanence of Mrs. Taylor's absence. Inside, despite the cozy, inviting furniture, and the walls hung with scenic pictures of mountains, trees, and flowers, the atmosphere in the house was cold and hollow. It was no longer a home. To its owner, it was merely a structure of white wood and brown brick.

Milton felt the death of his wife so acutely. He walked out of his son's bedroom and descended the stairs, barely able to take a breath without feeling his whole-body ache. The stiffness he felt after awakening from his second death, returned, though to a lesser degree. Milton moved in slow motion. He meandered across the entryway and shuffled through the dining room until he finally entered the family room. Everyone assembled was drinking coffee as they waited for Milton before starting the meeting with Dr. Amiel. The den was the only room in the entire house with the lights on, except for in Theo's bedroom, where a small shaded lamp glowed dimly.

Seven people sat in the den: Kapp and his wife Clare, Ray and his wife Charmaine, Dr. Robert Carter, Dr. Amiel, and Milton. The two couples sat on the sofa. While the doctors occupied the two recliners that flanked each end of the coffee table. Milton sat at the bar on one of three stools. They were there to determine whether divulging their secret to the Jewish doctor was in their best interest. To ensure the meeting went smoothly, Kapp and Ray revealed the secret to their wives shortly after their consultation in the backyard. For Clare, the disclosure vindicated the way she had been feeling since the accident. Charmaine's first response was fear. But after Ray displayed its physical benefits with his cigarette lighter, she became excited. Her excitement quickly turned sour and grew into jealousy once she learned that Clare was also endowed with the "invincible blood," as Charmaine labeled it. Clare noticed the sharp glances Charmaine passed her as the two sat next to each other. If Dr. Carter hadn't spoken when he did, Clare was ready to smack those cross-eyed looks off Charmaine's face.

"Why don't you tell us about yourself, Dr. Amiel?" Dr. Carter suggested.

"Yes, of course. My name is Benjamin Ezekiel Amiel. I was born in Frankfurt, Germany, on August 4, 1912. I am currently 43 years old. Like Milton, I am an only child. And like Milton's father, my father also died of Tuberculosis. It was my father's demise that motivated me to become a doctor in the first place. I was eight years old at the time of his death. My mother and I moved back home with her parents. My mother never got over my father's death. She was so distraught she was no longer able to function normally. So, it was my grandparents who raised me. The day after I graduated from medical school, my mother died in her sleep. Her heart just stopped beating during the night. My mother's death was a mystery. There was nothing physically wrong with her. My grandmother said my mother died of a broken heart."

Dr. Amiel shook his head remorsefully, then continued.

"After Hitler became Chancellor, the Nazis deported Jews to Poland, where they established the first ghetto in Lodz on February 8, 1940. I was sent there that same year in October. I was 28 years old. The conditions there were horrible. The Germans were slowly starving us on rations of only 300 calories a day. In the winter, we had no heat, and many of the sick and elderly, and small children, literally froze to death."

"In September of 1942, I and a Jewish senior medical student named, Adina Szwajger, made a decision that haunts me to this very day. To spare them from suffering a certain and ignominious death at the hands of the Nazis, we gave many infants, children, and elderly patients lethal doses of morphine. We told the older children that the medicine would relieve their pain. It did. They all died in their sleep. Adina and I escaped from the ghetto and joined the Polish Jewish resistance. As the only two members with medical skills, at many times, Adina and I often weighed the risk of being discovered by the Germans against the life of a patient. Should we sacrifice the one to save the many? That was the question that constantly plagued us."

"And what was your answer?" Dr. Carter asked.

"Yes."

There was a long silence before Dr. Amiel spoke again. "Both Adina and I survived the war. She stayed in Lodz, Poland, and I came to America. Once I came…"

"Why did you ask Milton if the Germans had performed experiments on him? What do you know about the Nazis' experimental program?"

Kapp was getting impatient. He wasn't interested in the doctor's entire life story.

"All through medical school and after I became a doctor, there was one physician who was constantly whispered about. The doctor was rumored to be inventing a serum that enhanced the human body's own natural healing process, giving a person the ability to overcome any and all diseases as well as survive fatal wounds to vital organs. The physician's name was Dr. Weiss."

"Josef Weiss," Kapp blurted out. He spoke the name under his breath as if he didn't intend for anyone else to hear. Everyone turned and looked at Kapp. But Kapp didn't notice them. He sat with his eyes focused straight ahead, peering at no one. It wasn't until Clare placed her hand gently on top of his clenched fist that Kapp noticed their stares.

Kapp glanced at his wife, then at everyone else. "I remember. That was the name of the doctor who the Nazi colonel introduced to Paulie and me in the castle tower. The old man had huge round eyes and wore round gold metal spectacles. He reminded me of an owl. He looked like a character out of one of those Hollywood horror movies. Only, the crazy coot wasn't acting. His insanity was real. He was a short man, only about five feet tall with fizzy white hair."

Dr. Amiel nodded his head vigorously up and down.

"That's him, that's Dr. Weiss. I know what he looks like because he was a guest speaker for one of my pathology classes in college. Many of my classmates, myself included, also agreed that Dr. Weiss resembled an owl. Several years later, the medical board took away his license to practice medicine. It was rumored that he gave the serum to his 15-year-old son, and his son died."

For several minutes, everyone looked at each other without speaking until all eyes finally rested on Dr. Carter.

"Okay, well, we have established that you know Dr. Weiss, and that he was the one that gave Kapp the serum. But what is it that you want? What do you expect to happen now?" Dr. Carter inquired.

"First of all," Dr. Amiel began, "my only reason for coming here was to find out if my suspicions were true. It's not every day that a physician sees an x-ray of a patient shot in the liver, severing a major blood vessel, and the wound to the liver has healed, leaving only a small indentation. The amazement and prospect that Dr. Weiss' experiment may have become a reality were enough to occupy my mind. Beyond that, I haven't considered anything else. But now that you pose the question, as a doctor, I want to understand how the serum works. How long will the serum last in the body? Forever? Or does it wear off in time? Can it be passed on through childbirth? No drug invented by humans comes without some side effects. What are the side effects of the serum? These are just a few of the questions that I'm seeking to answer. Doing so will require tests and observation of you, Mr. Taylor."

At first, Dr. Amiel glanced over at Milton. Then, he quickly turned his head and looked at Kapp.

"But wait, it was Mr. Johnson that was given the serum by Dr. Weiss first. Then when and where was Mr. Taylor injected with it?"

"That's not something we want to discuss at this time," said Dr. Carter. "This meeting was merely to find out what you know. We are not willing to disclose any more information until we are certain you can be trusted. It's been 11 years since the war ended. You are the first person outside of this circle that knows about the serum. We don't want publicity. Mr. Johnson and Mr. Taylor are not seeking fame. And they don't want to become guinea pigs for a lot of glory-seeking physicians. For white men to have this ability is one thing. For Colored men to possess it is another thing entirely."

"Yes, of course, Jews are also a hated race. Perhaps, not as vehemently as Negroes, but enough for me to understand your concerns. So, let me assure you, all of you, that I can be trusted. I don't want publicity either. That's why I didn't show Mr. Taylor's x-rays to anyone else at the hospital, and I don't plan to. I took them home with me where I hid them away in my attic safe. If I can have one desire concerning all of this, it would be that the genocide carried out on my people, or any other minority race will never happen again. Arab nations protest the Jews occupying Jerusalem ever since the formation of the State of Israel in 1948. Despite the war that same year, conflicts between the Arabs and the Israeli Jews have continued. The Arabs have refused to recognize Israel as a legitimate independent country. I am sure if the surrounding Arab countries had their way, the State of Israel wouldn't exist. They would dissolve the State of Israel tomorrow if they could and kill all the Jews. I will do anything, as would every Jew throughout the world, to ensure that doesn't happen."

As soon as Dr. Amiel finished speaking, Clare knew he regretted revealing so much, for, inside her head, she heard what the doctor told himself.

"You said too much, you fool," scolded Dr. Amiel's inner voice. *"But don't worry. They're just a bunch of niggers. I can outsmart the likes of them. I doubt they have even considered the possibility that the serum in Mr. Taylor and Mr. Johnson's blood may be passed on through a transfusion. Once I get my hands on their blood and transfuse myself and young Mittleman, my x-ray technician, we can begin finding an antidote to reverse the serum and administer it to Johnson and Taylor. No way Negroes can be allowed to have such power. We will be the only ones with the serum and can pass it on to other Jews. Then no one will ever again come against us or doubt that the Jews are God's chosen people."*

With her eyes fixed on him, Dr. Amiel noticed Clare eyeing him and flashed Mrs. Johnson a timid smile.

Clare quickly diverted her gaze for fear the doctor somehow sensed her ability to read his thoughts. The first time Clare discovered she could read people's mind was in the church basement when she read Nola's. Clare heard every word Nola uttered in her head. For Clare, it was like Nola was whispering in her ear. Clare wasn't startled by it. The power to read people's thoughts seemed natural. Clare had always been good at interpreting what others felt by observing their body language and facial expressions. Now, having the capability to hear what they were saying inside their heads made perfect sense. Every day her ability to read minds grew stronger. Although, so far, she could not read her husband's thoughts. Clare didn't understand why and hoped that limitation would change in time.

"I must go now," said Dr. Amiel as he stood up. "It's late, and my wife will worry where I am once she calls the hospital and discovers I'm not there."

Everyone else stood up too.

"I'll walk you to the door," said Milton, who slowly eased one foot in front of the other.

"That might take all night," Ray blurted out. A roll of laughter erupted from everyone. Even Milton broke into a smile. So did Dr. Amiel who put his hand to his mouth to stifle his chuckle.

"Okay, very funny," Milton stated. He immediately sped up his gait and led Dr. Amiel to the front door. Milton watched in the doorway with the porch light on as Dr. Amiel crossed the street and entered his dark green Rambler Rebel and drove away. By the time Milton closed the door, everyone else was sitting in the living room. In front of the walnut carved fireplace facing each other were two identical light brown sofas. Kapp and Clare sat on one couch while Ray and Charmaine sat on the other. Dr. Carter sat in the burgundy and brown paisley armchair across from the fireplace. Milton stood in front of the hearth with his back to the flames.

"I don't trust him," clamored Ray. "He just wants to steal the serum for the Jews."

"I agree," Charmaine nodded. "We can't trust the Jews any more than we can trust white folks. What have the Jews ever done for Colored people?"

Milton sighed. "As much as I hate to admit it, I don't trust Dr. Amiel either. And I regret telling him what I told him now. You heard what he said. When he and that medical student were faced with the choice of whom to save, the one or the many, they always sacrificed the one. Do we really believe that he wouldn't do anything to secure the serum for his people, even if it meant jeopardizing our lives? And how do we know he wasn't working for the Germans when he overdosed those children with morphine? Killing your people to stop the Nazis from killing them is doing the Reich's job for them. Either way, your people are still dead, and the Germans got what they wanted. And isn't it funny that after doing so, he and his accomplice were able to escape? Did he really murder his fellow Jews to save them from a horrible death or to save himself from one?"

"Yeah," Ray chimed in. "And what's that nonsense about him not showing anyone else Milton's x-rays? When do doctors take x-rays? That's done in the x-ray lab by a specialist. I'm sure the employee that took

Milton's x-rays looked at them before giving them to Dr. Amiel. Isn't that how it works, Captain?"

"Yes," Dr. Carter nodded. "The x-ray specialist would have seen Milton's film while developing the x-ray and revealed the phenomenon of the healed liver to the doctor. But all this talk about Dr. Amiel getting the serum is mute because we don't have the serum."

"That's right," said Kapp. "Dr. Amiel has to know we don't have the actual serum. So, he must think he can duplicate the serum by using our blood and that--Oh, God!"

"Exactly," said Dr. Carter, finishing Kapp's thought. "Or that the serum can be passed on through a blood transfusion. I suspected that possibility years before it was proven a month ago. Any first-year med student would reason the same. So, I'm certain Dr. Amiel has contemplated such a probability as well."

"So he didn't tell us everything he knows," said Milton.

"No, but more importantly, he lied," expressed Dr. Carter. "The question is, what are we going to do now that Dr. Amiel, and no doubt, at least one other person knows?"

At that moment, the look in Ray's eyes caught Clare's attention. She stared at Ray long and hard, reading his thoughts.

"Daddy!"

Everyone turned their attention to the stairs in the entry hall, where Theo now stood crying and rubbing his eyes.

Milton rushed to the stairwell, scooped his son into his arms, and carried Theo back to his bedroom.

Dr. Carter slowly rose out of the chair. "Well, I guess it's time to call it a night. It's been a long, sad day, and I'm ready for bed. I gather that we have all agreed that Dr. Amiel is not trustworthy, correct?"

Kapp, Clare, Ray, and Charmaine all nodded in unison.

"Good, then we can discuss what to do about him tomorrow," said Dr. Carter as he headed upstairs. Dr. Carter was sleeping overnight in one of the three bedrooms. Kapp and Clare gave up their bedroom to Dr. Carter. Milton would sleep in the room with his son, leaving Ray and Charmaine, Milton's bedroom. Kapp and Clare would sleep in the den.

Charmaine lifted her hands to her mouth and yawned. "Yeah, I'm ready to retire too. I hope you don't mind, Clare, darling, if I don't help clear the coffee cups from the den. I'm sure you and your 'invincible blood' can wash them up in a snap." Charmaine popped her fingers before flashing Clare a smug smile. She then switched from the living room into the hallway and up the stairs.

Ray followed.

Clare just shook her head and chuckled. "Why is it that good people are always the ones who die too soon, leaving the world to deal with all the bad people. It's not that I wish Charmaine were dead. I merely wish Olivia wasn't. Olivia and I got along. I see now that Charmaine is going to be nothing but trouble. I know that one day she and I are going to have to duke it out. And when I kick her ass, I want her ass to stay kicked. So under no circumstances are you to transfuse her with your blood. There's only room for one queen B around here, and that's me."

Chapter Twenty-Two

The Negroes of Montgomery seem to have taken a
lesson from Gandhi...
Their own task is greater than Gandhi's, however, for
they have greater prejudice to overcome. One feels that
history is being made in Montgomery these days...
It is hard to imagine a soul so dead, a heart so hard, a
vision so blinded and provincial as not to be moved
with admiration at the quiet dignity, discipline,
and dedication with which the Negroes have conducted their boycott.

Juliette Hampton Morgan

Montgomery, Alabama

After driving 13 hours and 751 miles from the windy city, Kapp, Clare, Milton, Theo, and the family dog, Goldie, arrived at Clare's parent's house on 1652 Hayneville Rd, at seven o'clock Wednesday evening. Clare's mother, Helen, had dinner ready for them when they got there. Driving his Chevy Bel Air, Milton and his son followed Kapp and Clare all the way to Montgomery. Olivia's unmarried younger sisters, Donna and Gloria, would live in Milton's house for now. Milton had no plans to sell it. Although he could no longer bear to stay there, Milton would keep the house as a homage to his wife and pass it on to Theo.

Milton promised to keep Dr. Amiel informed, but he didn't call the physician the day after Olivia's funeral to tell the doctor of his decision to move to Alabama. Neither did Milton have any intention of doing so once he arrived. Nor was the doctor discussed by Milton and the others any further. The dilemma of what to do about Dr. Amiel was unresolved. No one wanted to deal with that now. Wednesday was leaving day. That morning everyone woke up before dawn with the desire to get on with their lives. At 4:30 am, Clare and Charmaine were the first to rise. The two quickly cooked breakfast. Fifteen minutes later, they woke the others. By six o'clock, seven occupants descended the front porch steps of the residence--six lugging suitcases. Dr. Carter called a cab to take him to the airport to fly him to New York. Ray and Charmaine drove back to Detroit.

The next day, Thursday, March 22nd, was to be another day to remember in the history of the Civil Rights Movement. At his trial on March 19th, Dr. Martin Luther King was found guilty of initiating the boycott and violating an archaic law originally established against striking miners in 1921. Today, Dr. King was to be sentenced and was ordered to appear before the court. But Martin would not appear alone. The leaders of the Montgomery Improvement Association intended to accompany the Reverend to the hearing. The plan was for everyone to meet at Dexter Avenue Baptist Church by 10:00 am. From there, the over 90 indicted Civil Rights leaders, who had been charged but not prosecuted, would march six blocks from 454 Dexter Avenue, down Decatur Street to Madison Avenue, and continue to the city courthouse on 320 N. Ripley Street.

Kapp and Milton woke up Thursday morning in combat mode. They treated the event like a military mission they were assigned to execute as soldiers in the war. Their goal was threefold: first, to escort Dr. King and the others safely to the police station, second, to make sure no harm came to the Reverend once in custody, and third, if he was released, to ensure Dr. King returned home unharmed. They were to achieve this task without firearms or military gear. Kapp and Milton couldn't look like bodyguards either. They had to blend in with the crowd, which meant wearing a suit and tie. Both Kapp and Milton wore black suits and ties and were ready for battle. The prospect of a confrontation between the police or any white supremacists who might ignite trouble along the way was just the distraction Milton needed to keep him from agonizing over his wife's death. Since he left Chicago, Milton's focus was on the present, not the past.

It was a sunny day that March morning in Montgomery. A good day to walk to the courthouse with the temperature at 65.3 degrees Fahrenheit. By noon, the temperature rose to 70.1 degrees. At 9:00 am, Kapp and Milton were outside, ready to pick up Dr. King in Milton's Chevy. Now that Milton was here, Kapp no longer had to be driven to the King residence by Clare's father, Simon. Kapp and Milton were sitting in the car. Milton was about to start the engine when Clare came rushing out of the front door to the Chevy parked on the street in front of the house.

"Milton, your mother is on the phone. She wouldn't tell me what it's about, but it sounds serious," relayed Clare.

Milton looked at Kapp, and Kapp looked at Milton before Milton got out of his car and hurried back into the house. Kapp followed.

Milton picked up the receiver lying off the hook on the table in the entryway by the stairs.

"Hello, mom, what's wrong?"

Milton remained standing as he listened to his mother on the other end of the line. Kapp and Clare stood by waiting to discover what the call was about.

"You mean he's dead? When? How?" Milton asked. He listened a while longer. Milton then slowly lowered his body into the chair next to the table and placed the receiver down on the hook. Looking stunned, Milton sat, staring into the living room. His gaze rested on the 8 x 12 wedding photo of Clare and Kapp sitting on the fireplace mantel.

"What is it? What happened!?" Kapp and Clare both asked concurrently.

"Dr. Amiel was found dead on Lake Michigan beach early this morning. News reports say he was killed between 10:30 and 11:30 last night. The doctor left the hospital at 10:00 pm Wednesday to go home after performing surgery and never arrived, which led his wife to call the police."

"How was he killed?" Kapp asked.

"He was strangled."

"Well, I guess the question of what to do about Dr. Amiel is no longer an issue," spoke Clare. "Someone has taken care of that for us."

Kapp glanced at his wife. He was both astonished and disturbed by her response. It wasn't so much what Clare said as the way she said it. It was the unsympathetic tone in her voice and the look of indifference on her face that bothered him. Kapp blinked as if batting his eyelids would erase the image of his wife's apathy from his mind.

"You don't think Ray had anything to do with it, do you?" asked Kapp, peering down at Milton and refocusing his attention.

The question jolted Milton out of his stupor. "Ray left at the same time we did and drove back to Detroit. You remember, Clare's mom told us that Robert called from New York, and Charmaine called from Detroit to say they made it home safely. Helen told us that as soon as we arrived here Wednesday evening," answered Milton.

"Yeah, but it only takes five hours to drive from Chicago to Detroit," Kapp replied. "We all left at six o'clock yesterday morning. That means Ray got home about 11:00 am. He could have easily driven back to Chicago that afternoon in time to kill Dr. Amiel by ten or eleven-thirty."

"Aren't you two supposed to pick up Dr. King?" interrupted Clare. "It's almost ten o'clock. You better get going, or you're going to be late," Clare scolded before turning abruptly and walking into the dining room and then into the kitchen.

Kapp watched as his wife marched away. He was worried about her. Was he imagining it, or was his wife's personality changing? Clare was becoming secretive and insensitive. That business with Rosa Parks and now her callous response to the news about Dr. Amiel's murder was uncharacteristic of the woman he fell in love with in college. Kapp didn't like the difference he now saw in her.

Perhaps Clare was always this way, and I never knew it. Naw, after fifteen years of marriage, those personality traits would have manifested themselves long before now. She couldn't have hidden them from me for so long. Maybe it's a side effect of the serum. Dr. Amiel and said there probably would be side effects. Robert thinks one symptom is aggression. Maybe, but I don't care. I don't want my wife behaving this way, especially now that the baby is coming. I hope it will be a boy. But whatever the gender, the baby will need a loving and compassionate mother, not a female version of G.I. Joe. When I get home tonight, the two of us must sit down and have a long talk.

Kapp looked down at his watch. "Yeah, my wife is right. We better go," he said. "As much as I want to believe that Ray could not commit cold-blooded murder, my gut feeling says otherwise. So when we get to the church, you call Detroit," suggested Kapp to Milton as they headed out the front door. "There's a phone in the small office off the main hallway to the left by the front entrance. Ray will probably be at work but talk to Charmaine and find out what Ray did yesterday. Discreetly try to ascertain if Ray was home all day or if he left home and was away for a long time. The sudden murder of Dr. Amiel is too much of a coincidence. We have to know if Ray was involved."

Milton called Detroit when he arrived at the Dexter Avenue church but didn't get an answer. The walk to the courthouse was uneventful. The sentencing hearing of Dr. King lasted only an hour. Judge Eugene Carter presided over the trial. Dr. King's lawyers immediately informed Judge Carter of their intention to appeal the case. Judge Carter converted the $500 fine into 386 days in jail, which the judge suspended pending the appeal. Martin, therefore, could leave pending the outcome of the petition. To Martin's surprise, his wife Coretta was waiting for him right outside the door of the courtroom. She immediately greeted him with a big kiss on his cheek. When the couple walked outside, there was a burst of cheers and applause from a large crowd of association leaders and other black residents. News reporters and camera operators were everywhere. When an attractive blonde female reporter dressed in a powder blue, long-sleeved dress, approached Martin and Coretta with a microphone in her hand on the courthouse steps, Milton spread out his arms to block her access.

"No, she's okay," said Kapp, tapping Milton on the shoulder. "It's Nola Richardson from CBS. She's a friend of Bayard Rustin and Clare," said Kapp, who flanked Dr. King's left side.

Milton lowered his arms and stepped aside. He did so just in time to block another reporter, a young male, from getting too close.

"I'm with her," said the young man looking like a wealthy college student. The young reporter wore dark brown slacks with a matching brown, V-neck, cashmere sweater over a beige shirt and a gold silk tie. He was holding a pen and notepad in his hand. The reporter leaned over and whispered in Milton's ear. "She's my older sister, Nola, but that's a secret. I'm Adok, her apprentice."

Milton eyed his blonde hair then noticed another male holding a camera standing close behind Adok. Milton mistook the other fellow for a kid of sixteen until he noticed the light brown peach fuzz on his chin.

"Is he with you too?" Milton asked.

Adok looked behind him. "Yes. He's my, our photographer, Sands."

"Okay," Milton nodded and let them both pass.

"Did Martin expect you to be here?" asked Nola to Mrs. King.

"No, but I made plans yesterday for a babysitter. Unfortunately, the sitter was running late," said Coretta. "I arrived here as soon as I could. I took a cab. I wanted to be here to support my husband no matter what the outcome."

After three more minutes of questions, Martin and Coretta got into the back seat of Martin's black vehicle, escorted by Kapp and Milton. This time, Kapp drove, and Milton rode in the front, on the passenger's side. The Negroes of Montgomery treated the couple like royalty. The crowd smiled and waved to them as they drove by, which was a stark contrast to the way whites treated them. When Kapp stopped at a red light three blocks from the courthouse building, he saw a group of angry white men appear from an alleyway to his left. The mob ran towards them. Some were carrying large rocks, some bottles, and a few brandished baseball bats.

"Come on, light, change," Kapp whispered to himself.

Milton noticed the mob too.

The light was still red when one member of the gang hurled a stone that hit the vehicle door on the driver's side. Just an inch higher, and the rock would have smashed the window and hit Kapp in the head. Kapp had a choice; either wait until the light changed to green or drive-thru the red light. Kapp looked around. He saw no police cars and immediately pressed his foot on the gas pedal and sped away. Some of the mob chased after the vehicle. But Kapp drove too fast for them to keep up. The horde stopped giving chase finally, and instead, hurled their bottles and rocks at the car as they shouted insults: "go back to Africa, niggers!" Their invectives reminded Kapp of the day Jimmy Hodges chased his brother, Paulie, and him home from school, and he was hit in the nose with a rock while climbing a fence. Kapp shook his head.

The acts of hatred against us never change.

At the dinner table that evening, Kapp and Milton relayed everything that happened at the courthouse to Clare, Mr. and Mrs. Matthews, and Theo.

"Of course, the cops weren't there when the mob appeared," said Mr. Matthews.

"They never are when whites attack Negroes," expressed Kapp. "It's only after the assault is over that they miraculously appear. Or of course, when we outnumber the whites, the police are always there on the scene even when it's a one-on-one situation."

"Yeah, mighty whitey ain't too mighty when he's all alone," said Theo. Everyone laughed and nodded in agreement.

"I spoke with Charmaine today," announced Clare out of the blue.

Automatically the atmosphere changed from light-hearted to serious.

"Oh, what did the two of you talk about?" Kapp asked. "Milton called their house several times, but no one answered."

"That's because they were both working. Ray was at the plant, and Charmaine was at her beauty shop. They are working overtime and will be for the next week or two to make up for the five days they took off to attend Olivia's funeral." Clare passed a sympathetic glance to Milton and Theo, sitting across the table. "I phoned Charmaine at her shop around two o'clock."

Kapp noticed the look his wife gave Milton and Theo and was pleased. "And?" He said, sitting in the chair beside her.

"And nothing. Charmaine said the two of them have been working hard ever since they returned. She said Ray went into the plant several hours after they arrived home on Wednesday and worked two shifts back-to-back."

Kapp flashed a glance across the table at Milton, who shot a glance back at Kapp.

"Are you sure Ray went to work?" Milton questioned.

"I'm not sure of anything, but Charmaine is. She said she called the plant around eight-thirty that evening to see what time Ray was coming home, and Ray said he was working the late shift and wouldn't be home until around two in the morning."

"Are you certain she talked to Ray and not someone else?" asked Kapp.

"Well, that's what she said. I think Charmaine knows her own husband's voice."

Kapp sighed, relieved.

"If Ray was at work at eight-thirty, there is no way he could drive to Chicago to strangle Dr. Amiel by ten-thirty," Milton said to Kapp as the two sat on the front porch after dinner by themselves.

"Yeah, that's how I figure it also," Kapp replied.

Seconds later, the screen door opened, and out stepped Clare, Theo, Clare's parents, and Goldie, wagging his tail behind Theo. Theo sat on his dad's lap in the white painted rocking chair while Goldie laid at Milton's feet. Clare and Mr. and Mrs. Matthews sat with Kapp on the long, white, slatted swinging bench that hung from the porch ceiling by two white painted chains. The rocking chair and bench creaked as everyone moved back and forth in their seats while gazing up at the glow of orange and red streaks in the sky. It was 4:05 pm, forty-five minutes before sunset.

"Wow, I can't believe it's March, and it's warm enough to still sit out on the porch. So it doesn't snow in Alabama?" asked Milton.

No," said Helen. "Winters are generally mild here with temperatures around 70 degrees Fahrenheit during the day, unless it rains. That's when it gets frigid. It's usually a lot cooler a night too in the winter. But it's only 68 degrees now, which makes it just cool enough for a sweater."

"In Chicago, we would consider this summer, wouldn't we dad?" said Theo as he gazed up at his father's face.

"We sure would," Milton replied. "Your mother was sick of the cold. We talked about moving to California once you went off to college. She…" A lump formed in Milton's throat. No one spoke. Theo wrapped his arms around his father's neck as he laid his head on Milton's chest. One, two, three minutes passed. The silence was finally broken by the sudden shrilling sound of the telephone ringing in the entryway.

Kapp hopped up. "I'll get it."

Kapp walked into the house and picked up the phone. "Hello."

"Kapp, did you hear about Dr. Amiel?"

"Yes," said Kapp to Dr. Carter. "Milton's mother called him this morning and told him. How did you find out?"

"It's on the front page of The Jewish Weekly. We have many Jews working at the Harlem Hospital Center. It's one of the periodicals we subscribe to for employees to read in the lounge. I usually don't sit in the lounge. I prefer my office when I want to relax, but the staff was celebrating the permanent hire of two resident doctors this evening, and I was there to congratulate the physicians."

"The news reports say Dr. Amiel died of strangulation," revealed Kapp.

"I know, with a light blue lamp cord. The cord was still around the doctor's neck," said Dr. Carter.

"Milton didn't tell us that. Light blue, that's a strange color for a lamp cord."

"Not if it's a child's lamp for a boy's room. The base of the lamp is blue as well, and the shade is white with pictures of animals or cars outlined in blue. Sears & Roebuck sell the lamps for two dollars. My niece purchased one for her six-year-old son's bedroom. And if I'm not mistaken, I saw that same lamp in Theo's bedroom when I stayed at Milton's the day of Olivia's funeral."

Damn! Kapp's pulse quickened.

"So, what are you implying?" Kapp asked.

"I'm not implying anything," replied Dr. Carter. "I'm just stating facts."

"But Robert, you must have thought something when you read the news. What was your first reaction?"

"I hate to admit it, but my first thought was that we don't have to worry about Dr. Amiel anymore."

"Hmm. That was Clare's reaction too. Well, Milton and I were worried that Ray killed him. We have since ruled Ray out because he was at work at eight-thirty last night. Charmaine called the plant to see what time Ray was coming home. Ray answered. So there's no way Ray could have driven from Detroit in time to kill Dr. Amiel between ten and eleven-thirty. It takes five hours to drive that distance."

"No, Ray couldn't have driven there in time. But it only takes 45 minutes to fly from Detroit to Chicago. I know because I took a flight from Detroit to Chicago once. I have a first cousin who lives in Detroit. I was visiting my cousin last year and agreed to fill in as a guest speaker at a medical convention in the Windy City at the last minute. My cousin Sammy lives on Whitney. Ray lives on the next block on Columbus street. I have visited Ray many times while staying with my cousin. I know for a fact that Ray's 8-year-old son, Mickey, also has that same blue boy's lamp in his bedroom."

"So you have thought about it," said Kapp.

"Yes, but it wasn't my first thought. It was my second."

"Whether or not it was your first or second thought is academic. The question is, what are we going to do about it if Ray did kill Dr. Amiel?"

"If Ray killed the doctor, the answer to that question is simple--nothing," responded Dr. Carter.

"Nothing!?"

"Kapp, think. What can we do? Let's say we turn Ray over to the police. Ray is found guilty and gets the death penalty. If the authorities, electrocute him, shoot him, inject his veins with poison, Ray isn't going to die. Remember what I said in Straubing, Germany, after you rejoined C Company. If whites ever find out they can't kill one of us, all hell will break loose."

"So we just let Ray get away with murder? And what if he decides to kill someone else? Do we stand by and allow Ray to kill whoever he wants?"

"Hell, Kapp, I don't know! I don't have the answers any more than you do. I just know we can't turn him in. You know if Ray gets caught, he'll spill the beans on you, Milton, and Clare. Clare is pregnant. Do you want your wife and baby locked away somewhere? And what about me? I will be considered an accomplice. However, unlike the three of you, I can die. After the powers that be, beat whatever useful information I know out of me, they'll kill me for sure. Look, Kapp, this isn't a kid's comic book story we're living. And we're not superheroes dedicated to some higher purpose. This is real life, our lives, the lives of five black folks born in a country that hates us. The only higher cause we have is to ourselves and to our people."

"I don't condone what Ray did. If he did strangle Dr. Amiel, but I understand why he did it. I don't feel happy about the doctor's death, but I do feel relieved. And you probably feel the same way too, if you're honest. So let's stop making Ray out to be some fiend bent on ruling the world. Those were the people we fought and defeated in World War II--the Nazis. The same people that killed your brother and unintentionally injected you with a drug they invented to ensure their domination over every race on earth. Don't think for one minute that Dr. Weiss didn't administer his serum to German soldiers. How many Germans are over in Europe right now with the same invincible blood as you, Milton, and Ray? Who are they killing or planning to murder? For all we know, some may be here in the U.S. plotting mass destruction. They even maybe in Alabama planning Dr. King's demise. So let's remember who our real enemies are; it's not each other. I will not question Ray about Amiel's death. I'd rather not know. The less I know, the better. And I suggest you and Milton don't either. Let sleeping dogs lie as they say. And we shouldn't disturb dead dogs either since they can't talk."

Click.

Kapp suddenly heard a dial tone and was surprised that Robert hung up without saying goodbye. Kapp immediately placed the receiver on the hook. He felt overwhelmed. A thousand thoughts crammed his mind. Usually, whenever he spoke to Dr. Carter, he felt better. Not this time.

"Who were you talking to for so long?" Milton asked as he walked into the house, holding his sleeping son in his arms. It was now dark and much colder outside. Clare and her parents walked in behind Milton.

"I, it was Martin. He informed me that there is another meeting with city council members tomorrow. It will be held at City Hall in the Commissioner's Chambers at noon."

"Good, noon will give me time to register Theo for school tomorrow morning. Simon said that there is an opening at the brewery where he works, so I may stop by after I get Theo settled."

"Don't worry about coming with me if you have things to do tomorrow," said Kapp. "It's okay. Simon can drop me off at Martin's in the morning. You take care of your business."

Milton nodded and carried Theo upstairs to bed.

"Well, I guess we'll turn in too. I'm tired," said Mr. Matthews. "Like I use to tell Clare when she was little, the reason it gets dark so soon during wintertime is that God made summer for working and winter for sleeping. Goodnight, son." Mr. Matthews patted Kapp on the shoulder before he and Mrs. Matthews climbed the stairs together.

"Well, since all the kids have gone to bed, I guess that leaves the two of us to man the fort soldier," said Clare, flirtatiously gazing into her husband's eyes. She planted a long, passionate kiss on Kapp's lips then slowly slid her arms around his waist.

Kapp could feel his wife's growing belly, which seemed only to make him desire her more.

"What do you suggest, Mrs. Johnson?"

"That we slip into something more comfortable and kiss and cuddle on the couch in the den while watching TV. Ed Sullivan will be on at seven."

Kapp's first inclination was to retire, too, but he never could resist his wife when she displayed her ultra-feminine side.

"You had me until you mentioned the couch."

"I thought you might say that. So if you follow me up to our bedroom, I have a surprise for you."

Kapp obeyed, and when they entered their room that Clare painted azure blue when they first arrived, he was delighted to see a brand new, 22-inch TV sitting on a stand at the foot of their king-size bed.

"With Milton and his son staying here, I thought the den might get a little crowded, so I bought this today. Now, how about it, soldier? You want to kiss and cuddle?"

Kapp's lips spread into a big smile. "Definitely," he beamed at his wife. Instantly, his conversation with Dr. Carter vanished from his thoughts, as did all the other concerns on his mind. Clare turned on the TV. The two changed into their pajamas. Kapp and Clare intended to watch Ed Sullivan, but they never saw a minute of it.

It was well after midnight when Kapp awakened from a deep, restful sleep. With Clare lying in his arms, Kapp felt like a king. He was happy and content, especially now that he would be a father. But what woke him up? Usually, after a night of lovemaking, he slept until the morning.

After his eyes adjusted to the dark, Kapp looked around the room. His eyes first rested on Clare's face. Sleeping beauty, he thought. He then looked at the TV and next at the window where the glow from the outside streetlight shined through the sheer blue and white striped curtains. Although the window was closed, and the curtains were drawn, Kapp saw the curtain on the right move. When it stirred a second time, Kapp slid his arm out from under Clare's body and sat up.

"Who's there?"

Immediately, a young man stepped from behind the curtain. The young man's red hair resembled flames of fire. Hanging off his frail body were the tattered and torn rags of a blue and white striped prison uniform. The lad sauntered and dragged his left foot behind him as he slowly moved across the room toward the bed. Then, suddenly, the young man stopped and raised his arm. There was a pistol in his hand. The lad aimed it at Kapp's chest. That's when the walls of the bedroom came alive with thousands of tiny pale white lips.

"Shoot Hans, shoot!" The walls shouted.

Kapp jumped out of bed just as the gun went off.

Kapp woke up, panting and sweating. He threw back the covers and sat on the side of the bed. For many years after he returned home from the war, he had that same nightmare. Only in his past dreams, the walls never talked, and the prisoner's name was never revealed. After six years without nightmares, Kapp couldn't help but sense there was a reason for him dreaming that dream again now. Something was coming, something terrible. He felt it in his bones as Kapp sometimes heard his mother say when she felt a bad storm coming.

Kapp didn't go back to sleep that night. The need to run overwhelmed him. It was as if his body was forcing him. He felt the urge to run the way he did the night he escaped from the castle.

Quietly, so as not to wake Clare or anyone else, Kapp rose and donned his black sweats and gym shoes. He then cautiously made his way downstairs and out the back door. He headed for the woods behind the house. In three hours, Kapp ran the length and breadth of Montgomery, from the city streets to the country roads, clocking his fastest speed at 230 miles per hour. The more he ran, the faster he ran. Although Kapp's vision was blurry when he ran at top speed, Kapp always knew the direction of his parents-in-law's house. It was as if he had a compass inside his head. Kapp didn't know that Clare saw him go. Had Kapp only glanced back at the door, he would have seen his wife standing in the doorway. That night was a turning point for Clare. It was the first time she read her husband's thoughts.

What Kapp saw in a vision, Clare's mind expressed in words as she lay in his arms.

Kapp sees something moving in the curtains. It's a young man with flaming red hair wearing a tattered prison uniform. The young man is slowly walking towards the bed and dragging his left foot. The walls call out his name and tell the boy, Hans, to shoot. The young man raises his arm. He's holding a pistol and aims it at Kapp. The gun goes off.

As Clare watched her husband take off into the woods and disappear, she smiled. There was nothing she couldn't achieve now, she thought. Clare rubbed her tummy. She was having triplets--all girls. Of this, Clare was sure. That night she gave them names—Kenya, Keisha, and Kenzie Johnson. And not only were her girls going to be beautiful; Clare knew that just like their mommy and daddy, her daughters would be invincible.

Chapter Twenty-Three

The things that make us different,
Those are our superpowers.

Lena Waithe

8:30 am, Friday
March 23, 1956
Detroit, MI

On weekdays, Charmaine woke up at six in the morning, cooked breakfast, saw her husband off to work, and her son, Mickey, off to school. Now was her time to relax, catch her breath, and get herself ready for a long day of washing, pressing, and curling hair at the shop she owned and named Charmaine's House of Beauty. Charmaine sat down at her vanity table in her bedroom and applied her makeup. A lot of black women in her profession were good at making other women's hair look good but went to work with their hair unkempt. Charmaine believed beauticians should look the part. So she maintained a well-groomed and stylish appearance wherever she went. Charmaine acquired half her clientele by other women coming up to her and asking who did her hair. It gave her great pride to say she did, and then hand them a business card with the phone number and address of her beauty shop on 5477 West Grand Boulevard.

What Charmaine loved most about her job was the adoration she received from her clients when they stepped out of her shop looking better than they had ever looked, with a hairstyle that suited the contours of their face. Charmaine enjoyed being her own boss too. She also loved her first name. It was a name few people had which made Charmaine feel special and unique. As the youngest of eleven living siblings, six brothers, and five sisters, Charmaine was spoiled and accustomed to getting her way. As a kid, whenever she wanted something and didn't get it, Charmaine pouted and cried until her parents or older brothers and sisters gave in. Charmaine wasn't born the youngest. Her twin sister, Charlene, was born ten minutes after Charmaine. She and her twin sister both suffered from childhood asthma. It was the kind the twins would outgrow as they got older. But Charlene died at four-years-old from a severe asthma attack. From that day on, Charmaine's parents treated their surviving daughter like a precious China doll and gave her everything she wanted.

Like Charmaine's family, Olivia Taylor usually let Charmaine have her way too. That's why Charmaine liked Olivia more than Clare. Olivia treated Charmaine like one of her younger sisters. Clare wasn't as amenable. As the only child, Clare was also accustomed to getting her way. It didn't help either that Charmaine was jealous of Clare. Although attractive, Charmaine was two shades darker than Clare's medium brown complexion. Dark-skinned Negro women were considered less beautiful than Colored females with lighter complexions.

Although Olivia was fairer than both Clare and Charmaine, Charmaine never viewed Olivia as a threat. Olivia was thin with small breasts and didn't possess the "classic" black female body of broad hips and a big butt. Neither was Olivia feisty. Meek and humble was how everyone described the late Mrs. Olivia Denise Taylor. That meant Olivia often acted as the peacemaker between Clare and Charmaine whenever the two weren't getting along. Charmaine wondered who would serve as a go-between for her and Clare now. Charmaine knew they would need one. She was eager to have Kapp's invincible blood running through her and Mickey's veins. So was Ray. It was all the two talked about during the drive home from Chicago. But Charmaine knew Clare would oppose that. She knew it because Charmaine and Clare were a lot alike. If the situation were reversed, Charmaine wouldn't want her husband to give his blood to Clare, either. Determined to overcome Clare's opposition, Charmaine decided to be kind to her rival. She was prepared to suck up to Clare and play the loyal and dutiful friend. At least until she got what she wanted.

Charmaine heard the telephone ring and rushed downstairs to the foyer at the bottom of the staircase.

"Hello."

"Hi, Charmaine, this is Clare. I'm calling to let you know that Dr. Carter will be spending Easter Sunday here in Montgomery, April 1st. And you, Ray, and Mickey are also invited. I don't want you to think that we're purposely leaving your family out or anything like that."

"Oh, well, thank you. I appreciate the invite," expressed Charmaine with a smirk on her face. "I don't know if we will want to travel all the way to Montgomery just for Easter dinner, but I'll tell Ray."

"Oh, by the way. I told my husband and Milton that you said you called Ray's job at 8:30 Wednesday night, and Ray was there and answered the phone."

"Why did you tell them that lie?" Charmaine asked.
Hmm, so this is why she really called.

"Because my husband and Milton think Ray drove back to Chicago and killed Dr. Amiel."

"What!? Dr. Amiel is dead? When did that happen? And why do they think my husband did it?"

"Because Ray did murder him," said Clare without hesitation or doubt. "Dr. Amiel was strangled to death between 10:30 and 11:30 Wednesday night, and your husband did the strangling."

Charmaine didn't respond. She didn't know how to.

Ray went out at three o'clock on Wednesday. He told me he might go into work later that evening. But Ray didn't say where he was going when he left the house that afternoon. I didn't call Ray at work that night at 8:30. Ray called me and said he was at work. Maybe he wasn't calling from work. Perhaps he was calling from Chicago. Still, my husband isn't a murderer. He doesn't go around killing people. I don't believe it. But if Clare believes it, that's all that matters. Maybe I can use this to my advantage.

"So if I back you up in your lie, I want something in return. I want Kapp to transfuse Mickey and me."

"You can just keep wanting darling, but that's not going to happen."

"Then, I will tell Kapp and Milton the truth."

The Lebensborn Alliance

"Tell them," said Clare with a cocky air. "The lie I told my husband and Milton wasn't to protect me. It was to protect Ray. Do you think Kapp and Milton will still want Ray as a friend if they know your husband cold-bloodily murdered Dr. Amiel? How much trust in Ray will they have even if Kapp and Milton don't shun him and continue to associate with your husband?"

Damn it! She's right. "I'll tell Ray about your invitation," snapped Charmaine before slamming the receiver down on the hook.

"Ahh!" Charmaine screamed and stomped her foot. She thought if there were one person in the world she would like to kill, it was Clare Sandra Johnson.

Charmaine hurried back upstairs to finished getting ready for work. After donning a black pants suit with a white high-neck blouse, Charmaine slipped on a pair of black, side-zip-up boots, and a long, black overcoat. Charmaine's hair grew back to the exact length it was before the accident. She had plump cheeks with a small oval face. Her short haircut complemented her facial features with one large tapered curl resting across her forehead, and two smaller curls styled along both sides of her ears.

Charmaine took one last look at herself in the mirror and smiled. *As usual, I look good.* As Charmaine was admiring herself, she thought that perhaps she didn't need a transfusion from Kapp. Since her husband had the invincible blood too, why couldn't she and Micky get the blood from Ray? Charmaine's smile grew. Yes! That was the solution, she beamed. Why didn't she think of it before? Charmaine suddenly noticed the clock on the dresser and rushed downstairs and out the door. Her first appointment was at 10:30. It was now 10:15. Charmaine hopped into her little red Volkswagen parked on the street in front of her house. Her parents bought her the used car ten years ago for her twenty-first birthday. Charmaine started the engine, then shifted the clutch into first gear and sped away excited. She couldn't wait to tell Ray her idea tonight when he came home.

It was nine o'clock when Ray arrived home that night after working three hours overtime. Still, Charmaine had dinner on the table, a baked chicken surrounded on a platter of roasted potatoes, carrots, onions, and mushrooms with side dishes of creamed corn, and buttered broccoli. Mickey ate his favorite, spaghetti and meatballs, at 6:00 pm, the regular dinner time. He was in bed asleep by the time his father came home. As soon as Ray opened the door, his wife and the smell of food greeted him. Being the oldest and only boy born into a family with six younger sisters, Ray never had to worry about cooking or cleaning. His younger sisters adored him as their big brother and did all the housework. Ray was used to being catered to.

"How was your day, babe?" asked Charmaine as she planted a big kissed on her husband's cheek the minute he opened the door.

"Same as usual. Hmm, what's that I smell, baked chicken?" Ray asked, forcing himself to smile.

"Yep," Charmaine replied, noticing the sad look in her husband's eyes and wondering what was wrong. She helped Ray off with his coat, then led him into the dining room.

"Oh, babe, this looks good. I'm starving," praised Ray as he sat down at the head of the table. Charmaine sat to the right of him.

"You seem happy today," said Ray. What's up?"

"I'm excited because I thought that maybe we don't need Kapp's blood after all. Maybe Mickey and I can be transfused with yours."

"Yeah, well, you're on the late freight with that one babe. I already ran that possibility by Robert. He wasn't sure. But before we left Chicago, he took two vials of my blood to test it on mice in his research lab at his hospital. I called him on my lunch break today and got the bad news. He said that of the ten mice he injected with my blood, only one came back to life. The other nine died. Dr. Carter wouldn't recommend injecting you and Mickey with only a 1 in 10 probability of success. It's much too high a risk to take. He is certain that a transfusion would kill at least one of the two of you. If not both of you, he said. Dr. Carter thinks that only someone given the serum directly can pass it on through a blood transfusion with a high level of success. He examined my DNA and noticed that it differs from Kapp's. Robert said that a large circle surrounds each of Kapp's 23 chromosomes like a shield protecting each cell. But when he examined my chromosomes, the circle is a small 'o' attached to the bottom right side of each one. Robert believes that any children we have now will die if it doesn't inherit my genes."

Charmaine's heart sunk at the news. She was desperate for her and Mickey to get transfused.

"Clare called this morning with a bogus invitation to Easter dinner."

"Why is the invitation bogus?"

"Oh, so you're willing to drive all the way to Montgomery just to have dinner on Easter Sunday? I'm not. Besides, Clare never invited us to Easter dinner in Atlanta. Clare said Dr. Carter is coming, and she didn't want us to feel left out. But that wasn't the reason she called. She phoned because she wants me to back her up in the lie that she told her husband and Milton about you."

"About me! What lie is that?"

"That I called you at your job Wednesday night at 8:30, and you answered. Did you know Dr. Amiel is dead? She says Kapp and Milton think you drove back to Chicago and killed him. The doctor was strangled sometime between 10:30 and 11:30, and Clare is certain you did it. How dare she think that you would just up and kill somebody. I know none of us trusted him, but that's no reason to murder the man, is it?" Charmaine asked as she picked at her food.

When Ray didn't reply, Charmaine looked up from her plate and over at her husband. Ray was holding his glass to his lips. He took two, three, four sips of Manischewitz concord grape wine before setting his glass down on the table. Ray continued to eat and didn't look over at Charmaine.

Oh, My God! He did strangle Dr. Amiel. Ray doesn't lie. He avoids lying by simply not answering my questions, like now.

Tears began to well up in Charmaine's eyes. When she tried to sniffed them away, Ray finally glanced over at her.

"What's wrong with you?"

"You killed Dr. Amiel. That's what's wrong with me."

"It had to be done, babe," confessed Ray. He reached over and placed his right hand on top of Charmaine's left hand. "Kapp, Milton, and even Dr. Carter agreed."

"You mean, Kapp and Milton wanted you to murder him?"

"Yes, of course. You don't think I would have done it without their consent, do you?"

"But why were you chosen to kill him? Why couldn't Kapp or Milton do it?"

"I wasn't chosen. We drew straws. I pulled the shortest one. So, I had to do it."

"Then Clare doesn't know that her husband and Milton were in on it all along. She thinks they didn't know."

"That's right," acknowledged Ray. "You and Clare were never supposed to find out. I don't know how Clare did. She must have overheard something and took an educated guess because I'm sure Kapp wouldn't have told Clare about the plan directly. Anyway, you both know now. So, there's no need to discuss it any further. The four of us all agreed never to bring it up again. Now that agreement extends to you and Clare. You must promise me not to broach the subject again, not even to her," said Ray as he peered at his wife sternly. "Do you promise, honey?"

Charmaine nodded timidly. "Yes."

"Good. Now let's finish our dinner. Oh, and by the way. We will be going to Montgomery for Easter Sunday. Last year, our union negotiated that employees would get the Monday after Easter off. So after I get off work at noon on Good Friday, we will drive to Montgomery, stay Saturday and Sunday and drive back on Monday."

Chapter Twenty-Four

I'm doing my own thing from now on,
trying to keep out of trouble and get on with things.
I'm gonna live my life to the fullest.

Unknown Author

6:00 pm, Saturday
March 24, 1956
Montgomery, Alabama

Adok walked into the bar at the Molton Hotel in search of a good time. He just completed teletyping his brother two articles about the boycott and was tired of writing. One story highlighted the meeting between Dr. King and the other MIA association members with the bus transportation lawyers and city commission officials.

The longer story detailed the false public announcement made by the white city leaders on a settlement with the Montgomery Improvement Association to end the boycott.

Adok didn't eat and breathe the newspaper business like his brother. For Adok, being a journalist was just a job, not his life's ambition. Adok had no dreams other than just living. He had no aspiration of achieving anything of significance in his life. Falling in love and getting married was the only thing Adok looked forward to doing. But even marriage was not something he was interested in now. Adok didn't see himself settling down until his late twenties or early thirties. Until then, he wanted to enjoy himself. He felt the ordeal he suffered during the war gave him the right to indulge himself.

Wearing black slacks and a red turtleneck sweater under a black and gray tweed blazer, Adok sat down on one of the stools at the long wooden mahogany bar in the Molten Hotel.

"What would you like to drink, sir? I can mix you a killer Martini," said the bartender dressed in a red vest over a white shirt with a black bow tie.

"Do I look like an old man? I prefer a Rum Runner if you know how to make it," Adok requested.

The burly middle-aged bartender with black hair and a neatly trimmed mustache and goatee chuckled as he mixed Adok's drink.

"Where you from, coz you're not from around these parts?"

"Canada," replied Adok. "But I've been attending school in Boston at Harvard. You've heard of Harvard, haven't you? I know you Southern Rednecks don't cotton to your fellow Americans north of the Mason-Dixon line."

"Yeah, you're right; we don't. But what we dislike even more are people from other countries coming here and telling us who we don't like and calling us out of our names. So after you finished sipping down your Rum Runner, you can get your snobby, Harvard, Canadian ass out of here before I do it for you."

"Aw, Lucky! Don't treat the young alien that way," interrupted an older gentleman with salt and pepper gray hair and dressed in a tailored dark brown suit with his red tie undone and a bulging beer belly. He was sitting two stools down and quickly moved over and sat next to Adok.

"Show some hospitality. We don't want this young pup thinking southerners are not friendly. He may be Canadian, but he's our kind of folks. Aren't you, son?"

The older gentleman winked at the bartender as he rubbed the thick blonde mane on top of Adok's head.

Adok bit his lip as he pulled both sleeves of his blazer down to cover not only his wrists but half of his hands. Even more, than he disliked the old man touching him, Adok hated being called an alien. But something told him he shouldn't get on this old man's bad side. Lurking behind the elderly gentleman's wide grin and welcoming manner, Adok suspected there was a mean old coot. Besides, Adok wanted his drink, and he didn't want to search the city for another bar.

"My name is Eugene Connor," Mr. Connor extended his right hand to Adok.

Adok immediately shook Mr. Connor's hand.

"I'm the Public Safety Commissioner in these parts. Please to meet you, mister…?"

"Adok Wei-Makowski. I mean, my name is Adok Makowski."

Connor grinned and nodded. "Makowski, that's Polish, isn't it?"

Adok nodded.

"The Nowicki family is Polish. Do you know them? They have a son about your age named Drew."

"No. I don't know the Nowicki family," Adok replied.

"Well, then, I'll have to introduce you two. Drew has two brothers, real zealots for the cause."

Adok wondered what cause Connor was referring to but didn't want to ask. Whatever the cause, Adok had a feeling it wasn't right and wanted nothing to do with it.

"Once we become better acquainted, you can call me what all my friends call me."

"What's that?" Adok asked.

"Bull," stated Connor with pride.

You sure are a lot of that Adok wanted to say but didn't, controlling his urge to laugh.

The bartender placed an empty highball glass in front of Adok, then poured the orange-colored cocktail into the glass, dropped in a straw, and clipped an orange slice to its rim.

Adok immediately removed the straw and gulped down the drink until the glass was empty.

Bull Connor threw back his head and burst into a hearty laugh so loud that it made the few scattered customers seated at tables look over at the bar.

Bull slapped Adok on the back. "Now you most definitely can call me Bull. I don't trust a man that can't hold his liquor. Mix him another," ordered Connor to Lucky, "and put all his drinks for the rest of the evening on my tab."

Adok smiled and forgot all about the uneasiness he felt for the public safety commissioner. As the evening drew on, the bar filled up. By eight o'clock, every stool and every chair at every table was occupied. Adok was no longer seated at the bar. Bull invited him to share his booth in the rear of the room that seated ten. It was the largest booth in the establishment. Like a king holding court, Bull sat in the box and bestowed greetings or exchanged funny quips with every person that streamed by.

"Howdy King Bull," most patrons shouted. Bull knew everyone, and everyone knew Bull.

"Why do some people call you King Bull?"

"Because I recruit members to join our national social club."

"And what type of club is it?" Adok asked.

"The type of club that is perfect for someone of your caliber. But we'll discuss that later," said Connor. "Stick around another hour, and you will meet the Nowicki boys and some of the other members. Saturday is usually poker night whenever we're not busy with club business. Do you play poker?"

"Doesn't everyone? But I'm curious. What do you being called a king have to do with recruiting?"

"As I said, our social club is national. I'm the head of recruiting for the entire region, which includes all of Alabama, and that's the title given to regional recruiters."

"Oh, wow, that covers a large area. What did you say is the name of your club?

"I didn't," said Connor with an unexpected sharpness in his voice and a mean glare in his eyes. It was the first time the thin layer in Connor's southern charm cracked. Connor's hostile response to a question most people would ask confirmed Adok's first impression of the commissioner, and Adok suddenly felt a strong desire to leave.

"Forgive me, but I'm not up to playing poker tonight," Adok replied as he stood up from the table and was about to step from the booth.

Connor reached out his hand and quickly grabbed Adok's forearm. The old man's strength surprised Adok. The commissioner's grip was as tight as a vice, and his hand felt like a steel clasp around Adok's thick wrist. The commissioner tugged on Adok's arm, and Adok fell backward.

Flop! Adok's butt landed on the black leather seat.

"The king doesn't permit you to leave yet. Until I do, relax, and have another drink," said Connor as he motioned to Lucky at the bar for another round. "Besides, it's impolite to leave your host before the real party starts, especially when your host is paying your tab."

Adok hadn't felt this afraid since the war and his days at the Lebensborn home. Adok wished his brother was here or at least Sands. He needed backup. But Sands was busy developing today's film and declined to come.

Adok now regretted not taking his brother's advice. "Don't go anywhere alone," instructed Hans repeatedly while he drove Adok to the airport. But Adok didn't like being told what to do and what not to do. Such commands were an unpleasant reminder of the strict rules he had to submit to under Fraulein Hess during his ordeal at the Lebensborn home. That's why he now felt such a heightened sense of anxiety. He promised himself that he would never again be controlled like that by anyone.

Adok jumped up.

"No. I'm not staying, and I can pay for my own drinks," Adok stated in a firm tone. He reached into the upper left inside pocket of his blazer and pulled out his wallet. Just as Lucky walked up to the booth with a Martini and Adok's sixth Rum Runner on a silver tray, Adok pulled out a one-hundred-dollar bill and slammed it down on the table.

"Here is the money for my cocktails," said Adok to Lucky, "and whatever change is left-over, keep it."

Adok quickly departed without saying goodbye to Bull Connor or even looking Connor's way. Adok walked fast, wanting never to be in the safety commissioner's presence again. He exited through the glass door that led directly onto the street, instead of leaving the way he entered, through the hotel lobby. As soon as Adok stepped onto the sidewalk, a white Chevy pickup truck pulled up to the curb in front of the bar's entrance and out climbed three young men all dressed alike in dark blue jeans and light blue, open collard-shirts. All three of the men had blonde hair. But one of the young men had hair as yellow as the sun. On the top of his head, in the center, a portion of his hair stood straight up.

For a second, Adok stopped breathing when he saw the young male. It couldn't be, he thought. But unable to contain his excitement any longer, Adok blurted out:

"Casmir! Casmir! Is that you?"

"Sorry, but my name is not Casmir. It's Drew, Drew Nowicki. At least, that's been my name ever since a Polish American family adopted me," said Drew as his face spread into a wide grin.

Tears immediately filled Adok's eyes as he embraced his childhood friend.

Drew stepped back after a brief hug.

"Hey, none of that Adok, especially not in public," Drew rebuked jovially. "But it's good to know we both survived and escaped the whole Lebensborn experience."

His name may have changed, but Adok could tell Drew was the same sensitive boy that befriended him over eleven years ago.

"These are my brothers. The oldest is Drake on the right, and our youngest brother is Duncan, 17," introduced Drew.

"So you were at the Lebensborn home too? Drew use to talk about you all the time, and an older boy named Henrik. He said you were sweet on a girl named Alenka," mentioned Drake.

Adok didn't know what to say and just nodded.

Drew drilled Adok with questions as the two stood outside talking. "So what are you doing here in Alabama of all places? Do you live here now? When did you arrive in America? Were you adopted too?"

Adok answered most of Drew's questions.

"After Dr. Weiss died, his nephew, Hans, and I moved to Canada. I grew up there, graduated, and went to Harvard."

"Oh, wow! So you're a college boy and from Harvard no less. This Hans, he must be pretty rich to pay for your education at one of the most prestige's Ivy League schools in America," said Drew as he began to walk toward the glass door.

Adok followed. Adok didn't notice where they were going until he found himself back inside the Molton Hotel bar and seated at Bull Connor's booth along with Drew's brothers and several other men who must have arrived after Adok left. But Bull Connor wasn't there. Adok looked around and didn't see Connor anywhere.

"You gotta meet this older gentleman named Bull Connor. He's a hoot," said Drew.

"I've already met him. I didn't find him such a hoot. He reminds me of Fraulein Hess."

Drew's demeanor suddenly changed from jovial to concerned.

"He's not that bad. Look Adok. You need to try and be a bit more open to new ideas and more accepting of others. America is all about freedom. It's founded on that principle. No one in this country is forced to do anything they don't want to do. Bull Connor is one of the most important leaders in the community. So it would be in your best interest to get along with him. He can open a lot of doors for you. By the way, what was your major at Harvard? What brings you to Alabama? Do you have a job here?"

Adok froze and stared down at his watch. Once again, he wanted to leave.

There is no way I will tell Drew that I'm a journalist and here to report on the boycott. That may cause problems, and I'm not about to break off my friendship with Casmir now that we have found each other again. He and I are the same. Finally, I have someone my age that has experienced the same things I have. It's fate that I'm here. God has brought us together. But what will I tell Drew about why I'm in Alabama?"

"Excuse me, gentlemen."

Adok looked up and was relieved to see a Negro bellhop, dressed in a short gray jacket trimmed in red piping and wearing red pants, standing in front of the booth about to make an announcement.

"The poker game will be held in room 203, on the second floor. Mr. Connor is waiting for Y'all. So Y'all better get a move on, coz you know Bull Connor ain't the type of man who likes to wait for folks," the bellhop relayed.

Adok rose from the table before Drew and everyone else.

"Come on! I'm ready to play cards," said Adok taking Drew's advice. "By the way, Mr. Connor told me that he was the regional recruiter for a social club. Are you a member?"

"Yeah, my entire family are now members. My parents joined two years ago, Drake last year, and Duncan and I just joined in February."

"Good. I want to join too," Adok replied as he walked beside Drew into the lobby, and the two ascended a short flight of stairs.

"What is the name of the club?"

Drew placed his hand on Adok's back. He looked back to ensure they were alone. Then, Drew turned and flashed Adok a big smile before leaning over and whispering into Adok's ear.

"It's called the Ku Klux Klan."

Chapter Twenty-Five

There is an organization started called the K.K.K.
Members are joining by the thousands every day;
if they do not like it, they can say so.
But if you go once, you'll a member be.
It's nice to be a 'white man,' you'll very soon agree.

11-year-old Female, Unknown Author

10:00 pm, Thursday
March 29, 1956
In the woods, 25 miles outside of Montgomery, Ala

Alien is a nonmember of the Klan and/or anyone not a white, native-born Protestant

Grand Goblin is head of one of the nine domains for purposes of recruitment

Imperial Kleagle is a supervisor of Grand Goblins

Imperial Klonsel is a national lawyer for the Klan

Imperial Wizard is the national head of the Klan

Invisible Empire is the whole Klan

Exalted Cyclops is the head of a Klavern

King Kleagle is the head of recruitment for a region, under a Grand Goblin

Kladd is a conductor, in charge of initiating new members

Klavern is a local chapter

Klecktoken is an initial joining fee

Klonklave is a weekly meeting of a Klavern

Klonverse is a weekly meeting of a province

Klonversation is an event at which new members are "naturalized."

Klonvocation is a national or regional public event

Kloran is the Klan bible, setting out rules and procedures

Klorero is a large Klan gathering

Kludd is a chaplain

Naturalization is installing new members, and Naturalized are aliens that become members

Nighthawk is a courier and custodian of props who oversees new recruits prior to naturalization

Joyce Yvette Davis

Terrors are officers of a Klavern

Drew Nowicki stood in front of Adok in a small tent in full Klan attire. He was wearing a hood with the front apron raised, exposing his face and donning a white robe with a large Prussian cross sewn on the upper left side. A circle on the red, white, and black emblem surrounded the cross. The center of the cross was in the form of a diamond with a red mark shaped like a drop of water, symbolizing blood. A red tassel hung from the cone on his hat. Tied around Drew's waist was a white sash. Positioned a few feet behind Adok and Drew was a tall bamboo post with a small lantern placed on top.

"You nervous?" Drew asked.

Adok opened his eyes and nodded up and down. He wore an identical white robe holding his pointy-white hood that the Klan calls a helmet under his arm, trying to memorize Klan terminology.

"So was I for my Klonversation," admitted Drew. "Only, during my naturalization ceremony, I didn't have to go through it alone. Ten others became citizens with me. That made it less stressful. This is the first time the Exalted Cyclops, Rex Marwin, has agreed to perform an initiation for just one recruit. Bull talked Marwin into it. Bull Connor really likes you. He thinks you will be a great asset to the Klan."

Every time Drew said the word "Klan," Adok shuddered.

What am I doing here? I don't want to join this club. Hans will hit the roof when he finds out. How could I be so stupid not to realize the club Connor referenced was the KKK? That's why Connor turned hostile when I repeatedly asked him the name. Klan members are not supposed to reveal the name of the club to aliens in public. But it's too late to back out now. Even if I tried to run away, I wouldn't get far. There are at least a hundred men gathered outside. Besides, where would I run to? I don't know where I am, or which direction leads back to Miss Morgan's house. Damn it! What am I going to do?

Adok checked his wristwatch. It was now 11:15. Suddenly Adok heard singing. It was the sound of male voices singing "*The Star-Spangled Banner.*" Drew stuck his head outside the tent. Drew's oldest brother Drake was a Kladd and appeared at the tent's entrance.

"Take your assigned position," ordered Drake to Drew, looking severe and in a stern voice. Drew lowered the front apron on his helmet and left immediately.

Drake looked at Adok. "You ready?"

Adok gave a slight nod.

"When the singing stops, you step outside. But you are to wait at the entrance until the two Klexters escort you to the area where you are to stand in front of the altar. What are Klexters?" Drake asked.

"They are the two guards that stand outside the room or area where aliens for naturalization are kept," Adok explained.

"That's correct," said Drake, who put down the flap on his helmet and left.

For the first time, Adok was by himself in the dimly lit tent.

There's nothing more terrifying than to be all alone and afraid, uttered a voice inside Adok's head.

Adok realized the singing had stopped and quickly donned his hood and walked out of the tent. He was immediately greeted by the brisk night air and the heady smell of smoke. Adok gazed up at the gibbous-shaped moon, and then at the large assembly of white-robed Klansmen with pointy hats all standing like soldiers in battle formation. It was a spectacular sight to behold. At least a hundred Klansmen were assembled. The members formed a large square. Within the square, they formed a circle. Within that ring, they created an even smaller square. Inside the smaller square was the podium where Rex Marwin was to officiate over the Klonversation. A giant burning cross, twenty feet high, towered behind the platform six feet away. Lanterns burned around the encampment on tall posts.

Adok glanced at the Klexter on his right. To Adok's surprise, the eyes of Drew stared back at him. By the gleam in Drew's eyes, Adok could tell Drew was smiling.

Adok exhaled. Although still nervous, with Drew by his side he was less afraid.

When the assembly sang the "*Battle Hymn of the Republic*," the Klexters and Adok started walking. Adok walked between the two guards in a synchronized step. The singing stopped once Adok was standing in the center of the assembly before the Exalted Cyclops, standing behind the platform. An American flag draped the altar. A long sword laid across the flag with its hilt toward the Exalted Cyclops.

"Kladd of the Klan," called out Rex Marwin. "You will ascertain with care if all present are Klansmen worthy to sit in the Klavern during the deliberations of this Klonversation."

"I have your orders, sir," Drake responded. Drake approached each member who then made a countersign and whispered the password into the Kladd's ear. Drake verified the membership of each attendee. Adok was the last one to give the countersign and password, after which, he was drilled with questions and had to answer each correctly; he did. From memory, Adok recited the Klan oath and pledged to lead a life of cleanliness in mind, body, and spirit. Afterward, the Exalted Cyclops baptized him with holy Klan water by pouring a few drops on Adok's back. Rex Marwin then doused a few drops on himself, tossed some of the water in the air, and then moved his hand horizontally in a circle around Adok's head. Following the initiation, the entire assembly broke into a loud rendition of "*In the Cross of Christ I Glory,*" followed by "*Blest Be the Tie That Binds.*"

The ceremony lasted three hours. By the end, Adok felt a heightened sense of collective awareness. The word "Klan" no longer made him shudder. Just the opposite, he experienced an enormous and liberating sense of pride and purpose. Adok now thought of the robe as his armor and the emblem over his left breast as his shield.

I now have a secure and protected place in the world.

Twenty-year-old Adok Bohdan Makowski felt exalted and honored as he stood among his fellow brethren as the newest member of the Eternal Order of the Knights of the Ku Klux Klan.

Chapter Twenty-Six

*Church was never meant to be a place for gods to gather,
but for devils wanting to shed their horns for halos.*

Richelle E. Goodrich

April 1, 1956, Easter Sunday
Dexter Avenue Baptist Church

Although the Easter program was set to begin at nine o'clock in the morning, by 7:30 am, the church was packed. Some attendees stood alongside the walls and in the back of the hall. Those standing up were men and teenage boys who gave up their seats to women and small children. The congregation was a sight to behold as everyone assembled in their best Easter finery. Some women always wore hats on Sunday. But today, every female, five-years-old and older, donned a hat color coordinated to the exact match of their outfits in vibrate hues of pink, peach, yellow, violet, baby blue, and cream. There were a grand variety of hats to be seen, from satin and polyester feathered bucket hats to wide brim hats adorned with flowers and bows, and little girl's straw hats encircled with ribbons.

Clare and Charmaine were no exceptions. Clare wore a yellow and violet floral printed maternity dress with an off the shoulder ruffled trim with long ruffled sleeves paired with a butter yellow, bell-shaped hat, and heart-shaped diamond stud earrings. The 1920's style cloche cap was longer on one side than the other with the more extended flap covering the right ear. The hat was embellished with a gold rhinestone brooch pinned to a large knotted bow. Clare's black hair, curled under, flowed out from underneath the cloche and rested in a clump on her right shoulder. Charmaine was decked out in a tailor-fitted suit of light blue lace with a high-waisted, pencil skirt and a short jacket bejeweled with four round, glass buttons that fastened down the front and on the cuffs of her sleeves. Charmaine's wide-brim, baby-blue, saucer-shaped hat of sheer satin was cocked to one side and adorned in the front with a large rose of the same fabric and shade. Dangling from Charmaine's ears were a pair of long, pear-shaped, imitation pearl earrings.

Instead of the dark suits their husbands usually wore, today, both Kapp and Ray were clad in light-colors as were most men present. Kapp looked sharp in a double-breasted cream suit coat and curry-gold trousers paired with a gold shirt. On his paisley, walnut and mustard tie was a gold-chain tie clip. Tucked inside his upper-left coat pocket was a matching paisley handkerchief. Ray looked equally smart in a pecan brown, shark-skin suit and matching pecan shirt, accessorized with a burgundy diamond-pattern necktie, and a gold octagon rhinestone tie pin. In the buttonhole of Ray's upper-right lapel was a red carnation. But it was Milton who got everyone's attention when he walked in wearing an all-white suit contrasted with a cobalt blue shirt with a white collar. His white silk tie was embellished with a blue, oval sapphire tie pin. To top off his dashing appearance, Milton tilted his white Panama hat with the wide, cobalt blue band slightly downward, partially covering one eye.

"Who is that?" more than a few ladies whispered to each other. "I think it's Harry Belafonte," many replied.

Clare's friend, Maddie Wilkins, giggled as she leaned forward in her seat and touched Clare on the shoulder when she saw Milton strut in and stand against the wall next to Ray while Theo and Mickey sat together between

Clare and Charmaine. Maddie displayed her healthy bustline in a short-sleeved swing dress embellished with large roses of champagne pink. Her auburn hair flowed just above her shoulders in thick curls. On top of her head rested a small, matching pink, pancake-shaped fascinator clipped to one side with a feather hatpin. Both Mickey and Theo were clad in the same colors as their fathers. Eight-year-old Mickey wore light brown pants with red suspenders and a white shirt with a red bow tie. Theo, 10, sported a royal blue vest and trousers with a blue shirt and a white tie spotted with small blue polka dots.

Maddie sat directly behind Clare and Charmaine on the third row in the seats on the right side of the church closest to the center aisle with her younger brother, Stephen and his wife, Sissy, and two kids, Nicolet, 5, and Sam, 7. Ever since Milton arrived in Montgomery, Clare had been talking him up to Maddie. Clare thought the two would make the perfect couple. But Clare wanted Milton to land a job first and let a little more time pass between Olivia's death before she introduced the two. Now that Milton worked at the brewery with Clare's father, Clare invited Maddie to Easter dinner, and Maddie was excited and looking forward to meeting Milton and his son.

At 8:30, Martin and Coretta arrived with Kapp and the other pastors and the members of the Montgomery

Improvement Association, including JoAnn Robinson, Ella Baker, and Septima Clark. The three ladies, along with their husbands, sat on the first-row bench in front of Clare and her parents and Charmaine. The congregation was all smiles, and many clapped upon the entrance of the King family. Coretta donned a beautiful but modest pink dress and matching long coat with a flat, round, pink hat. Baby Yolonda looked darling in a multi-colored, pink, violet, yellow, and blue, short sleeve, dress with a large pink ribbon tied in a bow around her waist, and a pink ruffled bonnet with a ribbon fastened under her chin. Coretta sat with little Yo-Yo on her lap with the other pastor's wives on the first row on the left side of the church opposite JoAnn Robinson. Martin wore a navy-blue suit coat with light blue pants and vest, a white shirt with a two-tone blue striped tie. A white rose boutonniere garnished the upper, right-hand side of Dr. King's blazer. All the reverends and male MIA associates wore white rose boutonnieres.

Charmaine leaned over toward Clare. "Too bad Dr. Carter and his wife Linda couldn't make it. I think the two of them would have liked to have met Dr. King," said Charmaine. *If you did, invite them.*

Clare looked at Charmaine. "I did really invite them, but they decided to celebrate the holiday with their own families."

Charmaine looked at Clare flabbergasted and sat up straight.

Confusion occurred with the seating arrangements for the pastors and some members of the Montgomery Improvement Association. Twenty-four high-back chairs were arranged side-by-side in two long rows across the stage. Although there were 70 MIA members, only the male members on the negotiating committee sat with Dr. King on the first row. The choir sat on elevated, stair-step benches behind the committee members. The podium was positioned on the left flank of the platform. The podium was slanted at a right angle in front of the chairs and the choir so as not to block the occupant's seated on the stage view of the congregation. Dr. King sat in the chair in the center of the first row with Pastor Gardener Taylor seated on Martin's left, followed by Rev. Roy Bennet, Attorney Fred Gray, Rev. H.H. Hubbard, Dr. Moses W. Jones, and Rev. A. Wilson. Reverend Ralph Abernathy sat on Dr. King's right, followed by Rev. S. S. Seay, Attorney Charles Langford, Mr. J. E. Pierce, and Mr. Rufus A. Lewis. Only pastors occupied the second row. There were name cards on every seat. Except, when Edgar Nixon, President of the Montgomery Chapter of the NAACP, looked for his name card, he couldn't find it.

"Where am I supposed to sit?" Nixon asked. "Why isn't there a chair for me? I'm a member of the MIA."

Dr. King looked to his left then to his right but didn't respond, neither did the others seated with him. Nixon placed his hands on his hips and just stood eyeing them all with a tight lip.

Kapp grew concerned at the way Nixon glared at Dr. King and walked over to Edgar.

"Is there a problem, Mr. Nixon?" Kapp asked respectfully, aware of the growing friction between Nixon and the other MIA members.

"I need a seat," Edgar said.

"There is a space on the first row next to Mrs. Robinson," said Kapp, pointing to the end spot on the bench near the outer aisle among the section of seats on the right side of the church.

"No, I need a chair here with the other MIA members," proclaimed Nixon.

Kapp tried to reason with Edgar. "There isn't any space for another chair. Besides, most of the MIA members are not sitting here. There's simply no room for all of you."

"I'm not most members," Nixon protested, "I'm the treasurer, and I'm on the negotiating committee the same as the rest of them, not to mention one of the founders of the group, and I demand to sit here with the others," he shouted which got everyone's attention in the church. Both Milton and Ray hurried over to assist Kapp. With Milton and Ray now present, the three surrounded Nixon. Although Ray was the shortest of them all, standing only five feet ten inches tall, while the others were between six feet and six feet two, Ray took command.

"This is Easter Sunday. You don't mean to tell me that you are going to stand here, Mr. Nixon, and stage a hissy fit over where you sit on this of all days," spit Ray. "There's a space right there in the first row. Either plant your butt in it or leave. But there is one thing you are not going to do, and that is to continue to stand here and cause a scene."

The intense looked Ray gave Edgar Nixon needed no explanation as to what would happen next if Nixon didn't comply. Edgar sneered at the three, then at Dr. King. Martin was talking to Rev. Taylor and appeared to try to avoid even looking in Nixon's direction. Edgar huffed, then reached up and pulled out the white rose from the buttonhole in the lapel of his light gray suit and flung it at Dr. King. Before it hit Martin in the face, Kapp reached out his hand and caught it. Nixon then stepped off the platform and reluctantly took the seat in the first row next to the husband of JoAnn Robinson.

Charmaine leaned over to her left again. She whispered in Clare's ear. "What was that all about?"

"What it's always about when it comes to men--power," explained Clare. "You see, although Edgar Nixon initiated the boycott and is the head of the NAACP down here, he's uneducated. That is to say, he hasn't earned a degree. Every member sitting with Martin and on the MIA, except Mr. Nixon, has graduated from a university, even the female members. Nixon doesn't think the leadership positions should be held only by those with college degrees. Of course, none of the other male members agree. Kapp says Nixon is tolerated, but not very well-liked among the group. So, there is a bit of a class struggle going on, for which Mr. Nixon is losing. I don't imagine Nixon will last too much longer. If the Supreme Court rules in favor of desegregation and the boycott ends, I predict Mr. Nixon will probably go his own way."

"Oh, I see. So there is prejudice among the black Civil Rights leaders who are trying to stop discrimination and prejudice of Negroes by whites." Charmaine shook her head from side-to-side. "By the way, where is Rosa Parks? I don't see her here, do you? And it's 8:50, almost time for the service to start."

Clare forgot about Rosa. She looked around but didn't see Rosa either until someone shouted, "Rosa Parks is here!" At that moment, Mrs. Parks and her husband walked in. Her husband was wearing a tan suit while Rosa wore a two-tone, red and white, collarless blazer with a matching red pleated skirt, black pumps, and a black handbag. Usually, Rosa's hair was in a bun, today she wore it down in loose curls flowing over her shoulders with a small, round red feathered hat positioned on the top right side. A double string of tiny white beads adorned her neck, complementing a cluster of small white beaded earrings. No one had ever seen Mrs. Parks look so pretty. Ooh's and ah's rippled through the audience as Rosa walked down the center aisle and took her seat in the second row behind Mrs. King on the left side of the hall.

Clare noticed the forced smiles on the faces of Dr. King, and the other pastors and male MIA associates. She could read their minds. She heard many voices all speaking at once, but she blocked the others out and concentrated only on the voices of Martin and Ralph Abernathy.

"*Who does she think she is, sashaying in here, upstaging my wife just minutes before I give my sermon,*" said Martin.

"*I see now we are going to have to talk directly to Mrs. Parks from now on,*" pouted Reverend Abernathy. "*Talking to her husband is not working. We have to put a stop to Rosa's grandstanding once and for all.*"

Clare shook her head as she listened to their thoughts.

"I see that they don't much like Rosa Parks either, judging by the looks on their faces," whispered Charmaine to Clare.

Charmaine was observant. Clare had to admit that about her rival, if nothing else. Clare wondered if she was just as bias against Charmaine as the Civil Rights leaders were bias against Edgar Nixon and Rosa Parks. Clare tried to list the reasons she didn't like Charmaine, and to her surprise, she couldn't come up with even one defensible cause.

Did I dislike Charmaine simply because Charmaine was attractive and knew how to dress and carry herself? It was so easy to like Olivia. Olivia was soft-spoken and meek and didn't mind being a backseat passenger in our friendship. Charmaine is more like me. Charmaine will never settle for second place. And why should she? She has just as much right as I do to be in control. I know one thing, when the going gets tough, I want Charmaine on my side. She's a fighter. Hmm, perhaps I should persuade Kapp to transfuse Charmaine and Mickey with his blood, after all. And what about mom and dad and Kapp's parents? What's the point of living forever when the rest of your family and friends will die?

Suddenly the choir stood up and sung *At the Cross,* followed by *My Jesus I Love Thee.* Then, the entire congregation rose and joined in singing *When the Roll is*

Called up Yonder. Afterward, Reverend Abernathy opened the services with a prayer.

"Christ is more concerned about our attitude towards racial prejudice and war than he is about our long processionals. He is more concerned with how we treat our neighbors than how loud we sing his praises. A religion of compassion that's what God demands of us. God gave his only begotten son for us and resurrected him on this day as a testament of God's love for all mankind. God was not passive in His love for us, neither should we be passive in our love for Him or our love for one another," preached Martin Luther King, Jr. to the large congregation at the Dexter Street Baptist Church. The Easter Sunday service lasted three hours. Before Dr. King, Pastor Gardener C. Taylor of the Concord Baptist Church of Christ from Brooklyn, New York, also gave a rousing sermon. Pastor Taylor was a mentor and friend of Dr. King. He was also a Civil Rights leader in his own right.

Lunch was served downstairs in the banquet room. There was more than enough food because every black woman who could cook prepared at least two dishes. Clare helped serve and was surprised to see Nola standing across from her in the food line. Since Thursday evening, the young reporter who replaced Nola from the Vancouver Daily had been missing, and Nola and Sands were frantic in their efforts to find him.

"What are you doing here? I thought you would be celebrating Easter with Juliette at her church."

"I did for an hour. But services at a white church doesn't compare with the worship at a black church," said Nola.

Clare laughed and nodded. "So, has the cub reporter--what's his name--Adok, showed up?"

"No," replied Nola. "We haven't found him yet, but his brother is arriving tomorrow from Vancouver to help with the search."

"What do you think happened to the boy?"

"I think Adok is off somewhere boozing it up and having a good time with some little floozy he met at a bar. But of course, his brother doesn't believe Adok would stay gone this long without letting him know where he is. Hans thinks his little brother's a choir boy."

A crinkle formed on Clare's forehead. "Did you say the older brother's name is Hans?"

"Yes, Hans Weiss. He's the managing editor and owns the Daily. Not too many people know that fact, though. Why do you ask?"

Clare shrugged her shoulders. "Oh, I think I may have heard my husband speak that name, or maybe it was one of his war buddies. The soldiers Kapp served with, like telling stories about where they went and who they met during the war at the annual reunion of Kapp's tank battalion. We attend it every year."

Hans is the name I heard a voice shout in Kapp's dream. Hmm, I wonder. Nah, it couldn't be the same person. There are no doubt thousands of men named Hans in Europe.

"What does the police say about Adok's disappearance?" Clare finally asked.

"They don't seem all that worried about it either. I think the cops believe, as I do, that Adok's laid up in a hotel somewhere with a girl. They keep saying Adok will show up as if they are certain he will."

"Well, it's strange that the police aren't concerned. Colored men go missing frequently, and of course, the authorities could care less. But it's odd that the police aren't tearing up the town to find a white man."

"Maybe it's because he's a reporter," Nola replied. "I've noticed that most of the whites around here don't like the media. They think we're sympathetic to the Negro cause and not fairly portraying their side of the issue."

"Yeah, well, nobody complains louder than racists accusing others of being unfair to them," Clare interjected.

"So far, the police haven't gotten involved. Hopefully, that will change once Hans gets here. If not, I don't know how we'll ever find Adok," Nola admitted. After putting one of Clare's homemade dinner rolls on her plate full of food, Nola smiled at Clare, then turned and looked for a seat.

"My family is sitting over there at the last table on your right if you want to eat with us," said Clare.

Nola glanced back at Clare and nodded before heading in that direction. A second later, Maddie Wilkins walked up to Clare from behind. Maddie had been standing next to Clare serving until she took a restroom break ten minutes ago. Maddie gently grabbed Clare by the arm and pulled Clare a few steps away from the banquet table.

"Where is your husband?" Maddie asked quietly in Clare's ear.

"Oh, he's upstairs in the small office with Martin, Coretta, and Yo-Yo talking to Martin's parents. The senior Reverend King called to wish them a happy Easter. Why?" Clare inquired.

"You better go get him," said Maddie. "Three, hooded, KKK members are gathered outside in the back of the church. The restroom down here was full, so I went upstairs. And as I was walking to the sink to wash my hands, I just happened to glance out of the window overlooking the backyard when I saw them."

Clare turned and looked at Maddie with alarm. "What!? What were they doing?"

"Nothing. The Klansmen were just standing there watching the church. They were nestled between the trees in the wooded area. One had a rifle."

"Oh, God! It's just like the KKK to make trouble on a holiday," whispered Clare. "I guess they can't resist seeing this many Negroes happy and in one place. I better go tell Kapp."

Clare untied her apron and placed it on the table. She was about to walk away when she paused and glanced over to the right of the room where her parents were sitting.

Maddie noticed her hesitation. "What's wrong?"

"Kapp's two army buddies are sitting with my parents. My husband will need back up. But Nola is also sitting with them. Nola is going to wonder what's going on if I walk over and tell Milton and Ray that Kapp needs their assistance."

"Oh, you're right. Well, then tell Ray and Milton that Martin's car won't start and that Kapp needs their help trying to fix it," invented Maddie.

No," replied Clare. "Then Nola might wonder why, if Martin is leaving, where he is going while half the congregation is still standing in line waiting to get served. So you go and get Ray and Milton. You tell them that your car won't start and ask if they can see what's wrong with it. I'll continue serving. That way, Nola won't get suspicious if she sees that I'm still here."

"Okay," said Maddie. As Maddie walked over to Ray and Milton, Clare tied her apron back around her waist and resumed her position serving at the table. Milton and Ray stood up and followed Maddie out the door. First Nola, and then Charmaine glanced over at Clare. Clare smiled and waved to them before she wiggled her legs back and forth and held her stomach as if she was about to pee on herself. Then Clare abruptly turned and rushed out of the banquet room, still clutching her tummy. As soon as she entered the hallway, Clare headed upstairs.

Kapp, Milton, Ray, and Maddie were hurrying out of the office just as Clare stepped up from the stairwell. Not one of them noticed Clare as she followed the four down a short corridor to the back door. The door was locked. Kapp turned the latch as Ray, Milton, Maddie, and Clare stood behind Kapp in a single file. Slowly Kapp opened the door. Cautiously, one by one, Kapp, Ray, and Milton stepped outside and onto the back porch. Milton held out his hand, signaling for Maddie to stay inside. Maddie obeyed, but Clare stepped out from behind Maddie and lingered in the doorway beside Mrs. Wilkins.

Maddie noticed Clare for the first time and was startled.

"Shh!" Clare whispered to Maddie while placing her finger to her lips. Maddie nodded, and both she and Clare returned their attention to the wooded area, which began 30 yards away from where the church stood.

The Klansmen that Maddie saw earlier were no longer there. At least they weren't visible. After several minutes of standing silent and still, Kapp moved forward and descended the steps, never taking his eyes off the trees. Milton and Ray did the same. Kapp was in the middle with Ray on Kapp's left and Milton on Kapp's right. After all three men reached the bottom, they walked in unison towards the woods. They marched at a slow, steady pace the way lawmen in western movies walk headed for a showdown with outlaws.

As the three came within twenty feet of the forest, a coarse male voice shouted, "shoot!" Suddenly, a hooded, white-robed Klansman stepped out from behind a tree and aimed his rifle at Kapp and pulled the trigger.

Click! The rifle didn't fire. Click-Click! The Klansman fumbled with his gun, trying to get it to shoot.

"Pull back the lever, you fool!" Shouted the same voice that hollered "shoot."

But by that time, the Klansman's hands were shaking. He looked up. The three lawmen were walking faster and staring directly at him with mean, hard faces. "Ahh!" he screamed, then dropped his gun, turned, and ran. The other two Klansmen also fled, running back into the forest as fast as they could.

"Well, that was easy," said Milton.

"Yeah, no doubt because they were just a bunch of youngsters, and not the hardened, more experienced Klan members. Seasoned members all would have been packing guns and shooting at the same time. No, these were just kids, teenagers probably," said Kapp.

"Too bad," pouted Ray. "I was ready for some action."

Kapp picked up the rifle before the three-headed back to church. Examining the gun, Kapp turned it over in his hands. He recognized the brand immediately. It was the same model his stepfather owned. The same model he grabbed from behind the icebox the day Jimmy Hodges and his gang chased him and his stepbrother, Paulie.

"It's a Winchester 22 caliber, single-shot rimfire, bolt action rifle with a 27-inch barrel made in 1934. It won't shoot unless you release the pin like this," demonstrated Kapp as he pulled back the round clip. Kapp opened the chamber and took out the bullet. He then rubbed his hand over the rifle's smooth walnut finish before suddenly snapping the Winchester in two with his bare hands.

"Well, I guess the KKK won't be using that gun to shoot or kill Negroes anymore," said Ray.

"Nah, it doesn't look like it," confirmed Milton. The three lawmen laughed. Kapp handed one half of the broken Winchester to Ray and the other half to Milton.

"We'll pass a couple of sewers on the way home. Each of you drop your half down one of them," ordered Kapp.

Ray raised his right hand to his forehead. "Yes sir, Sarge," Ray saluted before breaking his half in two. Snap! Milton did likewise with his rifle piece.

Clare beamed at her husband with pride and awe. "Fearless" was the word that popped into her mind, which could only describe the defiant and determined way Kapp confronted danger. Even with a rifle pointed at his head, her husband didn't back down or flinch.

"That's my man," Clare gushed.

"And, that's, my man," uttered a voice that wasn't Maddie's.

This time, both Clare and Maddie were startled. The two glanced back at precisely the same time. Standing behind them was Charmaine, and behind Charmaine, Nola.

Clare shook her head. "What are you two doing here?"

"We came to find you," said Charmaine. "The way you held your stomach and raced out of the room, we thought something may be wrong. You are pregnant, you know?"

A burst of laughter roared out of Maddie's mouth. "It's no use. It's just no use," spoke Maddie shaking her head and moving her hands back and forth through the air. "Every time we try to keep something secret, the very people we attempt to hide it from, immediately find out about it. It's like trying to conceal our existence from God. I'm tired of all this sneaking around. No more cloak and dagger for me."

"I agree," said Kapp, as he, Milton, and Ray ascended the porch steps, still moving in unison. "However, I think this time, it was wise not to let too many people know what was happening until we knew the situation. As it turned out, the threat ended up being nothing but a group of teenage boys, which is usually not the case. So, no harm, no foul." After Kapp spoke, he passed his wife a look of concern as he walked up to the door. Without reading his mind, Clare understood her husband's silence and nodded her head.

"I will." Clare mouthed the words before embracing Kapp and kissing him briefly on his lips.

The three lawmen stepped inside, and the seven-headed back downstairs to the banquet hall after Kapp checked the office to find that Martin and Coretta were no longer there.

There was an awkward moment between Nola, Maddie, Clare, and Charmaine, when Nola's eyes locked on

Milton, and Milton responded with a smile. Nola blushed. Maddie cleared her throat as she glared at Nola. Maddie's face was on fire. The faces of Clare and Charmaine were just as red. Feeling the heat, Nola immediately looked away. As soon as they were all downstairs, Clare pulled Nola aside after the other five entered the banquet hall.

"Look, darling, let's get one thing straight, if you want to continue to strut around here like the Marilyn Monroe of the news media there is to be no, I repeat no involvement with you and any black man, especially not Milton. He's slated for Maddie. And let there be no misunderstanding, if it gets out that you are passing for white, your biggest problem won't come from black folks." Clare shook her head at Nola while simultaneously shaking her finger in Nola's face. "Oh, no darling. It will come from the members of the beloved white race you so desperately desire to claim as your own who will eat you alive and swallow your big mulatto butt whole. Because the worst thing Southern white folks hate more than every Negro they see, is a Negro they can't see, trying to pass himself off as one of them. You may be able to get away with being Caucasian in Canada, back East in New York or out West in California, but the Southern States of America is a country unto itself. And down here, racial intolerance is a religion."

In silence and defeat, Nola turned and walked away. Though Clare's words were harsh, Nola knew she spoke the truth. Back home, Nola never needed to confront the complexity of her racial heritage. In Canada, it seemed so simple, because she looked white; she was white. During the four years Nola attended Columbia University in New York, it was never an issue either. Everyone she met accepted, without question, what she said she was, a white girl. Although several times, she received second looks from the few black women that attended Columbia. None ever spoke out to challenge her nationality. But down here, almost every other day, Nola felt the pressure that her mixed heritage posed. If the truth about her mixed lineage were known, could she have gotten the job as a newscaster so quickly, if at all? If the executives at CBS discover that her father is Negro, would she still have a job? The voice inside Nola's head answered emphatically, *No*! Nola realized that she might have been better off working for the Vancouver Daily after all, where her father also worked, and her heritage was known.

Nola felt her eyes swell but fought back the tears until she entered the restroom. She was relieved when she found it empty. Nola immediately begun to sob uncontrollably. She wanted to go home and not have to deal with this anymore. She didn't want to choose. As quickly as she started, Nola stopped crying and lifted her head. She drew in her chest and inhaled one long, deep breath. She held it for a few seconds then slowly exhaled.

"I'm all right. Everything is going to be alright. So stop crying and pull yourself together, girl," she proclaimed, looking at herself in the mirror over the washbasin.

Nola turned on the faucet and splashed cold water on her face. From the spool just above the sink, she tore off a piece of paper towel and patted her cheeks. That's when Nola heard one of the six toilets flush. She looked to her left. To Nola's surprise, Clare's mother, Helen, stepped out of the last stall farthest from where Nola was standing. Helen walked over to the sink next to Nola, turned on the faucet, and began washing her hands.

"I guess it must be difficult being neither cold nor hot in a world that demands boundaries and doesn't tolerate ambiguity," said Helen.

I've just received a verbal whipping from your daughter, and I'll be damned if I will stand here and hear an instant replay from you, Mrs. Matthews.

"'Ambiguity,' now that's a word you don't hear rolling off the tongue of the average American Negro," Nola huffed. Nola quickly balled up the paper towel in her hand, tossed it in the wastebasket, and placing her left arm akimbo, switched out of the ladies' room before Clare's mother could form her lips into words to reply.

Nola knew she couldn't rejoin the party in the banquet hall now. So she headed upstairs. Nola intended to leave out the front entrance but hurried down the short corridor and out the back door when she heard the clap of high heels behind her ascending the stairs. Nola was afraid it might be Clare, and after what she said to Clare's mom, Nola dreaded what might happen if there was another confrontation with the audacious Mrs. Johnson.

Nola rushed down the porch steps. She parked her car on the side street adjacent to the church. As Nola walked hastily across the grass, a shiny gold object caught her eye between the line of trees. It was lying in a thicket of dry brush. At first, Nola was inclined to ignore it and kept walking. But the object kept twinkling like a star. Nola stopped and squinted her eyes to make out what it was. When she couldn't, her journalistic curiosity finally got the better of her, and she went to investigate. Within seconds, Nola was standing over the bush. The mysterious item was a 22-carat gold watch dangling from a gold chain. Nola picked it up and discovered that the first link was in the shape of a pig's head. How strange, she thought. The watch was still ticking and in excellent condition. Nola turned the watch over. On the back were words in a foreign language that read: "Dum Vivimus Vivamus."

What does that mean? Something about living. In Spanish, "vive" means live. Hmm, one of the boys must have dropped it. Whichever teenager did his parents is undoubtedly well-off. This is a Breitling and cost at least $1500.

Nola wasn't sure what she should do--leave it or take it with her. Finally, she put the watch in her purse and headed for her car. She wanted to show the Breitling to Miss Morgan, hoping Juliette might know which family in Montgomery was rich enough to buy their son such an expensive timepiece. Guests packed Juliette's house for Easter dinner. Nola tried but could not pry Juliette away. The few times Nola got close enough to talk to her, Juliette waved Nola off. "Not now, darling," Mrs. Morgan said. Nola finally gave up. Since she had eaten, Nola went to her room, resigned that she would have to wait until the party was over to show Mrs. Morgan the watch.

After church services, Kapp, Milton, and Ray escorted the King family home and stayed until seven o'clock before leaving two male volunteers from the congregation to watch the house. Clare and Charmaine greeted their husbands at the front door with a kiss while Milton looked on. It was a sight that made Milton long for his wife.

"Supper is on the table," Clare's mother, Helen, announced. Milton was the first to enter the dining room, less out of hunger than the need to escape memories of his life with Olivia. There were two table arrangements--the large table where the adults would eat, and a small round table placed in front of the dining room window for the children, Theo, Mickey, Nicolet, and Sam.

Mr. Matthews sat at the head of the table with Mrs. Matthews at the lower end. To the right of Mr. Matthews sat Kapp, Milton, Ray, and Stephen, Maddie's brother. To the left of Simon Matthews sat his daughter, Clare, then Maddie, Charmaine, and Sissy, Stephen's wife. Maddie caught Milton's eye when he took his seat. She sat directly across from him. It was as if he saw her for the first time. Maybe it was because he was missing his wife and needed feminine attention. Perhaps, but what Milton noticed most was the size of Maddie's breasts accentuated by a tight-fitting dress with V-neckline. Like the pink flowers on her dress, her breasts were in full bloom.

Maddie was a large woman, healthier than fat. She was what people called big-boned, the exact opposite of Olivia's tall, petite frame. As if hypnotized, Milton couldn't take his eyes off Maddie's bosom.

Maddie noticed, so did everyone else. Only after Kapp nudged his elbow into Milton's side did Milton realize his fixation.

"Oh, excuse me. I didn't mean...I'm so sorry," Milton apologized, flustered and embarrassed.

"No harm," replied Maddie sympathetically. "I'm used to it. My boobs, you know, are a body unto themselves. One day I think they just might get up and walk away."

Milton broke out into a hearty, full-throated chuckle. It was the first time he had laughed since Olivia died. Everybody else, including Maddie, joined in. The rest of the evening was much of the same, full of jokes and gayety. By the time the night ended, Maddie and Milton were a couple.

At midnight, the last of Miss Morgan's guests left, finally allowing Nola to speak to Juliette. The two stood in the study in front of the desk. Nola told Juliette about the incident that occurred with the KKK.

"Kapp, Clare's husband, thinks that they were just a bunch of teenage boys who got scared and ran away. I think one of them must have dropped this," said Nola. Nola retrieved the Breitling from her purse and handed it to Juliette. "Notice the pig's head, and there is an inscription on the back."

Juliette turned the timepiece over. "Oh, this is Latin, Dum Vivimus Vivamus means "While we live, let us live," interpreted Miss Morgan. "It's an Epicurean saying which comes from the Greek philosopher Epicurus. He believed living an existence of pleasure was the goal in life. Followers of Epicurus were hedonists."

Tap, Tap.

Nola and Juliette turned around simultaneously. The door to the library opened and in stepped Sands.

"Tessie asked me to find you, Miss Juliette. She said your bath is ready and that she is waiting for you upstairs." Sands suddenly noticed the watch in Mrs. Morgan's hand. He squinted his eyes as he stared at the Breitling.

"Where did you get that? That's Adok's watch. The pig's head is the symbol of the Porcellian Club that Adok was a member of at Harvard," explained Sands.

Nola and Juliette looked at the watch and then at each other.

"Oh, my God!" the two uttered in unison.

Chapter Twenty-Seven

Truth waits to be found.
It searches for no one.

Suzy Kassem

10:45 AM, Monday, April 2, 1956
Montgomery Regional Airport

Nola, Juliette, and Sands waited anxiously at the American Airlines terminal for Hans Weiss to arrive. The flight was thirty minutes late due to thick fog in New York, where Hans transferred from his Air Canada flight. The Canadian airline didn't fly to Alabama. Waiting for the delayed flight made the uneasiness the three felt about breaking the news to Hans even more acute. The three didn't know how they would tell Hans about Adok.

Juliette was nervous as she replayed, repeatedly in her mind, her words to Mr. Weiss, assuring him she would look after Adok like Adok was her brother.

When the flight finally landed, Hans walked off the plane towards Nola, Juliette, and Sands toting two suitcases, one in each hand. Hans was also carrying a newspaper in one hand. His suit coat was flung over his shoulder. His navy blue and white striped tie hung loose and crooked around his neck; his white shirt was wrinkled; his red beard was thick and unkempt, and his red hair uncombed. Nola, Juliette, and Sands quailed at the sight of his pitiable and distraught appearance. Juliette shook her head remorsefully. Nola bit her lower lip while Sands tried to clear the lump in his throat.

Hans set his suitcases down.

"So, Miss Morgan, is this how you watch out for your own brother?" Hans twisted the rolled-up edition of the New York Times in his hands as he stood glaring at the three one-by-one. He was in no mood to dilly-dally. He needed to blame someone for his brother's disappearance, no matter how unjustified the accusation. During the past two years, Hans' disappointment in Adok's behavior grew more acute with each incident, but nothing compared to this. Hans was afraid that all he feared was now coming true.

"Yes, I promised to watch over your brother like he was my own. But no brother of mine would be stupid enough to join the Ku Klux Klan," Juliette blurted out in her defense. She immediately put her hand over her lips as if she couldn't believe the words she just spoke came out of her mouth.

Hans stopped breathing. His eyes widened. Juliette, Nola, and Sands appeared to be holding their breath too as Hans stood stiff and motionless. Then, suddenly, Hans bent over, picked up his luggage, turned, and headed for the exit. Nola, Juliette, and Sands hesitated for a second, looking at each other. Sands was the first to follow Hans.

"Come on," Nola said to Juliette.

Nola drove Juliette and Sands to the airport in the Buick Riviera, now rented for her by CBS. But Nola was too nervous and didn't want to drive. So she handed the keys to Sands. She and Juliette sat in the back seat, Hans in the front. No one spoke during the thirty-minute drive to Miss Morgan's house.

Hans was immediately shown to his room by Tessie.

"Is this my brother's room?"

"No, sir. Your brother, Master Adok, sleeps across the hall, two doors down. He and Mr. Sands share a room."

"Master Adok! Who told you to call him that?

"He did, sir."

"Not while I'm here. From now on, you call him Adok, Mr. Weiss, or sir, but not master. Is that clear?"

"Yes, sir. Would you like to see your brother's room, Mr. Weiss?"

"Yes," Hans replied. Hans followed Tessie down the hall.

As soon as Hans entered, he rummaged through the dressers and closet, trying to find any clues that could lead to his brother's whereabouts. When he found nothing, Hans stood in the center of the room and scanned the bedroom with his eyes. *Where in the hell are you, Adok? I refuse to believe you left willingly and haven't contacted me. I refused to believe you joined the KKK. That's a lie. What would make you join such a hateful, racist organization as notorious as the Nazis'? I've raised you better than that!*

Hans closed his eyes tight and tried to concentrate. But no matter how hard he tried; he couldn't hear Adok's voice. He didn't understand why his hearing tuned in whenever something happened to the Colored soldier, Kapp Johnson, but not his brother.

"I don't even know Mr. Johnson," Hans uttered out loud to himself. "I only had a brief encounter with him in the castle tower 11 years ago when I shot him. But that dreadful interaction seems to have linked us together forever." Hans shook his head, feeling frustrated and mentally drained. Slowly, he walked to his room. Exhausted, he flopped his tired body down on the four-poster bed, laid back on the pillow, and quickly fell asleep.

It wasn't until Hans, Nola, Sands, and Juliette assembled again in the dining room at noon for lunch that their conversation about Adok resumed.

"What makes you think my brother has joined the Klan?" asked Hans to Juliette. Miss Morgan was sitting at the head of the table, Hans at the other end, and Nola and Sands sat on opposite sides directly across from each other.

"We don't know for certain that your brother is a member. Our evidence is only circumstantial. But it's the only explanation we can come up with," said Juliette.

"What evidence?" asked Hans.

Juliette looked over to her right at Nola. Nola gave Miss Morgan a nod and then told Hans about the incident that happened yesterday during the Easter celebration at the Dexter Street Church. Hans sat quietly, listening intently, looking at Nola as she spoke. When Nola finished, Sands reached into his shirt pocket and retrieved the expensive Breitling watch dangling from a 22-carat gold chain and handed it to Hans. It was Adok's all right. Hans remembered the day Adok showed it to him.

It was at breakfast on a Saturday two years ago during Adok's two-week Christmas break. That's when Adok proudly announced that he joined the Porcellian Club. The exclusive, all-male club was founded in 1791. It was first known as the Pig Club. That's why the club emblem is a pig's head. All Porcellian members wear either a tie clip or watch chain with the head of a swine on it. President Theodore Roosevelt and the renowned nineteenth-century poet, Oliver Wendall Holmes, were two of its most famous members.

Hans couldn't deny the implication of the evidence. Finding Adok's watch in the same location where the three Klansmen stood was too much of a coincidence. What other explanation could there be, other than, Adok must have dropped it when he and the other two Klansmen panicked and ran away?

Hans already knew some of what happened that day, even before Nola told the story. He heard portions of it. What he didn't comprehend until now was that Adok was involved. But when Miss Morgan blurted out KKK at the airport, Hans felt an awful feeling in the pit of his stomach. Hans was standing in the shower, washing his hair yesterday morning around nine o'clock when he suddenly heard someone yell "shoot!" followed by a click, then silence, and then two more clicks. He heard Kapp say that the assailants were just teenage boys. Hans froze when the voices started. He knew the sounds were not coming from the TV in his bedroom. The voices rang in his ears as if blasted on a loudspeaker from a place deep inside his body.

"Pull back the lever, you fool!" yelled the same person that hollered the command to fire. Shortly after that, someone screamed. Yesterday, Hans didn't recognize the screaming voice. Today, he realized the scream must have come from Adok.

My brother doesn't know how to fire a gun. He's never even held one in his hands before.

Hans sighed, then stood up from the table. He looked at Juliette, then at Sands, and last at Nola.

"I need to speak to Kapp Johnson. Take me to his house."

Nola shot glances at Sands and Juliette before gazing up at Hans with both surprise and confusion on her face.

"Kapp Johnson, I don't, umm. How can he help you? Don't you think it would be better to go to the police? I know the police haven't been helpful up until now, but now that you're here, Adok's brother, I'm sure they will be more responsive," said Nola.

"No, they won't, because they no doubt know where Adok is, because some of the members on the police force, if not all, are probably also members of the KKK.

That's a possibility that none of you have thought of I see."

"No, we didn't," said Nola shaking her head. "But still, what do you expect Mr. Johnson to do, and why would he help you? He doesn't know you. Why would he even want to talk to you? You and your brother mean nothing to him. You're strangers and not even American."

"Call Mr. Johnson. He'll want to speak to me. Tell him it's Hans, the young man from the castle tower."

Nola looked around at Sands and Juliette again, even more puzzled than before. "You mean, you know Kapp Johnson? The two of you have met before?"

"Call him," Hans repeated before walking out of the dining room and upstairs to his bedroom.

Reluctantly, Nola obeyed. She went into the study with Sands and Miss Morgan on her heels and called the Matthews' house. Nola would ask to speak to Clare, knowing that Kapp wasn't there and was on duty guarding Dr. King. But as Nola was dialing, she remembered telling Clare yesterday that Adok's brother was coming. Nola recalled how Clare reacted when she mentioned Hans' name. Clare said she thinks she heard Kapp speak the name Hans before.

Nola glanced over at Juliette and Sands sitting on the leather sofa in front of the fireplace. The two were seated on the edge of the couch, looking eager to know the outcome of Nola's conversation. Nola was about to tell them she thinks Hans and Kapp may know each other after all when, after the first ring, a voice on the other end of the phone said hello. To Nola's surprise, it was Kapp.

"Oh, Kapp. I didn't think you would be home this early. I thought you would be guarding Dr. King."

"Dr. King is relaxing with his family. As you know, Martin didn't have any meetings or appointments today, so I took the day off. But don't worry, I have a couple of men watching the house. I'm sorry, but Clare is not available now. She's taking a nap."

"That's okay because it's you I want to talk to."

"Oh, really? What about?"

"Well, I think Clare may have told you that Adok, the young reporter from the Vancouver Daily, sent to replace me, has been missing since last Thursday, and Adok's brother arrived this morning to aid in the search. His brother wants to meet with you."

"With me, for what? Why does he want to meet me? I don't know him. He needs to go to the police."

"That's what I told him, but he demanded that I contact you. He told me to tell you his first name. It's Hans, and he's the young man from the castle tower."

As soon as Nola repeated what Hans told her to say, Sands and Juliette jumped up and rushed over and stood in front of the desk. There was silence on Kapp's end of the line. The silence lasted one, two, three, four, five, six, seven, eight, nine, ten, eleven seconds.

"Bring him to Maddie's house around ten, no, you better make it midnight tonight. And Nola just bring him, no one else, understand. Also, I don't have to tell you that none of this is to be broadcast on the news, right?"

"Yes, of course." Nola heard a click on the other end of the line and slowly lowered her receiver down on the phone before leaning back in the chair.

"Well, what did he say?" Juliette asked.

"He wants me to bring Hans to Maddie's house at midnight."

"So Mr. Johnson really does know Mr. Weiss," Sands stated.

Nola shook her head up and down. "Kapp didn't say. But he must know Hans, or he wouldn't have agreed to meet him. They must have met while Kapp was a soldier fighting in Germany. Like most of Europe, Germany has a lot of castles. Perhaps American soldiers were stationed at one of those castles and used it as a command post or something."

"Hmm, well, I guess we'll find out tonight," said Sands.

"No, you won't. Kapp told me not to bring anyone else but Hans. And knowing how you occasionally double as a reporter, nothing about this is to be printed in the newspaper."

"I know that. I still work for the Daily, you know, and Hans is still my boss. You don't think I would dare report on something involving his brother without his permission. But you might be tempted to, seeing that you now work for CBS. So I think I should be the one to drive Hans to Maddie's."

Nola chuckled. "Yeah, right, you just go right on thinking that, and you can dream about it tonight while we're gone."

Sands huffed, then turned and left.

"You know, I expect you to tell me everything that happens at Maddie's," said Juliette.

"Of course, darling," Nola replied and passed Miss Morgan a wink.

Miss Morgan returned a sly grin.

Waiting for midnight to come was like waiting for a ninety-year-old woman walking with a cane with arthritis in her knees, to hobble across the street at a traffic stop during rush hour when your destination was fifteen miles away, and you had only seven minutes to get there. Nola fiddled away the time in her room doing a little of this and a little of that, like trying to comb her hair in a new style, polishing her toenails, or reading Eugene O'Neil's new book, *Long Day's Journey into Night*. But after several minutes, she stopped one thing and started another until she finally gave up altogether and laid on her bed and stared up at the ceiling. Nola imagined Hans engaged in similar wasted endeavors in his room.

When six o'clock rolled around, it was suppertime. Nola finally pried herself up off her bed and made her way downstairs. To her surprise, Hans was already seated, and so was Miss Morgan. The two were talking and stopped abruptly when Nola entered the dining room.

Nola flashed a smile at the two before sitting in the same chair she occupied at lunch. She looked across the table.

"Where's Sands?" Nola asked.

"Don't know. Tessie said he left thirty minutes ago," replied Juliette, shaking her head.

Nola looked at Hans.

"I don't know either," Hans responded.

"Hmm, it's strange for Sands to miss a meal since I know how much he loves Colored women's cooking," stated Nola. She then quickly changed the subject.

"So, are you ready for tonight, Mr. Weiss? How do you know Kapp Johnson, anyway? Did you meet him during the war?"

Hans passed Nola an expressionless glance. "I'm not the subject of one of your articles, or should I now say, news broadcast. So don't try to interview me, Miss Richardson, just eat your supper and shut up."

The sharpness in Hans' reply was unexpected. Nola never saw her former boss get mad or even raise his voice at any of his employees. She never knew Hans to be anything but calm and rational, especially when dealing with his brother, or hectic situations at work. Even this morning, when they picked him up at the airport, the way he spoke to Juliette was more out of frustration than malice. But there was an edge in Hans' voice now that Nola could only describe as hard, and the look on his face as he peered at her was mean.

Nola didn't know how to respond. She was afraid to, and so begrudgingly obeyed. No one spoke a word after that. After only twenty minutes, Hans was done eating and politely excused himself. As he walked out of the room, Nola rolled her eyes and stuck out her tongue at Hans when his back was turned. Juliette just laughed and shook her head at Nola's childish behavior.

Nola wanted to leave at 11:30 to make sure she and Hans arrived precisely at midnight. At eleven o'clock, she changed into a round-collared, gold-knitted sweater and a pair of black, tight-fitting, foot-strap pants and black loafers. Nola figured it would be a long night, and she wanted to be comfortable. After several attempts, Nola finally tied her thick blonde hair back into a ponytail before slipping on her dark brown, thigh-length peacoat with a wide, wrap-around belt. Fifteen minutes later, she was ready. Nola heard someone in the hall and rushed to the door. She thought it was Hans but opened it to find Tessie.

"What are you doing up so late?"

"Oh, I thought I would tidy-up the room Mr. Weiss is sleeping in while he's out," Tessie explained.

"Oh, well, you can tell him I'm ready to take him to Mrs. Wilkins."

"I'm sorry, ma'am, but Mr. Weiss left with Mr. Sands two hours ago while you were downstairs in the den watching Ozzie & Harriet with Miss Juliette."

"What!?" Nola grabbed her purse from off the bed and ran downstairs and out the front door, cursing as she went. Fumbling around in her purse, she frantically looked for her keys. She thought she may have left them on the dresser in her room until she found them in one of the side pockets. Nola was so anxious and upset, she dropped the keys on the ground and retrieved them several times before she finally opened the car door. She quickly backed out of the driveway and sped down the street.

I'm beginning to hate men. Nola looked at her wristwatch. *It's not even 11:30 yet. I'll get there in plenty of time. What if they changed the time? What if they changed the meeting place?*

"No! No!" Nola banged the palm of her right hand against the steering wheel and started crying.

Maybe I should have called Clare or Maddie before I left the house. Okay, Nola, calm down. Everything will be all right, just drive over to the farm as planned.

Twenty-five minutes later, Nola turned into Maddie's long driveway. It was twelve minutes to midnight. Nola fears immediately resurfaced when no other automobiles except Maddie's were there, and no lights were on in the house. All the curtains were drawn. *Maybe no one else has arrived yet.* Something told her that wasn't true. Nola couldn't believe how dark it was even with a full moon. But this was farmland. There were no streetlights, and the closest house in any direction was two miles away. Nola suddenly remembered that most rental cars store flashlights in the glove compartment. Nola leaned over and opened the compartment. Yes, there was a flashlight. Nola clicked it on and got out the car. She scanned the front of the house and called out, "Maddie!" several times. There was no response. Nola didn't know what to do next. Should she ring the doorbell? She walked around the side to check if there were any lights on in the basement. Kneeling, Nola peered through a basement window. It was dark inside. Nola then walked to the back of the house. The kitchen curtains were not drawn. Walking up the porch steps, Nola peeked into the window and beamed the flashlight inside. There were no signs of life. Nola checked her watch. It was now midnight. She let out a frustrated sigh. She felt herself about to cry again. Holding back her tears, Nola turned around and shined the flashlight around the backyard.

A large area of the yard was surrounded by a silver-wire fence four feet high. A dirt pathway divided the grassy area into two sections, with a teeter-totter on one side and a swing set on the other. Nola scanned the flashlight down the dirt path to the fence. That's when she noticed the open gate. Beyond it was a barn in the distance about a football field away. Nola immediately walked through the gate and headed for the barn. At first, she walked at a steady pace, then she trotted until finally, she ran. Just as she reached the barn door, Nola heard a creek. The barn door swung open and out stepped Kapp beaming his flashlight in her face. Frightened, Nola stopped in her tracks.

"Where is he?"

"Hans isn't here? He left the house hours ago with Sands. I didn't know he was gone until I was ready to drive him here and discovered he already left."

"Well, he hasn't arrived yet." Kapp looked down at his watch. "You better come in." Kapp stepped aside to let Nola pass. For another second or two, Kapp looked around outside before closing the door.

Inside was Clare, Maddie, and Milton sitting in foldable, wooden chairs arranged in a circle in the barn. Besides Kapp's chair, there were two empty chairs. Nola smiled, knowing that one chair was for her. She happily took her seat between Clare and Maddie. When and if Hans arrived, he would sit across from her between Kapp and Milton.

Like Nola, both Clare and Maddie were wearing slacks. Clare's was dark brown, complemented by a brown and white striped maternity blouse with a pointed collar that buttoned down the front. Over it, Clare donned a caramel trench coat. Maddie wore navy blue pants and a red V-neck sweater. Milton was dressed in army green trousers held up with a black wide-buckle belt and paired with a matching green, long sleeve, button-up shirt.

"We're missing two," observed Nola. "Where's Ray and Charmaine?"

"Back home in Detroit by now," said Clare. "They woke up before daybreak Monday morning and drove home."

"Oh, I see," Nola replied. Nola was about to say something else, but hesitated, wondering whether she should tell them everything she knows about Adok before Hans arrived.

"So, Nola, you think Adok has joined the KKK. In fact, you have some proof of that, don't you?" Clare blurted out.

Shocked, Nola looked at Clare. "What? I--how did you know that? Oh, I see, Miss Morgan must have told you about the watch that belongs to Adok that I found behind the church in the same spot those Klan boys were standing."

"Perhaps she did, or maybe I just read your mind," said Clare. Clare smiled at Nola, then winked at her husband.

"Is that true?" Kapp asked.

"Yes," Nola answered. She revealed what she knew about Hans' brother, even about the trouble Adok was involved in at Harvard. "A year ago, Adok and three of his Porcellian Club buddies, beat up the only Negro basketball player on the Crimson team. Adok was removed as one of the editors of the student newspaper because of the incident. So, it doesn't surprise me that Adok may have become a member of the Ku Klux Klan. You should see the way he treats Tessie, Miss Morgan's maid. Of course, Hans refuses to believe anything bad about his little brother."

Ten minutes later, Nola was still talking when she was interrupted suddenly by several loud raps on the barn door. This time Milton went to open it. As soon as Hans and Sands entered the barn, everyone stood up. Hans and Kapp immediately caught each other's eye. They both were wearing black pants and black turtleneck sweaters. Only their overcoats were different. Hans wore a beige blazer. Kapp sported a burgundy suede, zip-up jacket. The two men stared at one another in silence for several seconds as everyone else watched. Tension mingled with anticipation filled the air. Hans was the first to break the silence.

"Do you remember me?" Hans no longer had a beard or mustache. Sands took him to a barber to get a haircut and shave. Hans wanted to look his best and also make it easier for Mr. Johnson to recognize him.

"Yes," Kapp responded. "That night in the castle tower, you were wearing a raggedy prison uniform."

"Yes, that was me. Adok was there in the tower to that night, but he was in a separate room."

"Adok is your brother, the one who beat up the Colored basketball player, who tried to shoot up the church Easter Sunday, and who is now a member of the KKK?"

Hans cut a sharp sideways glance at Nola. Nola looked away.

"Yes," Hans admitted.

"Then your little brother isn't lost," stated Kapp. "He's right where he wants to be. And there's nothing you can do about it, and nothing I care to do about it."

"But I don't believe my brother would ever willingly join the Klan. He's confused. He's been brainwashed. Adok isn't a bad person."

"Bad people never believe they're bad, and neither do their relatives," said Milton. "So-called 'good people' do horrible things all the time. It's not creatures from outer space coming to earth robbing, lynching, raping, and killing humans. Martians didn't exterminate six million Jews. Every person that commits these crimes is somebody's nephew, uncle, son, father, and brother. Now your brother is one of them."

"Adok isn't his brother, not by blood or marriage," stated Clare out of the blue. Clare wasn't looking at anyone when she spoke. She stood with her head bowed, and her eyes closed. Her body was slightly turned away from the others. Rigid and still, with folded arms pressed tightly against her chest, Clare appeared to be in deep meditation. When she suddenly opened her eyes, her gaze immediately fell on Hans.

"Adok was with you and Kapp in the castle tower, that's true, but he was dead," Clare revealed.

Gasps escaped immediately out of the mouths of Nola, Maddie, and Sands, before silence, once again, invaded the room. Everyone's eyes dotted around the barn at each other. But Hans stared only at Clare as if he was searching for a reply to a question, he was too afraid to ask her and to which he knew the answer already. Hans then stepped closer into the circle, so he was only two feet away from Clare, Kapp, and Milton. Hans and Clare stood face-to-face while Kapp and Milton stood cater-corner to Hans on his right and left flank. Extending his right arm forward with his palm facing up, Hans pulled back the sleeves of his blazer and sweater, revealing his wrist. Without a word, first Clare then Kapp, and then Milton held out their right arms and also exposed their wrists.

Nola, Maddie, and Sands stood in a semi-circle behind the four. Nola shot a puzzled glance to Sands. Sands shrugged his shoulders.

"What's this all about?" Nola whispered to Maddie.

"Shh! Just watch and listen," Maddie whispered back.

Hans, Clare, Kapp, and Milton stared at each other's wrist. There was one physical trait the four all had in common. Pink was the color of their veins, not the usual blue healthy human veins appear to be. Adok brought this anomaly to Hans' attention years ago when Adok came home from school one day, bruised and crying. Some of the kids in Adok's 6th-grade class jeered and called him an alien because his veins were pink. It was a label that stayed with Adok through junior high and high school, one he fought many fights over.

"Are you a seer," whispered Hans to Clare.

"No," Clare tapped her finger against her temple. "And you?" Clare asked.

Hans pointed to his ear and mouthed the words "hearer."

Nola, Sands, and Maddie moved in closer to the four to hear what was being said. But the four quickly dispersed and sat down. Nola and Maddie took their seats while Sands stood awkwardly behind Hans.

"If Adok isn't your brother, then why do the two of you pretend to be, and why do you think Adok is confused?" Maddie asked.

Nola glanced at Maddie with surprise mingled with jealousy. Those were questions she should have posed.

Hans didn't hesitate. He told the story of how Adok was kidnapped and how Adok's parents and baby brother were killed by the Nazis.

"Adok spent two years in a Lebensborn home before my uncle chose him to come live with us. During those two years, he was indoctrinated with hateful, Nazi propaganda. He even refuses to eat chocolate candy or chocolate ice cream because he fears it will turn his skin black, that's how thoroughly they brainwashed him. After the war, and my uncle died, there was nowhere else for Adok to go. He had no other relatives, nor did I. So, I took him to Canada with me. To travel without being questioned or hassled, my uncle had legal papers drawn up, showing that we were related. That's how we've lived ever since, as brothers."

By the time Hans was done, sadness shaded everyone's countenance.

"Even if I were to agree to help you find and get your brother back, there's not much I can do now. I have promised to be Martin Luther King's bodyguard at least until the boycott is over, which will only happen if the Supreme Court rules in our favor."

"Yeah, and then there is the matter of money. My husband and I are expecting as you can see."

"I never expected your husband to do this for free, Mrs. Johnson. Money is no problem. I'm a rich man; I can pay for your husband's help. And I don't plan on sitting on the sidelines either. No man should ask another man to do what he is not willing to do himself. I intend to be involved in finding and getting my brother back as well."

"We may need more than just the two of us. Mr. Taylor here was a lieutenant in the war. He's excellent at strategy and tactical deployment. His skills might be useful." Kapp looked across Hans at Milton. "What do you think, Milt?

To Milton's surprise, the possibility of confronting the Ku Klux Klan was an exciting prospect. Now that his beloved Olivia was gone, and mainly since he knew his efforts would never result in his death, Milton felt the need to live more than just an ordinary life. "If Mr. Weiss can pay, you can count me in. We freed millions in Europe from the clutches of hatred and bigotry, what's freeing one more, especially when he's in our own country."

"Yes, I will pay you and whoever else the two of you know that may have extraordinary skills," said Hans, grabbing hold of his right wrist with his left hand while his right arm lay on his leg.

Kapp also gripped his right wrist and nodded to Hans as a sign he understood precisely what Hans meant. "I might have one more person willing to join the search," Kapp revealed.

"What about me?" Sands pushed in. "I want to help too."

"Really!? You can't even get to a meeting on time without getting lost," interrupted Nola with her arms folded, her legs crossed, and one eyebrow raised. "I doubt you will be much help."

Hans passed Nola a peevish glance. Sands noticed his boss's irritation.

"I can spy," refuted Sands boldly. "Most people don't pay any attention to me. They think I'm just a kid playing with my camera. That makes it easy for me to get in and out of places without suspicion, and why I always dress in blue jeans and a T-shirt. I may have a lead already on Adok's whereabouts. Ever since Adok went missing, I've been spending time at the bar at the Molton Hotel."

Nola interrupted with a scoffing sound. "You mean you are actually allowed into an establishment that serves liquor!? That seems highly unlikely since you say everyone thinks you're a kid."

This time not only Hans but also Kapp and Milton passed Nola the evil eye.

"Zip it or leave!" Hans insisted.

Nola pressed her lips together. She hadn't forgotten how Sands snuck off with Hans behind her back. She was still ticked off about it. But the looks of rebuke on everyone's face prompted Nola to hold her tongue.

In triumph, Sands flashed Nola a fake smile and continued. "I saw Adok coming out of the hotel a couple of weeks ago. So I've been going there every day at six o'clock. That's when the bar normally gets crowded. People getting off work come in for a drink or two. Today I overheard the commissioner, Bull Connor, say to the bartender that their newest club recruit is going to need a lot of training. Mr. Connor said, and I quote: "the boy can drink you under the table, but if the full moon were in shooting range, the lad would miss. So I sent him to one of our militia camps to get trained up." I'm sure he was talking about Adok. Mr. Connor's description of how well Adok can hold his liquor fits Adok to a Tee. In McMullin's Bar & Grill back home after hours, I often saw Adok gup down six High Balls in a roll without stopping. Unfortunately, Connor never said the name of the camp or where it's located."

Hans, Kapp, and Milton all nodded and praised Sands.

"Good work, soldier!" exclaimed Milton. "No rescue mission has ever succeeded without good intelligence. Once we find out the whereabouts of the T camp, we are going to need photos of the site and the surrounding area. We must know how to get in and out of the base and the best spot to lay in wait or take cover if necessary. So carry on."

"But be careful," warned Hans. "Spying is a dangerous business."

"That's right," Kapp agreed. "A good rule of thumb is to always follow your gut and don't get yourself into a situation that may cause injury to you or anyone else. That's our job. We'll do the heavy lifting."

Kapp looked over at Hans. "And speaking of heavy lifting, if you're going to be a part of this operation, you're going to have to beef up. We'll likely get into hand-to-hand combat, and you gotta be able to give, as well as take a punch. Like me, you have a boxer's physique, broad shoulders, and long arms. That's good. Boxing lessons, along with weight training, will give your body the definition and tone you'll need besides making you quicker and more agile. Working out will give you something to do while Sands is busy trying to locate Adok, and we wait for the Supreme Court's decision. I already know you can shoot."

"That's a good idea," said Hans. "But where can I go and who should train me? I can't be seen going to a Colored establishment. And going to a white one…." Hans paused, searching for the right words.

"You don't like the whites here, and you don't want to mingle with them," said Clare, reading Hans' mind. "You're afraid one of them may say something, and your reaction may give you away."

Hans looked at Clare and nodded his head up and down.

"If you buy the equipment, maybe we can rent this barn and set up the gym in here." Kapp looked over at Maddie. "If that's all right with you, Mrs. Wilkins? That way, Milton and I can train you ourselves. Milton was an amateur boxer when he was a teenager before he joined the army."

"Yeah. It was my mom's idea. I was such a scrawny kid. I was good at running away and avoiding danger, but my mom knew one day I would get caught, or there would be no place for me to run, and I would have to stand and fight. So at twelve-years-old, she took me to Gold's Gym and paid $5.00 a month for boxing lessons. Thankfully, that one day didn't come until I was fifteen. By then, training had put muscles on my lanky limbs and empowered me with the skills, stamina, and courage to defeat two 11th graders who tried to steal the brand-new baseball mitt my grandfather bought me for my birthday."

After Milton finished his story, Maddie finally replied. "Yes, it will be all right. With a padlock, you can lock the barn doors facing the house from the inside and enter and exit using only the double doors facing east. Park your vehicles on the east side of the barn. That way, my brother and sister-in-law won't know when you're here and come snooping around. Stephen and his wife don't permit the kids to play in the barn because it's too far from the house. So you shouldn't be disturbed."

"Even better, they can park their vehicles inside the barn," said Clare. "It's big enough, and there's plenty of room for at least three cars. That will eliminate any suspicion from occasional travelers driving by."

"That's an excellent suggestion," Nola chimed in. Everyone was contributing positive input. Nola felt left out.

"I'll go to Sears tomorrow and purchase the equipment. Should I have Sears deliver it, or should we pick it up?"

"We'll pick it up," both Kapp and Milton replied in unison.

"You can use my truck," said Sands.

"Nobody at Sears will be alarmed if Milton and I haul the equipment," stated Kapp. "They'll just think we're a couple of niggers working for a white man, as usual."

"And they'd be right," Milton joked. Everybody laughed.

Through all the joviality, Hans reached into the inside pocket of his blazer and pulled out a white, 4 1/8 x 9 ½, business-size envelope. He passed it to Kapp, who was still laughing. When Kapp saw the envelope, he stopped chuckling and took it. Looking over at Clare and then at Milton, Kapp felt the envelope but didn't open it. It looked full and felt thick. Kapp slipped envelope into the right-side pocket of his jacket.

Chapter Twenty-Eight

You can't teach a man anything.
You can only help him discover
It within himself.

Galileo Galilei

8:30 am Saturday
April 14th, Texas

"Whoever heard of niggers growing cotton. They're supposed to pick cotton, not grow it. I told old man Jenkins before he died, two years ago, not to give Toby Brown land in the first place--a house in the Colored section, sure, not twelve lush acres. But the cantankerous old cuss went ahead and did it anyway," ranted Mr. Wasserman, a city councilman from Kerrville.

"Why did he do it?" asked Charlie Mapps, Camp director. Adok, Drew, and Drill Commander, Wes Dixon, sat in foldable chairs around Mapps' desk in the camp director's office with Mr. Wasserman.

"On account of Toby's wife, Sissy Mae, is the daughter of his Colored mistress, Naomi Cunningham. Jenkins gave them the land as a wedding present. Also, because Jenkins knew he was about to meet his Maker soon and didn't want to go to his grave, having falsely accused Naomi's husband of stealing so he could take up with the man's wife without honoring Naomi's request to provide for her daughter."

"Okay, we'll take care of Toby Brown. He won't be growing any more cotton after tonight. I assure you of that," guaranteed Mapps as he stood up. He reached across his desk and shook Mr. Wasserman's hand. As soon as the councilman left, Charlie turned to Adok.

"Well, you've been itching for your first assignment. Here it is. I hope you're ready. You and your squad will hit the Brown farm tonight. Make sure nothing is left standing. Burn his crop, his barn, everything, including his house. Make sure nobody sees you, or else you know what you'll have to do."

At 9:00 pm, Adok loaded his squad of eleven recently trained Klansman, all clad in white robes, into two trucks and headed down the road apiece, 20 miles to the town of Kerrville to restore what the KKK deemed as the "balance and the natural order of white dominance and Negro subordination." It was the same highway he traveled with the Nowicki brothers when he arrived at camp. As Adok sat in the front seat on the passenger's side, gazing out of the window into the darkness, he recalled every detail that happened that night.

It was six o'clock Tuesday evening, April 3rd, when Adok, Drew, and Duncan were let out of the back of a milk delivery truck on some unknown backwoods' road in Texas--unknown, at least, to them. As the sun began to set, the temperate day became a chilly, breezy night. Mrs. Nowicki purchased identical red bomber jackets along with black, Timberland work boots, and a new pair of denim jeans for each to wear for the long ride. Their suitcases were sent ahead via UPS.

The young Klansmen departed at noon on Monday four days after Adok's Klonversation ceremony. They rode 846 miles for 16 hours and 26 minutes. The three limped out of the truck stiff, tired, and hungry. Each received only one 8-ounce canister of water to drink and one baloney sandwich during the entire journey. Adok and Drew instinctively knew that giving them only a small ration of food and enough liquid to keep them from severe dehydration was the first test in their training. Seventeen-year-old Duncan complained the entire way.

Duncan was the Nowicki's biological son, as was Drake. The teenager was unaccustomed to going without the daily necessities of life.

"Follow that road apiece until you reach a gate," said the driver, still sitting in his vehicle. The driver pointed a flashlight down a narrow dirt path on the opposite side of the two-lane highway where the boys stood. He then tossed the penlight to them before he drove away. Adok caught it.

"Where are we?" Duncan asked his brother.

"How should I know?" Drew responded.

"Come on, let's go. We won't find out languishing here," said Adok as he headed across the street.

Down the road apiece turned out to be a forty-five-minute track on foot. By the time they reached the six-foot-tall metal gate, Drew and Adok were holding up Duncan, who collapsed on the way seven minutes ago.

"Hello! We're here," shouted Adok. With the flashlight, he panned the area. Through the wrought iron, all Adok saw was a continuation of the dirt path and a forest of grass, bushes, and tall trees. Adok let go of Duncan's arm and walked up to the trellis and shook it; it didn't budge. Although it looked old and rusty, the gate was strong and sturdy. Adok spotted a key inside the lock on the other side.

"Here." Adok held out the flashlight for Drew to take.

"What are you doing?" Drew asked, taking the penlight.

Adok didn't answer. He walked ten paces back and ran forward, hopping on the fence and climbing up and over it in a blink. Once over, Adok turned the key and opened the gate. Drew struggled to get his listless brother to walk until Adok assisted.

"What do you think?" Adok asked Drew after locking the gate behind them. "Should I keep the key or take it with us?"

Drew shrugged his shoulders. "I don't know."

Adok hesitated for a second, then put the key back into the lock. He reasoned there might be more recruits coming to the camp that night. The three started down the clearance. All they saw were trees ahead and believed it would be another long track to reach the site. But the road curved to the right and then to the left before it ended, and suddenly, the three were rolling twenty-five feet down a slanted hill. When they reached the bottom, the illumination of floodlights suddenly clicked on, blinding them. Exhausted and in pain, they moaned and groaned while lying scattered on the ground like fallen tree branches with Adok on his back, Drew on his side, and Duncan faced down and barely conscious.

"Well, are you recruits going to lie there the rest of the night?" shouted a gruff voice from somewhere beyond the lights.

Adok and Drew could see only two feet in front of them. Adok stood up first. He wobbled from side-to-side a few times before finally gaining his balance by arching his back and straightening his shoulders to position his body upright. Drew followed slipping down to his knees once before slowly rising again and standing with a slight lean. Duncan had to be helped. Adok and Drew strained to lift Duncan to his feet. Following behind a muscular man wearing gray sweats and a gray infantry cap, the two carried Duncan two yards from where they had fallen into a bungalow with six empty bunk beds lined against both sides of the wall. A small single light bulb, hanging from a dangling cord, lit the entire barracks with a dim glow. As soon as they emerged from the long corridor into the sleeping quarters, Adok and Drew looked at each other. They were both thinking of how it reminded them of the dorm room at the Lebensborn home. It was as if they had traveled back in time.

With his back to them, the muscular man pointed to the three cots to the right of the door. After laying Duncan on the third cot farthest from the entrance, Drew flopped his body on the bunk next to his brother while Adok slowly lowered his butt down on the bed next to

Drew. Adok could hear his stomach growling even with the wind howling outside. Adok noticed the end table attached to the post on the left side of his bed. Curious, Adok leaned over and opened the top drawer. It was empty. He pulled out the second drawer, and to his surprise, he found two sandwiches wrapped in aluminum foil and two small cartons of milk. For a second, Adok just stared at the food, recalling the last time he was this hungry. It was the day he woke up at the Lebensborn home. Adok glanced over his shoulder at Drew and Duncan. Duncan was lying on his side with his back to his brother and Adok. Drew was lying on his back with his eyes closed. Adok noticed there were no end tables on either side of their beds. Adok picked up both sandwiches and unwrapped one. He inhaled. The smell of cooked baloney saturated his nostrils. He raised the sandwich to his mouth, ready to devour it when Duncan moaned.

"I'm so hungry, I can smell food. Do they ever plan on feeding us? I didn't come here to starve to death."

"Here," said Adok, placing the sandwich back into the foil and quickly rewrapping it. Adok turned and tossed Duncan the sandwich and then a carton of milk from the drawer. Drew immediately sat up in bed and looked over at Adok.

"We got food?"

"Yeah." Adok handed Drew the other sandwich and the last carton of milk before he rose and walked down the hall to the restroom and closed the door. There were six sinks and six toilet stalls with four urinals. To the left was the entrance to another room with twelve shower stalls, six on the north wall, and six on the south wall.

Adok walked over to the first sink and gazed at his face in the mirror. *I'll eat tomorrow,* he told himself. Adok didn't look at himself long. The self-condemnation reflected in his eyes made him divert his gaze. Also, pounding in his head was a voice urging him to leave. *"Get out of here before it's too late! This is not who you are."* But Adok was too tired and hungry to consider going anywhere tonight. Adok turned on the faucet and splashed his face with cold water. To appease his conscience, Adok told himself that he would leave tomorrow, with or without Drew and his brother.

Tomorrow came and went and came again, like the breeze that blew through the camp every morning, stopped midday, then stirred up again in the evening. It was now two weeks and a day later, and Adok was still there, immersed in his training as a Klansman to defend and protect the Aryan race. The voice of caution he heard that first night no longer spoke to him again after he became squad leader and the most revered and honored trainee in the camp. That happened the day after

Adok arrived when he woke up at 5:30 am to the shrill of a whistle and the loud, rough voice of Wes Dixon, the drill commander.

"Get your asses out of bed, you sorry sons of rednecks!" Dixon yelled.

Adok was the first to hop up and stand at attention at the foot of his bunk the way he had seen soldiers do in the movies. Drew was the next and then Duncan. Adok scanned the room with his eyes without turning his head. All the beds on both sides of the room now had young men standing in front of them.

Dixon stood with his legs spread apart and both hands on his hips.

The first thing Adok noticed about Dixon was that he had red hair like Hans, only not as thick, and styled in a butch cut. He was a large, robust man, over six feet tall, with a thick mustache and equally bushy eyebrows. On his stern face were thin lips, round dark brown eyes, and a pointed, wide-bridge Roman nose.

"My name is Wes Dixon, Drill Commander, God to you. And for the next six weeks, my words are law. When I say jump, all you ask is how high."

Everyone stood straight, silent, and still wearing the same clothes they arrived in last night. The drill commander walked over to Adok, looked him up and down, then asked him his name.

"Adok Makowski," said Adok.

The commander moved over to Drew. He asked Drew his name before nodding his head toward Adok.

"Did he give you something to eat?" asked the commander.

"Yes," said Drew.

"Yes, what?"

"Yes, sir," Drew repeated.

Dixon then moved over to Duncan and asked him the same questions.

"Yes, sir, a baloney sandwich and a carton of milk," answered Duncan.

The commander addressed each young man, all of whom had traveled in groups of three. He posed the identical questions to every Klansman without an end table connected to their bed rail.

When done, Dixon again took his position in front of the recruits.

"If you have not figured it out yet, everything you do here is a test to determine your strengths and reveal your weaknesses. There was a reason for leaving food in the end tables. First, to determine if the ones who had the table attached to their bunks were curious enough to open both drawers. You all passed. Second, to establish who among that group has what it takes to be a leader. A good leader must be willing to sacrifice and put his men before himself. A good leader would never ask his men to do something he was not also willing to do. The soldiers under his command must know that they can trust him, that he will do everything to help them succeed and keep them safe. Such a leader earns respect and loyalty from his men. Of the twelve, only Adok Makowski gave his companions the food in the drawer instead of eating the sandwiches himself. Therefore, Adok will be your squad leader. Besides taking orders from me, you will also take orders from him. Is that understood?"

"Yes, sir!" shouted everyone in unison, including Adok.

"Now all of you should shower and dress for breakfast. In the back against the wall, retrieve your suitcase, and put your clothes in the chest under your beds. You will find gray sweats, gray fatigues, and a cap inside. You were told to bring a pair of sneakers. I hope you did so. Always wear your gray sweats and sneakers in the morning. From morning till noon, you will engage in physical fitness exercises. In the afternoon, you will change into your fatigues and black Timberland's. Your new squad leader will determine which of you will shower first. Breakfast will be served promptly at 0700 hours in the blue bungalow. Don't be late, or you may not eat."

Dixon raised his right hand in salute. All the young Klansmen did the same.

"Dismissed," shouted Wes.

As soon as Dixon left, the other recruits gathered around Adok.

"Nice going," said Drew as he slapped Adok on the back. Duncan was next to congratulate Adok. Everyone else joined in too, except for one young man who stayed back. That trainee was looking for his suitcase against the wall. He retrieved it and was now at his bunk, taking out his sweats from the chest. Adok noticed the recruit out of his peripheral vision. The young man had his back to Adok. When the trainee turned around and walked toward the group with his sweats, clean underwear, socks, and sneakers in one hand, Adok stepped out into the aisle and blocked his path.

"Where do you think you're going?"

In defiance, the recruit answered. "Where does it look like?"

Adok looked the young man up and down. The Klansman was the whitest person Adok had ever seen. His hair was snow-white, his eyes a smoky gray. His skin looked almost transparent; it was so pale. Adok could see the blue veins bulging from his forehead as the trainee stared at Adok, tight-lipped and mean-faced. The young man stepped closer, so he and Adok stood toe-to-toe and eye-to-eye.

"Ich akzeptiere dich nicht als meinen Führer. Ich sollte die Führung übernehmen. Ich bin hier der einzig wahre Arier. Ihr amerikanischen Weißen seid eine gemischte Rasse – gemischt mit indischen und schlimmsten Negern," blasted the recruit in Adok's face.

"Ich bin kein Amerikaner. Ich bin Polin, aus Slupsk, Polen. Meine Eltern übergaben mich den Deutschen, als ich zehn Jahre alt war, um Germanisiert zu werden. Sie brachten mich in ein Lebensborn-Heim," Adok responded back.

The young Klansman was surprised to hear Adok speak German.

"This is America. We speak English here," interjected Duncan. He, Drew, and the other new converts now surrounded the pair.

"That's right," agreed a boy named Rocket Raymond. Rocket and Duncan were both seventeen, the youngest recruits at the camp.

The German Klansman made a scuffing sound.

"So you're Polish and a Lebensborn brat. So what! That still doesn't make you a leader worthy of commanding me."

"And what makes you think you're worthy of commanding me?" Adok replied.

"I am Garan Goring. My uncle was Hermann Wilhelm Goring, a military commander and a highly decorated Blue Max fighter pilot. You've heard of them, haven't you? Greatness runs in my family. I was born to lead. I am a true blue blood, as you can see." Garan tilted his neck to one side, exposing his external jugular vein, which was bright blue and visible on the right side of his neck.

"Let's see your veins." Garan suddenly grabbed both of Adok's hands and pulled them forward to expose Adok's wrists. Adok kept pulling them back.

"Why are you resisting? What do you have to hide? There is something wrong here. I see fear in your eyes."

At the word fear and the suspicious looks on everyone's face, Adok finally stopped struggling and relaxed his arms, allowing Garan to turn over his hands with his palms facing up. Garan stared down at Adok's veins as did everyone else.

"Mein Got! There pink, you have pink veins!"

Adok braced himself for the derision he knew was coming next. He had heard it all before. The claims that he was weird, a freak, an alien.

"Your blood must be truly pure to have pink veins!" Garan proclaimed with reverence and adoration.

Adok didn't know what to say.

"Yes, you are worthy of being my leader, of leading us all," Garan declared.

The truck rolled over a bump and jolted Adok back to the present. Drew drove another fifty feet before stopping.

"We're here," said Drew.

Adok looked around, slightly confused.

"Turn off your headlights before someone from the house spots us," Adok ordered.

Drew clicked off the lights. The dark blue truck was embedded between large bushes and trees behind the Brown house 70 yards in the distance. Twenty feet in front were two acres of a budding cotton crop.

Adok immediately lifted the walkie-talkie from off his lap, turned it on, and then hit the push-to-talk (PTT) button on the side. He waited two seconds before speaking.

"This is maintenance 1 to maintenance 2, copy," said Adok into the black and yellow device. Static was all Adok and Drew heard. Adok hit the PTT button again and repeated his words.

"This is maintenance 2 to maintenance 1. We have arrived at the problem site, copy," said Garan.

"Good. It is now 2200 hours. Your lights should be turned on in proximately three minutes. Once you've reached maximum illumination, head back to the station pronto, copy."

"maintenance 2, over and out."

The Lebensborn Alliance

Adok got out of the jeep first followed by Drew. Then Duncan, Rocket, Stewart, and Freddie Parker hopped out of the back of the cab with unlit torches in their hands. Each was also holding a two-gallon gasoline container. The other members of the six-man crew were with Garan. They would burn the two acres of crops in the front of the house.

"Hurry up, take your positions and spread your gasoline, but wait until 10:10 to light your fires," ordered Adok.

Adok put on his hood with the flapped raised, grabbed his container of gasoline, ran between a roll of cotton, headed towards the back of the single-story, white, wood-framed house. The plan was for Garan's crew to start their fires first in the larger cotton field in front of the house, on the other side of the dirt road, farthest from Toby's home. When Toby and his wife saw the flames, they would run outside to investigate, leaving the house vacant so Adok could enter and set their home on fire. Meanwhile, Drew would set fire to the barn, and Duncan and the others would torch the backfield.

Everything went as planned. As Garan and his crew drove away, Garan radioed Adok that Toby and his wife were outside, running toward the field with buckets of water. Immediately, Adok entered the house through the kitchen, where he dowsed the floor with gasoline. He was just about to light it up when he froze in place. There was a sound coming from one of the rooms. It was the sound of a baby crying. Adok crept through the hallway and entered the first door on the right. The bedroom light was on. Lying in a wooden crib was an eight-month-old baby boy. As soon as Adok peered over into the crib at the woolly-headed child, the baby stopped crying. With gleaming, button brown eyes, the child stared up at Adok in full Klan attire and smiled, then began to coo and flap his hands. The baby acted excited to see him. Adok quickly turned and rushed out of the house the way he came. Jumping off the back porch, Adok looked around. The fire was everywhere. He coughed. Through the smoke, Adok saw Drew running towards him out of the burning barn.

"What happened?" Drew asked. "Did you set the fire?"

"No! There's a baby inside," shouted Adok. For a second, the two stared at each other.

Adok thought he knew what Drew was thinking. "I'm not going to kill a baby. If you want to, you do it. The Nazis killed my baby brother, but I will never kill a child, not even a Negro child."

"I don't blame you, brother. I wouldn't either." Drew glanced back at the house. "Okay, then, let's get outta here."

The two ran around the flaming field of cotton to reach their truck, but suddenly, Adok stopped.

"Oh, no! I left my gas can on the kitchen floor."

"Leave it," Drew said. "No one will know who put it there."

"No, but Wes will know I left it. He won't like me leaving evidence behind, traceable or not. Besides, I'll be the only one who didn't bring back their container. I must get it. You go on. I'll be there shortly."

Adok ran as fast as he could back to the house. With one long leap, he sailed over the five steps onto the back porch and entered the kitchen. He spotted the tin, red and black gasoline canister sitting near the entrance to the hallway. Adok rushed over, picked it up, and turned to leave. Squeak. Once again, Adok froze. He slowly turned his head to his right. Out of the corner of his eye, he could see a Negro female standing at the doorway of the baby's room. She was pointing a rifle at him. Adok lifted his left, then his right hand, holding the can of gasoline high over his head. The woman was sobbing.

Leave! Just walk away. She's scared. She'll never shoot. You're a white man. She knows better than to kill a white man.

Adok lowered his hands. He hesitated for a second, then walked in a brisk pace towards the door. Once outside, he pulled off his hood and inhaled. He was relieved and happy to breathe the smoke-filled air until he noticed a figure standing below on the ground. The figure was Toby Brown, a young man in his twenties. Brown was not very tall, but he had broad shoulders and muscular arms. He looked like he could more than hold his own in a fight. Toby was pointing a rifle at Adok's head. What stuck in Adok's mind was the mean, hard, look in Toby's eyes. Brown was wearing the look of a man determined to protect his family and his land at all costs.

Bang! The sound of the rifle going off exploded in Adok's face. Suddenly, Adok felt a hole burning into his forehead. He felt his skull splitting apart. Then, almost as quickly, the splitting feeling stopped. Adok saw the bullet drop from his forehead and land at his feet then rolled down the porch steps until it stopped at the feet of Toby Brown. Toby stared at the slug and then gazed up at Adok in horror. Vanished was the mean, hard look in Toby's eyes replaced now with a look of overwhelming fear. Toby's entire body was trembling and shaking uncontrollably. The rifle in Toby's hands slipped from his fingers and fell to the ground. That's when Adok retrieved his shotgun slung over his right shoulder and pointed it at Toby Brown's head. Adok smiled, feeling exhilarated by the sense of control he now felt pulsating through his veins. Adok never experienced such a sensation before, a sensation that made him feel all-powerful and invincible. He liked the feeling. Adok released the lever and fired one shot into Toby Brown's skull. At impact, some of Toby's blood splattered on Adok's cheek. Adok wiped the blood away as Toby fell straight backward. Thump! His body hit the dirt and laid breathless and still.

"Ahh! Ahh! Ahh! Toby! Oh, my God, no, no!"

"Be quiet!" Adok lifted his left hand balled into a fist without looking back at Toby's wife. "You have your son and your home, Mrs. Brown. Be thankful for that. But there is to be no more cotton grown on this land or any other crop, understood? You've been warned. Don't let me have to come back."

Adok walked down the steps slowly with pride and poise, like a man just crowned king and the ruler of the world. As the fire blazed in front of him, Adok stepped into the flames unafraid. A strong wind suddenly stirred, blowing the ambers away from his body as if by the sheer force of his will. Adok quickly reached the truck.

"Did you just step through that fire?" Drew asked, staring at Adok in amazement as Adok open the door on the passenger's side. Curls of smoke emitted from Adok's robe, but none of his flesh was burnt.

"What happened?"

Drew was in the driver's seat while Duncan and the other members were sitting in the open cab bed chattering to each other about how they executed the burning of Toby Brown's farm.

Adok ignored Drew's questions. "Let's go," he ordered after entering the vehicle and closing the door. Adok touched the center of his forehead. There was nothing there, not even a swollen scar. *Thank you, Dr. Weiss.* Adok rolled down the window and gazed into the night. The moon was full; the stars were out. It was a warm, breezy evening, much like the night eleven years ago when he, Hans, Dr. Weiss, the Nazi colonel, Dag, and Arnulf traveled on the highway to Switzerland.

Hans. Adok said the name repeatedly in his head as he leaned back in his seat with his eyes closed. But no matter how often he pronounced Hans's name, he couldn't picture his brother's face in his mind's eye. It was as if the physical representation of his brother had been erased from his memory. Adok felt nothing when he uttered the name now--no deep affection, no connection. Adok soon gave up and opened his eyes. Suddenly Adok realized Hans probably heard him fire the shot that killed Toby Brown and became afraid. He looked down at the blood on his fingers and knew there was no turning back for him now.

Chapter Twenty-Nine

Never doubt that a small group of thoughtful,
Committed people can change the world.
Indeed, it is the only thing
That ever has.

Margaret Mead

6:30 am, Monday
April 23rd, Montgomery, AL

"It's about time you guys got here," said Kapp as he greeted Ray. He and his family drove up just seconds ago and parked in front of Clare's parent's house. Kapp stayed up all night, waiting for their arrival.

Ray got out of his gold Ford Fairlane. Charmaine was asleep, and so was Mickey, covered with a blanket and laying across the back seat.

"We thought you guys would arrive last night."

"Yeah, I thought so too, but we didn't leave from Charmaine's grandparent's house in Columbia, Tennessee until 1:45 this morning. Neither Mickey nor Charmaine wanted to leave. They wanted to stay two more days. But I told them nobody was paying me to stay in Columbia, and Mickey shouldn't miss any more school."

"Hmm, I never thought of you as the sensible one."

"When it comes to making money, I'm all sense--dollars and cents, that is. So, when do I meet our employer?"

"Midnight tonight," said Kapp.

"You said there was a house we can rent?"

"Yeah, Sylvia Latimer's house right next to ours on the left. Mrs. Latimer's husband, Todd, died a year ago of a stroke, and Mrs. Latimer moved to New Jersey to live with her daughter and son-in-law two weeks ago. She's renting it fully furnished and ready to move in. All you and Charmaine have to do is unpack. With the furniture included, the rent is $275 a month. You can't get a better deal than that. The house is even painted gold, which matches your Fairlane."

Ray glanced over at the house and chuckled.

"It looks well maintained. I would have thought Milton would have rented it."

"That was the plan at first. But Milt and Maddie Wilkins surprised us and got married on Saturday. It was a simple and quick ceremony performed at the church by Martin. Only Maddie's brother and his family attended, along with Theo, Mrs. King and little Yolanda; Clare and I, and Clare's parents."

"Oh, wow, Milton didn't waste any time, did he?"

"Well, when you've been married for over fifteen years, there are certain habits that are hard to break."

"Yeah, ain't that the truth. And speaking of habits, let me wake up mine." Ray got back into his car and nudged his wife.

Charmaine stirred, yawned, then opened her eyes.

"Wow! We're here already?" Charmaine asked, looking around.

"Yep, after four and a half hours of nonstop driving," said Ray. "Come on, babe, let's go see our new home."

"I'll get Mickey. You and Charmaine go on in," said Kapp.

As Ray and Charmaine walked to the Latimer house with a suitcase in each hand, Clare appeared on the front porch of her parent's home looking more than just four months pregnant.

Clare smiled at Charmaine. She walked to the far end of the porch.

"You're going to love the house. Sylvia has it decorated beautifully in various shades of beige, gold, and burgundy. Once you guys have unloaded your suitcases, come over. Mama and I are cooking breakfast."

Charmaine was taken-a-back by Clare's warm and friendly manner. *Hmm, what's going on? Clare actually seems glad to see me.*

"No, Charmaine. There's nothing wrong with me. I can be warm and friendly sometimes, even to you," Clare chimed before she turned and walked back into the house.

Charmaine looked at Ray. "How does she always know what I'm thinking? It's uncanny. It's like she can read my mind."

Ray didn't respond as he opened the unlocked door. *If I can run faster than a locomotive, maybe Clare can read minds.*

"Man! Clare was right. This is nice," acknowledged Ray as soon as he stepped inside. The wood floors throughout the house shined like newly minted pennies. Charmaine quickly inspected their new home. To the left of the living room was a hallway leading to three bedrooms and one bathroom, straight ahead was the dining room, which led into the den and the kitchen. The kitchen also led to the bedroom hallway and to the back porch.

Kapp brought Mickey in and laid him on the beige living room sofa. He was still asleep.

"Well, I'll leave you guys to get unpacked. Come over when you're done. Breakfast should be ready in about twenty minutes."

"I wonder why this is only a one-story house," commented Charmaine when Kapp left.

"Because that's how the builder's built it," said Ray.

"I know that, but usually, they build like houses on the same street. At least, that's the way homes are built in Detroit. And that's how it is on my grandparent's street. All the houses on their block are two-story. Don't get me wrong. I like this house; it's just that we're accustomed to living in a multi-level home."

Ray chuckled and shook his head. "You can't fool me, babe. We've been married for too long. You're bringing this up only because Clare's parent's house is a two-story, aren't you?"

Ray didn't wait for his wife to answer. "Why don't you wake up Mickey while I put the suitcases in the bedrooms. Then we can eat. I'm hungry."

After breakfast, Kapp and Ray went to pick up Martin for the weekly MIA progress and financial meeting held every Monday in the basement of the Dexter Street church.

"Is Milton going to meet us there, or do we have to go get him?" Ray asked.

"Neither," Kapp replied. "Milton and Maddie are honeymooning in Florida. They will return sometime this afternoon."

It was ten o'clock when Kapp and Ray arrived at the meeting with Dr. King. All the members were present except Attorney Fred Gray. Gray always gave updates on pending legal matters. Rev. Abernathy phoned Fred several times, but there was no answer. The members waited an hour and then began without him.

Martin Luther King, sitting at the head of the table, stood up. "I now called this meeting of the Montgomery Improvement Association to order." Martin looked down at the far end of the long desk to his right at Edgar Nixon. "Our treasurer will now read the accounts report." Martin nodded to Edgar, then sat down.

Nixon opened the black, 8 x 11, folder in front of him, but immediately closed it. Then, with his right hand, he slid the folder down the table to Martin. Martin looked at the notebook but didn't pick it up. An awkward hush fell over the room.

"I'll read it," said JoAnn Robinson, finally. JoAnn was sitting directly across from Nixon. She rose from her chair. The tension and silence in the room made the click of her heels more audible as she retrieved the folder and walked back to her seat and sat down.

"Last week, we took in $225 from cake and pie sales. Direct donations from the Dexter Church members was $37.53. Direct donations from Holt Church members was $22.10. Direct donations from…"

Before Mrs. Robinson could complete her sentence, the door swung open and in rushed Fred Gray breathing heavily but smiling.

"The Supreme Court has just ruled that bus segregation is unconstitutional. We won!"

Everyone jumped from their seats, clapped, cheered, and hugged each other.

"We must tell Rosa," said JoAnn to Fred in tears.

"I already have. I've just come from Rosa's house. As the plaintiff in the lawsuit, it was only right that she be the first to know," said Gray.

Ray and Kapp were standing against the wall behind Martin, smiling and clapping also.

"Great timing," Ray whispered. "Now, we can begin our other job in earnest and make some real money."

Kapp nodded. To his surprise, he was also eager to move on. His concern now was when to tell King.

I won't tell Martin today. I'll wait until the end of the week. And maybe I should call off the meeting with Hans tonight. I'll phone him later this afternoon and tell him we'll meet on Tuesday night instead.

Monday, April 23, 1956, seemed more like a Sunday. Every Negro in the city was in high spirits, giving thanks and praising God. JoAnn Robinson, Ella Baker, and Septima Clark got the word out by telephone that special services would be held tonight at the Dexter and Holt Street Churches, and the First Baptist Church of Montgomery. The three women figured that everybody would want to come together to celebrate the Supreme Court decision, and one church couldn't hold them all. Everyone also expected to hear Dr. King speak. So the three women suggested that Rev. King give a short speech at all three churches, starting with First Baptist at six o'clock, Holt at 6:30, and Dexter at seven o'clock. Martin agreed. Kapp and Ray escorted Dr. King home to rest and to prepare his speech. Martin would give the same address at each church. JoAnn recommended that Martin limit his oratory to one page then leave. Otherwise, the services would last well into the night, and people had to get up and go to work the next day.

Kapp called the two backup bodyguards designated to watch the King house when he wasn't there. Kapp decided he and Ray should go home and get some rest too. Escorting Martin to three locations on the day Negroes won a significant battle against discrimination would anger a lot of white folks. The Klan would like nothing more than to kill the leader of the Civil Rights Movement, on this of all days. Kapp knew he had to be especially alert and vigilant tonight.

"Here, I just found this on the floor in the men's restroom," said Ray as he and Kapp got into Ray's Ford to drive home. Ray handed Kapp a folded piece of paper. Kapp unfolded it.

"What does it say?" Ray asked. "I didn't have time to read it."

"It's addressed to Martin." Kapp read the entire letter out loud.

Joyce Yvette Davis

Rev. M. L. King, Jr., President
Montgomery Improvement Association
530-A South Union Street
Montgomery, Alabama

Dear Sir:

This letter is addressed to you and the Board. I am tending you my resignation as treasurer of the MIA to be in effect _____ or sooner.

Since I have only been treasurer in name and not in reality, it will not be hard to find someone to do what I have been doing, even a school boy. I resent being treated as a newcomer to the MIA. It is my dream, hope and hard work since 1932, and I do not expect to be treated as a child.

I shall not attempt to go into all the details of the things I dislike. Whatever the reason for my resigning, shall not effect my respect for the organization that is bigger than I or any of its members. I regret to have to make the decision, but if it will help the organization, I am gald to make the sacrifice.

With every good wish.

I am Fraternally yours,

"It's not signed, but the name E. D. Nixon is typed at the bottom," Kapp said.

"Well, that comes as no surprise."

"Yeah, Edgar must have typed this himself," said Kapp. "He misspelled the word 'glad.' He typed 'effect' instead of 'affect.' He left out the word 'it.' And he's missing commas in several places. There's no way Jo-Ann, Ella, or Septima would have made such errors. Edgar also didn't say when he was leaving, so he hasn't entirely made up his mind yet. This letter is just a rough draft."

When Ray and Kapp arrived home, Ray's parking space in front of his house was taken. A brand new Chrysler DeSoto Adventurer occupied the spot. The car was burgundy with a white hardtop. Ray had to park on the opposite side of the street.

"Who's the hell car is this?" Ray questioned as he got out of his Fairlane and walked over to look at the DeSoto, admiring it.

"Mine," came a loud voice. Kapp and Ray looked up and saw Milton standing on the front porch of Kapp's in-law's house. Milton walked off the porch and over to his car and stood beside Kapp.

"Wow! You're full of surprises, aren't you? Ray commented. "I guess with a new wife, you figured you needed a new car as well."

"Something like that," responded Milton. "There were too many reminders of Olivia in my old car."

Kapp placed his hand on Milton's shoulder. "We understand man. You did the right thing."

"Yeah, I see what you mean. Your Olivia was a good wife. But she's gone, and it's time to move on. You got a big, healthy woman to keep you warm at night now."

"That's right, and I don't even need a pillow," Milton gushed.

The three burst into laughter.

"Speaking of moving on, I'm sure you've heard that the Supreme Court ruled against segregated buses," said Kapp.

"Yeah, we heard it over the radio when we were driving home. Every Negro motorist on the highway honked when they passed by another Colored driver. So I guess this means you'll no longer be Martin's bodyguard."

"Yes, but I'm going to wait until Friday before I break the news to Martin and his father. You see, it was Rev. King, Sr. that hired me. It's only right that I inform the elder reverend as well. In the meantime, we have to worry about tonight. Let's go inside, and I'll give you the details."

Clare, her parents, Charmaine, Mickey, Maddie, and Theo, didn't attend the special service at Dexter Church. The three wives decided it was better if their husbands had only the protection of Dr. King and Coretta to consider. They all gathered at the Matthews' home and waited for the events to end. It was midnight before their husbands returned. They were greeted at the door by their wives and Clare's parents.

"How did everything go?" Maddie asked Milton, anxiously, with one hand on her new husband's shoulder and one hand caressing his cheek. "Were there any problems?"

"There were threats of violence by whites--you know, shouts of "go back to Africa" and such. Some of the Klan were walking the streets or driving around in full garb shooting off their rifles. But that's not the reason we're late. Martin didn't stick to his script. The plan was for him to give a ten-minute speech at each venue. Instead, Martin spoke an extra thirty minutes at First Montgomery, seventy-two minutes at Holt, and an entire two hours at Dexter," replied Milton.

"Yeah, Martin was really on fire tonight," said Ray. "Listening to him, you couldn't help but think that the roof of the church would miraculously disappear, the sky would open, and Jesus would descend to take the Reverend straight up to heaven."

"I guess if that could happen to anybody, it would happen to Dr. King," interjected Mr. Matthews. "And now that the three of you are home safe and sound, Helen and I are going to bed. Goodnight, everyone."

"We're right behind you, Pop," said Kapp.

"Where are the boys?" Milton asked.

"Oh, they're asleep on roll-away beds in the den," answered Maddie.

"I think you should let them sleep there tonight," said Clare. "And Milton, you and the new Mrs. Taylor can sleep in what will soon be our baby's room. We haven't removed the big bed out of there yet."

Maddie blushed when Clare called her Mrs. Taylor.

"That's a good idea. I don't feel like driving back to the farm tonight anyway," said Milton.

"Yeah, we can get Mickey tomorrow. It will be nice to have our new home all to ourselves the first night," said Ray, flashing a winked to Charmaine. It was now Charmaine's turned to blush.

"There's a car coming down the street," said Kapp. "The driver is moving slowly like he's searching for a house. He's getting closer. Hit the lights, babe."

Clare obeyed and turned off the lights in the vestibule and the living room. While his wife and the others were discussing the sleeping arrangements, Kapp heard an automobile, walked into the living room, parted the drawn curtains, and peered out.

Everyone hurried into the living room and found a spot to look out of the large picture window themselves.

"Who can it be at this time of night?" Clare asked. Although she didn't want to say, her first thought was the KKK. Kapp, Ray, and Milton retrieved their handguns from inside their black suit coat pockets. The black Chevrolet was continuing down the street at a slow speed until it finally reached their house and stopped. Someone inside the car beamed a flashlight on the front porch. Immediately, Kapp and everyone else stopped looking out the window.

Ring, ring, ring.

No one moved.

Ring, ring, ring; ring, ring, ring; ring, ring, ring.

Finally, Clare tiptoed into the hallway and picked up the phone.

"Hello," Clare whispered into the receiver.

"Clare, tell Kapp Sands found out that Adok is at a militia training base in Texas. Tell everyone to meet me tomorrow at the barn at 6:00 pm."

"Ok, Hans. Is there anything else, perhaps something about Adok?"

"Don't tell me you can even read my mind over the telephone."

"No, at least, not yet. It's just that you sound so sad, even though you've found out where your brother is located. You should be happy, and you're not. Have you heard from Adok?"

"Yes, but not directly. I don't want to talk about it. And I would appreciate it if you stayed out of my head altogether. It's not good to always know what your acquaintances and relatives are thinking. It can cause a lot of problems. Your powers should be reserved for people we don't know, and of course, our enemies. I'm sure your husband and the others would agree."

Clare got mad and seethed with anger inside. *How dare you tell me how to use my power. I'm not telling you how to use yours. Isn't it just like a white man to want to restrain Colored people's abilities for their own benefit? We're all on the same team now. But how long will that last? A white man will always be a white man. We can help you fight your wars, work your farms and businesses. But at the end of the day, you still hate us and try to keep us down. Oh no, darling, I'm going to read your mind and everybody else's. Knowledge is power, so I've heard. So while my husband is out there helping you get back your brother, I'm going to acquire the knowledge that will make my family as rich as the Rockefeller's.*

"All right," said Clare calmly, without divulging her true feelings. "I'll give him the message."

Clare placed the receiver back on the hook. When the driver of the Chevrolet Nomad continued slowly down the street again, Kapp ran upstairs to his bedroom and retrieved his binoculars from his dresser drawer. He rushed to the window and peered down at the automobile with his binoculars. As the Nomad passed the street light, Kapp read the license plate number.

"The car has New York plates," Kapp told everyone as soon as he went back downstairs.

"Who else do we know from New York beside Captain Carter?" Kapp asked.

"Nobody," said Milton.

"Maybe that was him," Charmaine replied.

"No, the Captain has our phone number. He would have called me first and let me know he was coming. And he wouldn't arrive here this late, not with the racial situation so volatile."

"I guess we won't be spending the first night in our new home after all. We should bed down here tonight just in case the driver comes back," said Ray.

"I agree," said Milton. "Charmaine and Maddie should sleep in the extra room upstairs. The three of us will stay down here and keep watch."

"Let's move the boys upstairs in that room, too," said Kapp.

"That's a good idea," said Ray.

Maddie and Milton, Ray, and Charmaine rushed into the den to get Mickey and Theo. Ray and Milton folded up the roll-away beds and carried them to the bedroom as their wives helped their sleepy sons upstairs. Theo and Mickey quickly settled in their beds, and in no time, were fast asleep again.

"The boys are all tucked in," said Clare as she entered her bedroom. Kapp was sitting on their bed, changing into a pair of blue jeans and a black T-shirt.

"By the way, who was that on the phone?"

"Oh, yeah, I almost forgot," said Clare. "It was Hans. He said Sands found out today that Adok is at a militia training camp in Texas. He wants you guys to meet him at the barn at six tomorrow evening."

"Man, this has been quite a day. All the dams are breaking at once. I guess I'm going to have to tell Martin and his dad that I can no longer be a bodyguard sooner than I thought."

Chapter Thirty

Conflict is inevitable
But combat is optional

Max Lucado

2:00 am, Wednesday
May 5th, Klan Militia
Base Camp, Kerr County Texas

Duncan and Drew huddled in the foxhole they dug 50 yards from camp last night. Rocket and Philip also shared a foxhole.

"How long are we supposed to wait?" asked Duncan.
"Until they come," said Drew.

"Who are they, and how does He-im-Heimdall know we're going to be attacked tonight?" Duncan asked, struggling to pronounce the code name for Adok.

"I don't know who they are or how Heimdall knows. He just does," said Drew.

The day after burning Toby Brown's farm, Adok insisted no one speak his name but use a code name instead. Garan immediately came up with the designation, Heimdall.

"Heimdall is a god with the power to see for a hundred miles," said Garan. "The German military used it doing WWII to indicate long-range radar."

Adok smiled. *If you only knew, Herr Garan, how accurately the label applies to me. Now all I have to do is change the sound of my voice,* he told himself. "Yes, that's a perfect code name. And from now on, that's the name I want to be called," said Adok, straining his vocal cords and restricting the movement of his tongue.

"You sound like a bad imitation of Frankenstein and Donald Duck rolled into one," giggled Duncan. Everyone except Garan joined in the laughter. Adok immediately passed them all sharp looks, and the laughing stopped as abruptly as it started. That was three weeks ago.

2:00:01 am...

"Where's Adok?" Duncan asked a second later after yawning. He was lying against the dirt wall of the foxhole.

Drew didn't answer. The order was not to reply if anyone called Heimdall by his real name. But Drew knew if he didn't respond, his younger brother would stubbornly continue to say Adok.

"He took Garan, Charlie, Wes, and Stewart further into the woods," said Drew. "You know you are not supposed to say that name. Use his code name, or I'm calling Drake as soon as this mission is over. And that's in addition to the butt-kicking Heimdall will give you. You see how good Heimdall is now at Karate. He's even beating Wes."

And the more Adok fights, the more vicious he becomes, Drew thought to himself. *Adok seems to relish it. I thought he would choke me to death when we were practicing the other day. Adok has changed. Ever since our first mission, he's become mean and bossy. He's even telling Mr. Mapps and Mr. Dixon what to do. He's no longer the kind and sensitive little boy I knew at the Lebensborn home.*

Those days seemed like a million years ago, Drew thought as he gazed out into the darkness with only the glow of the full moon as light. Terrorizing and killing

Negroes was not the life he dreamed of living. Two years ago, when his parents joined, the Klan seemed like a fun way to meet people, especially girls. Their family attended parties and dances with other Klan families. There were picnics and outings to amusement parks. In that respect, the KKK was like a social club. The organization didn't emphasize the militant side until after you joined. Sure, Drew knew the Klan preached white supremacy, but Drew thought it was only in the abstract sense. He believed whites were superior to blacks in every way. He believed in keeping the races separate. And sure, Drew thought it was necessary to put the Colored's in their place occasionally. Threats, beatings, burning property, harassment, banishing, and shooting off guns were what Drew had in mind. He never imagined it would go so far as cold-blooded murder. Drew was proud of Adok for refusing to burn down Toby Brown's house with Brown's baby inside. That was the Adok he knew. Drew's delight was short-lived. Two days later, he learned that Toby was dead, and Adok killed him.

If I hadn't been kidnapped and taken to a Lebensborn home, I would be in Poland now with my real mother and father.

Drew missed his parents, especially his mom. He wondered if they survived the war. Occasionally, a picture of his mom flashed in his head. He inherited her blonde hair. His mother's hair was long. It hung down the length of her back to her butt. But she always wore it braided and pinned in a ball on top of her head out of the way. Drew was happy the day he was adopted. He thought himself one of the lucky ones. Now he wasn't so sure. Drew closed his eyes and sighed.

If only I'd obeyed the first time mother insisted I come inside.

2:00:25 am…

No matter how intensely Hans concentrated, he couldn't pick up Adok's voice. It was as if his brother dropped off the face of the earth. The night Adok burned Toby Brown's farm, Hans heard everything. Since then, nothing. Hans was frantic, wondering what his brother was doing. Adok surely knows by now that he's in America and with Kapp Johnson. His brother may even be watching him at this very moment as he, Kapp, Ray, and Milton make their way to the camp on foot. Dressed in dark green fatigues and green ski masks with revolvers holstered to their shoulders, the four were spread out tracking through the woods blind since they all agreed Sands wouldn't take photos of the area. With Adok's ability to see, no one wanted to chance Sands getting caught or killed. Suddenly, Hans heard Adok's name and stopped walking. He stood motionless, not even breathing, anxiously waiting to hear his brother's name spoken again or his brother's voice.

"Did you hear something?" Kapp asked in a low tone.

Hans looked to his right. Kapp was crouched down, walking towards him.

"My brother's name, that's all. The voice sounded close."

"How close?"

"Within a mile radius, I'd say."

"In what direction?" Kapp asked. "Can you tell?"

"No, the voice was too low," Hans replied.

Hans and Kapp continued. The two walked in a line 20-yards from each other. While Ray was 20 yards away to the left of Hans, Milton walked 20 yards away to the right of Kapp. Cautiously, the four proceeded through the woods.

2:05 am...

"Where's Adok?" Rocket asked. Rocket was standing over the foxhole, looking down at Drew and Duncan, beaming his flashlight on the two.

"What are you doing!? Turn off that light and get back to your station before Adok has your ass!" Drew shouted, so agitated, he forgot to use Adok's code name.

"We've been huddled down in these dirty holes all night. I need to relieve myself."

"Well, go ahead. You're in the woods," snapped Drew.

"I need to do more than piss. I'm going back to camp to use the restroom. I'm not about to take a chance on getting bitten in the ass by a gopher or worse, a snake. If Adok comes back, tell him where I'm at."

2:05:30 am...

"Psst...Kapp. We're going in the wrong direction. The camp is that way," said Hans, pointing west.

Kapp ran over to Hans, as did Ray and Milton.

"How far?" asked the three simultaneously.

"A hell of a lot closer than I thought, less than a mile. The length of eight football fields," said Hans. "Kapp, since you can run extremely fast, why don't you run ahead."

"I can run fast, too," Ray revealed. "I used to run track in high school."

Kapp peered suspiciously at Ray. Ray never mentioned he ran track before.

"Kapp is a speed demon. He runs over 100 miles per hour. My brother has seen him. I doubt you can run that fast."

Ray noticed Kapp and Milton pass each other looks and realized he was in a dilemma.

If I show, I can run as fast as Kapp, Kapp, and Milton will know I could have traveled back to Chicago and killed Dr. Amiel.

"Wow!" Ray said, trying to sound astonished. "I don't think I can run that fast either. But I know I can run faster than you two," said Ray, pointing to Hans and Milton.

"Then why don't you go southwest and Kapp go northwest while Hans and I proceed straight ahead, west," said Milton.

Kapp nodded. He smirked at Ray before disappearing in a poof.

Ray suppressed the urge to do the same. It took all the restraint Ray could muster not to match Kapp's speed. As soon as Ray was out of Hans and Milton's eyesight, Ray let loose.

"We should be off too. We need to get to the camp as soon as possible," said Milton.

Milton and Hans started running.

High in an oak tree, 300 yards away, Adok watched the scene. Once he saw Kapp zoom away, he quickly climbed down to warn Charlie, Wes, Garan, and Stewart. The four rose from the tall, thick shrubberies they nestled behind. They met Adok in the center of a small clearing surrounded by six massive southern oak trees towering thirty feet high.

2:06 am…

"Three are coming this way," said Adok in his altered voice. "But one is headed to the camp from a different direction. *Kapp is probably already there by now*, Adok thought.

"I'm worried about Drew and the others. I don't think they can handle him," said Adok.

With practice, Adok no longer sounded like a cross between Donald Duck and Frankenstein. His voice was now two octaves deeper with a slight Southern accent.

"It's only one man. They should be able to handle one invader. Otherwise, all their training has been for not," said Wes.

"Yeah, but this one was a soldier in the second war, and he has special skills."

"How do you know so much about who's attacking us?" Wes inquired.

If I reveal one is my brother, coming to get me, they may not want to fight. Charlie and Wes may want to talk to Hans, hoping to persuade Hans to join. Hans would never join the Klan. He's too humble, emphatic, and self-righteous for that.

"We don't have time to discuss that now. Just take your positions. I'm going back to help Drew," said Adok.

Adok paused a second.

Kapp is strong. Goring is the only one who can fight as well as Wes and me. It will probably take all eight of us to capture and secure Kapp since we can't kill him.

"I'm taking Garan with me," Adok finally said, glancing at Garan standing between Charlie Mapps and Stewart.

"Come on," said Adok, waving his hand.

Charlie Mapps parted his lips to speak. Adok flashed him a mean, squinted stare. Charlie immediately closed his mouth without uttering a word.

Adok and Garan quickly ran to the black military-style jeep hidden several feet away behind another cluster of trees.

Adok hopped into the driver's seat and Garan in the front next to Adok. Then suddenly, Charlie, Wes, and Stewart appeared and jumped into the back seat. Adok noticed the defiant looks on each of their faces and decided not to challenge them.

"We gotta hurry up. Kapp is already at the camp, and all hell has broken loose," said Adok. He angrily slammed his open hand against the steering wheel, realizing he just spoke in his normal voice.

2:06:22 am…

Hans stopped in his tracks when he heard his brother speak and grabbed Milton by the arm.

"Adok is 200 yards from here. But he just drove away. He knows Kapp is at the camp and is headed back there. Adok was talking to someone. So, there is at least one other person with him."

"Then we better push it," said Milton.

2:07 am...

Tommy Tippins, Jack Copper, Craig White, Freddie Parker, Philip Hunter, Rocket Raymond, James Brewer, Drew, and Duncan each unloaded their guns into Ray Wilson and Kapp Johnson. But the bullets went straight through the two. Neither Kapp nor Ray stumbled, faltered or fell as the two ran towards the boys from opposite directions. Now the eight were fighting Ray and Kapp in hand-to-hand combat.

Instead of ambushing the intruders, the intruders ambushed the recruits. The siege began minutes before after the first shots rang out, in rapid succession. The shots came from the camp. Abandoning their foxholes, Philip, Duncan, and Drew hurried back to the base. They found Jack, Craig, Freddie, Tommy, James, and Rocket standing back-to-back outside the bungalows with rifles in hand firing into the darkness. Three fired upon the cliff while the other three shot into the woods in the opposite direction. Several rounds went off before the six stopped and stood, shaken and afraid. Crouched down, Drew, Duncan, and Philip ran out of the woods.

"Who are you shooting at?" Drew asked Rocket, who was still pointing his gun up on the cliff twenty-five feet above them.

"How the hell should I know," snapped Rocket. "We know at least two, if not more, are somewhere out there. One is on the bluff, and at least one is in the woods behind us. We can hear them, but we can't see them."

"Whoo, whoo, whoo." Kapp made the sound of an owl as he looked down from behind a tree on the cliff. The sound made the other three Klansmen facing the opposite direction turn around and also stare up at the hill. Kapp silently chuckled. Even from that high, he could tell the recruits were scared. They were just boys and didn't know what they were doing. Abducting Adok would be easier than Kapp thought. But which of them was Adok, Kapp wondered. Just then, Ray rushed out of the woods behind the eight screaming like an Indian on the warpath. All the young men quickly turned around and fired at Ray.

"Heehaw!" Kapp yelled as he ran from behind the oak and jumped twenty-five feet down off the cliff, landing on his feet.

Drew turned and saw Kapp. "There's the other one," he hollered. "Shoot! Get him! Kill him!"

Duncan, Rocket, and Philip switched directions and fired at Kapp, spraying him with bullets. The eight hurled their guns at Kapp and Ray when their rifles ran out of ammunition. Kapp and Ray used their arms to deflect the blows, and the fistfights began.

Ten minutes into the fist-de-cuffs, Adok came racing out of the woods. Straight ahead, Adok saw Drew and the others fighting two masked men. One Adok knew had to be Kapp. The eight were no match for the two. But Adok could tell, Kapp and his accomplice were not seriously fighting. The two were grinning as they slapped away the blows, ducked and evaded the nine recruits punches.

I'll wipe those smirks off their faces, Adok vowed as he veered the car left toward the hill and dived out of the jeep. His body hit the dirt and rolled several times before his forehead slammed into the iron flag pole. Dazed, Adok lay on the ground. It took several seconds before he stood up and joined Drew, Duncan, Rocket, and Philip in fighting Kapp. The driverless vehicle continued with Stewart, Garan, Wes, and Charlie still inside.

"Oh, Sh_ _!" the four yelled, then jumped from the jeep before it crashed into the hillside.

Garan wasted no time, once he stumbled to his feet, he drew his hand gun and fired his first shot dead center into the back of Ray's head.

Ray felt the heat of the bullet as it drilled a hole into his skull. Ray stopped fighting. The blows from the other five boys came fast and furious, but Ray didn't feel a thing. The feeling was all in his brain. His head felt like it was about to explode. For a millisecond, fear gripped him; Ray thought he was going to die. Then, suddenly, the burning ceased. A tinkling sensation rushed through Ray's body, from his head to his toes. Ray felt the bullet drop out of the back of his head. Ray's body shook. He felt energized and acutely more aware of everything around him. It was as if he died and came back to life-- He had. One of the young Klansmen was about to hit him in the face, and Ray rammed his fist into Tommy's jaw. As Tommy fell, Ray twisted Tommy's head, horizontal to the boy's right shoulder, breaking Tommy's neck.

Freddie, Jack, Craig, and James ran at the sight of Tommy lying dead. Ray then retrieved his revolver from his shoulder holster and shot each before Ray swung around and shot Garan between the eyes. The energy Ray felt was matched only by his anger. He was one of the few WWII veterans never injured in the war. *I have to come home to get shot.* That made Ray mad. He wasn't playing anymore. Ray reloaded and killed, Stewart, Wes, and Charlie the same way he shot Garan. Ray aimed his gun at Philip several feet away. Philip had been knocked out by one of Kapp's blows and was on the ground just regaining consciousness.

"Stop!"

Ray looked over his shoulder and saw Hans and Milton running out of the woods towards him. But before the two reached him, Ray put a bullet into Philip's head. At first, Ray thought Hans would be the one to protest, but Hans hurried over to where Kapp was fighting his brother, Drew, Duncan, and Rocket.

"Adok! It's me," shouted Hans, lifting the mask off his head. Adok responded by attacking him.

Ray shook his head at Adok's reaction, then watched as Milton walked towards him. Milton took off his mask. Ray pulled off his ski cap and checked the bullet hole in the back of the cap before slipping it into his pants pocket.

"You didn't have to kill that boy," said Milton with a stern, disapproving glare.

"No? Well, they didn't have to kill Toby Brown and burn his crops. They didn't have to kill Maddie's first husband either or Emmett Till, and all the other countless Negroes lynched, burned, and beaten to death over the decades. We didn't have to get shot at driving home that night from the reunion, but we did."

"All those wrongs still don't make this right."

"No," replied Ray, "but it makes it even."

Milton shook his head. He knew it was no use talking to Ray. Milton glanced over at Kapp and Hans fighting

Adok, Drew, Duncan, and Rocket before he looked around at all the dead bodies scattered about.

"Did you and Kapp do all this?"

"Yep," Ray nodded.

"That's a lie! It was just you," said Milton.

"If you knew the answer, why ask the question?"

"To see if you were going to tell the truth," Milton replied.

"What is truth? Pontius Pilate asked Jesus."

Milton looked at Ray speechless. There was no doubt in his mind now that Ray killed Dr. Amiel. Ray was going to be a problem. Who could control him? Ray was going to do what Ray wanted, and to hell with everyone else.

Kapp fought Drew, Duncan, and Rocket while Hans and Adok duked it out. After another three minutes of fighting, Drew threw up his hands and shook his head.

"No more," Drew told Kapp. Drew fell to his knees, huffing and puffing, trying to catch his breath.

"Come on," prodded Duncan to Drew. "It's three against one."

"It's no use. We can't beat him. We haven't laid a glove on him. So let's just stop. You too, Rocket, stop it!"

Rocket obeyed and raised his hands. Kapp backed off, pulled off his ski mask, and walked over to where Milton and Ray stood. Hans and Adok were still fighting. Adok landed most of his blows. It was evident Hans didn't want to hit his brother and was dodging and deflecting many of Adok's punches.

The three boys huddled together. They were stunned after finally noticing the bodies of their friends. Seeing the three Negro men made them even more afraid. Duncan spotted Garan and ran over to Garan's body lying near the wrecked jeep. Drew and Rocket followed.

"They've killed them all, damn niggers," Duncan whispered to Drew with tears in his eyes. Duncan bent down and took Garan's revolver from his hands.

Ray was watching the three out of the corner of his eye.

Duncan rose. The three were facing the hill with their backs to Ray and the others.

"Don't," whispered Drew, realizing what his brother was about to do. "It's over. More killing won't bring any of them back."

"We can't just let them get away with this," Duncan argued. Duncan glanced at Rocket.

"You're right," Rocket agreed. "We may not be able to kill all four, but we can at least take out one. The one closest to us. The darkest one."

"Brother," said Duncan, "you turn around and face the three standing over there. Rocket, you continue facing this way."

Drew and Rocket obeyed. Rocket was taller than both Drew and Duncan. As soon as Drew turned around, Duncan also turned around with Rocket blocking Duncan from Ray's view.

"When I count to three, Rocket, you step aside," said Duncan. Rocket nodded.

"One…two…three."

Ray was ready. He had his gun aimed at Duncan before Duncan raised the hand gun to pull the trigger. Drew reacted when he saw Ray pointing his revolver at his baby brother and jumped in front of Duncan, taking two bullets in the chest. As soon as Adok heard the shots, Adok turned from his hand-to-hand combat with Hans and looked over his shoulder. He saw Drew fall.

"Nooo!" Adok rushed to Drew's side. He held Drew's head in his hands. "Casmir! Casmir! Don't… You're going to be all right, brother. You're going to be…"

Casmir slowly shook his head from side-to-side as he gazed up at Adok's tear-drenched face. "I was wrong," Drew said as he coughed and spat blood. "We didn't escape Lebensborn after all, did we Adok?"

A gasp of air escaped from Casmir's mouth. Lifeless and still, his blue eyes remained open, fixed in place like two glass crystals. Duncan was on his knees beside Drew crying.

Adok threw back his head and screamed. "Ahhhh!"

The scream was so loud the leaves on the trees appeared to shake from the shrill.

Hans ran over to console his brother, but Adok pushed him away, stood up and rushed towards Ray like a bull towards a bullfighter.

"No!" Hans shouted as he ran after Adok. Hans grabbed Adok from behind.

"Stop it, Adok! It's time to stop this nonsense and come home."

"I'm going to kill that nigger!"

Hans switched positions with Adok, blocking Adok's path to Ray.

"You can't, brother. He's like us. The three of them are like us. You can't kill them."

Adok's jaw tightened as the pink veins in his forehead and neck swell.

"Damn it! You gave those niggers the serum."

"I didn't…" Hans stopped himself. He was about to refute Adok's accusation and say he would never give niggers the elixir.

If I ever use that word or imply mistrust of Kapp, Ray, or Milton, that will be the end of our alliance. Then, who will I turn to for help?

"I…" Before Hans could utter another syllable, Adok slammed his fist into his brother's jaw. Hans blocked the next punch and the next, but Adok jumped up, swished his legs through the air, and landed a drop-kick. The maneuver was unexpected, and Hans fell backward on the ground. Hans shook off the blow to his chin and snapped to his feet. Adok kicked him in his crouch and pounded Hans with a battery of blows to the face. Adok was fast, maybe even as fast as Milton. Although Adok's punches didn't hurt, they came in rapid succession, too quick for Hans to counter. Finally, Adok swung and missed. That time Hans ducked. Just as Adok was about to throw another punch, Hans felt a firm hand on his shoulder pull him backward. Adok's fist would have hit Hans right between the eyes, but Kapp's large, round, balled, tightly-clenched fingers rammed into Adok's knuckles instead.

Crack!

The power of Kapp's blow knocked Adok down. He landed on his butt several feet away. Adok's hand was numb. He could no longer make a fist. When he tried to lift his arm, he couldn't. It was limp. Every bone in Adok's right arm, from his shoulder clavicle bone to the bones in his fingers, was broken.

Adok snarled and cut a mean look at Kapp standing over him.

"You dirty, stinking Nig…"

Kapp raised his fist. Adok paused.

"That's right; you better shut up little white boy before this black man pounds your racist ass into the ground, and who will save you then?"

Kapp reached down with one hand and grabbed Adok by his shirt collar and pulled the boy to his feet. Hans, Ray, and Milton gathered around Adok and Kapp. Milton held both of Rocket's hands secured behind the boy's back while Ray held Duncan at gunpoint. Suddenly, there was a buzzing sound. Everyone looked up but saw only the yellow streaks of sunrise in the sky. Still, the noise grew louder and louder.

"There!" Rocket shouted, tilting his head eastward.

Emerging just over a cluster of trees was a black helicopter. Before anyone could react, the copter was upon them. Kneeling and leaning over the side of the copter were two figures dressed in black wearing long coats with hoods. Each had a rifle. They both fired two darts. One man shot Hans and Kapp. The other man shot Ray and Milton. The tranquilizer darts took effect immediately. First, by paralyzing the four, then by knocking them out. Instantly, Kapp, Ray, Hans, and Milton collapsed. Kapp was the first to come to a minute later, then Ray. Hans and Milton woke up together. Still drowsy and shaken, they stood up one-by-one. Hans looked around. His brother and the other two boys were gone.

"Ha, ha, ha," came a loud sinister laugh. The helicopter hovered in one spot.

The four looked up at a menacing figure staring down at them. Hans shuddered as he glanced over at Kapp, who returned Hans' gaze. Although stark white with sunken eyes, pencil-thin lips, and gaunt cheeks, Hans and Kapp recognized the face of Nazi Colonel Otto Strauss. He, too, wore all black, but no hood covered his head of stringy brown hair. And tiny pimples still dotted his face.

"I have Adok now. You thought you could keep him from me, but he's mine, mine! Ha, ha, ha. If you think World War II was horrific, wait until World War III. It's coming. I won't rest until Hitler's dream of a New World Order ruled by Aryan Super Humans is realized. Don't think you can stop me; you can't. It's going to happen. Where Hitler failed, I will succeed. Ha, ha, ha; ha, ha, ha; ha, ha, ha."

As the helicopter moved away, Adok appeared also wearing a long black coat with a hood. Adok raised his right arm, bent his elbow back and forth, and flexed his fingers. He shot a mean gaze at Kapp then at Hans before slowly lifting his middle finger.

Hans felt a lump form in his throat. He was overcome with sadness and despair as he watched the helicopter fly out of sight with his brother as a willing passenger. Hans felt like crying. He wanted to die, but he was also angry and wanted to fight.

There's no way I will let it end like this. Adok is my brother, mine! I raised him. I didn't raise a hateful, racist, murderer. I didn't. And whatever it takes, I will get my brother back.

"So, where do we go from here?" Milton asked. The four men stood in a circle facing each other.

"Germany," Hans and Kapp replied in unison. Hans looked at Kapp and smiled. The strange connection he felt with Kapp Johnson from afar was even stronger now that they were together. Hans didn't know what was linking them. He just knew they had a special bond. For some unknown reason, he knew he could always count on Kapp. That was good because Hans needed to rely on someone. He was tired of not having friends. For eleven years, it was Adok and him, and now Adok was gone and had become his enemy. Not in a million years did Hans think their future would turn out like this.

"Going to Germany is all well and good, but if we can't kill that madman and your brother, how are we going to stop them?" Ray asked.

"We may not be able to kill them, but we can prevent them from killing innocent people and dragging the world into another war," said Kapp.

"Yeah, well, that's going to take a lot more than just the four of us," Ray said.

"For once, I agree with Ray," said Milton. "Who knows how many others there are. The doctor who invented the serum may have injected hundreds of Germans."

"No, he didn't," Hans rebutted. "The doctor that invented the serum was my uncle. I was there. I know how many others received the serum. Only two German soldiers, besides Adok, Strauss, and myself, were injected. I believe the two that shot us with the tranquilizers are Dag and Arnulf. They were with us in the castle and drove us to my uncle's house in Switzerland the night Kapp was mistakenly given the serum and escaped. When he died, Uncle Josef told me to give the remaining vials of elixir to Colonel Strauss. But Adok and I destroyed all the bottles and burned the formula. We even burned down Uncle Josef's laboratory shed. If Uncle Josef gave the serum to others, he would have told me. He trusted me. I was his only living relative."

"Wow, okay. Then it's four against four. That we can handle," said Milton.

"Even if we do only have to contend with four like us with invincible blood. That Nazi can still enlist others who can come after our families. My wife and son are not invincible. Neither is Theo and Maddie." Ray glanced at

Taylor. "I don't think you want to lose another wife much less your son; do you Milt? So the only way I'm going to Germany is if my family is invincible too. Otherwise, you guys can count me out. Saving the world is fine, but not if I lose Mickey and Charmaine in the process."

"You're right," said Hans. "It wouldn't be fair to ask you two to continue without protecting your families, and the only way to ensure their safety is by making them invincible. I have no problem with that. Unfortunately, I burned the formula. But wait…how did you two become invincible?"

Ray and Milton simultaneously pointed at Kapp.

"They, along with my wife, were transfused with my blood," Kapp confessed.

"Oh…oh my God! Is it that easy? I never considered it could be passed from one person to another by a simple blood transfusion. That puts a different light on things. I hope Strauss hasn't figured that out. If he has, we may be dealing with an army of invincible men, not just four."

"Nah, I didn't get the impression that the colonel was that smart during my brief encounter with him in the tower. He appeared to me to be a man desperately trying to be more than his mental or physical capabilities allowed. How he got to be a colonel, I don't know. But I doubt it was because of his intelligence."

Ray rolled his eyes. *I don't care how intelligent the Nazi is. What about the blood?*

"So you two agree before we go to Germany, my family and Milton's will get transfusions?"

Hans and Kapp nodded.

"Okay then, let's go," said Ray.

"Wait," said Milton. "We must burn and bury the dead first. We must burn the bodies, so they won't be easily identifiable if discovered. We should bury them a couple of miles deeper into the woods. The graves will be harder for someone to find. If we leave them lying here, they are sure to be discovered. And you know who will get blamed. The police will automatically assume a bunch of angry, renegade Negroes are on the loose with enough guts to slaughter white men."

The four were silent as they passed each other looks.

Finally, unable to control himself, Hans responded. "And they'd be right," he said with an outburst of laughter.

"ha, ha, ha," Ray, Kapp, and Milton joined in.

Three hours later, the four were on the highway, headed back to Montgomery in Sands' pickup truck. Hans drove. Ray, Kapp, and Milton sat in the open cab bed. Every time a police car drove by, the policeman looked but never stopped the vehicle. The officers merely nodded to Hans and continued, assuming the three Colored passengers were the white driver's employees.

…And they were right.

To be Continued…

Printed in Great Britain
by Amazon